A welcome invitation…

"My place?" she asked.

Sweet cinnamon bear, full of humor and fire and strength. "Any place you like," he said, rumbling low.

She didn't respond as she headed toward the parking lot, a ragged asphalt patch crammed full of cars in what had become true dusk. She looked over her shoulder, found him watching her and smiled—and she didn't wait. Not playing games, just matter-of-fact *check yes or no*.

Ruger took a deep breath of the night air, found it scented with leftover heat and sage and creosote. It tasted like anticipation. The hair on his nape bristled, a tingle on his skin.

He followed her.

Books by Doranna Durgin

Harlequin Nocturne

**Sentinels: Tiger Bound* #142
**Sentinels: Kodiak Chained* #150

Silhouette Nocturne

**Sentinels: Jaguar Night* #64
**Sentinels: Lion Heart* #70
**Sentinels: Wolf Hunt* #80

**The Sentinels

DORANNA DURGIN

spent her childhood filling notebooks first with stories and art, and then with novels. After obtaining a degree in wildlife illustration and environmental education, she spent a number of years deep in the Appalachian Mountains. When she emerged, it was as a writer who found herself irrevocably tied to the natural world and its creatures—and with a new touchstone to the rugged spirit that helped settle the area and which she instills in her characters.

Doranna's first fantasy novel received the 1995 Compton Crook/Stephen Tall Award for best first book in the fantasy, science-fiction and horror genres; she now has fifteen novels of eclectic genres, including paranormal romance, on the shelves. When she's not writing, Doranna builds webpages, enjoys photography and works with horses and dogs. You can find a complete list of her titles at www.doranna.net.

SENTINELS: KODIAK CHAINED

DORANNA DURGIN

HARLEQUIN®

entertain, enrich, inspire™

Recycling programs
for this product may
not exist in your area.

ISBN-13: 978-0-373-88560-2

SENTINELS: KODIAK CHAINED

Copyright © 2012 by Doranna Durgin

THE GATEKEEPER
Copyright © 2012 by Slush Pile Productions, LLC

CONTENTS

Dear Reader,

As we prepare to ring in the New Year, we have some exciting news to share with you. Starting in January, Harlequin Nocturne is unveiling a brand-new look that's a fresh take on our paranormal covers. Please turn to the back of this book for a sneak peek.

Our stories still feature powerful, mysterious alpha male heroes facing life-or-death situations as they battle for the heroine's love. But we will be increasing the page count to allow for a wider breadth of story, subplots and heightened sensual and sexual tension.

New York Times bestselling author Heather Graham gets Nocturne off to a great start with the launch of the thrilling new miniseries The Keepers: L.A. And Rhyannon Byrd returns to Nocturne with another title in her popular Bloodrunners miniseries about a pack of very alpha wolves.

So don't miss out on your favorite series. Look for the newly repackaged Nocturne titles starting in January wherever you buy books.

In the meantime, be sure to look for this month's reads: *Holiday with a Vampire 4* by Susan Krinard, Theresa Meyers and Linda Thomas-Sundstrom and *Sentinels: Kodiak Chained* by Doranna Durgin.

Happy reading,

Ann Leslie Tuttle

Senior Editor

SENTINELS: KODIAK CHAINED

Doranna Durgin

This book is unquestionably dedicated not only to those people who were involved in making it happen, but to those special people who MADE it happen: the readers who let me know how much they wanted to see a book for Ruger.

Chapter 1

If a bear...

Like Ruger hadn't heard all the jokes. Bear, woods, yeah, yeah, yeah.

But he wasn't alone. From where he stood among a small patch of trees, he'd looked down on the unexpected plaids and bagpipes and sporrans and kneesocks, smelled the scents of whisky and wool in the cooling air, and heard a pipe-and-drum band squalling up into full sound over all.

And he'd looked down on this woman.

If a bear finds another bear in the park during a Celtic festival, does anyone notice?

He sure did. And so did she.

She stood outside the whisky-tasting tent with its miniscule cups of tasting whisky. If any of the humans standing near her had a clue, they would have treated her with more respect. They wouldn't have casually bumped into her on the way to the open tent flap—or failed to see the strength in her short houri form, the beauty of nut-brown skin and black hair and smoky eyes.

She smiled faintly at Ruger and lifted her tiny plastic

cup of honey-gold liquid in a quiet salute. Ruger lifted his chin in a subtle salute to the lady bear and eased back into the trees of the hill—not quite ready to give up his woods, thin as they might be.

If a bear...

Especially a Sentinel shifter bear looking for quiet the night before a field assignment in the continuing fight against the Atrum Core. One trying to pretend that he wasn't quite himself, still recovering from what hadn't killed him, but had maybe killed who he was and had always been.

Healer.

Never mind the Atrum Core ambush that had put Ruger out of action for months. *The bite of Flagstaff's night air, their team gathered in the hotel parking lot where the Atrum Core had been seen, Maks' hand pushing against the hotel door, their tracker's cry of warning—*

The astonishing flash of stinking, corrupted Core energy blooming from the room to take the team down.

Ruger's bruises had healed long before he'd woken from the induced coma. And theoretically, his singed senses were, in fact, recovered.

Theoretically. He could sit up here on the crest, thin, gritty soil beneath the seat of his jeans, and he could feel the accumulated ills and ails of the festivities below. He just couldn't do anything about them.

A woman on chemotherapy, smiling brightly to a friend. And there, a middle-aged man whose lungs sat heavy in his chest, and on the far side of the festival, amidst children clustered at a game under the mercury lights, was a youngster with sickness lurking in his bones. Ruger couldn't see him—even a Sentinel's night vision had its limits—but he could feel it well enough.

On a normal night, he could ease the man's breathing, offer the woman energy, and—

No, the child was what he was.

On a normal night...

Ruger closed his eyes, absorbing the taste and feel of the ailments and knowing—*knowing*—he could help. Knowing that if he channeled the healing energies that had once come so readily to him, he could...

Soothe...

Ease...

Mend...

He reached, and found nothing. He reached deeper, and found only a deeper nothing, a profound and echoing inner darkness.

Deeper—

The pain came on with the inexorable nature of a gripping vise, increasing to sharp retribution in an indefinable instant. Ruger grunted with the impact, momentarily stunned by it.

And then he was sitting up on the crest of the hill, startled by the sensation of warmth trickling from his nose and into his mustache.

Again.

He pulled a bandanna from his back pocket and wiped away the blood, sitting still in the dusk until he was sure the nosebleed had stopped.

Not so much the healer after all.

Well. He was still *warrior.* And he was still *bear.* And Nick Carter, Sentinel Southwest Brevis consul, still counted on that fact—counted on it enough that he'd pulled Ruger back into the field.

Not that he or Nick had much choice—not when mere weeks after the hotel ambush, the entirety of Southwest Brevis had been crippled in the aftermath of Core

D'oíche. Ruger wasn't the only one who didn't know how much of himself he'd recover but who had things to do in the meantime. He could still offer his knowledge—and, unique among healers, he could damned well watch his own back.

And he needed to prove it. To his teammates, to himself.

Ruger got to his feet, shadowing through the woods quietly enough to startle those at the edges of it when he emerged. There, just down the hill…the lady bear still waited. Too much of a coincidence to believe, much too enticing to ignore. A bear in the swirling midst of the Celtic fair, tossing back what remained of her whisky, throat moving with her swallow.

She spotted him immediately and pitched the sample cup into the trash, moving away from the side of the tent to come his way—and scooping two more samples from the table beside the tent as she did. So many of the bear shifters were exceptionally tall, on the burly side—plenty of hair, rugged features. Ruger not as much as some, despite his Kodiak nature when he took his bear. *Little black bear,* he thought suddenly, and knew it true of her—the comfortable amble in her walk, her black hair glinting in the light, thick bangs cut to frame her face and her skin with enough tone so many would assign to South India what came from the bear. She was sturdy and rounded, her eyes large and dark and her nose just a little bit long, her mouth wide and chin gently notched below. Not plump, but plenty of hips and breast packed into a petite form.

Not a woman who would break easily.

She watched him watching her, making her way through the crowd as if the whisky tent rowdies weren't there at all, and when she got there she said, quite matter-of-factly, "You took too long to come over."

Not a shy creature, the bear.

"Just thinking about who you might be," he said, looking down on her—accepting, without thinking, the sample cup she proffered him. It felt too small in his hand—but then, so many things did.

Maybe she wouldn't.

He'd definitely been cooped up in brevis medical for too long.

She watched him, her large, dark eyes thoughtful, and he hoped his unbidden thought hadn't shown on his face.

Or maybe, given the speculative light in her eye, he hoped it had.

Then she smiled, just a curve at the corner of that wide mouth. "I'm on loan from Colorado. I knew you were in this area…but so far at brevis it's mainly been wolves and big cats." She frowned in thought. "Though I'm pretty sure that one guy was a weasel."

Ruger grinned, scratching his fingers through the beard beside his mouth. Full beard, short enough to be tidy, long enough to obscure the landscape of his lower face. "Pine marten," he told her. "He prefers to be called pine marten."

She shrugged. "He'll have to watch where he puts his hands, then."

Ruger's hand closed around the tiny whisky sampler; his jaw tightened, ever so slightly. Not that she was his to care about, but…

She laughed, as if she'd understood perfectly well. "I took care of it." She nodded out at the milling crowd. "Lay odds *he'll* learn better tonight, too."

Ruger cut his gaze out toward the whisky tent, and found the man in question readily enough. Mid-thirties, a wiry guy who probably thought that scruff at his chin counted as a beard, and who had buckled an ostentatiously large sporran over his jeans—most likely to hold the flask now in his hand. He looked bored with the fair, but not the least bit bored with the sight of Ruger's new companion.

"It happens," she told him, sipping the whisky. Her eyes widened appreciatively; Ruger could smell the peaty nature of the liquid from his own sample. She shrugged, still looking at the man who'd noticed her. "You know how it is. They can tell something's different. They're not sure just what…but they think they want it." She cocked her head at him. "Or maybe you don't know. You've got that forbidding thing going on." She nodded at the thinning crowd.

He didn't look; he'd already seen them. Ladies' night out, three friends in their late twenties who'd struck the right note of agreeably Celtic and casual, ostensibly admiring the silver rings they'd each purchased. A decade younger than he was—none of the scars, none of the same realities.

They had no idea of the battle that had so recently raged across this region, or of his part in it.

He took the whisky, letting it sit on the back of his tongue a long moment before it warmed his throat, and when he lifted a shoulder in a shrug, she smiled, understanding.

He was already talking to the one person in this park who interested him.

She said, "I'm still finding my way around here. I hit the Making Tracks bar last night—I thought I'd see more of us there."

"We're spread thin right now," he said. "If we weren't, you wouldn't be in this region at all."

"To be honest," she said, "I was hoping to find you there. Annorah from brevis communications suggested this place when I didn't."

Of course she'd known of him. There weren't so many bear shifters around that it was hard to keep track. And one *did* keep track, when entering a new brevis. "Wouldn't be here if I'd realized the Celtic fair was here. Those trees normally make for decent privacy."

"Oh?" She raised her brow, her gaze back to his before it drifted across the breadth of his shoulders, lingered on his face…went briefly lower.

In an instant, every muscle in his body tightened. She smiled, just a little.

Bears. Not game players. Predators. Knew what they wanted, when they wanted it. "I'm heading out tomorrow," she said, as if she could read his mind. Maybe she could—some blooded Sentinels did—but he thought not. It wasn't a talent for bears.

Of course, neither was healing. Usually.

He nodded slowly, and agreed, "It's that kind of night."

"I figured I'd be on my own," she said. "But I'd be happy if I wasn't."

He nodded again, this time with something of a smile. There were a number of teams heading out in the morning…and any number of Sentinels who didn't want to be alone tonight. "Like I said. It's that kind of night."

She studied him, inhaling deeply—slowly. Taking the measure of his scent and closing her eyes briefly. "Bear," she said, as if to herself, but when she opened her eyes she looked directly at him and smiled. "It's been a long time."

Hell, yeah.

And here he came, moving in from the crowd: Mr. Way-Over-His-Head, mid-thirties, wiry, and chin scruff. And—bonus!—plenty of hard alcohol on his breath. "Hey there," he said to her. "Thought you might like to dance to some Wicked Tinkers with us."

She cut a quick glance his way. "No, thank you," she said, as politely as it could be done.

"Hey, if you don't know how, don't worry about it. We can teach you all the moves you need." He mimed a quick Highland step, and it held way too much thrust.

She gave him another glance, more deliberate this time. "I'm not into it, thanks." This time, there was meaning in her glance at Ruger. He read it easily enough, for all that he didn't yet even know her name. *I'll deal,* it said.

"C'mon, honey," the guy said. "You'll make me look bad in front of the guys. Besides, you'll like it. You just met this guy; I been waiting for the right moment all night."

"You missed it."

"Just a dance or two," he said, getting bolder, a little more reckless—more desperate, with a glance back at his smirking buddies. "That's what you came here for, isn't it?"

Ruger clamped down the rumble in his chest.

I'll deal. Her look was a warning…and a request.

Ruger closed one hand into a fist and stood down.

She spoke quietly but clearly, glancing over to the trio of women-witnesses, at that. "I don't know you. I don't want to talk to you. Please leave me alone now."

Maybe the guy didn't hear her; maybe he didn't care. He took her arm, and not gently.

Oh, the little bear could move. Ruger saw it, but he doubted the guy did. A twist, a shift, the flat of her palm with just the right force in just the right place…the guy blinked at her from the floor.

"Oh!" she said, with a certain suspicious clarity and

lack of emotion. "I'm so sorry! I was so startled when you grabbed me!"

The women smirked.

The guy's friends threw aside their whisky tasters, bristling en masse—taking a step forward.

Ruger shifted. That was all it usually took—the movement. The distinct moment when they realized that he filled more space than they'd expected, that he moved with the easy power of his kind.

In the instant they hesitated, the lady bear spread her hands in a mollifying gesture. "No big deal, fellas. He startled me. Wouldn't want to turn it into something noticeable, right?" She sent a significant glance at the security guard most definitely headed their way, a man in kilt and hose and arms that no doubt stood him in good stead when it came time for the caber toss. "After all, there's still whisky to be tasted."

That did it. They hauled their friend to his feet, brushed him off and dragged him away. One of the women offered a thumbs-up and said, loud enough to be heard over the distance between them, "He's always an asshole at these things."

"Could have been worse," Ruger said, but his eyes were on the lady bear, and the lurking humor in her eye. Not for a moment discomfited; not for a moment concerned. "Someone could have gotten broken."

They laughed and moved on, not quite taking him seriously. The lady bear did, eyeing him for a long moment, a smile in the corners of her dark eyes. "Mariska Banks," she told him, and the humor took on a certain gleam. *Invitation.*

"Ruger James," he said, and did the little whisky a grave injustice by tossing it back. "But you knew that."

"My place?" she asked.

Sweet cinnamon bear, full of humor and fire and strength. "Anyplace you like," he said, rumbling low.

She didn't respond as she headed toward the parking lot, a ragged asphalt patch crammed full of cars in what had become true dusk. She looked over her shoulder, found him watching her, and smiled—and she didn't wait. Not playing games, just a matter-of-fact *check yes or no*.

Ruger took a deep breath of the night air, found it scented with leftover heat and sage and creosote. It tasted like anticipation. The hair of his nape bristled, a tingle on his skin.

He followed her.

Through the musicians, past the collection of Celtic dog breeds on display, past the sheep and even a few Highland cattle. By the time they reached the parking lot, he'd caught up; by the time they walked to the unlit far end where Ruger had parked, evening had found its way into nightfall.

The guy's friends probably thought they couldn't be seen in the dark, with their semicircle blocking the way to Ruger's short-bed Hemi. Sentinel night vision tinged the men blue, but left them crystal clear—along with the crowbar, the baseball bat and the tire iron.

"We thought about it," one of them said as Ruger and Mariska stopped, backlit by the fair. "And we decided it was a big deal after all."

Ruger exchanged a glance with Mariska. "This time," he said, "we share."

This time, someone got broken.

Mariska jammed her key in the lock of the small house, her brevis accommodations for this Tucson assignment. Like all Sentinel temp homes, it sat right where the

city abruptly gave way to desert: a place where a bear—
or wolf or javelina or big cat—could roam.

Ruger stood up close against her back, one arm reaching over her shoulder and propped against the stucco
house, his breath stirring her hair and his presence stirring her body.

He'd fought with her. *Beside* her. He'd known her
strength; he'd trusted her training. And he'd embraced
it, not grown wary with it.

After a lifetime of feeling too bold, too strong, too
much, Mariska quite suddenly didn't quite feel alone
anymore.

The brush of his body warmed her from the inside—
a ruffled feeling that trilled down her nape and tickled
along her skin, gathering heat low in her belly, tightening down along the backs of her thighs. Greedy and un-
abashed.

Because now she knew—it would end soon enough.
She hadn't intended it when she'd come here; she'd imagined herself needed—*wanted*—in the field beside him.
She'd had only to meet him to understand how personally he'd take her presence—to sense the pride of him.

Maybe he'd understand. Maybe he'd see it had nothing
to do with her respect for him—the famous Southwest
healer of both brawn and compassion—and everything to
do with what she wanted from life, and a little bit about
what he deserved.

In any event, it hadn't been hard this morning to convince Nick Carter to send her out as Ruger's backup on
the coming field op. He hadn't been proven in the field
since the Flagstaff ambush; they couldn't risk him.

Not that they ever should have been asking so much
of him in the first place.

And it was an opportunity—a chance she'd never been

afforded on her home turf, where too many had seen her grow up and still thought of her as little Mariska.

The bear in her went after what it wanted.

What she wanted now was one night when it didn't matter that she was strong and practical, exotic but not beautiful. *Different.* She was the one the men approached out of curiosity and not because of any true interest; she was the one who looked short and stumpy next to the sleek Sentinel women who shifted to big cat form, the one who embarrassed even Sentinel men with her strength, never mind her vigorous nature in intimacy.

No little wonder she'd come looking for this singular man—the man she'd watched and admired and come to know through reports. A man who would be her physical match, and whose underlying nature might just match hers. If nothing else...*just for tonight.*

Tomorrow, everything would change. He wouldn't tolerate what she'd done for the sake of her place in this brevis. No bear would.

As soon as she twisted the doorknob, he pushed the door open—looming over her in a way that made her feel not threatened or crowded, but claimed. And when he moved forward, she pushed back—contact enough to strengthen the lure when she did move away.

She laughed when he growled an undertone of response. "Ruger," she said, trying out the taste of his name, and tossed the house keys onto the low bowl shelf by the entry.

He pushed the door shut and took her shoulders from behind—an aggressive move not so different from that of the man at the festival. But for Ruger she turned easily, fluidly, enjoying the strength in his hands and the assumption in his touch. She drank in the sight of him, too-wiry sable hair just long enough to grip when the moment called for it, beard trimmed closely enough to guess the shape of his jaw, and no need to wonder about pale brown eyes or strong brow and cheek, the full shape of his mouth. No need to wonder about the breadth of his shoulders, well above hers, or that bit of hair peeking out at the unbuttoned neckline of his shirt.

She ran her hands across the rough nap of the material, absorbing the warmth beneath, the plane of muscle—the hint of nipple.

He inhaled sharply. "Whatever you want of this night, tell me—" he took a deep breath, let it out "—now," he said. "Tell me now." *While I can still think.* The unspoken sounded clearly enough.

She didn't hesitate. "What I want *is* tonight. All of it."

He looked at her long enough to make her doubt— to hold her breath as he searched her gaze. And then he brought his hands up to cup her jaw, tangling his fingers in her hair, tipping her head up to take her mouth in no uncertain terms. No shy attempt to get acquainted, no hesitant questions. He brought her into it strong and hard, holding her right where he wanted her as he slanted his head for a deeper connection.

It took her no time at all to grab him back, hands skimming his ribs, finding his flanks and kneading hard to pull him up against her. She was too short; he was too tall. It didn't particularly seem to matter. She felt his response all the same, and she stood on her toes to reach his kiss, full of bursting internal exclamations and enthusiasm. When they broke apart to breathe, she tipped her head back and laughed for the pure exhilaration of it.

"Hell, yes," she told him, and kicked off her leather walking flats, flipping the snap on her pants even as he came back for her, leaving barely enough room for her hands at his zipper, fingers on automatic as she drank up the scent, the touch, the very presence of him—kissing hard and strong and deep, her hair and her nerves already mussed beyond all redemption by his stroking hands.

She stepped out of her pants, right there in her foyer—no lights necessary, with her night vision showing perfect detail. She reached for the jeans now hanging low on his ass—and for the first time he startled her, both with the low and demanding noise in his throat and with his hands as they slid away from her hair, her shoulders, coming to rest at her waist—picking her right up off the floor with no effort at all to flip her around.

She found her balance with her hands braced against the half wall between the foyer and the great room, and she understood right away. Even in the thrill of it—the strength of him, the anticipation—she whirled back around. "No," she protested. "I want to touch—"

Just like that, she was facing the wall again, his body pressing against her—but he leaned down, the side of his head against hers, the stiff brush of his beard against her jaw and her hair tangling between them. "Next time," he said, and quivered up against her, restraint in the hands that tightened at her hips and the sudden gust of breath in her ear. And then he waited, no more than a heartbeat—a space for protest.

Next time.

"Hell, yes," she said, bracing her arms against that wall.

"Protected?" he asked. Sentinels were, as a matter of course—those who couldn't ward themselves had it done for them.

His hands ran over her belly, up to her breasts, learning them, kneading them—lightly at first, until she arched into his hand and said, "Hell, yes."

His arm crossed her chest—supporting her, continuing

to play her breast; the other dropped back to her belly—splayed there a moment, pressing them together while Mariska tipped her head back and hummed, a low and uninhibited sound. A bear sound. Her legs parted and he took full advantage, cupping her; she cried out in surprise at the sudden rush of pleasure and heat, and again as his fingers pressed into her.

"Ready?" he asked, and this time his voice came strangled, the tremble of him surrounding her.

"Hell—" she breathed, and got no further, for he lifted her hips and found his way home, his exclamation of surprised pleasure in her ear, his legs stiffening until he found his balance again.

"—yes," she whispered, wanting so badly to touch him in return—but her arms knew better, absorbing the increased weight while she held her breath in expectation, waiting to feel the fullness and size of him in motion.

Except he just stayed there—holding her, fingers tightening around her body, his breath a convulsive gasp in her ear—while she finally realized he was grasping for control.

Who the hell wanted control?

She squirmed.

He growled, holding her tightly—so tightly, his head pressed to hers and his hips suddenly plunged against her.

Except he somehow had the wherewithal to grab back control—he played with her, little thrusting increments of sensation. She gasped in outrage and then at the spiraling, clawing sensation, drawing on the nerves from her spine to her tightly curled toes. And she gasped in delight—at the understanding that she was claimed, that she was in the hands of the strength and power she craved.

With a cry, she pushed back at him, squirming inside and out. And yes, he made a harsh, startled noise, a fierce noise—a sound of wrenching pleasure as he lost control again and pounded into her without restraint. Her own delighted whimper rose in volume as her feet came right off the floor and hooked around his legs and—

Oh, hell, YES—

He caught her as she stiffened and trembled—and then he shouted as if the moment took him completely by surprise. His knees gave way, and there they were on the floor while she sat back in his lap, clinging weakly to the half wall.

As the aftershocks of hellaciously superb sex faded away and Mariska's stunned fog of pleasure eased, a short laugh snorted its way out. She clapped a hand over her mouth, sagging precariously close to the wall, but couldn't help it; she did it again. And of course he felt it—the clench of her internal movement around him, her slipping position.

He pulled her upright, finger-combing the hair away from her face as he tucked his mouth in beside her ear again, and this time his voice was a growl. "What?"

"Just—" she said, and waved her hand at them, at the wall, at the foyer littered with her clothes and her shirt somehow hanging open and her breasts free. "Just—" she tried again, and gave it up and laughed right out loud.

She felt him relax slightly. "Lady bear," he said, and nipped at her ear.

"Does that make you a gentleman bear?" she asked, twisting to look back at him, his face so close to hers.

He offered a wry smile from within that beard. "Not for a long, long time."

"About tomorrow—" she said, not having planned it in the least.

But he shook his head. "Tonight," he told her, "is always. No matter what happens tomorrow."

Her heart clenched, much as her body had clenched only moments earlier. "An always night," she whispered. No matter tomorrow.

Eventually they got past the foyer. Not before Ruger spread his shirt on the rough textured paint of the half wall, set her on it, and provided what she'd clearly wanted the first time—the chance to fondle and stroke.

He'd meant for things to go slower, then—a chance to admire the sturdy bones of her, to marvel that he hadn't worried about crushing her or frightening her, and the certainty that she'd been able to brace herself against that wall no matter how he pounded into her. A chance to run his hands over full hips and full breasts and her curvy, flat and tight waist, and to marvel at her perfect proportions. Not tall, not long and lean and slender, not any of the things that so many men ogled.

But all the things that Ruger ogled.

And it didn't go slow at all.

So eventually they made it past the foyer...but only as far as the sprawling couch, where they finally fell asleep. She, sated and lightly snoring...he, completely smitten.

But when he woke in the morning, covered only by a soft cotton blanket that had slipped down far enough to threaten modesty, the light streamed in the windows of the airy Southwest home and Mariska the lady bear was gone.

Chapter 2

That she'd left didn't surprise Ruger. She was on assignment today; she'd only ever asked for the night. She, like all of his kind, was clearly wont to an independent nature, not needy on the morning after.

Besides, she'd left him out some tea makings and a protein shake.

Ruger didn't bother to head for home—a tidy little trailer in the foothills of the Catalinas. He dug out the little overnighter kit from his truck's half-cab storage, brushed his teeth, and helped himself to a quick shower, relieved at the neutral scents of her soap and shampoo.

But the shower did nothing to clear his head; his senses reeled in the aftermath of Mariska—and in the surreal but inescapable fact that he was about to report for field duty without his healing skills. He stared at the lightly fogged mirror and felt as though he saw someone who had been, not someone who was. Strong in body once more, a man more big than beefy or hulking, a man with strength in arms and torso and defined muscle all the way down to the towel that draped his hips.

But still only part of what he'd been.

He tugged on his shirt, stepped into his pants, grabbed the protein shake, and headed out to the truck with the heat of the early morning soaking into his shoulders. Thinking changes and forward as he started up the truck. Maybe that was why he pulled into the barbershop when he saw it. When he stepped out, his hair was only a smidge more crisp around the edges—but his bared cheeks sensed the slightest breeze, and that untanned skin tingled in the sun.

As if facing the world without a beard for the first time in his adult life would distract him from things still missing.

He still had his knowledge. His herbs and creams and brews. But those would no longer be infused with the healing energies—and they hadn't ever been the reason for his demand in the field.

Not to mention that brevis liked a healer who could look after himself. Counted on Ruger to do so, instead of using their depleted manpower. Until Flagstaff, when he'd walked into that Atrum Core ambush just like the rest of his team. Then when Core D'oíche had hit not so long afterward, he hadn't been there to help the wounded.

So damned many wounded.

But he shouldn't be thinking about that now. *Now* was about forward. First stop, Brevis HQ, where he'd join the briefing on his new assignment in Arizona's high timber region, following up on whatever Maks Altán had uncovered.

Brevis itself hid in a deceptive handful of stories on the edge of Old Town Tucson, where the building foundation dug down deep into caliche to hide invisible subterranean floors below. Apartments and offices and meeting rooms above; medical, the amulet lab and so much of their archived history below. A complete and tidy headquarters for a race of earthbound sentinels unknown to the world at large.

Ruger parked the pickup in his assigned slot and headed for the high conference room outside Nick Carter's corner office—a room draped with local plantings and replete with the astringent scents of the desert. Ruger pretty much knew what he'd find there—the vast window, the carpet thick underneath and the conference table holding a bottomless pot of herbal tea. Businesslike and still welcoming.

He'd find Carter and possibly Jet, the wolf who'd discovered her human side through Atrum Core experiments, as well as the other members of his team—all new to him, he suspected. He was ready for that.

He wasn't ready to open the big wood door and find Mariska sitting at that table, her expression more of a wince than a welcome, her eyes widening slightly at the sight of his newly shaved face.

He might not have known she'd be on his team, but...

She'd known. He could see it on her face. She'd known, and she hadn't said anything. And he couldn't think of any reason why not.

At least, not any good reason.

He gave her a wary nod, yanking out a chair at the end of the table—the one he always took, not because of any stupid alpha game, but because in a room of men made big by their Sentinel nature, Ruger stood the largest... and took the most leg room while he was at it.

Nick sat at his desk, two computer monitors in play and a stack of folders threatening to slide over the edge. Annorah leaned over to scoop them up and deposit them in the middle of the table, shoving one in Mariska's direction and another at Ian Scott, the amulet specialist who'd briefly worked with Maks in Pine Bluff. One to

Ruger, and one to a woman Ruger didn't know—a wards or shielding specialist, most likely.

Ian flipped his folder open and began an immediate doodle in the margin—impatient with such meetings as ever. Sardonic in nature, his snow leopard showing strongly in his pale hair, striking eyes, and the flow of his movement—at least, when he wasn't acting like an overcaffeinated cat. "If we're all up to speed on this," he said, "let's skip to the good part."

Ruger made a subliminal grumbling noise that the others nonetheless perceived very well, his normally amiable nature tangled by his reaction not to Mariska's presence, but to her guarded expression.

"Not everyone comes at this from the inside," Nick said mildly, ignoring Ruger's mood and responding to Ian. As alpha as they came, that Nick Carter—full of wolf and full of innate pack understanding. But an alpha didn't need to posture or dominate…an alpha just *was.* That mild voice meant plenty.

Ian sighed and flipped his pencil against the table a few times. "Okay, sure," he said, sitting back. "What've we got, then?"

"Mariska, I am Jet." The whisky voice belonged to the woman with whisky eyes, Nick's fiercely beloved Jet. As usual, she hovered by the window, restless and graceful. As usual, she tended the social necessities first. More wolf than any of them, Nick included—wolf born and human made, escaped from the Core, bereft of her pack, and now forever with Nick. "I'll be scouting wide."

Ian raised his hand. "Ian Scott. Amulet hotshot." He tapped the folder a few unnecessary times. "I'll be supervising amulet recovery in the installation Maks has found."

Annorah crossed her arms. "Annorah. Communications central, here at brevis." If she looked defiant, Ruger suspected it was only because she wanted to be out in the field again. It wasn't likely to happen anytime soon; she'd lost that privilege in Flagstaff when her inexperience-driven fear had nearly sabotaged the mission.

Nick leaned back in his office chair. "Nick Carter," he said, pale green eyes astute as he watched them all. "Boss."

Mariska hesitated, her troubled gaze flicking from Nick to Ruger. She cleared her throat. "Mariska Banks, on assignment from Western Brevis. I'm personal security."

Ruger's subliminal growl went loud, as all the implications of the situation hit him at once—and then combined with her guilty expression to make sense.

She was there to look after *him*.

And she'd known about it while he hadn't. *Hell, she's bear.* She'd likely made it happen in the first place. He looked past her to Nick. "That's not the plan."

"It's not," Nick said easily. "But early yesterday, Mariska came to me with some compelling points. This rogue has been too active—too unpredictable. We need to catch him as soon as possible, and to do that we need to understand him as soon as possible—the contents of this bunker will allow us critical insight. So it would be best if you aren't distracted by security issues while you're tapping your healer's perceptions at the new bunker."

Hell, yes, she'd made this happen. She'd insinuated herself into this field op...she'd supplanted the one thing he could still offer to brevis. He couldn't help his utterly flat voice, or the way it did nothing to disguise his anger. *Betrayal.* "I can take care of myself."

"Whoa," Ian said. "So can I, but I'm thinking this is a conversation I don't need to be part of."

"There is no *conversation*," Nick said. He eyed Ruger, and if his gaze was still easy, it was also implacable. The decision had been made.

Ruger clamped down on his growl, but it didn't stop him from sending a dark look at Nick. *Personal security.* It was the last thing he wanted or needed—especially when it was coming from a woman he suddenly no longer trusted. Not because she'd had the idea, or because she'd gone to Nick with it. But because she'd understood better than any of them—bear to bear—what it meant to him, and she'd never said anything.

She'd been fierce and gorgeous and astonishingly joyful and giving with her body…and he'd given the same back. And yet—

You should have said something, Mariska.

The final member of the team cleared her throat, a little more loudly than necessary. "Allesandra," she said, and even in his ire, Ruger saw the coyote in her buff blond hair and amber eyes. "Call me Sandy. Given what happened to Ian the last time he was in Pine Bluff, I'll be working wards on our hotel. You'll all be responsible for personal shields." She gave Nick a wry look. "Normally I'd be working with my partner to make sure we could cover both, but we all know how it is these days."

"That's all of you," Nick said. "Now listen up—if you take anything from this briefing, let it be caution. Don't underestimate the man behind the installation you'll be studying. His name is Eduard Forakkes, and he's likely still in the area. We're almost certain he was Fabron Gausto's amulet tech—and the Core's recent advances with silent amulets are most likely his doing. Physically, he's unassuming—but he's as treacherous as Gausto ever was."

"Trust me on that one," Ian said—as dryly as ever,

and likely without any awareness of the pain that tightened his face.

Sandy pushed at her folder. "What evidence do you have that he's still there?" she asked. "Maks found this bunker abandoned, aside from the leftover animals."

"Because he isn't anywhere else," Nick said. "Because the Core, as much as they'll embrace him if he comes up with something they can use, has branded him rogue. Because this bunker may not be a primary installation, but it was clearly in active use at the time of its discovery. And because—"

"Maks said so," Jet said, an atypical insertion from her spot near the window, one uttered with complete confidence in the Siberian tiger who had helped free her from Gausto six months earlier.

"If anyone knows Forakkes, it's Maks," Nick finished, a flash of fury rising to the surface so quickly that Ruger blinked—only to find it gone again. A little reminder of what lay beneath their consul's calm exterior.

It wasn't enough to deter Ruger from the pending argument between them—but it was enough to keep him quiet for now. Especially since he understood Nick's wrath all too well—he'd read the material in this folder from front to back already; he knew Forakkes had been active in the Core for a startling number of years.

A decade and more ago, he'd been trying to breed Sentinels for his own purposes. Young Maks had survived escape from that situation. His mother had not.

Yes, Maks knew Forakkes. But Maks was still sorting himself out up there in the White Mountains with Katie Rae Maddox. He would no doubt join Ruger there, but only briefly.

Sandy accepted the assurances matter-of-factly. "Okay, then," she said. "He's still there. Then we'll find him."

"And don't forget Katie's visions," Ian said. "I know they're vague, but her sense of foreboding goes far deeper than the local situation."

"Second that," Annorah said. "She's got a reputation as a lightweight. Don't you believe it. If you took the form of a little deer, would *you* want to attract the attention of the rest of us?"

"Exactly so," Nick agreed. "She fooled me for years. We'll let you know if anything else comes through for her, but until then, keep her report in mind—*and don't get cocky.*"

"Cool," Ian said, hitting a quick beat with his pencil. "Well, this has been uplifting, but I've got a silent amulet to secure before we go. And oh—by the way, watch out for those, too. If you're used to sensing the stink of the things, the new silent ones will take you by surprise."

Mariska frowned at her folder, quiet as she absorbed the nuances of the team. She hadn't truly understood the significance of this situation, that was clear enough. And *that*—there on her face, the faint frown of her brow and the worry in her eyes—*that* was doubt. *Self-doubt.*

It pissed Ruger off that he could read her so well.

"That's it," Nick said, as if he didn't see it. "Head down below and get geared up; I want you in Pine Bluff by midafternoon."

"Halfway there," Ian said, on his feet and reaching for the door handle while the rest of them still shifted in their chairs—Sandy reached for a last swallow of her tea, Annorah stretched, and Ruger...

Ruger just glowered.

Mariska gathered her folder and stood, tucked together in a tidy button-down blouse with the wood buttons and natural material that meant it was Sentinel kosher—it would follow her if she took the bear, absorbed by the earth magic until she needed it again. Her slacks held the wrinkle of natural cotton; Ruger would bet she wore the moccasins he'd seen the previous night. Mariska Bear came prepared.

And she'd known what she was doing when she pried her way onto this team. She'd known what she was doing to *him*.

She'd taken away the one thing he truly had left to give them.

She met his current glower with uncertain honesty— with a note of pleading. "Ruger—"

He wanted to growl. He didn't. He leaned back in the chair, one arm hooked over the back of it, his legs sprawling into the space left by Ian's departure.

"Ruger—" Mariska said again, dismay in those big dark eyes and on that wide mouth.

Ruger only shook his head. "Just one night," he said softly—knowing the others would hear, and not caring.

Mariska cared. The woodsy brown tones of her skin went a shade paler. She pulled her folder off the table and left, moving with a stiffness that hadn't been the least bit apparent any of the times they'd made love the night before.

Just one night.

But it would never be enough.

"Ruger. You wanted to talk to me?"

Of course Nick knew what was coming. And Jet, too; she gave them a glance over her as she headed out the door, leaving Ruger alone in the room with Nick.

So Ruger didn't mince words. *"No,"* he said. "I don't need any damned babysitter. Especially not one I can't trust."

"I trust her," Nick pointed out.

Ruger stood, going from sprawled to upright and tense, his anger hitting the surface faster than he'd ever expected. "This isn't about whether I need help— I damned well don't. This is her bid for something bigger than Western Brevis has given her. That's not the right reason!"

"Doesn't mean she can't do the job." Nick didn't react as Ruger reached the desk, looming tall; he rocked back in his pricey office chair, still relaxed—except Ruger knew him well enough to see the wolf bloom to life behind those pale green eyes.

"It does if I won't work with her," Ruger said. "She lied to me. She *used* me."

"Is that what this is about?" Nick said, and now his voice was soft enough for Ruger to take notice. "Your pride?"

A rumble of anger pushed at his chest; Ruger ground his teeth, fighting to keep it to himself. "It's about," he said distinctly, "the fact that I don't trust her."

"Then you have a problem," Nick said. Oh, yeah. Far too relaxed in that desk chair, the desk between them and the dual monitors off to the side, the rest of the surface populated with neat paperwork. But even as Ruger struggled with anger, Nick sighed. "If I didn't think you could take care of yourself, you wouldn't be going at all. But she made some good points when she came to me yesterday morning. You need to be able to concentrate on what you're doing—to go deeper than is possible if you're watching your own back, and to work faster. There's too much at stake for us to take chances—we've lost too much already."

Exactly. They were shorthanded; they were licking their wounds. They needed every active field agent they could get—and that meant not wasting extra manpower

on an assignment with which Ruger didn't need help—
didn't *want* help.

Didn't want the help of a woman who had already
thrown away the heart he'd so rarely offered.

"I don't need her there," he growled at Nick. "I don't
want her there. And no good will come of having her
there."

Nick inclined his head. "She's yours," he said. "Make
the best of it."

Once, Ciobaka had been a dog—immersed in the *now*
of being canine, his world full of scents and natural cinders crunching under feral paws.

Now he was dog, and yet more. He saw more, heard
more, comprehended more…but understood nothing.

He sat in the cage that had once easily held him, but
now required lock and key. The cage sat in a vast and unnatural underground space, the ceiling arching overhead
and sly sky tubes bringing in enhanced sunlight to turn
darkness into an illuminated artificial cave. At night there
were fake lights, driven by a thing called solar power.

Human things surrounded him—a stack of crates and
cages, a dissection table, a long wall full of things elec-
trical and whirring. To the far end, the men slept in cots;
beside that section, Ehwoord had his own den. There was
a tiny place where the humans snatched food, and a tiny
toilet closet. Crammed beside this stood a black, molded
chest with a lid and drawers and foam, and it held shiny
metal weapons that stunk of oil and acrid powder, and
none of the men touched it at all.

Ehwoord's places were brightly lit at all times. No
one would guess at the man's importance otherwise. He
was of advanced years and weakened body, although
it seemed to Ciobaka that Ehwoord grew strangely

straighter with the passing days, his sparse hair thickening, his lines softening, his voice growing sharper even as his temper grew more erratic.

Ehwoord fussed endlessly with metal disks and leather thongs, and he captured and caged many small creatures with thin crunchy bones and juicy meat. He didn't eat them, as only made sense; he *changed* them—and changed them again.

"Ehwoooor," Ciobaka said, as much as lips and tongue would allow. "Wahwaaaah."

One of Ehwoord's subordinates—Tarras—smacked the metal bars of Ciobaka's enclosure with a baton. Ciobaka snarled horribly; the man flinched.

"Tarras," Ehwoord said, his voice tight as he barely glanced aside from his current scratching notations, "don't annoy Ciobaka. Ciobaka, don't frighten my people. And the phrase you're looking for is *want to*. Not *wanna* and certainly not *wahwah*."

Ciobaka pushed breath up toward his nasal passages. "Wahnaaa."

"Freak," Tarras muttered, and went back to the task of cleaning small animal cages. Like Ehwoord's other subordinates, he had swarthy skin tones, dark hair pulled back into a short club at his nape, and shining silver pieces at his ears and neck.

"An improvement," Ehwoord said of Ciobaka's enunciation. "But you nonetheless may not have this gopher. He and his little friends are doing me a great service with their deaths."

"Toopit," Ciobaka said with some disgust. He flattened his dingo-like ears, his lips pulled back at the corners in canine disapproval.

Ehwoord gave him a sharp glance. "You will not think so if my success with them spares you."

Tarras reached for the prey food pellets. He picked up the pellet scoop and said, "I liked the thought of surprising those Sentinel bastards with your workings to change *our* forms. This, I don't get."

Ehwoord's voice grew very tight for that moment. "Finalizing that working under these crude conditions has proven impossible. At this moment, what we need is redemption in the eyes of the Septs Prince—he who holds sway over all our regional *drozhars*." He smiled gently, an expression Ciobaka found even more frightening. "Once he's captivated by our success, our positions will be secure. And I'm sure he'll agree—if we can't have Sentinel powers, then neither will they."

Chapter 3

I don't need her there. I don't want her there.

Mariska shouldn't have lingered at Nick's office, reorienting to the elevator and the quietly classy earth tones of the hallway. No, she shouldn't have lingered at all. Not when her hearing was as acute as any Sentinel's.

Apparently, she'd somehow fooled herself into hoping that Ruger would understand.

Silly bear that she was.

It had all made sense when she'd spoken to Nick about the assignment, twelve hours before she'd even gotten close to Ruger. No doubt she should have said something when she'd found him at the park…but the moment had been so perfect, the opportunity so rare, the man so engaging…

Well, so be it. She'd take the elevator down to the gear room to augment her own minimalist duffel—a couple of high-power stun guns, a collapsible baton, a blackjack… everything it took to manage Atrum Core goons without leaving bodies behind.

When it came time to leave bodies, she had only to call on her bear.

Not that the Core played fair. They carried guns and they carried amulets, and they pretended they were only protecting the world from Sentinels run amok with their own prowess—the connection to the earth that had given their druid ancestors the ability to shift form, and then further specialties besides. Healers, like Ruger. Trackers and warding specialists and earth power wranglers.

Mariska had none of that. She was strong and able, a powerhouse packed into a curvy little body. And she continued in the tradition that had started two thousand years earlier, when that first shape-shifting druid had faced his fratricidal half-Roman brother—a man who had then founded his Atrum Core clan, so intent on stealing power and influence that they'd only helped shape the Sentinels into what they were today—strong, confident protectors.

What did you expect from me? The thought held a bitterness she'd felt more and more often in recent days. Take a bear shifter, train her in that tradition, keep her just a little bit bored and a whole lot eager, and then turn her loose in front of opportunity?

"What did you *expect?*" she muttered, out loud this time, as she gave the elevator call button an unnecessarily savage punch. The little plastic cover made a faint cracking noise. *Well, hell.* She needed the activity, anyway. She'd take the stairs.

"You smell like Ruger." The voice came so close, so unexpected, that Mariska startled away from the elevator. *Jet.* Of course. Only wolf-borne Jet could take a Sentinel unaware. Not that Mariska had been at her best, so full of introspection and unexpected emotions. She put on her calmest face, casting Jet a glance. "Is that polite?"

Jet paused to think about it, wild whisky eyes beneath

black hair, feral features unbothered by the implied criticism. "Is it *not* polite?"

A little off balance all over again, Mariska said, "It's private."

"*Private* is a thing that others can't perceive," Jet pointed out. "The scent of Ruger is an obvious thing."

"You're supposed to pretend," Mariska muttered, taking a step for the stairs, uncertain how this woman fit into the hierarchy of Southwest Brevis—other than being more wolf than anyone, other than providing invaluable insight to the Core…other than being Nick's chosen.

"Pretend what?" Jet tilted her head slightly; her posture changed, ever so subtly, and Mariska froze, seeing the threat behind it.

Mariska knew the rules about taking her bear here in the hallways of brevis. She wasn't so sure about Jet.

"Pretend you weren't lovers?" Jet asked, with no apparent self-consciousness at all. "Pretend you didn't share that part of yourself with him, before you came in here this morning to hurt him so?"

"I'm doing what I think is best," Mariska said, irritation rising. She hadn't understood, until she'd seen that look in Ruger's eyes, that her presence would do more than annoy him. That it would undermine him—and it would do so in front of his team. But her reasons for doing it? Still sound. Still important. "For both brevis and Ruger."

"And for you."

Mariska felt her eyes narrow. "You were right at the head of the line when they handed out *blunt,* weren't you?"

"I don't know what that means," Jet said. "And I don't think it matters. The thing that matters is how Ruger looked when he saw you in Nick's office."

"Don't tell me you think he should be working this without protection." Righteous indignation lent a snap to her voice. "Maks just barely survived what he fought up there—*Maks,* your own best bodyguard. Ruger is a *healer.* Just because he's a bear doesn't mean he should go up there alone."

"Pack is best," Jet said, agreeing so readily that it took Mariska by surprise. "But you didn't have to hurt him to do this, and you did. How does that make you the best person to watch his back?"

"I—" Mariska's certainty fled, leaving her floundering and frustrated. "I'm only doing my job."

Jet looked at her with something akin to scorn. The sting of it tightened Mariska's throat in a combination of familiar bitterness and old despair. *"Pack,"* Jet said, "is everything. Until you come from that place, you cannot do your job at all."

"That's not fair," Mariska muttered—but she did it to Jet's retreating back, seeing in her tall, lithe form everything that she wasn't; seeing in her graceful movement everything she had wanted to be.

No, she told herself. What she wanted to be was seen for herself, accepted for herself, valued for herself…given the chance to prove herself.

She'd thought this was it. She'd thought Ruger might understand; she'd thought she could be of important value to this team.

But now she'd seen that look on Ruger's face; she'd heard his fierce need to support his friends and his beleaguered brevis…she understood that she'd taken that chance from him.

And now she'd watched them discuss things she'd only before read about. Now she'd seen the grim expression in Ian Scott's eyes when he spoke of the amulets, and the concern on Sandy's face. She'd seen them all trying to be matter-of-fact about circumstances that were so obviously grave, and she'd seen them reacting to a seer's visions that she'd so readily shrugged off after reading about Katie Maddox's lightweight history.

Mariska looked at Jet's retreating form, and for the second time that morning, swallowed back the fear that she'd been terribly, terribly wrong.

Ruger tossed his gear in the back of his assigned short-bed pickup truck, grateful that brevis motor pool hadn't tried to cram him into the hybrid BMW SUV that had put that brief, slightly manic grin on Ian's face.

Grateful, too, that after they'd dumped their gear into the pickup, his two amulet flunkies had trailed Ian over to that vehicle, along with Sandra and Jet. At least, he was grateful until he did the math, and jerked his head up to see Mariska hoisting her own gear into the back of the truck…with no seats left in the BMW.

"Yeahhh," he said. And, "No. Trade out with Sandy."

Mariska cast a meaningful glance over her shoulder to where Ian had already put the car in gear and peeled out—too quickly—into Tucson's rising midday traffic. "I was hoping we could talk."

"I was hoping we wouldn't," Ruger told her, yanking the door open and adjusting the driver's seat back as far as it would go without even trying to get in first.

"Don't you think we should?" She stood solidly in the other doorway, the sun glinting so brightly off her dark hair as to be painful, nothing even hinting of hesitance in her manner. Lady bear, and everything about her was still just what he wanted. His body knew it, his brain knew it, his heart knew it, and damn, it made him mad. *So close…*

"Look," he said. "I get it. You went for what you wanted with brevis. You went for what you wanted last night. It turns out to be different from what I wanted, but I don't guess that's your fault. But it also turns out I don't trust you because of how you went about it, and *that* would be your fault. Don't expect me to feel any differently about it. And don't expect me to play nice so you can pretend it's all fine. You wanted to ride with me? Let me know how that works out for you." He climbed into the truck and slammed the door closed, making final adjustments to the seat.

When he reached for the seat belt, she was right there beside him already, tucking her small personal backpack off to the side, flipping the air vents the way she wanted them. "It's not like that."

He snorted, with no effort to make it kind. "It's exactly like that." The motor started smoothly, and he reached for the radio.

She turned it off.

"Ah, hell," Ruger said in disgust, and put the truck into gear. "Awkward silence it is."

"Look," she said, and she sounded exasperated. Exasperated, but trying to moderate it. "I did what I did, and it's done. But I didn't mean to mess with you."

He snorted again. "What did you mean, then?"

"I just wanted—"

"I got that part," he said. "You *wanted.*"

"So did you!" she said, temper rising in a sudden spurt—her nostrils flared, the color rising on the angle of her cheek, coming through the tone of her skin. "You *wanted* several times, as I recall, and it seemed to me you were happy enough with what you got!"

Ruger sat in silence a moment, his foot on the brake, his body twisting to check behind the truck before he backed up. He regarded her steadily, his heart beating stupidly hard, his chest tightened up with equally stupid hurt. He said, "I did. And I was. And I somehow managed not to sacrifice you along the way."

Her eyes widened; her mouth flattened, and he suspected she bit the inside of her lip. After a long moment, she said quietly, "None of that means I'm not right for this job."

"It *means* I don't trust you." He pulled out into traffic a lot more steadily than Ian had, heading for Route 77 northwest out of Tucson. "And that means you can't do the job."

"Sure as hell is going to make it harder," she muttered, crossing her arms over her seat belt, looking away. "Maybe you're just a big dumb bear after all."

He slanted a quick scowl at her, keeping his attention on the road. Even Sentinel reflexes were good for just so much in city traffic. "How exactly do you figure that?"

"I *figure*," she said, "that it's in your best interests to be a team player. I *figure* it's in your best interests to work with me so I can watch your back."

"That's your mistake." Ruger braked for a light, and took advantage of the moment to look over at her— catching her by surprise, and catching, too, the faint hint of misery on her face—right before her mouth firmed up and her eyes hardened, and she met his gaze straight on. He didn't soften his tone in the least, letting the words come out distinctly, hitting each one and watching the impact of them in her expression. "Because I don't need anyone to *watch my back* at all."

This time, when he switched the radio on, she left it.

Mariska climbed out of the truck to take a deep breath of pine-scented air, looking out over the achingly clear

skies of Arizona high country. Their accommodations—
a cluster of seasonal tourist cabins twenty minutes out
from the tiny town of Pine Bluff—sat nestled against a
rugged hillside, and Sitgreaves National Forest spread out
before them. Mariska's bear stretched within her, eager
to sink claws to earth.

The SUV had arrived some moments before, its oc-
cupants spilling out over a minimalist parking zone of
hard dirt, natural cinders and pine needles spread everywhere. Sandy already stood to the south of the cabins, her
posture too erect to be casual, her face lifted slightly to
the sky, her eyes closed. *Already setting the wards.* Ian's
people had scattered across the grounds surrounding the
two neighboring cabins, their expressions full of focus.

Not that there would likely be amulets seeded anywhere nearby when they'd only just arrived, but Mariska
understood well enough that familiarizing themselves
with the taste and energies of the area would make it
possible to locate amulets should they be placed later—
especially if they were of the new crop of silent amulets.

Ruger, too, disembarked from the truck, standing
much as Mariska had—scenting the air, visibly longing
to indulge in his bear. Yesterday she'd seen him as tall
and burly; she'd loved the curl of his hair, so obviously
only tamed by the cut, and she'd loved the rugged nature
of his beard. It had been all too easy to imagine the vigorous nature of their bodies joining…and it was all too
easy to remember it now.

But today she saw beyond the first impression, and
realized how much of it was just that—an impression,
driven by his very nature. Today she saw the masculine
beauty of a body that was large and strong, but not over-
built; today she saw that the beard had hidden the lean
features of his face, long dimples carved into his cheeks,

a jaw that was strong without going wide, and pale brown eyes shadowed by dark and expressive eyebrows.

She realized her palms had gone damp, and surreptitiously wiped them along her thighs.

Jet came out of the cabin in front of the truck, wearing nothing but a long T-shirt and a necklace of braided leather and gleaming metal. Her bare feet moved soundlessly over the ground, and she stopped before Mariska. "This is our cabin," she said. "You, and me, and Ruger." She glanced at the second cabin. "The others will stay together so they can talk amulet things."

Mariska winced inwardly—but of course she'd be housed with the man she was here to guard. "Thanks," she said. "Going out already?"

"To run," Jet said with such longing that Mariska felt an immediate sympathy. It was one thing to keep her bear at bay when she'd grown up doing so, when she hadn't even taken the bear until she was twelve. It was another to be born wolf and linger as human. Jet added, "And I want to check this land."

"Are those—" Mariska stopped herself from reaching to touch the metal-thick, satin disks with chunky edges that looked like a gift, but also looked like "—dog tags?"

Jet laughed. "Wolf tags," she said. "You can wear your special clothes and have them change with you. I run without."

Ian joined them from the other cabin, looking satisfied with the housing and satisfied with the inspection. "So you play pet, if someone comes on you?"

"Not pet," Jet said, and bared her teeth.

Ian laughed and held up a defensive hand. "*We* know that, darlin'," he said. "But try not to scare the natives, okay?"

"They won't see me," she assured him, and headed for the woods.

"Ready to take a look around?" Ian asked Mariska. "We're meeting Maks in half an hour."

Mariska looked over the hood of the truck to Ruger, who had come out of his reverie to head for the back of the truck. "Go ahead," he said, grabbing the first three bags and easily slinging them from the truck. "It's more important for you to check the place out. I'll do my own recon when I get the chance."

She heard nothing in his voice but matter-of-fact practicality, but she winced a little inside anyway. And then, as Ruger's shoulders filled the doorway, she wondered how they would both possibly fit into the same cabin, no matter how large it was.

Jet ran the woods. She ran as wolf, stretching her legs and lowering her head into the pure glory of it. Indulging in the hot, dry scent of the towering pines in the afternoon sun, the breeze ruffling her black fur...the silence in her head.

So full of talk, the humans. So full of thinking they knew what they wanted, and then not being happy when those things happened.

Her tongue lolled out in a ridiculous pant; she pulled herself down to a trot, scrambling up the loose scuff of a rocky outcrop to circle behind and above the cabins. No wise wolf wore herself out on indulgences when she needed to stay sharp against the enemy. Always in the form of man, that enemy—once because she had been wolf, and now because she called the Sentinels her pack.

It was to her relief that Ian had asked her to stay here at the cabins while they went off to meet Maks Altán at the place where he now lived and to follow him into the forest to Forakkes' bunker. Not just to stay, but to learn the area in all its scents and sounds and lay of the land so she might be alert to any hint of incursion by the Atrum Core. "We'll be working hard and fast," he'd said. "When we come to ground, we'll need to know it's safe."

She'd promised him that. And if later, they needed her to stand sentry at the bunker, she would do that, too. Wolf again.

She only regretted that she was not *wolf again* with Nick, whose uniquely hoarfrost hair fooled people into thinking he was prematurely gray. *Foolish people.* They had only to look, and they would see it wasn't. They had only to look in his eyes to see the gray wolf lurking there.

She saw the bear in Ruger easily enough. She'd spotted Mariska's smaller bear right away. And no matter that they'd showered…they smelled of one another, and of lingering lust.

Mariska, she didn't know. But she had never seen that hurt in Ruger's eye; she had never seen him closed and angry…and yet still obviously wanting. It was the *wanting* that was the problem. It meant Mariska could hurt him again, if she wanted. Or even if she didn't want, but didn't pay enough attention.

Blunt, Mariska had called her.

Jet's teeth weren't blunt. Not in the least. And if Mariska Banks wasn't careful with Jet's pack, she would learn just that.

Mariska stood behind Katie Maddox's weathered log home and even more weathered old pole barn, looking out into the embracing forest—and even with the team and Maks Altán right there beside her, found herself so in the thrall of the place that she almost forgot why they were there.

Like Ruger, Maks was a big man—a Siberian tiger lurking visibly beneath, his eyes green and his hair white at the temples with darker streaks running through the deep chestnut. Like Jet, the wildness of his nature flaunted itself, running quiet but steady in every move he made. His uneven movement stood out in stark contrast— the hitch in his stride, the stiffness in his torso. Sentinels healed with astonishing swiftness—but only when it came to saving their lives. Beyond that point, they had to pull themselves together one day at a time, like anyone else.

Or at least, almost like anyone else.

On the surface, Maks didn't hover over Katie, his slender love, and he didn't evince any threat or subtle warning—but Mariska quickly realized that no matter how they shifted in conversation, he always stood between her and the team.

With good reason, at that. No Chinese water deer would find herself happy in the presence of so many predators. Ian's two assistants were too light of blood to take a change form, but two bears and a snow leopard were quite enough.

All the same, Katie Maddox—long-legged, graceful, and touched by cinnamon in her hair, her eyes and even her faint freckles—didn't look intimidated. She looked, in her way, fierce. Protective. And while Mariska puzzled over it, Ruger narrowed his eyes, traded glances between Katie and Maks, and said, "You two didn't waste any time."

Only when Katie looked at him in surprise, her hand touching her abdomen, did Mariska understand. She immediately accorded Maks another notch of respect for his quiet restraint, and took a step farther away from Katie.

Maks chose not to acknowledge Ruger at all; he lifted his head to the woods, drawing their attention west.

"We bought the neighbor's land," Katie said. "And there's forest on all sides of us. So as long as you head out in this direction, no one will see you." She ran a hand over the electronic ATV sitting beside her; four of the machines hunkered by the side of the old pole barn well behind the house. "You'll be hooking up with an old logging road for most of the ride. Don't be seen—nothing with a motor is allowed in this forest."

"Then why use them at all?" Mariska was the first to voice the unspoken, although she tried to put humor behind it. "You didn't think the bears could keep up with the cats?"

Maks only smiled, quiet as it was. "Up to you," he said. "I'm riding."

Ruger sent her a look, a thread of incredulous response reaching her from what was most likely a lingering result of their time together. Only then did she understand, even as Maks shifted the weight from his recently injured leg, and winced as she opened her mouth to apologize— except she couldn't read the expression that crossed his face just then, a sudden dazed distraction.

"Maks…" Katie's voice sounded odd, faint and distressed; her eyes had lost focus. If Mariska had had any doubt about the nature of their relationship, it would have disappeared before the sight of the tiger gone stupid and dazed beside her, caught up in whatever gripped her.

Ruger reached Katie just as her eyes rolled back, scooping her right off her feet, his legs braced but otherwise showing no particular effort—as though he could stand there forever.

"That's a powerful thing for a *vague little seeing*," Ian said, always that little sardonic tone behind his words.

"Could be the pregnancy," Ruger said, carefully shifting so Katie's lolling head found support against his shoulder. "Could be she's been hiding this much from us."

Maks took a staggered step forward, caught his balance, and shook off whatever had gripped him, looking far too vulnerable for a tiger. His voice came a little rough. "No. This is new." He reached for Katie with purpose, but it was too late; she stirred in Ruger's arms and then made a startled, frightened noise, stiffening against him.

"Katie Rae," Maks said, but he didn't crowd them; he only put a hand on her leg. "Ruger is safe. Let it be."

"Maks," she said uncertainly, clutching at Ruger's shirt as if that would hold the world still, too.

"Let it be, Katie Rae," Maks said again. "If he frightens you, I'll have to hurt him. And we need him right now."

"Oh," Katie said—still breathless, but no longer quite sounding frightened. "Okay, then." But then she hesitated, looking up at Ruger as if she saw him for the first time—reaching to touch his face with a sympathetic empathy that took Mariska by surprise. "Healer," she murmured. "I'm sorry."

Mariska fought a shock of envy at the way he received Katie's touch, accepting both it and the sentiment she offered. He set Katie gently on her feet, relinquishing her to Maks.

Katie held tightly to Maks' hand. "Just like before," she said, her gaze still a little distant. "This foreseeing has always been about more than Maks' presence here… that was just part of it. The *first* part. But…there's a foreboding…there's terrible grief, there's—" She stopped and shook her head. "Can I try to show you, please? My seeings have never translated well to words."

"Can you do that?" one of Ian's assistants asked. Mariska hadn't seen them at the meeting, hadn't ridden with them in the tidy little BMW SUV, and now, with some resignation, simply thought of them as Heckle and Jeckle.

"I can try," Katie told him. "But I need hands." She extended hers, and Maks put his over it. Ruger, too, and that left Mariska and Ian and Sandy, exchanging glances with a mutual reluctance but finally adding their hands to the physical nexus along with Heckle and Jeckle.

"Ready?" Katie murmured. "Here it comes…"

But Mariska wasn't ready.

The wild, yipping howl of a bereft wild dog, the wash of a vile stench, tasting foul in her throat. A hollow huffing sound, followed by a clacking, the surge of fear…a tremendous explosion. And then an entire chorus of grief, animal skins fluttering to the ground like sodden laundry. Wolf and bear, panther and boar, wildcat and stoat and deer. Crumpled up and discarded, and a nation of grief splashing in to wash it all away—

Ian swore under his breath, jerking his hand from beneath Mariska's and sending her tumbling back to reality. Tumbling back *in* reality, as she struggled to reorient and found herself steadied by a pair of familiar hands—familiar and big, and a touch her body knew instantly.

Not until she'd blinked and recovered her equilibrium did he step away, leaving an ache where his warmth had been.

"You see," Maks said, glancing at Katie. "You see why it matters."

"Yes," Ian said, and his words sounded a little strangled. "Whatever that was, it sure as hell matters."

"That sound," said Heckle—short, bandy-muscled, and not strong enough of Sentinel blood to take the change. He cupped his hands over his mouth to imitate what words couldn't quite convey. *A hollow huffing sound, a clacking...*

"What *was* that?" Jeckle asked, but not as if he expected to get an answer. Like Heckle, he likely saw little of fieldwork, but he was a solid sort, old enough to have a wealth of experience behind him.

Mariska exchanged a glance with Ruger, looking for and finding the wince of awareness that told her he'd recognized it, too. "Bear," she said finally. "Frightened black bear, with teeth and breath."

Heckle gave her a skeptical look. "What frightens a bear?"

Ruger said flatly, "Not much," and Mariska realized she was chafing her upper arms, chilled to the bone in the rising warmth of the late-summer day.

"Great," Ian said. "Now the bears are spooked."

"Good," Katie said, her tone unexpectedly practical. "You should be."

Ruger made a rumbling noise; Mariska thought it might have been dark humor. Katie shot him a look. "And maybe you'll all be *careful*." She shivered, giving the woods a wary look.

"The boundaries are up," Maks told her. "I'll know if anyone approaches while we're gone." He sent a look Ruger's way that Mariska interpreted as a warning. *And once I take you in, you're on your own.*

Chapter 4

The ATVs moved along in eerie silence, and the old logging road unrolled in uneven waves until it slipped along the side of a more significant ridge. By then they'd hit their first Core-imposed obstacle, the thick layers of determent workings that filled Mariska first with the impulse to turn aside and then a rising anxiety.

But Maks led them steadily forward, and the effect faded. Eventually, Maks took them off the trail to a little hollow, and they huddled the machines together and cut the engines. By the time Mariska dismounted and grabbed her gear bag, Maks had already snagged the waiting camo net and flipped it over the ATVs.

Heckle and Jeckle were the last to get out of his way, fumbling their heavily padded amulet storage bags. Maks gave the net a final flip and it settled into place. Rather than heading down the road, he circled aside to move slantwise along the slope of the mild ridge they'd just passed by, his limp more pronounced with the marginal footing—a cautious approach.

"I thought this bunker was abandoned," Mariska said, keeping her voice low as a matter of course with the assumption that someone—anyone—might be in these woods close enough to hear.

Maks looked back at her with some surprise, leading them upward. "This is *Core*."

"He means," Ruger added, "we don't take anything for granted."

Mariska gave herself a little kick. *Of course not.* She simply wasn't in step with this team yet.

Wouldn't be, if she didn't stop second-guessing her own decisions.

Maks took them over the crest of the ridge. "I don't know if anyone remains," he told them, a note of apology there. "The scents are strong enough. But I didn't go in."

Ian's voice held some hint of exasperation. "I should hope not. We'll need to sweep for amulets before we so much as touch the damned door. Tell me you knew that."

"I knew that," Maks said, mild in response. Like Nick, Mariska thought—with enough confidence so he had no need to bristle back. But let someone threaten Katie…

She wondered, quite suddenly, what it would be like to have someone at her back so fiercely. Not because she needed it. Just because of what it would feel like.

Maks led them around the jagged stump of a fallen pine and tipped his head at the cut of ground breaking way before them, though there was no structure evident. "There," he said, and crouched—started to, at least, until the one leg buckled, and he put his knee on the ground with the compensatory grace inherent in all the big cat Sentinels. "The bunker."

The ground dipped halfway down the ridge and rose even higher on the other side; otherwise, it was unremarkable. Just a rocky little swale covered in stubby, twisted scrub oak and the ancient skeleton of another fallen tree.

But Mariska wasn't going to be the first one to say there wasn't anything there. Instead, she moved into position beside Ruger, turning her senses to their surroundings—even if that meant no more than noting the pine siskins *fweet*ing overhead and a singular squirrel rustling around in the pine needles some hundred feet away. The local energies were quiet—no scent of Core amulet corruption, everyone's personal shields drawn tight. Maks' was the loudest of those, his shields so much stronger than she ever would have expected, even knowing of his personal strengths.

"Ah," Ian said suddenly. "I see it now. How the hell did you ever find it?"

"It stinks of Forakkes," Maks said, and his voice was no longer casual at all. "And others, once close."

And still Mariska didn't see it—not until she quit searching the details and instead looked at the little swale as a whole. The slight convex curve of the ground, the occasional hard-edged shadow, immune to the sway of the breeze. This time she couldn't stop herself. *"How—"*

How had he buried this structure, and left so little sign of it on the surrounding environment?

"It's been there a long time," Ian said, with no trouble following her line of thought.

"The old logging activity would have been a perfect cover for its construction," Jeckle observed. "The question is, how do we get *in?*"

"In the rocks across from us," Maks said. "I didn't try it."

"Smart," Ian said again. He glanced back to Heckle and Jeckle. "Let's drift on over there, boys. Stay quiet on your feet, and when I say to hang back, then damned well hang back. No one's asking you to be field Sentinels overnight."

Maks looked over to Ruger. "Don't underestimate him," he said. "*Forakkes*. He is a man without soul."

"I know what he did," Ruger said grimly, and Mariska got the impression that they were alluding to something other than the events in the operation field reports—the details of Forakkes' amulet workings from the time of Core D'oíche, including those that had caused the ultimate if inadvertent demise of the former local Core prince, the *drozhar,* of this area. Forakkes had gone on to create the monstrous javelina-creature Maks had battled at so great a price—and he'd nearly succeeded in his intent to kidnap and enslave Katie Maddox.

But this was something else—something grimmer and even more personal. If she hadn't known it by Maks' eyes, she would have heard it in Ruger's voice.

Maks pushed off from the ground—he'd barely faltered before Ruger reached him, one strong arm steadying him the rest of the way up. Maks' expression was more annoyance than pain, and he said to Ruger, "No matter. Katie will see to it." Mariska was instantly caught by their easy camaraderie, by Ruger's instant response to a teammate's need. By herself, *instantly the outsider.*

She had only herself to blame for the intensity of that feeling. Jet had been the only one to confront her so directly, but they all knew Ruger had been stunned by her presence on the team—they all knew it was personal.

Maks started back down the slope, and she quickly smoothed away the little curl of envy that tightened her mouth. Ruger turned to her, his dark expression enough to warn her. "Nothing happening here for a bodyguard, you may have noticed."

"I'm patient," she told him.

He snorted. "I doubt the hell out of that." He bent and scooped up his pack. "If you were *patient,* you wouldn't be here. You wouldn't have talked your way onto this team, when Nick damned well could have used you elsewhere."

But I wanted to work with you. And I believed in what I told Nick. "I wish we could start over," she said abruptly, shifting her own pack. "I wish you could look at me and see whatever it was you saw in that park yesterday evening."

He looked at her for a long moment. "So do I," he said, and for that moment his voice was devoid of blame and bitterness, holding nothing but honesty—and maybe a touch of sadness. "Dammit, Mariska—so do I."

Across the swale, up on the high ridge, Ian waved to them; it was enough of an invitation that Mariska tentatively made herself more receptive to sent communication, and she wasn't surprised when she felt the tickle of his thoughts.

::We can see it,:: he said. ::We're heading in.::

::We'll wait,:: Ruger said, not so much as glancing to see if she agreed. ::I'm getting something from inside, though—not human, not well. I'll try to make sense of it.::

Her resentment flared. *Hello, you could have discussed this decision with me.* But staying here made too much sense. Besides, if he was heading into some sort of healer mode, she could hardly move out on her own after making such a big fat bear deal about being here.

And if she was going to be honest with herself, she'd have to admit her crankiness came from resentment—from the slowly dawning awareness that she'd just plain screwed up.

::Got us a door,:: Ian said. ::Nicely integrated with the Core amulet equivalent of ice-cold water balancing in a bucket overhead. Gonna be a few minutes.::

::We'll wait,:: Ruger said again, although this time his attention seemed divided, his gaze distant. His brow drew with concentration—with some subtle effort. "Not *unwell*," he muttered, and she wasn't sure if he spoke to her or if he just spoke. "But not *right*. I can't— *Hell*." He jerked as if he'd needed to catch his balance against the nonexistent movement of the ground, and Mariska put out an impulsive hand to steady him—but pulled back before he noticed, as he abruptly turned away, one palm pressing against his brow.

She gave him that physical space as he yanked a colorful bandanna from his back pocket, broad shoulders stiff.

"The brief said your healing was still affected," she said. "It didn't say how."

He turned back to her, stuffing the bandanna away. "Does it matter?"

"I don't know," she told him. "Does it?"

He glared at her a long moment, then muttered a curse—a capitulation of sorts, if not a happy one. *"Affected,"* he said, "is a euphemism for *can't*."

It shocked her more than she expected. "At all? But I thought—"

He shook his head, a vicious motion that cut her off short. *"Can't,"* he repeated. "I can still feel the wrongness of things—like in there." He jerked his head at the obscured bunker. "But I can't heal it. I can't touch those energies any longer, never mind guide them."

"But you're—" They were thoughtless words, and she stopped herself just in time. *You're Ruger. The bear who heals—and who does it better than anyone else in the field. The one who needs backup just because he's too important to risk, never mind that no one should have to do those two things at once.*

She might as well not have bothered. He clearly understood the direction of her thoughts. "Not anymore," he told her. "I'm here to analyze, that's all."

"I don't understand." She didn't, and it troubled her; she didn't bother to hide it. "Then why would Nick give me the impression you'd take the healer's role—that you'd need me?"

Ruger snorted; it was a throaty sound. "I don't have the faintest idea. Because he's giving you the chance of your career, to be in on this operation? Because he's pissed at me about something?" But he stopped, and shook his head. "No, that's not fair. If Nick's pissed, he comes at you head-on." He sent her a direct stare, a challenge from pale brown eyes. "I only know one thing for sure—*I don't need this.* And we're spread thin enough. Nick should have put you somewhere else. On some*one* else." The challenge didn't ease in the faintest. "Someone who you haven't lied to yet."

"I didn't—" she said hotly, but stopped. Not just because she pretty much *had* lied to him, even if it was both simpler and more complicated and that. But because he'd gone still, staring down the hill. Not still as Maks or another big cat would do, the stalking calm—just plain *still.*

And then, before she could ask, he started down the slope. There was something about the angle of his head that caught her attention, spiking concern.

"Ruger," she said, pitching her voice as a warning.

He didn't seem to hear, and maybe it was just as well she hadn't distracted him. For an instant later, when a camouflage-obscured figure behind the fallen tree exploded into motion, Ruger barely startled at all, even when Mariska yelled his name—this time imbuing it with alarm as well as warning, all the *dammit, this is what I'm here for* she could manage in one word.

At the park, he'd respected that. He'd wordlessly left her the room to do her share of the brawling.

Now he ignored her completely—even though he could easily see that the man had reacted in panic as Ruger's path downward narrowed his escape route from this swale. And he could damned well see that if he stepped back, he'd create the man room to get past, leaving him completely open to Mariska's full-bore approach from the side.

A bear in full-speed charge was nothing to trifle with, whether in her human or animal form.

But no, Ruger crouched slightly, weighting himself to earth—taking those few necessary steps to block the man's way. And then he just *was,* rooted and unmoving. He ducked one shoulder in a perfectly timed block, and Mariska found herself floundering to shift gears. She cursed, slipping in the layered old pine needles, and righted herself to discover that the fool of a Core minion was fighting back—and doing it in the cowardly way that the Core did best when they couldn't manage an ambush.

With firearms.

"Gun!" she cried, barely hearing Ian's mind voice with its bemused ::What the hell is going on over there?:: as she spotted the weapon on its way out of the shoulder holster hidden beneath the forest-patterned camo jacket. *"Gun!"*

::Idiot,:: Ruger snarled, a personal thought gone public—or at least gone to Mariska—as he yanked the man up and off his feet, gave him a good shake, and dropped him to slap the gun away. "Stay *down.*"

But by then Mariska was close enough and still running on strong, and she could see the man had no intention of doing any such thing. He fumbled in his jacket pocket even as he crabbed away—a classic amulet grab—

and Ruger said, "Ah, *hell*," and threw himself down on the minion.

"No, no, *no!*" Not when there was no way to tell what the amulet would do if it made contact, what it would do even if it didn't.

The dull snap of bone stopped her short. Ruger rolled away from the man, ending up on his hands and knees and already poised to thrust up and away. A big man, nimble on his feet.

But then, she already knew that.

Amulet corruption shredded the air, far thicker than carrion; the man had time for only a faint gargle of horror, a quick and spastic thrash toward death before he subsided.

After a moment, Ruger climbed to his feet, nothing of haste about it.

::Ruger?:: Ian said, obscured by terrain and structure. ::What the hell?::

::We're good,:: Ruger said, an absent sending that didn't distract him from circling in as he brushed himself off. ::Back with you in a moment.::

"Good?" Mariska said, aghast at the shrill note in her voice. "We're *good?*" By then she was close enough to reach him—she punched him solidly on the arm. "This is what you call *good?*" She looked down at the minion—the former minion—and discovered his elbow bent the wrong way, his hand stuck in his pocket as it clutched the amulet…and his body as mummified as any creature left dead and undisturbed in the desert sun. "What were you even *thinking?*" and she threw another punch into his arm, full of frustration and fury.

Ruger turned with a quickness belying his size, his hand closing around her wrist—closing hard. His eyes, so matter-of-factly amiable—*so filled with heat*—had gone hard, hard enough to make her gasp. And he said nothing, but she heard the growl rumbling deep in his chest.

She responded without thinking, offering the quiet sound in her throat that meant a bear's acquiescence—but only for the instant before she managed to cut it short. Then she yanked her wrist free and glared at him. "You should have let him go. I would have had him—that's why I'm *here*." And when he said nothing, she found herself flinging out words, rushing to fill that void, wanting something—*anything*—from him in response. "Last night in that parking lot, you would have let him past. You would have worked as a team. You should have known—"

"Last night," Ruger interrupted, "we *were* a team."

She blinked back unexpected emotion, and made her voice hard. "We're still a team. You have your job, and I have mine. Don't get them mixed up again."

::Guys?:: Ian said. ::Hate to break up your little whatever-it-is, but have I mentioned I want to know *what the hell is going on?*::

"We had company," Ruger said, out loud as much as through his mind's voice. "Our company accidentally fried himself with his own amulet."

::Purely by coincidence, I'm sure. Keep sharp, then. We're just about through here; come on over and we'll get a look inside.::

::Coming,:: Mariska said—but when she lifted her head, she discovered that Ruger was already on his way.

The brief, acrid stench of stolen Core power burst through the underground workshop, making Ciobaka sneeze. "Wowoww."

"What are you complaining about now?" Tarras

slammed the door of the recently emptied cage nearest to Ciobaka's.

"No," Ehwoord said, the snap of annoyance in his voice. "He's right. Yoske triggered one of his defense amulets."

Ciobaka tilted his head, studying Tarras as his mouth clamped shut and his body stiffened in anticipation of repercussion. But Ehwoord continued quietly grooming amulets for the next round of impressions, no more prepossessing than he ever was with his slight stature, his belly going round, his hair gray and his skin lined with wrinkles of a strangely stiff nature—as if parts of him had forgotten they were old and the rest of him was ancient. Sometimes Ciobaka thought his mind worked in that same pattern, shifting from coldly efficient to something just a little less sane.

Tarras asked carefully, "You felt it?"

"It's my amulet," Ehwoord told him, as if that was explanation enough.

"Then they've found the overflow installation."

"Perhaps. Or Yoske became careless between here and there." Ehwoord's mouth tightened. "I needed that network up and running. I *need* those cameras. After a time, if Yoske doesn't return, you'll see to it."

Tarras cleared his throat. "Of course. I'll take a team and—"

"No," Ehwoord snapped, and Ciobaka blinked at his emphatic tone. Interesting, to see Ehwoord ruffled. Interesting, to see that Tarras feared. "We hardly need half a posse tramping around in the woods if the Sentinels have found the installation. You may, however, take Ciobaka. He can warn you of Sentinel presence long before you detect them. They are, at all times, far too cocky about their presence in woods such as these."

"Wahnnah!" Ciobaka said, and barked an exclamation as his tail quivered in anticipation. "Ouwwtah!"

"Out," Ehwoord said, flaunting his human tongue and lips. "And yes. Of course, you will wear the collar—and you still bear the obedience amulet within you. If your behavior is less than exemplary, there will be punishment upon return."

Ciobaka flattened his dingoesque ears, crouching slightly in the submission that Ehwoord wanted to see. But he flexed his newly mobile dewclaw thumb, pondering the buckle to his electric collar—and made sure Ehwoord saw that not at all.

Chapter 5

In truth, Ruger had only meant to stop the Core minion from pulling the amulet from his pocket. If the man
hadn't triggered the thing in hand, he'd still be alive.

He'd been a handsome man—as were many of the
Core, in a snake-oil kind of way. Not because of their
strikingly swarthy skin—more olive than Mariska's stunning complexion, not as dark—but from the affectation
of their hair, slicked back into a short queue and always
black, whether natural or dyed. And the silver jewelry,
heavy at wrist and neck and ear.

And their ubiquitous suits. Especially in the high-level
posses—those serving the regional *drozhar* or even the
Septs Prince, leader of them all. High sheen, beautifully
cut…always just a little bit *I think much of myself.*

Not that this man was any of those things any longer.
His black hair had gone dry and brittle; his skin taut,
dry walnut stretching over bone. His clothes had been
woodsy enough, the camo jacket over fatigue pants and
a black T. But whatever else he might have had to tell
them, they'd lost it when his tongue dried up. All they'd

ever know was that this place wasn't quite as abandoned as they'd thought it to be.

"He's safe," Ian said, coming to inspect the man now that he'd cleared the installation's entrance of security workings. "I'll leave the rest of it to you."

Ruger hadn't expected Mariska to display any squeamishness over the chore, and she didn't. She leaned over to search the man, displaying her truly fine ass in the process. Ruger watched until he realized the riveted nature of his gaze, and scowled as he moved off across the swale. "I'm going to take a look inside with the AmSpecs. Let us know what you find."

"Nothing so far," she said, all business, her voice muffled as she bent to her task—and as he put distance between them. "Whatever he was up to, I don't think he's going to give us any clues."

One of Ian's poorly introduced AmSpecs waited by the entrance. It turned out to be a substantial door set within the rocks at the base of the opposite slope, obscured by light and shadow and a truly clever camouflage of combined paint and netting. Of course, Forakkes wouldn't expect anyone to get this close, given the deterrent workings he'd had set in the area—and likely no one had, until now.

"Jack Ivers," the man said, as Ruger approached. "AmSpec grunt. Glad to meet you." He grasped the inset latch and twisted, and then put enough effort into shoving the heavy metal door that Ruger propped a hand over his shoulder and pushed, speeding the process considerably.

Of course, then he had to duck. Not even the Core, with its typically lavish appointments and luxuries, would dig an underground hallway any larger than it absolutely had to be.

This one sloped sharply downward, with fourteen-inch circles of solar tube lighting overhead—eventually they'd find the discreet plastic domes that served to collect and amplify the light. Darkened LED lights also lined the sides of the hall and the center of the ceiling. Wire mesh served to reinforce the packed dirt walls, anchored and slightly concave. The good, clean scent of dirt went a long way toward cleansing Ruger's head of the inevitable stink of Core workings.

The stink when they entered the installation was another thing altogether. Harrison, the other AmSpec grunt, stood off to the side, his complexion gone a little gray. "All clear so far," he told Ruger. "We've checked the amulet station and the animals." He nodded at the place, a cavernous Quonset structure also lit by solar tubes, subdivided into distinct areas, and full of such dim corners and visual clutter that Ruger couldn't immediately make sense of it all. "This is where they work; they don't need to trip over their own amulets every time they turn around."

Ruger merely made a noise deep in his throat, an absent acknowledgment. He understood, for the first time, what they faced in this newly emerged rogue—Forakkes, a man who currently defied his own Core as much as he defied the Sentinels. And he understood, for the first time, the truly terrifying nature of Katie's vision. The pain of this place hit him in a miasma of feeling—all the wrongness, all the misery, all the reeling desperation, striking hard against his healer's perceptions.

And I can't do a damned thing about it.

He stood rooted, all his energy focused on just one thing—filtering out the *need* of this place so he could think.

"I left our friend outside the door," Mariska said, speaking from behind him before she reached his end of the tunnel. "I didn't find anything, but maybe a closer look— Oh, hell." She came up beside Ruger and stared, openly stunned, at the structure spread out before them.

Crates lined the wall on the far end; in the corner stood shelving stacked with aquariums and terrariums. Additional shelves bore bags of esoteric kibble, and one organizational niche held a sophisticated and complex computer station while another held autopsy tables and a third held a wooden worktable and a series of wood cabinets. Closer to the entrance, several completely enclosed spaces looked as if they'd once been private quarters, and a large cage of stout bars still held not only straw and troughs, but the notable stench of javelina.

"What is that *smell?*" Mariska asked, wrinkling her nose.

"Collared peccary times ten or so," Ruger told her, absurdly pleased to find he had complete control of his voice. "The creature Maks fought must have lived here. But there's a lot more here than that."

She nodded. "Death, for one."

"Death, for one," Ian echoed. "No kidding." Then he pointed out the wooden worktable to his assistants. "That's where we'll want to start. I don't want to touch anything today—it's enough to see what we have to work with. We'll make a plan and come at it tomorrow." He headed that way, glancing over his shoulder at Ruger. "I suggest you do the same. Go slow."

Mariska watched him—hesitating, for once, before she charged forward.

Then again, so was he.

"Look," Mariska said, as they closed in on the rack of stacked crates; she nodded to the shelving that held the small animal cages. "Fresh bedding. They all have water. Maybe our guy was here to take care of them."

"Doesn't make sense." Ruger pulled his thoughts together, pushing away the assault of misery. No wonder it had grabbed him so hard from the outside looking in—demanding help, demanding mercy—drawing him past the perception of the woes and into a subconscious attempt to *fix* them. "If this is an active installation, where is everyone? *Anyone?*" He looked back to the largest cage where the mutated javelina had stayed. "It's been weeks since Maks killed that thing, but someone's been tending these animals." He paced the length of the stacked crates, finding them empty—albeit with obvious signs of past occupancy.

"It's as though they're abandoned and yet still part of some experiment," Mariska said, and frowned as they approached the aquariums, slowly coming to a stop, her entire body a signpost of reluctance. "Ruger—"

"Yeah," he said, his voice gruff—agreeing with her, seeing what she saw. This, then, was part of the reason for the odor that permeated this place, interlaced with the misery he'd felt until he could barely tell them apart. It wasn't an odor of death so much as it was an odor of dying.

The first aquarium held a flat rock that barely rose above several inches of water. A limp form sprawled on the rock, its fur mattered and coming away in patches; sections of rotting skin peeled away from beneath. The animal's head was under water, its eyes huge and dull, its gills expanding and contracting as if it gulped for air, never quite getting enough.

"Is that…" Mariska's voice grew tentative; she blew out a breath with an uncanny resemblance of sound to the frightened black bear in Katie's vision. "Is that a squirrel?"

Ruger made a noise deep in his chest. ::Yes,:: he said

between them, not quite trusting his physical voice. An Abert's squirrel with gills, trying not to drown and trying not to rot in the unrelentingly watery environment it hadn't been born to manage.

"But," she stammered, "but…*why?*"

He almost reached for her hand, wanting to wrap it up in his and offer the best comfort he could. And then he remembered that she was here because she'd thought herself ready for it—so ready for it that she'd used his situation as an excuse to be here, never mind that her maneuvering had torn away the one unique thing he'd had left to offer brevis.

So he kept his hand to himself. "Because it's who they are," he said shortly. "It's what they do. It's what you got yourself into when you talked yourself onto this team."

"I—" The word came hot out of her mouth, her temper rising to the moment—and then, with visible effort, moderating into restraint. "That still doesn't answer the question. No matter how wretched the mind behind this, there was also *reason* behind it. The Core bends people—and animals—to its purpose without consideration, but it does have *purpose*."

Zing. She had him there. He scrubbed a hand over his face, still somewhat surprised to find smooth skin where the beard had always been. "In Tucson," he said, "Gausto's purpose was to create a working that allowed those in the Core to change shape—to put them on even ground with the Sentinel field agents."

Mariska snorted. "Even if they could change to a bear, they wouldn't *be* the bear. Not like us."

"No, not like us." Ruger stepped on to the next aquarium, found a snake with stumpy legs and tentacle toes twisting itself into a knot of confusion, and found himself looking at Mariska instead. "But as close as they could come."

"I read the details on that," she said, her expression troubled. "The instability of the working…that's how Fabron Gausto died. They still haven't replaced him with a new *drozhar,* either."

"Still looking for someone with a balance of ambition and common sense. Gausto was all ambition, and look where that got them." *One failed scheme after another, each one tipping the delicate detente between factions further out of balance.* He left the aquariums to check the larger crates, and should have known better. Mammals with feathers, birds with fur and creatures so mixed up he couldn't be certain how they'd started. All of them sick and miserable. Their need hammered against him, an unending and plaintive demand for mercy. And the healer in him fought to respond, leaving Ruger with an aching head. He dabbed at the dampness on his upper lip, half expecting to find blood and relieved when it was still merely a cold sweat.

"Eduard Forakkes was behind that working," Mariska said. "He escaped, came up here…and what? Kept developing it?" She nodded at the animals. "It doesn't make any sense. Not with that Frankenstein javelina, and not with the animals here."

"We thought that was his purpose, when Maks found the javelina," Ruger said. "The question is, are these animals somehow a by-product of that same purpose? Or did he change what he was doing? Or…did we have it wrong all along?"

Mariska's worry came through loud and clear. "What I want to know is how it ties into Katie's vision."

Ian's voice filtered out from the amulet work section. "Get over yourselves," he said. "We're here to gather information. Leave the brevis analysts *something* to do, huh?"

Ruger growled out loud, an ominous sound in the cave-like interior, and Ian laughed. "Back atcha, fella," he said without rancor.

"He's right, I suppose," Mariska said under her breath.

"He's right," Ruger said. "And he's not." He touched the crate where a bird with no beak flicked its tongue out at a cup of mashed seeds, its freakish little nostrils flat to the remaining face and twitching with distress. "I'm a *healer*. Gathering information…that's not the half of it."

"No one expects you to heal these animals," Mariska said, her tone surprised and sharp.

"*I* expect me to heal them." He thought he'd been ready for this—to be out in the field applying what medicines he knew, acting the part of emergency medic without relying on that lifelong innate ability to channel healing energies.

But he hadn't realized how much he'd feel their pain. And he'd underestimated the ongoing impulse to do something about it.

"You must be kidding." Mariska's blunt voice held nothing but honesty—every bit the same lady bear he'd met the evening before.

Now those blunt words beat against him, one by one. "You could be one hundred percent, and you'd never be able to help these animals—to put them back the way they were. You sure can't help them now—the only thing you can do is put them out of their misery."

Ruger stiffened, turning away from the crates to find her close—to draw himself up so it became obvious how much he towered over her. Kodiak and black bear—so similar in nature, so different in effect. "I don't need you here, little bear. I don't want you here. I don't even think you belong here. Do me a favor and don't be in the way."

Her eyes narrowed, darkened with emotion; her chin, surprisingly, revealed that emotion in a little tremble. But she said nothing; she merely turned from him, her shoulders stiff, and walked away.

Ian's mind-voice found its way to Ruger. ::Bastard.::

Ruger shot back a quick response. ::Yeah,:: he said. ::But I'm not wrong.::

He'd taken care of himself outside the installation; he'd take care of himself in here. He had more hours in the field, as healer and fighter, than she'd even imagined. He didn't trust her, and he didn't need her.

He didn't need her at all.

Chapter 6

*B*astard, Mariska thought, and didn't care if she thought it loud enough for the world to hear. But no one sent any startled glances her way as she stalked away from the animals, heading for the office area simply because no one else was there.

She'd only meant to help. To *console*. And even if she'd done it in her blunt bear way, if anyone could understand that...

She muttered a growl between her teeth, her face burning with humiliation, her stomach a cold, hard knot around the hurt that wanted to make her throat ache except she damned well *wouldn't let it*.

::Hey,:: Ian said, low enough to be private. ::Look, little bear, I think you screwed up big-time, but we all know you didn't deserve that. Take it easy.::

She send him back a silent growl, and heard him laugh quietly out loud in response. But, after a pause, he said, ::The man's hurting. You walked right into that hurt and you played him for a fool while you were at it. Give him space.::

::I *never*—:: she snapped at him, but stopped short. She

hadn't; she never would have. What was so complicated about it all? She'd wanted to meet him; she'd hoped for his interest. She'd hoped for everything they'd had together. It had nothing to do with position on this team. *Nothing*.

Except she hadn't told him about it.

::Yeah, you played him,:: Ian said, bent to his work as if they weren't having a conversation at all. ::Now give the big guy space, okay?::

She sent him a reluctant assent. Give Ruger some space, okay. Or as much as she could, considering she was supposed to watch his back when he was distracted by work.

She had to admit he hadn't been distracted by work out on the hillside when he'd taken on the Core minion. He'd spotted the man first, even though he'd been actively probing the installation—even though he'd clearly struggled for doing so.

None of those thoughts made the hurt go away. If anything, it came closer to the surface, making her eyes swim—making her think about how he'd been with her the night before. How could he have been so…*involved*… so fiercely tender…and now turn on her so strongly?

Because, little bear, he was *so very involved. So very tender.* Because he'd let himself care, just that fast.

She hated it when her little voice was right. Even if some part of her was just as pleased by it. Even if that part of her wanted *more*.

Right. Give him space.

She slanted a glance his way, hesitating outside the office area. If she wasn't mistaken, he was tagging those animals who needed immediate mercy euthanasia. She closed her eyes, took a deep breath, and entered the office area.

Cr-aack!

The packed dirt floor lay hard beneath her back; the solar tube circles danced brightly overhead. Ruger's voice echoed strangely in her ears. "Mari! Don't move!" And Ian's voice joined it, tangling their words together. "Amulet—don't move—be okay—*Mari...*"

The next thing she knew, someone's pack propped her up; a vile-tasting drink trickled down her throat without her permission, and Mariska choked and coughed and spat it out with vehemence.

"She's awake!" Heckle called, although Mariska barely dared to squint her eyes open.

"I thought so," Ian said—not from anywhere nearby, and deep in concentration. "I'm going to say I called it—a sentry working, triggered when she passed the threshold." His voice grew slightly louder. "Mariska, dear, when did you hear any of us clear that area?"

Oh, hell.

"Never mind," Ian continued. "Trick question. We didn't."

"It's okay," Heckle said, leaning in closer—a big fuzzy face in her vision. "You just got a bad shock."

"Just," she managed, her tongue thick.

He shrugged. "Relative to what it could have been. Now drink the rest of this. It's horrible, but it's one of Ruger's—and that means it'll help."

"Ruger," she said, somewhat stupidly.

"Drink," Heckle said, tipping the sports bottle to her mouth and filling her mouth so it was either swallow or spit. She chose swallow, but wasn't convinced she'd do it again. He looked over her head. "Did you find anything else here?"

Ian made a noncommittal noise in his chest, and Heckle leaned in, a confidential posture with his voice low. "That means they've been tricky."

"There's something here to protect," Mariska said.

"Yeah." Heckle wrapped her hand around the sports bottle. "Drink this. Or I'll get into trouble." Even as she thought, *No, I will not,* he leaned even closer and muttered, "He's right *here.*"

Great. Mariska drank a few more swallows that were thick and gritty and tasted like dirt. Or worms. Or both. But with each swallow, she felt the warmth spread through her numb body, bringing it back awake. A familiar warmth, a familiar trickle of energy.

She lifted her head, still squinting slightly in the too-bright light, and found Ruger not far away. He sat with his back to the wood plank divider of the amulet station, his arm resting over one upraised knee and a dazed expression looking back at her, his mouth not looking quite right. She squinted a little harder and then was sure of it—the glint of bright red smeared over his upper lip and dribbled over a well-formed mouth to drip off his chin.

Her eyes must have widened. He blinked, swiped a hand over his chin, and swore resoundingly as he caught sight of his smeared fingers. A minute of rummaging, and he pulled the bandanna from his back pocket to mop up his face.

Familiar, that bandanna. He'd already pulled it once, as they stood outside this installation. How convenient that it was already a *red* bandanna. "Ruger, what's going on?"

He pushed himself to his feet, stuffing the cloth away and gesturing at the bottle in her hand. "Watch you don't spill that stuff. There's a limited supply."

"I'm fine now, thanks," she said sharply, as he turned his back on her to head for the animals.

He laughed, short and humorless. "Little bear," he said, "I know exactly how you are. Just because I can't *heal* doesn't mean I can't feel it."

It took a moment for the realization to hit, and then she was up on her knees, staring after him—staring out to the end of the installation where the crates and cages sat. "You mean—"

"Every one of them," he said.

Oh, HELL.

"Hey," Ian said, stepping back from his amulet and workings search to stare at the mundane matters of routers and Ethernet cabling. "These computers are networked out to somewhere."

"Touch those machines and I'm not going to fix you when Nick finds out," Ruger said without heat.

"Give me some credit," Ian said. "But I'm sure as hell going to pull the cable. If Forakkes wants access to this setup, he isn't going to get it."

Mariska scrambled to her feet, leaving the amulet team inspecting the computer area. She took one last swig of the gritty brew, pushed the spout closed and followed Ruger back to the animals.

"You might as well finish it," Ruger said, not looking away from the cages to meet her eyes. "It doesn't keep once it's mixed."

"But it's—" she started, then pulled back on the words.

He looked at her again for the first time since she'd woken—directly at her, his light brown eyes disconcertingly perceptive. "Right," he said. "It's from before, when I could add something to the value of the herbs and restoratives."

She held it out to him, feeling a stubborn mood settle in. It was better than humiliation. "Do you need some, then?"

Perceptiveness darkened to a glare—but then he looked away, schooling himself back to something approximating neutral. "Healer, heal thyself? Sorry, it's been tried. In theory it's doable, but when you're feeling it from both sides, it gets a little dicey." He shrugged, a restless gesture. "That's assuming the healer can tap that energy in the first place, which I can't."

"But this is already made up. And…you didn't look well. You were *bleeding*." She still held the bottle out; she could hold it out all day if she had to.

He took it with an abrupt snag, caught the spout with his teeth to open it, and tossed back the contents as easily as he'd tossed back the whisky they'd shared. When he returned it, it was empty.

"There," she said, somewhat defiantly. "Not so hard."

He made a noise in his chest. "Persistent, aren't you?"

"Of course I am," she said. "That should have been obvious from the start."

He made another sound she couldn't decipher—and then lifted his head to eye the tunnel entrance. Embarrassed warmth washed across Mariska's cheeks. *She* was the one who should have been the most attentive to noises and clues and signs of intrusion. By the time she located Sandy at the entrance, Ruger had already relaxed and turned away.

Maybe he'd been right all along. He was a healer, but he was also a warrior—and he had spent years in active fieldwork. While Mariska had years working personal bodyguard to those from the mundane world—sometimes clandestinely, at that.

Not the same at all. No matter how she wanted it to be.

"Outer wards are set," Sandy announced, coming into the structure to eye the cages. "What the hell is this little freak show?"

"You know what we know," Harrison said from inside the office. Ruger stepped back from his work, waiting to see if he needed to wait on interior wards. He was in enough trouble with his healer mojo—he didn't need to work through additional ward-setting interference. Harrison poked his head out to gesture vaguely at the areas they'd cleared. "The amulet station, the animals, and this area are good to go, but we haven't checked the far end yet."

"No problem." Sandy rocked back on her heels, her hands clasped behind her back. "I can wait right here. The last thing we need is some unwitting clash of new wards with old workings."

Fine. Good. Ruger rubbed the flat of his hand across his cheek, still feeling the bare strangeness of it, and turned back to the animals.

He'd already started assessing them—pulling out those in such irreversible misery that they needed immediate release. Even through the faint ringing in his ears and the lingering thump of exaggerated pulse in his head—his reward for the stupid, instinctive attempt to pour a healing into Mariska—he had no trouble discerning which of the caged creatures before them still lived only because it hadn't yet figured out how to die.

If he'd had his skills, he could have shown them the way. Not an active euthanasia so much as opening a door to offer the choice. Quiet…peaceful.

But he didn't. And he didn't have a CO_2 chamber, and even if he had the necessary drugs, he had no idea where to find a vein on these twisted pieces of nature.

Nor did he realize Mariska had left his side—until she returned, hefting a—

He gave it a double take. *Hatchet.*

"You shouldn't have to do this," she said simply, tossing aside the gear pack from which the hatchet had come.

He couldn't quite look away from them—less *Island*

of Doctor Moreau and more *Frankenstein*. "I can't heal them," he said. "So I owe it to them—"

"You couldn't heal them no matter what," she said. "Some things can't be done. And we *all* owe it to them to fix what's been done here."

"I should…" He let his words trail off, wondering when he'd lost his matter-of-fact grasp on the obvious even as he rued the rest of the obvious: even though she was right, he still should have been able to offer them some relief, some surcease from the misery their existence had—

"Stop that," she said, and hit him—a short, sharp backhand rap of her knuckles across his ribs. "Your nose." She tugged the bandanna from his pocket and pushed it into his hand—and then she crouched beside the first cage, removed the water-breathing squirrel with a firm but gentle hand, and placed it against the dirt. "I am so sorry," she told it. "This isn't the least bit fair." And with a quick, assertive stroke, she ended its suffering.

Ruger must have made some sound; she looked over her shoulder and told him, "Sandy might have some preservation warding we can use until we can deal with disposal. Go ask her, and leave me to this."

Astonishment warred with guilt. This wasn't a job he could rationalize away…definitely not something he could just leave in someone else's hands simply because he no longer had the means to do it as he otherwise might.

"*Stop* it," she said again. "Don't you get it? I'm damned well going to do what I came here to do, even if it means I'm protecting you from *yourself!*"

He turned away before she could reach for the next cage. "I'll be outside," he told Ian on his way past. "Come get me if you need me."

* * *

The team wouldn't be long; Ruger knew that much. Just long enough for him to stretch into his bear. He should have been thinking about what they'd seen inside; he should have been thinking about the best way he could contribute, or pondering Forakkes' intent—or whether the man had any intent at all, or was simply completely and entirely out of control. He should have—

He was beginning to hate the word *should,* that was what.

So he did none of those things. He sat beside the shirt he'd removed rather than destroy because it wouldn't change with him thanks to its plastic buttons, and he groomed an itchy spot between his massive toes, and he sifted back through impressions and sensation.

Mariska.

Warm and strong and incredibly responsive, so full of life it practically burst out of her and right through him, so full of honesty that she hadn't shied from what they'd found together the night before.

Mariska.

A mere twelve hours later, and already she had the power to wrench his emotions with her casual betrayal. She'd gotten what she wanted, all right. In all respects.

Warm brown skin and flashing eyes and the heady scent of arousal, soft in all the right places and muscled in all the right places and the sweetest damned cry of release—

Ruger grumbled a low groaning growl and stood, shaking himself off with a massive roll of fur and muscle—pushing away the pure physical yearning.

Honesty and betrayal combined…it was a dangerous, dangerous combination.

One he wanted more of…and one he didn't dare.

Chapter 7

Mariska stood on the crest, looking back down on the installation with the rest of the team—thinking of what they'd found there, what had happened there, the faint ache of her head in the wake of the amulet slap…Ruger's need for some space from it all. *From me.*

"Wards are good," Sandy said, her gaze veiled as she slipped into ward view to double-check their work. "Just in case this place isn't as abandoned as we thought it was."

"*Some*one's been feeding the animals," Mariska reminded her, more absently than she should have—looking over to the opposite hill, where flashing blue-white energies marked the moment of Ruger's transition from the bear to the human as he came to join them. "It might not be active, but it's not abandoned."

Sandy shrugged. "The wards won't stop them from coming back, but it'll sure stop their workings from getting in." She grinned, a light expression perfectly suited to her coyote nature. "And the very physical lock Ian put on the door will keep them out of the structure."

Ruger navigated the opposite slope with a casual

stride, the bear still clear to Mariska's eyes—the unhurried manner of his movement, the loose-jointed strength. His shirt hung from one hand, and she knew it wasn't made of the all-natural materials that would have allowed it to change with him.

"...should be clear," Ian said.

Mariska gave him a startled look. "I'm sorry, what?" And then rolled her eyes at his knowing grin. She smiled back at him, ever so sweetly, and full of teeth.

Ian laughed out loud. "The interior," he said again, "should be clear. But I'd like to go over it again first thing tomorrow. I really wasn't expecting them to have such stringent measures in place within one of their own installations—especially one this remote."

"They're done," she told Ruger as he joined them, question in his eyes—and tried to keep her voice less grim than it wanted to be. Wearing a predator's skin didn't make it any easier to take the life of something small and innocent and suffering.

"Thanks," he said. "Though I could have—"

"There was no reason you had to," she told him, impatient all over again.

"I hear there's a great steak house on the main drag," Ian said. "Let's grab some food and sleep. I need to send some images back to the lab, and I'd like to get an early start tomorrow. Those amulets are a treasure trove, and they'll have to be packed like china."

Ruger snorted. "China hand grenades, you mean."

"Something like that. I think we should haul the computers out of there, too—let's get them back to brevis for a look."

"Be good to take a look right here, if we can," Ruger

said. "If we're going to understand what's going on here, even file headers might help give us context."

Ian hesitated, an uncharacteristic thing. "I'll check with Nick. None of us are experts, and there's no telling what unauthorized access could trigger."

Mariska looked down at the underground installation, thinking of the security layers they'd already encountered. "Forakkes doesn't seem like he'd leave a vulnerable flank."

"Dammit," Ian said. "Now I'm *really* thinking about steak. Let's get out of here and into that restaurant before I go all leopard on somebody's ass."

Ruger slipped into his shirt and led the way without comment—at least until they had nearly reached the little cut-through access back to the ATVs. Even as he stopped there, Mariska felt it, too. Undefined, intangible… *presence.* Obscured but definite, just the hint of a scent and the hint of Core stench.

She stood there for a silent moment while the others waited, hunting detail…hunting a more accurate impression. *Nothing.* Whatever had been here since they'd left, it had come protected. She exchanged a frustrated glance with Ruger; he shook his head, no more successful than she.

They moved on without discussion. As if that moment of accord had been the most natural thing in the world, hardly even worth noting. Only as they reached the ATVs did it hit her—that this was what she'd truly wanted all along. *This* was what she'd come so close to having, in those initial hours of discovering Ruger, of their accord and instinctive understanding.

But thanks to how she'd handled things, this was also what she would now experience only in such sweet, fleeting moments as the one that had just passed.

* * *

The steak had probably been good. In fact, to judge by the cat-ate-the-ibex expression on Ian's face, it had been impressively delicious.

Mariska hadn't noticed one way or the other. She ate in silence, watching Ruger's easy camaraderie with the rest of the team. And when they returned to the cabins, she watched Ian take Sandy and his team to their cabin to put their heads together over amulets and wards, and she didn't fail to notice that Sandy and Heckle—*Harrison*— fell together in close proximity, their body language all flirt and obvious intent.

Nothing unusual or untoward in that. The Sentinels as a people were open about their sexuality, nonjudgmental about choice and preference, and happy to give and take pleasure. None of it necessarily meant commitment or even an interest in getting together again.

She'd thought to have the same with Ruger. A night together without strings. *What happens in Tucson, stays in Tucson.*

She'd obviously thought wrong.

She headed for the cabin, her personal gear pack slung over one shoulder and her eyes gritty in the long desert twilight. Ruger still stood beside the truck, pulling his own gear from the back…taking much longer than necessary.

I didn't mean to mess things up, she thought at him, but pressed her lips together on the words as a black wolf ghosted between the cabins, head low and whisky-colored eyes intense. "Jet," Mariska said. "We're back for the night. You?"

Jet merely sat, as tidy and upright as a wolf could be, and regarded Mariska without comment. But she didn't come any closer, and Mariska took that as clue enough. "Do you need anything? Have you eaten?"

Jet's jaw dropped in wolf amusement, and Ruger came up to the porch with Mariska to observe, "I'd say that means yes." He told Jet, "There wasn't much to the day—we got in, we took some notes, and we're going back first thing tomorrow. Forakkes is up to something, no question about it—but so far it's not making much sense."

Mariska found herself bemused to consider this summary of the day. But Jet took his words at face value, stood, tipped her head at them a moment with something sparking behind wild whisky eyes, and then trotted off into the woods.

"I'm not sure we'll see any more of her than that," Ruger said, but he headed into the cabin with a grin tugging his mouth.

It was first of those she'd seen all day, and it stopped her in her tracks. Surely he'd smiled like this at some point in the previous evening—his face hidden in that neat, full beard. She just hadn't seen it—or felt the impact of it, the sudden openness of clean and rugged features.

She felt it now, all right. Right down to her toes.

Great.

She shrugged off the moment and followed Ruger into the cabin—her first good look at it since arrival. Kitchenette with eating bar, tiny loft room with a bed, tiny bedroom down below, bathroom, and a tiny common area with a faded couch and a token television set. Several fans sat off to the side, but here in the high altitude temperatures and in the shade, she felt no impulse to pull them out. Braided rug, homemade curtains, big picture window looking out to the woods behind them…

They weren't here to be charmed, but she felt the lure of it nonetheless.

"Top or bottom?" Ruger asked, and then stood still a moment—a *long* moment—and very carefully rephrased the question. "Do you want the loft, or the first floor?"

"Loft," Mariska said, and dropped her bag at the bottom of the steep, narrow stairs. "Listen," she said, taking a deep breath to do it, turning to face him and finding him waiting with his expression turned neutral—that grin gone, his eyes distant. "About what we felt on the way out of that installation…it was subtle, but I think…" She stopped, her thoughts fractured by impulse—one she gave way to. "Dammit, I'm sorry!"

His expression opened with surprise; she couldn't blame him. She hadn't expected to say those words, and she hadn't expected to leave the stairs and walk right up to him—close enough so his height and size had an impact. Her body remembered both height and size, not to mention touch and his groaning, whispered response; it teased her with echoes of pleasure.

His surprise grew wary as she reached him, and then again when she didn't stop; he took a step back, and another—his legs came to rest against the couch so he abruptly sat. Still she didn't stop, climbing right up to straddle his lap. "I'm *sorry,*" she said. "I didn't realize it would be so difficult for you. I didn't understand that I would be stepping on your toes so hard. I didn't *want* to understand—because I wanted you, and I wanted this chance, too." She settled against him. He shifted beneath her, his breath catching, his eyes closing.

He didn't open them when he spoke. "Just because you're bear enough to go after what you want doesn't mean you're always going to get it." But the muscles of his neck corded, and his hands had come to rest on her hips, whether he realized it or not.

"I was wrong, okay?" She moved closer, her breasts

brushing his chest and her breath brushing his mouth. "I should have known it wouldn't be okay, but I didn't want to see that. I was wrong and I'm really...*really* sorry."

His jaw tightened; he thrust slightly against her as if in spite of himself, and his hands had closed in a bruising grip. She moved in response, her body full of spreading heat—trying to maintain her train of thought when she really just wanted to revel in how he felt beneath her, from hard thighs to muscled torso to the clench of his biceps and what it did to his chest. And his mouth. She wanted to feel his mouth... She whispered, "I'm sorry."

A faint tremble ran through his frame, and she felt the hope of his reaction to her. His head tipped back; his breath briefly stuttered.

But still he shook his head. "I get that," he said, his voice strained. "I believe that. But you still did what you did, and that means...it's just the way you—" He gave up, let his head rest back against the couch, his heart beating fast enough so she could see the movement through the shirt he'd only ever half-buttoned into place. He swallowed hard, and started again. "That means...it's just the way you think."

She stilled, a spear of rejection turning hard in her chest.

He opened his eyes—light brown gone dark with his response to her, and yet his expression struggling for distance. "I've got things to sort out, Mariska. I don't want this now."

"You do," Mariska said, because in spite of the chilling effect of his words, she couldn't believe them. *Didn't* believe them. Not with the way he'd enjoyed their time together the night before. Not with the way his body moved beneath her even now, his hips flexing ever so slightly in spite of his words. "You do, and you know it. You want *this*."

"Yes," he said, and the admission seemed to be a relief. "I want to turn you over and cover you and take you—" He took another sharp breath, maybe realizing his words had been a mistake as his body responded once more, aroused and hard enough that he had to be aching as much as she. He finished his sentence with a strangled determination. "Take you hard."

But then his hands fell away from her, and he shook his head. "I want. But I don't *need*."

Mariska pushed herself away from him, swiping thick bangs away from her face. "Oh, God," she said. "You mean it. I just— I thought… Oh, *hell*." Her face grew hotter than she ever thought it could, and she scrambled back to find the floor, horrified to get tangled in his feet. "Oh, *hell*."

"Hey," Ruger said sharply, grabbing her arm before it was quite out of reach and holding so firmly that she would have to turn to an honest fight in order to disengage—and though she jerked back with that impulse, she instantly subsided. She owed him this much. She'd pushed him and shoved him and moved in on him, and if he chose to respond with the same physical assertion—

It was only fair.

"Don't go there," he told her, reading her humiliation with an accuracy that only layered in more of it. "Just *don't*."

"You must be kidding." She laughed bitterly on those words, looking down at where he sprawled back against the couch, his erection straining his jeans, his eyes still dark and the stubble of his beard making an evening comeback, defining the strong lines of his face—his expression in control again. "How can I *not?*"

"Because," he said—and even though she steeled herself for bear-blunt words, he still took her by surprise, "I don't want to have to deal with it. There's already enough going on here, and if you indulge in a wallow of regret or embarrassment or whatever, it's going to be hard on everyone. Own it and go on."

"Own it and go on," she repeated numbly.

"And go on," he confirmed. And then added, "I will."

She stepped back, and this time he let her go. "The question is," she murmured, looking at him somewhat askance, "is that a promise, or a threat?"

He lifted his shoulders in a languid shrug. "Go ahead and grab the bathroom, if you're ready to turn in. It's going to be a few moments before I feel like moving."

Own it and go on.

Mariska squared her shoulders and found her determination, and walked away.

Jet curled up in a hollow between two scruffy, twisted little oaks, tucking her nose over her tail and perfectly happy to be out in the night. She had some curiosities left from the day—wondering what had put that look in Ruger's eyes, and seeing the faint and atypical worry in Ian as he disembarked, glancing over at Mariska.

She'd drift in close enough in the morning to catch Ian—to interrogate him with wolfish eyes and whatever persistence she needed. Tonight, she left them alone to absorb whatever it was that they'd found.

Besides, they still carried the faint stench of Core, whether they knew it or not. She'd had enough of that to last a lifetime.

She flicked her ears forward, moving nothing else but

her eyes—looking down on the cabin she could have been sharing with Ruger and Mariska, if she'd wanted. Never mind her own preferences; she'd have been out here regardless, just to give them space.

Two bears, trying to figure themselves out…she didn't need to be in the middle of it. No matter the furrow in her brow when she thought of the look on Ruger's face when he'd seen Mariska at the briefing. There were other things, too, behind that hurt and betrayal. There was longing. There was deep, deep *want*. And Mariska… what she'd done had been wrong and hard and even stupid, but it hadn't been done with intent.

Jet, too, was an outsider. She knew what that felt like. She could give Mariska time; she would give them both space.

Besides, the more she stayed out of things, the more anyone watching the team would think them complete as they were.

Chapter 8

Ruger opened his eyes unto the birdsong of early morning and found himself still on the couch.

Not that he'd intended it. He'd watched Mariska make her way up the stairs—everything about her rounded and strong, dark hair dragged back into a French braid that brushed her shoulders, teasing him with a glimpse of breast and strong cheekbone before she disappeared into the loft—and he'd thought to wait until the effect of their...*conversation*...faded before he moved from the couch.

It had taken longer than expected. And eventually he'd fallen asleep, and now he found himself blinking awake to classic morning wood and the sight of Mariska leaning back against the stair railing, her arms crossed and her brow raised.

He rubbed his fingers over his eyes, pressing a little harder than he probably should have, and swore.

"Good morning to you, too," Mariska said, and something in her voice alerted him. He dropped his hand to look at her more closely, and to see the little furrow between her brows just barely visible behind her bangs.

"You okay?"

"Do those cures of yours come with a hangover?" she asked, clearly having decided not to query his sleeping arrangements.

He centered himself in his damaged healing space and felt it from her—the lingering headache, the touch of malaise. He pulled back just in time, stopping himself from any attempt to soothe her. *Dammit*.

She must have seen it—she shook her head with emphasis. "Uh-uh," she said. "None of that. I just need coffee. Something tall and strong and with plenty of sugar in it."

"Whatever you're feeling isn't from the restorative," Ruger said. "More likely it's from the hit you took in the first place. Be more careful today, huh?"

"You think?" she asked crossly.

"You don't have to go," Ruger told her. "If you're not well, it would be best to stay here and recover."

The look she sent him was eloquent answer enough, dark temper behind brown eyes. He held up his hands in a gesture of defeat. "Hey," he told her. "Believe it or not, it's my job to look out for the health of the team. When it comes to field fitness, I've got last word out here."

She narrowed her eyes, understanding that not-so-subtle threat. "You wouldn't."

He stood from the couch, stiffer than he liked from the night on old springs and old stuffing. "I would," he told her, not rising to her temper. "If I felt it was absolutely necessary. But today…it's up to you."

"Even though you'd rather not have me at your back." She didn't quite believe him, that was clear enough. Her voice was flat, her mouth was flat, and for the moment her brewing anger overrode the discomfort showing on her brow.

"That's personal," he said. "Totally different thing."

She deflated, rubbing her forehead. "Damn." She sighed. "If you're going to be reasonable about it…"

"Professional," he said. Except for the part of him that still felt the betrayal, and the part of him that didn't want her on the team at all—and the part of him that wanted her back on his lap. *Right now.*

A bear of conflict. Never a good thing.

"There's jerky in my pack," he said. "That'll help until we get to breakfast."

She snorted. "Is it going to taste like that drink you gave me?"

"It's going to taste salty and pretty damned hot," he said. "Annorah makes it."

He saw in her expression the moment she let herself think of the tang of tough meat and spices, the salt on her tongue…a certain longing, and all the primal bear showing through. He lost every bit of ground he'd gained—distancing himself from the state in which he'd woken.

Great. Apparently his body had plenty to say about Mariska, and had no compunction about ignoring his better judgment, or even giving him a break. He reached to the end of the couch and snagged his backpack, tossing it her way even as he headed for the bathroom. "Chow down. I'll need ten minutes for a shower."

Or half an hour.

But no cold shower would be long enough.

"Nick wants us to grab those computer hard drives," Ian announced over breakfast—a diner just short of fast food where they piled on the protein and fruit. Ruger dug in as heartily as any of them, but it took a scowl at Mariska to make her reach for anything but the raspberries on the fruit plate. Ian eyed her and went on without comment. "We'll also set up our satellite connection today—while we're at it, we'll see if there are any networks active in the area."

Sandy bit a sausage in half. "Sounds like we should have someone from tech support up here with us."

Ruger shook his head. "They're all light-bloods, strictly in-house work. The few who aren't are out on assignment already."

"Doesn't matter," Ian shrugged. "Any one of us can take out hard drives or find an active network. We don't have to hack it—we just need to know it's there."

"Right," Mariska agreed. "If there's anything within range out there, it's going to be Core. Do you want me to tackle the hard drives?"

Ian gave her another hard once-over—seeing what Ruger saw, perhaps—her subdued nature and lackluster expression. "If you don't mind, I'd really rather have you run another security sweep of the installation."

She frowned. "Amulets? But I—"

Ian grinned. "Amulets, no. I'll do that—outdoors and in. I don't want to take any chances after yesterday. I'm just asking for regular security stuff."

Relief brightened Mariska's expression. "Sure," she said. "First thing."

Good. Ruger didn't need her crowding his every move. He didn't need her there at all.

Just keep telling yourself that.

Through breakfast, through the ride into the woods… that was exactly what he did. Even as he stood waiting for Ian and his team to inspect the site for new amulets.

But it didn't quite offset the rise of the sensible inner voice suggesting that while he didn't in fact need someone watching his back, Mariska *was* here. And he was the one who could make it easier on both of them, or harder for everyone.

It made him cranky.

Cranky enough so he hardly noticed that Ian's team had completed their sweep of the area, declared it undisturbed, and now waved them down to the entrance. Mariska made an offhand noise in her throat, a thoughtful little bear-hum, and Ruger pulled his attention back to the moment at hand to follow her in.

But the moment he entered the facility, he stopped short, wrinkling his nose. "I thought you warded those animals," he told Sandy.

"I did!" Her expression of distaste said it clearly enough—she smelled the decay, too. Nothing so profound that a purely human nose would have detected it, but distinct to Sentinel senses. Ruger headed straight for the creatures Mariska had dispatched the day before—specimens, now—but before he'd even reached them, he realized he'd gone past the source of the odor.

Mariska had come to the same conclusion—turning slowly in one place, hunting the source of this new dismay. "They were all good when we left last night," she said. "They had food and water and—"

"Over here." Ruger found it—the beakless bird, motionless in the shavings below its perch. He pulled the cage from the shelf with brusque, no-nonsense urgency and placed it on one of the area's worktables. The lid came off easily.

Mariska bent to watch as he scooped it out from the cage, the slight frown of her headache turning into something more profound. "What the hell? Ruger, it doesn't have a…a *face*."

Ian stood back far enough to stay out of the way, close

enough to be in on the conversation. "Didn't we know that?"

"No—I mean—" Rattled, she took a step back; Ruger reoriented the stiff little body in his hand. "Before, it didn't have a beak, but it had a weird little flat face. Now—"

Nothing.

No beak. No eyes. No nostrils and no mouth. Just a round, closed little head covered in fine iridescent blue feathers, faint indentations indicating where those features would have been located.

Nothing at all.

Ciobaka curled up in the far corner of his cage, past his toilet area and into the dim section where the overhead daylight didn't quite reach. He hid his nose under the tip of his brushy tail and left his ears flat against his skull.

"Still sulking?" Ehwoord asked, but not in the voice that suggested he wanted a response. "Failure merits punishment, Ciobaka. Tarras understands that."

The day before, they'd gone out to find one of Ehwoord's pack members dead outside the other buried structure. This morning Tarras had looked distinctly pale; he didn't quite stand erect as he moved about his chores.

Ciobaka knew that what had happened wasn't his fault. He knew that being unable to enter the other installation because its securities had failed wasn't his fault, either.

"Fortunately, Yovan was successful in restoring the camera network." Ehwoord adjusted his huge monitor, no doubt still obsessing over the flat, grainy moving images on it. "I'll continue my work from here—in fact, I already have. I believe our friends are just now beginning to understand."

"Is that—" Tarras hesitated, obviously looking for better words than *Is that smart?*

Ehwoord didn't give him a chance. "Careful," he said softly, and Tarras turned away.

Ciobaka turned away, too. Biding his time.

Chapter 9

Ruger looked at the deformed bird with sick disbelief—unable to voice any cogent remark, unable to come to any conclusions. Just frozen there in that horror.

Mariska's hand came to rest on his arm. She gently removed the bird from his hands, adding it to the other specimens, and Sandy stepped up to apply the preservation warding. Only then did he look down at his hands, finding them fisted and shaking with tension. "When I find him..."

"When *we* find him," Mariska said. She swiped the bangs away from her eyes and rubbed her forehead with two fingers, her eyes closed.

Ruger turned back to the installation as a whole, looking it over as if he might see some sign of Eduard Forakkes right here and now. "I thought this place was warded," he said. "I thought it was supposed to be *secure*."

"It *is*," Sandy protested before Ian could do it. "Inside and out."

Mariska looked at the shelves, full of Frankencreatures. "We should check the rest of them. Maybe whatever Forakkes did here, it's still in progress."

"Ongoing mutations?" Ruger shook his head. "Surely we would have seen some sign of it yesterday."

"We had other concerns," she reminded him. "We may have been here for a while, but we weren't keeping that kind of eye on them. Who would? It's not something any nominally sane person would even look for."

The rage rumbled deep and hot, a counterpoint to the ongoing, subtle tug of arousal she invoked in him. *"When I find him..."*

"We," she said automatically, and headed for the shelves.

"Breakfast seems to have been a big *fail*," he said. "Let me do something for that headache."

She shot him a wary glance. "But you can't—"

Brief amusement lightened his mood. "Over-the-counter analgesic," he told her, a smile twitching at his mouth; it turned into a genuine grin at her palpable relief. "Did you really think I spent all my time wielding mystic healing powers? Hell, woman, I trained for this. I even throw a pretty neat stitch."

"Sorry," she muttered. "An aspirin would be nice. Maybe two."

"Maybe two," he agreed, and headed for the field kit. "But don't feel obliged to make me prove the stitches." He unzipped the canvas kit and poked through bandages and blood clotting sponges, antiseptic and sterile packaging—as ever, doing a silent inventory check on the way by. His fingers closed over a two-pack of aspirin, and he tugged it from its mesh pocket—and then froze, caught in astonishment at the faint scent of Core corruption.

"Ruger—" Mariska said, as Sandy came to abrupt

attention and Ian cursed resoundingly. "You'd better—Oh, *hell*—"

She didn't need to say anything else; she was already backing away from one of the cages, her expression not one of fear, but of horror.

"Ian," Ruger snarled, "get this facility fucking *secure*."

"It fucking *is*," Ian snarled back, but frustration laced his tone.

"It *is*," Sandy said, closing her eyes and adopting the peculiarly alert posture of a Sentinel in ward view. "I can't see a damned thing!"

"Don't tell me this is some *new* silent working," Jack said, annoyance mixing with the alarm in his voice. "Hell. I don't even want to know. I'm going to go after those hard drives while we still can."

"Ruger—" Mariska said, but by then Ruger was there, and he pressed the aspirin into her hand just to get it out of his own as he tugged the affected cage out away from the others—a medium rodent cage containing a vole with bird's feet.

He'd gotten there just in time. The little creature emitted an astonishingly loud squeak and fell over, thrashing wildly; Ruger set the cage on the worktable and crouched before it, trying to see amid the flurry of wood chips and limbs—until finally it lay still, its tiny chest heaving.

"It's still alive," Mariska whispered, bending over right there beside him.

He didn't respond right away—too intent, and not quite willing to allow that the moment was over. But the vole righted itself, tottering, and gave itself a quicksilver shake.

"Well?" Ian demanded—too impatient to stay quiet, for all that he'd held back to be out of the way.

Ruger shook his head. "I'll be damned if I know—"

And then he saw it. That the vole no longer struggled to maneuver on bird's feet, but that it tottered around on no feet at all.

Mariska gasped at the same time Ian swore; Sandy made a strangled noise.

And Ruger only stared, his grim expression making his features hard, his jaw so tense she expected to hear his teeth grinding.

"You can't fix this," she said, keeping her voice low. "You're not here to do the impossible." He didn't respond; he didn't look away from the unsteady little vole. Thank God it didn't seem to be in pain. "Forakkes is up to something—Katie's visions told us that much. The only way we're going to stop it is to figure out what it is. *That's* why you're here."

His mouth thinned briefly; something indefinable changed—a shift of his body, the degree of tension. Mariska heard Ian release a breath.

Jeckle screamed.

Mariska whirled to him; only in that instant did she absorb what she'd heard the instant before—the quiet *snick,* the *shoosh* of a sliding metal mechanism. And still she couldn't make sense of him, sprawled across the floor of the office area, entangled in something…blood spreading across the hard-packed dirt floor.

Heckle was the first to reach his friend, cursing a steady stream. "Jack," he said, a desperation already edging his voice. "What the hell have you done?"

By then Mariska was there, fully able to see the scimitar-like blade impaling Jeckle's torso, and the gap in the solid metal desk from which it had come. Fully able to see the stunned expression on Jeckle's face—the

look in his eyes as his blood poured out and his breath
came impossibly short.

Ruger pushed past her. She made a grab for his arm;
his shirt slipped through her fingers. "Ruger, no—" Only
afterward she realized she'd been trying to spare him
the impossible.

Sentinels didn't die easily. But they died.

Heckle looked up from where Jeckle's hand had closed
convulsively around his. "Do something," he demanded.
"Dammit, *do* something!"

Sandy drew in a breath; Ian wasn't as subtle. "Harrison," he said, and shook his head, his tone one of final-
ity. He nodded at Jeckle, his meaning clear. *Tend your
friend while you can.*

Heckle sent Ian a glare; he sent Mariska a glare. He
all but growled at Ruger, some lurking light-blood instinct coming to the fore. He turned back to Jack and
said, "You dumbass."

"Didn't—" Jeckle said, his body trembling convulsively around the sleek metal.

"Just be still," Heckle said as Ruger knelt on the other
side of the downed man, big, competent hands already
at work—shifting clothing, gently touching wrist, chest,
neck. "Sentinels are harder than this to take down."

No, they aren't. Mariska swallowed hard. And Jeckle
wasn't a fully blooded field Sentinel; he not only didn't
take another form, he didn't even come close enough
to guess which form might have lurked beneath his humanity.

Jeckle shook his head with vehemence—more than
Mariska would have thought possible—and turned to
Ruger. *"No,"* he said, struggling for air. *"Listen.* Didn't
touch anything."

Mariska got it first—looking at the tools scattered on

the floor around them, at the angle at which Jeckle lay. He'd said he was coming after the hard drives. He'd come toward the desk with tools in hand. He'd touched nothing. There'd been no evidence of Core workings. And yet the computer tower now sizzled and smoked, the scent of hot metal in the air.

"They have eyes on us," she said, her voice low and horrified.

Jeckle caught her eye with an expression of gratitude, his body relaxing around the blade…his breath easing out in one impossibly long sigh.

Heckle swore.

Only then did Mariska realize what Ruger was doing. As before—as with her—not even thinking about it, but reaching out. Looking to heal, where he no longer could, blood trickling from his nose, a thin stream of it from his ear, his face gone pale—

She hit him, a fast backhand slap to his upper arm—knowing it would take just that to save him from himself. "Stop it," she said, fierce with her concern. He didn't even rock with the blow. "Ruger!" She hit him again, this time closing her fist. ::*Ruger!*::

"Ah, hell." Ian stepped in—or would have, crowding the already tight space, but Mariska didn't wait for him. She grabbed Ruger's shoulder, jerking him around and winding up for a good hearty slap, and then another—until suddenly he looked at her with startled eyes.

But only until they rolled back in his head, and he fell with enough impact to declare again his solid size.

Ian muttered a string of curses, his voice rising along the way until his precise, furious diction became completely comprehensible. "—ing son of a *bitch*."

"What the hell?" Heckle demanded, disentangling his hand from Jeckle's with a care that belied his expression.

"Be *quiet*," Mariska snapped. She wanted to stay there beside Ruger, her hand resting on his chest to feel the steady rise and fall of his breath, her attention focused on the rugged lines of his face, she wanted to wipe away the blood and reassure herself that the trickle had stopped.

But she sat back from him, pushing herself to her feet.

"What the hell, *be quiet?*" Heckle said, his voice rising.

::She's right,:: Ian said, loudly enough to make Mariska wince—but it got Heckle's attention. ::They can see us—maybe even hear us.::

Mariska headed straight for her gear bag. This had been her assignment this morning—checking this installation for networks and electronic incursions—and instead she'd let herself get distracted.

Heckle stood to glare at her, his hands fisted by his sides, his fury palpable. ::You should have—::

::Stop it,:: Ian said sharply. ::Yes, she should have. And Jack should have waited for an all clear before heading for such a critical area. This is Core turf, dammit, and we need to act like it!::

Sandy's mind-voice was softer than her physical voice, and much less certain. ::Forakkes can see us,:: she sent, still trying to fathom it. ::He triggered that attack remotely. He took out the hard drives….::

Ian said nothing, waiting for Mariska—and Mariska pulled out her full-range wireless camera detector and paced down the center of the cavernous installation.

It only took a moment before the scanner slowed, tightening in on an exact frequency—and then another moment to pick up the feed, duplicating it on the diminutive screen in the handheld. Mariska found herself looking down the length of the installation—Ian's lean form, Heckle's lingering fury and grief, Sandy off to the side and Mariska's own short, sturdy self standing closest, studying the device in her hand. "Here," Mariska said, and traded the scanner for a smaller device as Ian came up behind her. And there it was, blinking back at her as she peered through the small viewfinder—the tiny red flashing light of a networked camera.

She held the detector up, carefully maintaining its orientation, and Ian muttered, "Got it."

Way too high to reach.

::We'll have to find the point-to-point wireless bridge,:: Sandy said. ::If we even can. And I doubt we came equipped to jam that— Oh.::

For Mariska went to the gear bag, pulled out the first small, hefty item she came to, and whipped it at the camera with pinpoint accuracy.

"Okay," Ian said, returning the detector, the corner of his mouth lifted in a hint of the dry humor that so suited him. "So much for that one. But if there's one, there's more. Find them."

Mariska glanced over at Jack—and over at Ruger, who hadn't yet stirred.

"Find them," Ian repeated, but he gentled his voice. "And then we start thinking this thing through from the top."

Mariska went to work.

Ruger's arm hurt. So did his face, stinging along the newly exposed surface where maybe he shouldn't have shaved his beard after all. He grumbled to himself, bearish sounds of dissatisfaction.

"Ruger." That single word held relief and maybe a little bit of something else. Sorrow.

He cracked his eyes open to find he was leaning against the office partition with Mariska kneeling beside him. He gave her a bleary and suspicious look. "You hit me."

"I did," she said promptly, and still the sorrow hid behind her eyes. "Don't make me do it again."

He remembered, then—how natural it had been to respond to the crisis by sinking into that healing trance. He couldn't remember what had happened then, but he could guess. The skin of his upper lip felt cool and scrubbed; his neck itched beneath his ear, and when he touched it, his fingers came away damp with almost-dried blood. "Hell," he said. "Maybe I do need protection. From *myself.*"

"Maybe you do," she told him, but she looked no less sad. "Ruger, I'm really sorry. I feel like I keep saying that, but…this is different. I get it now. Watching you work—"

"*Try* to work," he said, and couldn't hide that bitterness.

"Watching you," she repeated. "Seeing what you've lost…" She shook her head, dark-chocolate eyes full of regret. "And I came in and yanked the rest of it away."

"Don't," he said, more harshly than he meant to—simply because she hit too close to home, and he couldn't deal with it. Not here, in the middle of an active operation, the team all around them and Jack dead not far away. He pushed back at the twist of pain in his throat.

She took a breath, almost said something…sat back on her heels. "I can't fix all that now. I can only do the job I was sent here to do." She made a face, sent him a slantwise look. "And I *will* stop you the next time you do something like that."

"You'd probably better." It should have been the end of the conversation—Ruger with his thoughts still dazed, Mariska with the headache that obviously wouldn't quit, Ian and what remained of his team muttering in the background. But neither of them moved, and after a moment, Ruger reached out to put a hand over hers.

After a moment, she sighed, and turned her hand over beneath his so their fingers intertwined.

For a few minutes, that was enough.

Finally, Ruger glanced over to the dark, damp spot where the dirt had soaked up Jack's blood.

"Sandy put a stasis warding on him," Mariska said, and pushed a finger against the bridge of her nose, clearly pulling herself back to the matters at hand. "We were being watched. I've disabled the cameras—"

A snort from Ian let them know just how illusory their personal privacy had been. "She means to say that she *obliterated* the cameras."

"—and we're jamming the network, too—at least until we can find the tech. That's how they got Jeck—I mean, Jack."

"Watching through the cameras," Ruger said, as if he didn't believe it. "Manually triggering the blade."

"Freaking *Raiders of the Lost Ark,*" Ian grumbled from the amulet area.

"I don't know what he hoped to accomplish," Mariska said, a hard expression taking over her features—not an expression any smart man would want to face. "He hasn't stopped us. And who would even use such a barbaric thing? He already had the hard drives wired—they're smoked. Useless."

"He was making a point," Ruger said darkly. "And he was making us hesitate."

"Damned right," Ian came up behind Mariska. "Mariska got nailed yesterday. We lost Jack today. The hard drives are gone. Have we even been here twenty-four hours? We've totally underestimated this man."

"Overestimated him," Ruger muttered. "We gave him

too much credit for being human. We should have known, once we saw those animals..."

"I want to grab what we can and get out of here as soon as we can," Ian said. "We'll analyze what we gather back at brevis, and we'll blow the hell out of this place. No more playing on Forakkes' home ground."

Mariska climbed to her feet, holding her hand out for Ruger. "You're okay?"

"Hungover," Ruger said, and at Ian's skeptical expression, closed his eyes long enough to do a quick internal review. He did, at least, have that much skill left. "Seriously. I'll be fine." He accepted Mariska's hand; he accepted her strength. In the warmth of her hand against his, he felt a fleeting echo of their bodies tangled and pounding; her eyes widened slightly, and she pulled her hand away as he came to his feet.

Ian shook his head and muttered something, and went back to the amulet section. "I'll be the rest of the morning packing up these blanks," he said. "Mariska, would you take your gear outside? Make sure we're not being watched out there?"

"Of course," Mariska said—but she gave Ruger an uncertain glance. "I'd prefer it if Ruger came with me, if that's okay. I'd rather have someone at my back if I'm going to be concentrating on techie tricks."

Ian merely looked at Ruger, waiting.

And Ruger straightened, watching Mariska with narrowed eyes—examining her expression for any sign of pity, condescension or manipulative overtones. ::I'm not for sale,:: he said, a private voice that went to her alone.

::I'm not buying you,:: she said without hesitation. ::I have a helluva headache and I don't want to have to split my attention.::

"Sure," Ruger told Ian, who waited so patiently that it

couldn't have been more obvious he knew there'd been a private exchange. "Whatever's happening with the animals, we clearly can't stop it. I'll take stock when we get back inside." He looked over to that end of the installation and shook his head. "I just hope we can figure out what he's up to before we run into those workings in the field."

But Katie Maddox's shared vision whispered urgency, and so far they didn't have a clue.

Chapter 10

We don't know anything. Not nearly enough.

Mariska stood outside the cabin with the day of work behind her, letting the cool night air wash over her face. Dinner sat uneasily in her stomach; her skin felt tight and warm.

If she hadn't been Sentinel, she'd have said she was coming down with something. But she was...and Sentinels didn't. They didn't get colds or the flu; they didn't carry viruses and they weren't vulnerable to bacteria. The same preternaturally robust nature that allowed them to heal swiftly from near-fatal wounds also protected them from common—and uncommon—ailments.

Of course, get a little scratch and it took nearly as long to heal as any average human would. Sentinel bodies didn't waste energy on the little things.

All of which explained the lingering headache and every other small price she still paid for blundering into an amulet the day before.

Ruger likely felt the same from whatever damage he'd done himself with that knee-jerk attempt to save Jeckle.

Jack. She'd seen him gulp down not two but four ibu-profen over dinner, as casually as he'd tried to hide it.

Unlike the evening before, dinner had been a somber affair—one less Sentinel at the table, and plenty of stories being swapped between Ian and Heckle, while Sandy's pale complexion highlighted her red-rimmed eyes and Mariska found her voice going ragged at the most unexpected moments.

Even Jet—alerted to the situation through Annorah—had been subdued, showing herself only from a distance, and fading quickly back into the woods.

They hadn't found additional surveillance gear during their sweep of the bunker area, and then they'd spent the rest of the day cataloging Forakkes' offenses against the creatures once in his care.

They still hadn't made any sense of it. And once Mariska destroyed the cameras, there had been no more workings triggered. Sandy lurked around the edges of the work, furious that her wards had somehow failed to prevent those workings and determined to figure out how.

All in all, it was a day of win for Forakkes.

Although it *had* felt good, taking out his cameras—knowing he was watching it happen and helpless to stop it. One tiny win for Mariska.

Ruger stepped onto the porch—his shirt unbuttoned and shirttails flapping free, feet bare. Light filtered out from the cabin to paint highlights and shadows over the planes of his chest, picking out the dark hair that barely tapered as it traced a line down abdominal muscles and disappeared behind the black jeans hanging low on his hips.

She didn't need to see any more than that. Her body remembered. Her skin reminded her of just that, tightening with a prickle of wishful anticipation. She greeted Ruger with a tired smile. "All quiet?"

"Everywhere except inside my head," he said, an honesty she hadn't expected. "I keep seeing…"

"All of it," she finished, when he didn't. "Does Ian really mean to pack up and leave before we find Forakkes? Or is my inexperience just showing again?"

He joined her by the porch rail. "I'm not sure what he'll do. Right now, I think he believes our best bet is to take back what we can and give the brevis teams time to analyze what's going on."

"To be more prepared before we go looking any harder," she guessed. He nodded, but he didn't look settled about it. She straightened, trying to interpret that slight frown. "You don't think it's the right thing to do?"

"I'm not going to second-guess how Ian handles his team," Ruger said shortly—and closed his eyes, shaking his head briefly. "I'm sorry. I'm just feeling…"

"Bearish," she said, finishing the thought for him again.

He flashed her a quick smile; she swallowed hard and pretended it hadn't so easily quickened her pulse. Not when she'd so thoroughly muddled what might have been between them. "Bearish," he agreed. "Truth is, I'm not sure we have that luxury of time. Maks obviously only drove Forakkes deeper into hiding, he didn't stop him— though he hurt him."

"His amulets," Mariska said, remembering the reports—that Forakkes, to Maks' memory, hadn't aged at all in the years since he'd once held Maks-the-boy and his mother captive in a breeding program. Not until his amulets were destroyed in a confrontation with Maks, at which point he aged so rapidly that it had been hard to tell if he was seventy or a hundred and seventy. No doubt he had reapplied his workings, to whatever effect they might have had.

"The amulets," Ruger agreed. "But it doesn't seemed to have slowed him down at all. If anything, I'd say the opposite. He's not truly hiding any longer. Or he's frantic to complete what he's started."

"And he's flaunting what he can do," Mariska said. "That stuff with the animals this morning—that was neener-neener as much as anything else. It seems like a change of style."

Ruger made a noise in his chest—disgruntled agreement.

"You don't think we can afford to leave him alone long enough to figure out exactly what he's doing before we try to stop him."

"I think," Ruger said, looking out over the darkness much as she had been moments earlier, "that Katie's vision is pretty damned convincing. I think what happened today is pretty damned convincing. He's got to be stopped, not given time to play."

"Even if we're not ready." She wasn't disagreeing—wasn't arguing. Just stating it out there clearly.

"Maybe especially if we're not ready. Maybe we'll never truly be ready."

Before she'd come here, Mariska had felt ready. She'd felt as though she could handle anything. "Jet was right," she said. "You were right. I don't have the experience for this kind of fieldwork."

He straightened to look at her with surprise.

"I interfered with the team cohesion," she said, weary and achy. "I interfered with you. I took the first opportunity to walk into a trap. And the only way I've protected you is by *hitting* you."

"Ah," he said. "Mariska Bear, you're just tired and hurting."

"But I'm not wrong," she said sharply. "Don't go patronizing me."

He made a gesture of surrender, and when she relaxed slightly, reached out to take her hand. "You need a good humming."

"Excuse me?" But she followed the tug of his hand into the cabin and its small common space, back to the couch where she'd found him that morning. Before she knew it, he'd turned, scooped her up, and sat with her on his lap.

Alarm struck her—surely he wasn't going to try more healing—and she started a scramble to her feet. Astonishment replaced alarm when she went absolutely nowhere at all—when she realized the ease with which he restrained her. Since when did that ever happen to Mariska Bear?

And why did part of her like it? His assertion, his strength—and her underlying knowledge that if she'd truly wanted to go, he'd let her.

Instead, she subsided, although her voice held a sullen note. "If you do a healing thing, I *will* hit you."

"I'm not," he said, and pulled away the band securing her short French braid. "I won't."

"You'd better not." But she was already tipping her head at the utter luxury of sensation—his fingers scraping through her hair to work it loose of the braid, combing and touching. Every tug on her scalp felt like a caress; every incidental brush of his hand against her cheek sent a thrill down her spine.

"Uh-huh," he said, and the sound hummed against her from his chest.

"Oh," she said, as he took a slow, deep breath, slow enough so the contentment of it seeped right into her; she relaxed into his lap. He tipped his head, resting it against

the side of hers; his breath stirred her hair and shivered
down her neck. One hand rested across her lap to encom-
pass her hip while the other slipped from her hair to rub
the back of her neck. Mariska released a contented sigh,
and said again, "Oh. *Humming.*"

"One bear to another," he told her, shifting beneath
her, but not tensing—not building expectation, even as
she felt him harden. Just a gift of comfort and closeness.

"Oh," she said, one more time, and her voice was
suddenly, unexpectedly thick, "I don't deserve this. Not
after—"

"Hush," he told her, a murmur in her ear. "I'm not sure
you do. But I *want* to. And I've got you."

No question of that. She blinked away tears of emotion she couldn't quite label, and let him tuck her against
his shoulder—letting herself absorb the comfort of his
touch, and the comfort of being held in such strength.

"Better," he said, stroking her shoulder, down her
arm…petting her into submission. His other hand shifted
from her hip to her stomach, resting there with a splayed
possessiveness.

She wasn't sure when he'd slipped it under her shirt,
his palm warm against her skin. Or when his thumb had
drifted up to stroke the side of her breast. She found herself arching to it—and then stilled. He'd slipped down on
the couch, offering her more security, her body angled
over his—she'd never felt delicate before. She'd never
felt so *held*.

She'd never felt so aware that she didn't deserve such
a gift.

"Shh," Ruger said, close enough to nuzzle her ear.
"I'm being selfish."

"Not smart," she responded, somewhat breathlessly.

Oh, hell—not just breathlessly, but completely without air or assertion.

"Not smart," he agreed, and did something with his lips behind her ear that sent a sudden shiver through her body. "Just selfish." His thumb rounded her breast, encroaching more sensitive areas. His breath washed her neck.

She forgot to think. She only ached and shivered and throbbed beneath his hand, clutching at him. She found the gap in his unbuttoned shirt and slid her hand along his ribs, absorbing the crisp rub of his hair against her fingers, the landscape of muscle across his torso.

Somewhere along the way his hand slid down her stomach and unfastened her slacks and gently cupped her—so gentle, so quiet. He touched her with whispers, unexpected from those big hands and devastatingly effective. She breathed a moan as her head dropped back, and he took advantage of her bared throat, licking along her jawline, breathing over it, his hips rolling up against her bottom.

"Ruger—"

"Shh," he said, even as she shuddered, as heat and pleasure gathered and built around the movement of his hand, fingers encroaching. His voice came as a wash of heat against her skin. "It's a moment, little bear."

Little. To him, maybe she was. And yes, she felt held and gentled and safe to be who she was, knowing she wouldn't hurt him, knowing he could handle her. As though for once she could simply…

Let…

Herself…

Go.

She found herself gasping and limp in his arms, his shirt crimped in her fingers, his breath humming against her neck, his touch turned soothing. "Ruger," she said, as if that was supposed to mean something.

He pressed a kiss against her forehead. "Shh, now." He moved his hand back to the bare skin of her stomach, shifting to settle her more securely—as if she could ignore the great big erection she sat against. She opened her mouth to say something—he covered it with a kiss. A sweet kiss, not demanding. "I'm fine, Mari. Just…give me the moment."

Confusion cut through the soft haze of fatigue and satisfaction—the impulse to be doing something, saying something…the feeling that she should be chagrined or abashed, the realization that she wasn't. In the end, she gave him the moment, and she fell asleep in his arms.

Ciobaka lingered at the rear of his caging area, gnawing a span of deer ribs with his back to the work area.

"Not still sulking, are you?" Ehwoord's voice came like the ripple of cold water over rock. Cold, cold water.

Ciobaka stopped the movement of his jaw without removing his teeth from bone; his ears went flat. "'Ite 'oo."

"There will be no *biting,*" Ehwoord said, without concern.

Ciobaka lifted his lips in a nasty, nasal snarl, still looking at the wall.

"You think it unfair to have been punished for circumstances that were beyond your control?" Ehwoord did something on his worktable, heralded by dully clinking metal, the susurrus of material shifting. "In fact, you were not."

Ciobaka went back to his ribs.

"Like our friends the Sentinels, you believed I would not. Or could not." Metal slid across the wood of the worktable. Always the thick, dull metal of Ehwoord's amulets. They filled his pockets; they hung at his neck. And in some way, he had been using them to change who he was—his gray hair now showing streaks of black, his skin less stretched…his form less stringy even as his moods grew more varied. "For that reason alone, you deserved punishment."

But Ciobaka had an inbred sense of canine fairness, and he knew better. A proper dominant did not punish simply because he could, or simply to prove he would.

Ehwoord stopped what he was doing, and sat back in his chair; the squeak of it sounded across the room, cutting through the moans of the caged animals with which he'd been working this day. "They shouldn't have broken my cameras," he said, his voice more strident. He glanced at the molded black chest, where for once the lid stood open, and Yovan handled a long metal construct with a certain reverence, putting it to his shoulder, fiddling with settings…making notations in a small notebook. "After tomorrow, they'll understand that. And if they don't leave this area—" He stopped, and Ciobaka knew without looking that he pressed his thin old lips together, that his face had flushed—that he would either kill something in this moment, or he would regain his temper, and there was no point in watching either way.

When Ehwoord spoke again, his voice had regained its cold control. "Well, then," he said. "Maybe I'll test this new working sooner than I had planned. Then we'll see what happens to a Sentinel who is no longer a Sentinel at all."

Chapter 11

Ruger woke with a crick in his neck, his legs weighted down and his body slanted over the couch that wasn't quite big enough to hold him in any position. How it had held two of them through the night, he couldn't begin to imagine.

Mariska lay warm in his arms, her bottom snug against his groin, her hair splayed over her face and his arm—thick and black and scattered, her bangs askew. Her cheeks held a flush, barely evident beneath the nutty tones of her skin or the naturally dark sootiness of her eyelids.

His body responded to her, of course—a deep, aching pull, both sweet and merciless. Waking this way, finding her with him this way…it couldn't have felt more right.

He had no idea what the hell he was doing.

He couldn't trust her. He didn't doubt her sincerity; he doubted her judgment. He didn't doubt her intent; he doubted her inexperience—with teamwork, with deep fieldwork, with this level of Core perfidy.

Eduard Forakkes was no minion. And Mariska wasn't

here on her own, a single bodyguard working with a single principle.

But she was here, and her judgment and her inexperience left the team vulnerable. Never mind her clear determination to fulfill her role here.

But she was here, and she had the power to ruin him. Whether she meant it or not.

And still he bent to wake her with a brush of his cheek against hers—one final moment of selfishness, indulging in that which he couldn't afford. "One day," he said, when she opened sleepy eyes, "I *will* wake up in a bed again." And he stood with her in his arms, turning to redeposit her on the couch. By then she was fully awake, her body gone from relaxed to tense—but remaining quiet as he settled her down, careful not to interfere.

"Gotta shower," he said, and didn't mention it would be another cold one.

He had the feeling she knew.

When he emerged, she was brushing her teeth at the sink, and she grabbed up her toiletries bag—the no-nonsense clutch of a woman used to travel—and disappeared into the bathroom.

Ruger brewed a stinging peppermint tea, grabbing a handful of the jerky to head out to the porch. Harrison stood behind Sandy on the porch of the other cabin, his arms linked around her waist in a gesture that was both comforting and possessive. He heard snatches of Sandy's distress that Jack would have to wait for a recovery team—and the recovery team was waiting for them to finish with the installation.

He yanked off a bite of the jerky and chewed, satisfied to grind his teeth over it.

Mariska joined him there, scented with mild cucumber

soap and shampoo, her wet hair drawn back into its braid. She drew breath to say something, but hesitated on it.

"Hey," Ruger said, offering her a piece of jerky. "None of that. Unless you're mad at me. If you are, then just hit me and have it over with."

That surprised her. "Hit you?" she said, taking the jerky and taking a much smaller bite than he had. "Why would I hit you? I'm a big girl, Ruger. If some part of me hadn't wanted what happened last night, I would have stopped it. I just don't know where it leaves us."

Ruger didn't respond right away. When she reached for his tea, he absently handed it over, watching her mouth as she sipped—the movement of curved lips, just plump enough, a natural dark red in complement to her skin tones.

She raised her eyebrows at him.

He grabbed at the thoughts he'd been gathering. "It leaves us in this middle of this assignment, for starters. Just maybe, it leaves us back where we started."

"Taking advantage of the moment," Mariska said, not quite looking at him. "Like that first night."

Ruger was the one who had to look away. That wasn't what he'd felt after that first night with her. He'd felt the start of something then. He'd *wanted* it. "The moment," he said out loud, as casually as he could. He didn't believe it—not of himself. He knew himself too well—knew he'd been too hurt by her, and that meant he'd already gone past *the moment*.

But they had to get through this assignment somehow. If that meant pretending a friends-with-potential-benefits relationship, he could do it. Sentinels as a whole had perfected that particular byplay, just as Sandy and Harrison had done.

"Right," Mariska said, returning his tea, her dark eyes

holding a sadness he hadn't expected. "And thank you. I know you've got every reason to make things harder for me."

"Under the circumstances, that would make me a dick," Ruger said. "I try to avoid being a dick."

She snorted faint laughter, and he grinned back down at her, and thought maybe he'd get through the day after all.

They approached the installation with caution—knowing Forakkes was still here somewhere, still lurking with intent. Maks had known it, too—he'd been tiger when they parked at the old Williams place and skirted the back corner of Katie's property with the ATVs. Tiger, moving with a limp and occasional lurch, but tiger nonetheless glowering and on patrol.

Quiet as the ATVs were, Ruger and Mariska withheld conversation—but her arms tightened around his torso as they rode past Maks, understanding the implications.

Maks, too, was on high alert.

They disembarked to the side of the trail and tossed the camo netting over the ATVs; Ian went ahead, casting for amulet sign, and Mariska followed in his wake.

But where Ian moved steadily forward, Mariska stopped, her expression uncertain. Ruger moved up beside her, questioning her with a glance—and then not truly needing her explanation, not as he drew on the bear, and the scent of Core visitors hit his nose.

"Do you—?" Mariska asked, and stopped as she saw his head lifted in concentration. "Oh, good. I wasn't sure—"

Ruger snorted. "Yes, you were. You just didn't want to say it. The hell with that, little bear. Just because things haven't gone as planned doesn't mean you don't know your job."

Her eyes widened slightly; she chewed her lip, then let it go. "Okay. The problem is, I don't scent them from any particular direction. It's as though they were everywhere. At least three of them. And it's all muddled up with—"

"Skunk," Ruger said flatly.

Sandy had come up on their heels. "I'm not getting any of it but the skunk."

"Take your coyote and you would," Ruger said, without concern. None of them had human senses as acute as those of their other forms, even if they were still better than any mundane human could expect. But in either form, a bear's sense of smell was second to none. He looked down at Mariska. "Once we get settled inside, I think you and I should take a look around. Bearishly speaking."

"I think *one* of us should," she responded, her tone pointed.

Sandy help up her hands in a gesture of peaceful retreat. "This one's all yours, Mariska."

Mariska looked straight at Ruger, and he wasn't sure if the apology in her eyes made things better or worse. "You said I knew my job. Well, this *is* my job. Yours is inside, figuring out what's going on with those animals."

"We *know* what's going on with those animals," he growled.

"We don't," she shot back at him. "We know what's *happened* to them. We don't know *why*. And now that Forakkes has slagged the hard drives, those animals are all we have to work with."

"Then we're screwed," Ruger told her. "I can't read that man's mind, and I'm sure not going to do it while I'm worried about the security of this place."

"Then you'll have to deal with it, won't you? Because the security of this place isn't why you're here."

"Little bear—"

She raised her lip in a human snarl, her legs braced, her hands fisted at her sides, color on her cheeks. He met it with eyes narrowing, head tipped in warning—for long moments they faced off, Ruger's temper rising to an intensity he rarely allowed simply because it was so. Damned. *Hard*...

...to think straight.

"Fine," she said, so matter-of-factly it threw him completely off balance. She took a step back from him and reached into her bag, pulling out the satellite phone while he struggled to regain his equilibrium. "I'll see what Nick thinks."

It slapped his temper down fast enough—left him stunned all over again. "That's what you want to do? Make good at my expense again?"

"No," she snapped. "It's what you're forcing me to do because you don't truly respect my skills, no matter what you said. Would you argue with Ian about amulets? Would you argue with Sandy about wards?"

He floundered in defensiveness, knowing only that he'd done it again—left himself far too open to this hurt. "It's not the same, little bear." He used the words deliberately this time, offering a moment of his own bared teeth. "I don't do wards or amulets. I damned well know how to watch my own back."

"It's not *why you're here*. And dammit, I don't know that you do. Look at all the chances you take with healing—God, Ruger, you could have killed yourself trying to heal Jack!"

"I wasn't trying to *heal* him," Ruger said, dropping

his voice into its deep lower register, a human growl. "I was just trying to help him *survive*."

"And still you bled from your ears," Mariska said, and the tremor in her voice sounded like fear. "You passed out, and you didn't exactly bounce right back, either. What am I *supposed* to think, Ruger? That this is your very best judgment? That you've adjusted to what happened to you? It doesn't look that way from here!" She displayed the phone, holding it out in a neutral position— her meaning clear enough. *Your choice.*

He straightened, stiff with the impact of her words, and stared at her with a gaze that should have melted whatever chill thing she was made of. She met it without flinching.

"Put the phone away," he said, and left her there to do it as he headed for the installation.

Mariska made her way through the door and down the tunnel in solitude, finding a comfort in the scent of dirt and the enclosing walls. *Damned stubborn man. Damned stupid man.* She tried to think of a way that encounter might have gone better...and couldn't.

Then again, it couldn't have gone worse.

She couldn't quite bring herself to enter the installation. Not yet. Not when the others had likely heard almost every word of that encounter.

Not when she wished she could be more certain that she'd been right to pull out the nuclear option, brandishing the sat phone with its connection to Nick Carter. The look on Ruger's face...the hurt, the fury...

The murmur of voices within reassured her; the team was going about its business. She admired the smooth efficiency of their exchanges, the ease with which they fell to work with one another.

She'd thought to find that for herself here. One of the team.

Then maybe it would have been good not to start by undermining the one they all love. The one she had only belatedly—far too late at that—realized that she could love, too.

The quiet commentary stuttered short on a sharp sound, the voice deep and surprised. *Ruger.*

Mariska forged forward into the installation with her heart suddenly pounding, seeing it differently than she had the day before. No longer a benign space with secrets to uncover, but a space of lurking dangers and arcane threats. But even before she emerged to assess the situation visually, she'd absorbed the lack of fear in the air, the less than desperate response. She found Sandy and the amulet specialists converging on Ruger, who stood—unharmed, his scowl evident from the set of his shoulders—in front of the cage shelves.

"What's going on?" she asked, merging into the group as Sandy and Heckle caught up to Ian.

"They're dead," Ian said, disbelief in his voice.

"All of them," Ruger said, his anger barely suppressed. "He killed them *all.*"

Mariska understood immediately. "We took away his eyes. That made them of no use to him."

"Wrong," Sandy said, her mouth tight with disgust. "He used them, all right. To make an impact on *us.*"

Mariska wouldn't have thought of it. But Sandy was the one who liked knots and puzzles and wards, her clever coyote mind always at work. The moment she said the words, Mariska knew the truth of them. "That man is a monster."

"Of that, we can be assured." Ian looked at the carnage of little bodies. "But he's arrogant, too, and we can use that. Sooner or later."

Ruger glanced over at Ian with enough intensity in his expression to stop Mariska short—to fill her with both respect and an instant, longing ache. "We'll use it," he promised. Only as an afterthought did he send a quick look Mariska's way. "When you're done outside, I could use some help. Someone to take notes."

"My shorthand is nonexistent," she told him, keeping her voice as steady as she could—as casual as she could. "But I'll be glad to help." She took a breath. "I'd like a group consensus on this, though—the way the trail is muddled up out there—"

"And the *skunk*," Sandy added, wrinkling her nose to rearrange her freckles.

Mariska made a face in response. "It's obvious they did it on purpose. Even as the bear, I won't be able to sort things out in short order. Would you rather I spent the time unraveling what they've done, or do you want me to secure the immediate area and come back for this?"

"The question is whether they're just trying to tie us in knots—use you up that way—or if they're hiding something." Sandy looked over at Ian. "I think it would be best not to get caught up in their game. To just secure the area with extra care. Do one pass with your hands and your tech, and the other with your bear and your nose."

"That should cover it," Ian agreed.

Mariska didn't want to glance over at Ruger—to see how he felt about it, or about her—but her eyes did just that.

He wasn't looking at her at all. He kept his gaze on the cages, on the animals within the cages.

She almost wished he had his beard again. Then she wouldn't have been able to see the hard muscle of his jaw or his throat move when he swallowed. And she wouldn't have realized, with blinding clarity, just how much she'd hurt him. Again. She almost opened her mouth on the sudden, overwhelming impulse to suggest that he come out with her. The two of them would work faster, would provide twice the coverage…and it wouldn't be the same as if he'd been insisting, judgment-blind.

But the moment passed, and she didn't have the courage after all. "I'll be back as soon as I can," she told them, and figured she didn't hide her misery any better than Ruger had. But there was a monster out there, killing animals, working up to kill the Sentinels—and she was here to stop him.

Chapter 12

Mariska emerged into the woods with some relief, grateful she'd worn shifting clothes today. White clouds already tumbled together in a gathering storm, carrying in the next monsoon front. She set her water bottle and detector tech off to the side of the entry and took her bear, right then and there.

Oh, to be bear—full of strength, more nimble than she ever got credit for, her senses sharper than anyone ever assumed. Sight and scent and hearing, the strong swipe of a claw, the sprinting speed to rival any creature. She stretched hugely, yawned a great noisy yawn to shed stress and ambled straight to the nearest tree just to see how high she could mark it. *High. Satisfyingly high, little black bear.* For the first time since she'd triggered the amulet on herself, her headache faded; her skin no longer felt tightly hot.

She shook off with a flap of glossy pelt and headed out, stretching her legs—not trying to follow any given scent, but making note of them all…the tracks she crossed, the scent in the air, the skunk obscuring all. Nothing stood out; she found only the aimless, crisscrossing patterns of several men, calculated to confuse and annoy.

She shed the comfortable skin of her bear to grab the detection gear, but didn't expect to find anything. None of the men had hesitated long enough to *do* anything, perhaps not realizing she could detect as much from the scent pools. They'd simply been on the move.

Only when she finished did she realize that the headache had returned, that her joints felt strangely rusty. Maybe that was why she had the growing urge to be back inside with the others. It was with relief that she met Sandy's friendly greeting upon entering the facility. "All clear?"

"Looks like they were just messing with us," Mariska said. "A whole lot of tromping around to do nothing and go nowhere." She stowed her gear. "The clouds are building—I think we'll get a good storm this afternoon."

"Any rain is good rain," Sandy said, the automatic response of a desert dweller. She nodded at Ruger, who had laid most of the little creatures out in rows on the worktable. Ian and Harrison were sequestered off in the amulet section, packing the amulets into sturdy, sectioned cases. "I've been helping Ruger, but Ian will need me to help ward those cases when they're full. I'd swap with you if we could."

The kind thought cheered Mariska considerably. "Thanks. I'm sure we'll manage."

"It'll be fine," Sandy said, lowering her voice to a confidential level. "Don't you back off, either. Just because this is hard for him doesn't mean you're not right."

Mariska found herself floundering for words—and by then Sandy had left her with a meaningful look and a sauntering gait, joining up with the amulet team. She smiled to herself—just a flicker of warmth at that camaraderie—and then headed to the grim scene at the end of the cavernous building.

Ruger handed her a thick, padded spiral-bound note-book, the paper smooth and narrow-lined. It was with some surprise she realized it was a journal—a healer's professional journal. While she didn't feel comfortable flipping through it under his scrutiny, she got glimpses of the contents as she hunted the next clean page—a bold, clear hand scribing case notes, surprisingly accurate and simple sketches of plants and notes about their unusual effects on Sentinel bodies, field notes on amulet injuries, Sentinel healing tendencies…and the occasional disgruntled editorial remark.

She felt as though she was holding Ruger in her hand.

If only she'd had the chance to read these notes before they'd met, maybe she wouldn't have blundered so hard. If only she had the chance to read them now…then she'd be able to carry him with her wherever she went, no matter how things went between them in these next days.

He gave the book a meaningful glance—one that told her he'd prefer it if she didn't pry—and handed over a pen of such perfect weight and balance that she knew it would glide more beautifully over the paper than any pen she'd ever used before.

She almost thrust the whole thing back at him. It felt too intensely *his* for her to be welcome there. But he'd already moved back to the worktable, and she closed her hand around the pen and smoothed the paper down, making herself look ready. Only then did she take a close look at the animals, and blurt, "He's changed them *all*. How did he—? Right through the wards!"

"That's one of the things we need to figure out," Ruger said, and his tone was nothing but professional—no sign of lingering anger, no resentment. She relaxed, grateful—

and a little embarrassed that she'd expected less from him. "Although I wouldn't say he's *changed* them. I'd say he's *un*changed them."

She looked at the untenable mutations laid out before them, fur and feather and scale, each of the animals missing something critical to its survival. The bird that had once carried fur everywhere but its wings now lacked all skin in those areas; the gopher with scales patterning its back and sides likewise looked skinned. "Wait a minute," she said. "You're right! I mean, of course you're right, but…look. Nothing's changed now except what he had already changed in them before, right?"

"Not that I've seen." Ruger looked at the skink curled stiffly in his palm and gently set it aside, giving his attention to Mariska instead. "What are you thinking?"

She rested the notebook against her hip. "Sandy's never seen any sign of workings slipping through her wards, right? What if that's because he'd already changed them once? What if he established some sort of connection with them? The working wouldn't have to get through the wards, not really. It would more or less already *be* here."

Rather than responding, Ruger looked out into the installation. "Ian, you hearing this?"

"Hell, yes," Ian said. "I've never heard of any such thing, but when have we seen this sort of experimentation before? You just keep thinking out loud, Mariska."

"Well," she said, looking at the animals and flipping back to the previous day's notes—Ruger's clear hand and clinical descriptions of what had been done to the animals, "I think what you've been doing is compiling details—what these animals were when we got here, what they are now…"

"That's where I'm starting," Ruger agreed, and the

earlier relief she'd felt at his neutral tone faded as she understood the price it exacted—the distance it had put between them.

Loss constricted her throat; her thoughts stumbled. *It doesn't mean I'm not right. It doesn't mean I'm not doing what's best for him. For the team.* She took a breath and persisted. "I'm wondering, what's the point? He changed them, and then he *un*changed them without actually restoring them. So what's he *really* doing? In the big picture?"

"Being insane," Heckle muttered as he hauled a heavy packed-and-strapped amulet case to sit by the exit.

Sandy snorted, but Mariska had eyes only for Ruger's reaction—the wary understanding behind his expression. "Whatever he's doing," Ruger finally said, "the end goal is to help the Core—probably by hurting us, but not necessarily."

Mariska closed her eyes, thinking back to the reports of the raid on Gausto's compound—the massive beast he'd become, the havoc he'd wreaked—and the horror of his death when the amulet failed. "He's already seen how badly it goes when the Core uses amulets to change their own nature."

"Total suckage," Heckle said on the way back to the amulet section.

Mariska touched the fur on one stiff little body. "So if this is about hurting us, and it's about changing but not about changing *Core*—"

"God," Ruger said. "He changed them not to prove he could—he's known that for a while. He changed them so he could *un*change them. That's what this is about—*unchanging* us. It's about *taking away what we are*."

"Katie's vision," Mariska whispered. *The wild, yipping howl of a bereft wild dog, the wash of a vile stench, tast-*

ing foul in her throat. A hollow huffing sound, followed by a clacking, the surge of fear...a tremendous explosion. And then an entire chorus of grief, animal skins fluttering to the ground like sodden laundry. Wolf and bear, panther and boar, wildcat and stoat and deer. Crumpled up and discarded, and a nation of grief splashing in to wash it all away—

She saw in Ruger's eyes the same horror she felt—the same understanding. She found herself reaching for his hand, not even thinking about it—just craving the strong warmth of it, the ease it might give to the sudden increased throb between her eyes and the strangled feeling in her throat.

Maybe he noticed. Maybe he didn't. He didn't close the distance between them; he didn't look at her at all. He looked out across the installation, his gaze not focused on any of it at all. "He's out there somewhere," he said, and his pale brown eyes were haunted with understanding. "And he's figured out how to kill us all."

Ruger walked away from the worktable—walked away from Mariska, from her bereft expression and the hand she'd held out to him.

Maybe he was a bastard for not reaching back—not when they faced something that made their personal differences irrelevant, not when he so deeply shared that which she felt.

But he had nothing to give her. Not when it took everything in him to resist going straight at her—an all-out confrontation as bear, head to head, to resolve their conflict once and for all.

Or when it took just as much restraint to keep from sweeping her up, throwing her across that table, and making her cry out again and again—making her quiver and moan as she had in his arms the very night before, making her lose control as they both had on the night she'd brought him home.

Either way, it was a very good reason for him to not be here at all. Or for her to not be here at all. It mattered little how right she was in any given moment if her presence disrupted the team so badly that he couldn't function.

Except he had.

No, *they* had. Together, they'd skipped hours, maybe days of painstaking notes, and gotten to the heart of the situation.

Eduard Forakkes was creating a working that would strip Sentinels of their *other*. Ian without his snow leopard, Sandy without her coyote, Harrison without whatever slight vestige of *other* he carried buried within.

Mariska without her bear.

He tried to imagine being without that part of himself…couldn't. In his heart, he knew they wouldn't survive it—not any of them. *He's figured out how to kill us all.*

Without turning around, he raised his voice and asked, "Can we counter this?"

"Not in time," Ian said flatly, the only one among them who could answer at all. "Not without losing lives to the process."

"Then we have to stop him."

"We have to *find* him," Sandy pointed out.

"We have to tell brevis," Mariska said, and her voice sounded odd, strangely breathy.

At that, Ruger turned, giving her his healer's eye—reaching out in a way he'd been avoiding, if with more of an edge than behooved the process. Sandy, too, had turned to Mariska, standing on the edge of that amulet work area, her mouth open on words yet unvoiced.

But Ian glanced overhead at the arc of the ceiling and the layers of dirt and foliage over that. "Not even the sat phone will get a signal from here," he said. "I'll go make a call. Mariska, would you—" He stopped, frowning. "You all right?"

"It's just the shock of it," she said, not the least bit convincing. "Thinking about it. I'm fine."

"You're not," Ruger said, hardly considering his words as he strode back toward her. "You're flushed. You've *been* flushed."

"Stop it." Her voice was low, holding just a bit of a desperate growl—she skewered him with a look as if she thought this was personal. "Leave it alone. It's a bug or something, and I'm just not used to it. None of us are."

"There's a reason for that." Ruger's response didn't diminish her defensive anger in the least. "We don't get *bugs.*"

"He's right." Ian reached the middle of the cavernous space with long strides, grabbed up Ruger's field kit, and passed it over like a basketball. "I'm thinking less bug and more amulet."

Ruger caught the kit and dropped it onto the table with a solid thump, already rummaging for the last of his restoratives even as he assessed her. If he'd been able to reach out fully to her…even her reaction to a more active healing energy would tell him so much more than he knew now.

But no; he could do little more than any other Sentinel, connecting to feel the uncomfortably feverish sensations in her body, the ache in her bones. He could help the symptoms, but he couldn't address the causes of her malaise. He couldn't do the subtle exploration that would allow him to figure it out.

He couldn't take away the suddenly frightened look in her eye.

"More *amulet?*" she repeated, her voice thinning a little. "I thought that was just a stun amulet. I thought I just needed a day or two to get over that. Are you saying that the working is still *in* me?" She looked down at herself in horror, her hands brushing at her body as if it crawled with insects.

"Not actively," Ian said, with no reassurance in his voice at all. "But that doesn't mean it didn't start something that's still in process."

"Ruger?"

He stopped rummaging long enough to meet her eye, but with no more reassurance than Ian. "I'm sorry," he said, making himself face the words. "Whatever it is, I can't just make it go away." He found the vial of restorative and added reduced infusions of yarrow and basil, both preserved and enhanced by the energies he'd once been able to control. "Let me have your water."

Mutely, she pulled the sport bottle from her belt; he dumped the vial into it and closed off the top to give it a vigorous shake. "This should help until we figure out what's going on. It may even be enough to carry you through."

She took the bottle as he held it out to her. "You don't believe that, though."

He shook his head. "I'm not making assumptions, that's all. If I could still feel what was happening, I'd tell you." But Ruger glanced at Ian, knowing what Mariska didn't—that she'd asked the wrong Sentinel. Ian was the one who knew amulets—and Ian was the one who didn't believe.

Ian confirmed it a moment later, a private sending to Ruger. ::We need to get her back to brevis.::

::I know. She's not going to like it.::

Ian's gaze flicked to Mariska and back, the faint twist of his mouth allowing that he well knew it. ::Talk her into it, then.::

::Me? I don't think so.:: Ruger forgot to hide his alarm and Mariska gave him a sharp look, her eyes narrowing as she gave the water a wary sniff, raising it for a drink.

Ian said out loud, "Brevis definitely needs an update. I'll go out and grab a signal. Sandy, you want to come?"

"Sure, I'll watch your back," Sandy said, grinning—sending Ruger a knowing glance. "I need a chance to stretch my coyote, anyway."

Ian shot Ruger a look—*you owe me*—and said privately, ::I'll save your cowardly ass and get brevis to request security on the amulets we're shipping back. You can thank me later.::

Ruger only scowled as the impact of his own reaction hit home. *Much later.* Because it meant she'd go, all right.

And he didn't want her to. No matter that he couldn't and didn't trust her.

"Oh!"

Mariska's gasp stopped them all in their tracks—Ruger most of all, two long strides and he was at her side as she doubled over, the water bottle bouncing in the dirt beside her. He reached out to her without thinking—and stopped himself with effort, limiting himself to what he could feel of her, the faint echo of pain radiating from her belly.

It was enough. He wrapped an arm around her waist, supporting her, and looked over at Ian with the grimmest of expressions. "She's reacting to the infusions."

"But that didn't happen before!" Sandy protested.

Ian said, "The working wasn't truly throughout her system before."

Mariska's hand closed over Ruger's at her waist, clasping his fingers. "Then you're right," she said, jerking slightly as pain shot through her belly; he felt the echo of that, too. Just enough of the healer left to know. "It's from the amulet, and it's—" She winced. "It's bad, isn't it?"

"It's not bloody good," Ian said, when Ruger only pulled her closer, wrapping his other arm around her to kiss the top of her head, trying to remember if he'd ever felt so helpless—and so desperate.

Harrison was the one who said it out loud. "This is ridiculous. We've lost Jack, and Mariska needs help. We've got most of the amulets packed and we think we know what's going on here. We need to call for extraction and get a strike team up here to find Forakkes."

"He'll know they're coming," Mariska said, straightening cautiously, her hands still clamped onto Ruger's arms.

Sandy didn't hesitate. "Then get the strike team on its way while we hang out as a distraction."

"Coyote," Ian said approvingly. "If Carter takes this as seriously as he should, they can scramble a team up here within two hours. I have reason to know, don't I?"

"That's how long it took when Forakkes sent that working after you last month," Mariska guessed— proving once more that she did, in fact, do her homework.

"Minute by minute," Ian affirmed. "Think you can hang on that long, Mariska?"

"Hell, yes." She straightened a little more, not quite shrugging off Ruger's arms even if she no longer leaned on him. "As long as I stay away from that potion."

"Someone ought to drink it," he said. "It's the last of the restorative."

She winced. "Sorry about that."

"There's no way you could have known you'd react

to it. I didn't, did I?" He tightened his arm around her in brief reassurance, and felt her relax a little. He thought that once again, they were somehow where they were supposed to be with one another—this place of physical familiarity and comfort that had come to them right from the start. Only this time, he knew to expect the inevitable sense of betrayal; he knew it would come.

It didn't stop him from leaving his hand along the warm curve of her waist.

Ian tossed the sat phone in the air—and for an instant, he looked like nothing more than a cat playing. "Sandy," he said. "Let's put out the call. Harrison, can you finish up this round of packing? We'll place final wards when we get back in—and then we'll see what's left to us, depending on what Nick has to say."

Harrison headed for the amulet area; Sandy preceded Ian to the exit, her step light with the anticipation of taking her coyote. Mariska bent away from Ruger's grasp, snagging his notebook and pen from the floor and wiping off the pages as she set it on the table. "Sorry about that," she said. "It's such nice paper, too."

His indulgence, that notebook, that pen. His nod to how much his profession meant to him. "It's sturdy," he told her. "That's the point. I like sturdy things."

She glanced over at him, and her eye sparked a little brighter over her flush. "As it happens," she told him, "so do I. And I feel better—I think it's passed. How about if you let me go, and I'll find the water bottle. You're right—someone should take advantage of it."

"It'll hold," he said, although he released her nonetheless, stepping back from his lingering but token support. "The preservation spells carry over from the dry herbs. That might even have been what you were reacting to—we should try releasing those and see how it goes, if you're up for it."

"Damn right I'm up for it." She took it as a challenge, and Ruger grinned as she immediately bent to look for the sport bottles, making no effort to avoid staring at the rounded shape of her ass. "Where the hell—"

Thunder cracked above them; Mariska startled upright. "It's too early for that storm—"

Another crack, a rumble—the ground shook. Harrison yelped a warning as something crashed to the ground at the other end of the facility; Ruger crouched slightly, balancing himself against the unsteady ground. "That's not thunder—"

The arching Quonset roof groaned as something slammed down above them. Metal buckled; dirt trickled down to bounce off the worktable. Several of the little animal bodies vibrated off the table, and still another explosion ripped loose overhead. The shelving swayed, crates and cages clattering; Mariska jerked around, her eyes gone wide—but Ruger was faster, leaping between the shelves and Mariska and wrapping himself around her as they both went down.

The shelving hit hard enough to knock the breath from his lungs, a slicing pain mixed with the impact and chaos. Another explosion rocked the land above them; the facility screamed with twisting metal. They rolled free of the shelving with Mariska above him, shielding his face— shielding what she could.

The roof gave one last wrenching groan overhead as one of the metal panels sheered away—Ruger saw it coming and flipped them over one last time, covering Mariska in whole as they came to rest under the worktable.

The world rained down upon them.

Chapter 13

Curiosity was a small mouse rustling in grass; it was sweet berries dangling on a bush overhead. It was the cool gurgle of water in a monsoon-made stream.

Ciobaka's curiosity held nothing near such promise, but all the same...he unfolded himself from the back of his caging area and sat attentively by the door, his head cocked and his big ears scooped forward.

Ehwoord looked good this day. There was less gray on his head, more movement in his step, even if his face stayed stiff and strange. "Wha?" Ciobaka asked when he couldn't stand it any longer. *"Wha?"*

"Those who work against me," Ehwoord said, not so much as cracking his eyes open, "eventually die. Our Sentinel friends have just learned this lesson." Then he did look at Ciobaka, one of those direct looks that set Ciobaka's hackles on end no matter how unwise.

This time, Ehwoord merely laughed. "You still have use," he said, and Ciobaka narrowed his eyes to a canine squint. "But the Sentinels...if I don't have access to my work, then neither will they. I eliminated their opportunity to study the living animals. Among other things."

Ehwoord said it so matter-of-factly it took Ciobaka a moment to understand.

"Deah?" he asked, startled.

"Yes, dead." Ehwoord tipped his head, pushing the headphone disk with one finger and squeezing the button that meant the mike curving to his mouth would let him talk to others. "Deploy the veil working, and then fall back. Once you return, monitor their wards. When the woman who set them dies, they'll fall—then you may use the remaining workings to fully obliterate any remaining evidence of our presence there."

The corners of Ciobaka's mouth pulled back. Months ago, he wouldn't have understood the significance of this conversation—not any of it. But now, as Ehwoord left his desk to toss a limp quail into Ciobaka's cage, he understood it all.

But as he glanced at Ehwoord from the corner of his eyes, chewing vigorously at a feathered wing, he knew one other thing, one very important thing.

Ehwoord didn't know that he knew.

The noise went on forever, and Mariska saw none of it. She buried her face in Ruger's shoulder—she had no choice. She couldn't even see the table above them. She could only hear the groan of earth and metal, the crash of things falling from the ceiling, tipping over from the walls. Falling dirt made a softer noise, an uneven patter of earth rain that finally...*finally*...faded to a trickle.

"Get *off*," she said when he didn't move. His uneven breathing gusted near her ear, his body so tense it trembled—still waiting for a final blow.

But the table had held. And if she couldn't yet make sense of the visual chaos around them, she could at least tell they'd have dim light to work with—the ceiling ripped through to the sky and daylight filtered dully through the dust of the cave-in.

"Ruger," she said more gently, another nudge.

He released a long breath and raised himself to hands and knees, his back bumping the table, his body still caging hers. "Hell," he said, his expression heavily dazed. "They fucking *blew us up.*"

"Ruger," she said, *"get off."*

He looked down at her with dawning comprehension—and still he didn't move. Still protecting her. She showed her teeth at him and shoved.

"No," he said, unmoved—still not sounding completely with it, and she wondered how hard the shelves had hit him. The sting of her own injuries made themselves known—nothing more than bumps and cuts and a few deep bruises. He added, "Not quite yet," and sounded a little more sensible about it—especially given the belated crash of something not far away.

So for the moment they huddled together, breathing, waiting for the world to settle. Ruger eased back down over her, propped on his elbows; she searched his face, trying to understand what she saw there—wondering if he could feel her heart pounding just as she felt his. Another nearby crash and the table shifted; he stiffened, hunching slightly as if to protect her.

"Shh," she said, and reached up to touch the side of his face—sweaty and dirt-streaked and just a little wild. It startled her—she hadn't realized she had that kind of gentle reassurance in her. And she hadn't realized that he needed it.

But he dropped his forehead to hers, his voice broken. "Mariska," he said. "God, Mariska—if you'd—"

"Shh," she said again, and stroked his hair, short and wiry and the hint of curl against her fingers.

She wasn't surprised when he kissed her.

She was surprised by its gentleness, by its care—a kiss imbued with a tender, thorough care. His hands framed her face, capturing her without imprisoning her, and he kissed her mouth, he kissed her cheek, he kissed her brow—and her mouth again, while she felt a hot trickle of tears escape to run into her hair simply from the purity of what he offered.

He pulled back without releasing her—watching her with concern, trying to read her. With her thumb, she wiped away the moisture from beneath his eye and whispered, "I'm sorry."

"Do you suppose," he told her, "I would ever be happy with someone who didn't have the strength to do what she believed in?"

Her eyes widened as the impact of his words rolled through her—unfolding in her body as a fluttering lightness of spirit, the intense relief of an underlying tension she didn't know she'd been holding. And still— "But the things I did—"

"Shh," he said, and bent to kiss her again. This time neither of them startled when something crashed nearby, and though her body warmed to him—and she felt his response just as clearly—neither of them rose to that, either, instead reveling in the tenderness.

It couldn't last forever—it couldn't last for more than a moment, with the world still trickling down around them. When he eased back, she said, "I'm going to make you mad again."

He grinned down at her, and it, too, held something of teeth. "I'm going to make you mad again, too."

::Ruger? Harrison?:: Ian's communication came filtered through a certain amount of confusion, a distinct stab of pain. Ruger winced—feeling it more than she did, Mariska realized.

::We're here!:: Mariska replied for them. ::Under a table. We can't see anything yet.::

::Too dark in here even for Sentinel eyes,:: Ian said. ::We're under…:: His mind-voice trailed off, as though he was only then making assessment—or as though he'd become disoriented. Ruger tensed above her, his head tilted with a fierce concentration that told Mariska he was gleaning everything he could through his diminished healer's skills. Finally Ian said, sounding more true to his dry nature, ::…a helluva lot of crap, that's what. Smack in the middle of the tunnel.::

::Sandy?:: Mariska asked, so Ruger didn't have to.

::She's out cold—half-buried. I can feel her breathing.::

She thought of broad, clawed paws working against the dirt and debris of the tunnel. ::Can you take your leopard?::

He responded with a short, sharp snapshot of what he saw, what he felt, bypassing words for the immediacy of *choking dust, utter darkness, shifting rubble, Sandy's back warm and her breath hitching, the profound pressure of dirt, the stabbing pain of something sharp and invasive, the gouge of crumpled wire.*

Ruger breathed a curse, his head dropping as he absorbed all, including Mariska's gasp of dismay.

::Got it,:: Mariska said faintly. Shifting under such circumstances would only incorporate the fallen materials into his body. She looked out from beneath the table to the shaft of filtered sunlight, picking out the far edge of the structure, the crumpled shelves that had slammed down against Ruger, the jumbled mess that comprised the rest of the installation; she sent it to Ian and felt his faint curse in reply. ::I don't get it,:: she said. ::What the hell happened?::

::You tell us.:: The reply came from Heckle. ::You're the one who checked out this area.::

Mariska's glad response at his mind-voice—dazed as all of them, but laced with anger rather than pain—faded instantly. ::I *did* check this area,:: she said, and rather than going defensive, she felt her own slow burn of anger—and to her surprise, she felt a trickle of the same from Ruger. Not blaming anger—not at all. But on her behalf, his hand squeezing slightly against her arm as he remained propped on his elbows above her.

::You obviously missed something!::

::That's enough,:: Ian said, and it was the weariness in his voice that stopped Mariska short. ::Start thinking in terms of ordinance.::

::Ordinance…:: Mariska repeated, not quite able to wrap her head around it.

::Hand ordinance,:: Ruger said, withdrawing from his healer's mode to join the conversation for the first time. ::Or RPGs.:: *Rocket-propelled grenades…*

::Makes sense,:: Ian said, sounding more distant. ::Once we were all underground, they had a clear field, right through the wards.:: He hesitated for so long that Mariska was about to ask if he was okay—and didn't, because how stupid was that? None of them were okay. When he spoke again, she felt the effort of it. ::Harrison, are you injured?::

::No.:: Heckle's prompt reply was as convincing as his words. ::But there's no way I'm getting out of here without help.::

Another long hesitation—way too long—and Ian said, ::They're here, and they're hunting…and we're the only ones who know what they're up to. Brevis needs to know. We don't know how much time we have before Forakkes…his working…::

Ruger's thought filled the silence. ::Ian?::

::Here,:: Ian said, if barely so. ::Reach Annorah. Let brevis know. And Ruger…::

Ruger waited, shifting above Mariska as patience snapped to concern. ::*Ian!*::

::Don't take that tone with me, bear. Just got to…rest awhile. Now go…find…them.::

"Dammit!" Ruger pushed away from her, removing the table from overhead by the simple act of hunching his shoulders, planting his feet on either side of her, and rising up beneath it. It crashed down a few feet away, upended and in pieces among the debris from which it had sheltered them.

Mariska scrambled to her feet, but not before snagging the water bottle she'd been after in the first place—just barely accessible in the shadow of the table's protection. To her relief, the initial intense, cramping response she'd had to her first few swallows had completely eased; the herbs may even have done some good in the wake of them, for her fatigue had lifted, her generalized aches receded.

Or it could simply have been the adrenaline still pounding through her body—adrenaline released anew as she looked around at the destruction of the installation. Dirt and metal piled between this end and the area where Harrison now waited; the exit was crumpled and buried. Lighting hung from the ceiling from stretched wiring; metal struts still popped and snapped, groaning under the stress. "It's not stable," she said, words absently spoken out loud.

"Not in the least." He turned a circle, inspecting the area. "We've got to get help up here."

"Annorah?" Mariska suggested. And then, "Ruger—your back!"

He twisted as if he could look over his own shoulder. "Thought I felt something sharp."

"You *think?*" She dropped the hard-won bottle, stepping up to hold him still with a hand at his side, the other tugging at the blood-dotted shirt over his broad shoulders. "This needs to come off."

"Leave it," Ruger said, pulling away to turn around. "It's not that bad."

She grabbed the belt loop at his hip to jerk him back where he'd been, still trying to assess the depth of the slashing wound and growling a warning as she did it.

He subsided, but barely, impatience radiating through him so palpably that she abruptly understood it was only for her that he stood still at all. "Mari," he said, "there's *nothing we can do about it.*"

She followed his gaze around the wreckage of the facility—looking to that central spot where they'd piled their gear upon arrival. *Buried.* Including the medic's field kit. His herb kit, too, was beneath the rubble—closer by, not as deep, but nonetheless buried.

She released a frustrated breath and snatched the bottle up. "Here," she said. "Drink what's left of this, at least." She glanced at the location of their erstwhile gear. "It may even be the last water we have for a while. I'd suggest we split it, but…"

"But," he agreed, and took the bottle, tipping his head back to take the contents in deep, long swallows. When he was done and wiping the liquid from his chin, he gave the bottle an uncertain look, glancing at the rubble around them.

Mariska took it from him and set it firmly on the floor rather than tossing it aside. "We might need it."

He snorted, and surprised her by wrapping an arm around her shoulders, pulling her off balance for a rough, half hug and kissing the top of her head while he was at it. "All right, little bear. What first?"

"Adveho," she said without hesitation, referring to the Sentinel Mayday call. "If any situation ever justified its use... Then we can work on getting Heckl—I mean, we can see about getting Harrison out of there. And he can help us with Sandy and Ian."

"It may take more than we have," Ruger said, giving the collapsed tunnel a worried glance.

"It might," she agreed. "We're not going to not try, though."

He closed his arm around her for a quick squeeze. "Go ahead and assess this place," he said. "I'll send the *adveho.*"

She agreed, leaving him to sit in the place where they'd once lain together, his expression already heading inward as he went deep for the necessary focus. She turned to pick her way through the mess, flinching at another rain of pebbles and setting herself to task.

Not for long. Ruger made a surprised sound—a pained sound. She jerked back around to find him frowning, his face tight and his palm pushing between dark brows. He looked up before she could ask. "I can't get out. There's some kind of wall...it stinks of the Core."

Can't get out... "We can't reach Annorah. We can't get help...and we can't warn brevis." Mariska frowned, flexing her fingers in a barely conscious claw-threat at Forakkes. "Are you all right?"

"Hurts like hell, actually," Ruger said, with no particular heat to his voice. "But I don't think any of us are *all right* at the moment. It'll fade." He climbed to his feet, looking up at the bright tear in the roof. "What do you think?"

Mariska gestured at the debris around them. "If we can get to Harrison, we'll have more manpower—but he's not injured and doesn't need immediate help. If we try to reach Ian and Sandy, it'll be trickier—tighter space, more chance of triggering dirt fall. But Ian has the sat phone, and both of them are in critical need of rescue."

"One we might not be able to give them even if we free them." Ruger's words fell more heavily than hers. "And if we don't stop Forakkes, we could *all* die."

Mariska's gaze locked onto his, finding a steady pale brown full of regret and full of awareness. *If we leave, our friends might die. If we don't leave, our friends will die. And so will we.*

She nodded, and that was it. Decision made. "Let's see if we can find anything useful before we go."

Ruger made a sound of agreement in his chest, but looked overhead again to their only exit—the distant gap in the ceiling, surrounded by sharp, torn metal. "Going," he said, "may not be as simple as that."

Chapter 14

Ruger prowled the cluttered remains of the structure, ducking against yet another trickle of shifting earth.

We can't reach Annorah. We can't warn brevis. And we can't take the chance that Forakkes will do what he means to do to us.

The fact that Forakkes had escalated so significantly, so suddenly...

Not a good sign.

Mariska didn't think so, either. She'd tugged a gear bag from the debris—lunch, MREs and some personal items, as it happened, including the gloves she quickly appropriated. She'd dumped all but two of those meals, filling the bag with several shards of metal she'd partially wrapped with cloth torn from another, less fortunate bag—makeshift weapons. She included the empty water bottle, the jacket Ian had so carelessly discarded upon their arrival, and tucked her own cell phone away in a side pocket.

They weren't likely to find a signal out here. But just in case...

Ruger spent his time nudging at Ian to no avail, unable to absorb any information about his injuries—or Sandy's—while they were unconscious. Harrison offered the occasional short comment, his out-of-breath thoughts reflective of his own efforts as he targeted an escape route and began removing debris.

In fairly short order, Ruger and Mariska stood together looking up at their single exit: a small hole in the metal roof two-thirds of the way up its arc, a pile of shifting rubble their only access.

"It's going to take bear to widen that hole," Ruger observed.

"I don't think that mess is stable enough for *bear,*" Mariska said, the stubborn note in her voice. "We might be able to slip through as human."

"*You* might be able to slip through as human." But even as Ruger spoke, the pile shifted slightly.

Mariska gave him a wary look. "I'll go first. I'm least likely to disturb that crap, and most likely to get through. If it seems stable enough, you can follow as bear and make yourself as much of a hole as you need." She visibly braced herself for his response, her mouth tight and her chin lifted.

"Good plan," he said, shrugging out of his shirt.

She tipped her head, examining him for signs of hidden resistance; he only grinned back and gave in to impulse, gently rubbing a thumb over her smudged cheek and tucking back hair that had tugged loose from her braid. "Hey," he said. "If it's good, it's good."

She relaxed, and stole a glance at his back—but didn't ask if he was okay. There wasn't any point, and he was right—the wound was long and slicing, but shallow enough. And they still had to get out of here; they still had to find Forakkes.

And if they couldn't reach brevis along the way, they still had to stop him themselves.

Mariska put her hand out for the shirt, waiting—guessing that it wasn't one that would take the change with him, as seemed to be his habit.

Ruger handed over the shirt and she tucked it away in the gear bag, unable to interpret the look he sent her. Thoughtful, for sure. She twirled her finger in a helicopter motion, a silent imperative. With some resignation, he turned around, showing her that which he'd been hiding. "Healer, heal thyself," he said, bitterness lacing his voice. "Or not."

Mariska kept her voice even, seeing the diagonal slash across his shoulder blade; it stopped just shy of his spine. Blood still trickled from the lower end, forging a stream down the roll of muscle paralleling his spine, but it was thin and already easing. "I thought that was hard at the best of times." She couldn't help it; she put one finger against smooth, warm skin, pressing just enough to shift the lip of the wound so she could see the depth. *Not deep. World's worst paper cut.*

"It is," Ruger admitted. "We feel it from both directions…the patient, the healer. That's why it's always been so important—" He cut off his own words, and she knew it was for her sake—for the sake of peace between them. *Why it's always been so important that I can take care of myself.*

But the silence hung heavily between them after that, and Ruger turned to look at her. "Screw that," he said. "Not saying the truth just because it's hard felt as fake as hell, and I'm not doing it again."

She bared her teeth at him, and only in retrospect

did she realized what she'd expected him to understand. *Don't play nice for me. I can take care of myself, too.*

To judge by his returning grin, he understood it perfectly.

"Well," she said, "it's nearly stopped bleeding anyway. So take your bear already, and let's get out of this place. The sooner we're out from under Forakkes' influence, the sooner we can get help to them." She couldn't help a glance at the obscured and twisted exit doorway.

Ruger stepped back—and back again—as the change bloomed out in billowing clouds of strobing light and energy, easily filling the space between them. *Big man. Damned big bear.*

Only then did she realize it was the first she'd seen of his other—the glossy brown pelt, towering size and hunched shoulders of the Kodiak. *Alaskan grizzly.* No sign of the white V-collar he'd had as a younger man, just breadth and strength and a mighty flap of pelt as he settled into himself.

She took a single step forward—he'd ended up that close to her—and ran her hand over the short hair at the side of his face, over the side of his sensitive muzzle, meeting warm brown eyes that held the faintest hint of laughter.

She stepped away, embarrassed to have been so readily entranced, and adjusted the bag over her shoulder. "All right, then," she said. "Let's go. Just give me a chance to assess the footing, okay? I'm used to thinking in terms of *my* bear's size."

He released a huff of amusement, and Mariska turned to the slope of rubble before her and started to climb.

The footing shifted beneath her, making her glad for the sturdy soles of her light hiking boots—but she didn't take a single step for granted. Ruger would have no such protection. Only once did she hesitate, looking at the impossibly steep climb, the stretch from the newly formed slope to the rent in the roof and the forest-filtered sunlight beyond.

She tackled the crumbling slope. In short order she made the transition to all fours—clambering, grabbing handholds, testing them, discarding them…trying again. And then again she found herself climbing.

At the top she jammed her feet against the thin support of buried metal and slowly stood upright, her heart pounding in her chest. Below, Ruger looked impossibly small. The facility should have stretched out below her; instead it was truncated a third of the way down its length, burying the office section beneath what looked to be an entire tree—half the crown and a jagged section of root. *Harrison's behind that.*

She froze with a sudden light-headedness, vertigo snatching at her sense of self. *Bear,* she thought with panic. *I am solid, strong bear. I am myself, and I am* right here.

Ruger made an encouraging noise; she latched onto the remembered strength of him and found herself.

After a moment, when she was sure, she fixed her gaze on the tortured remains of the roof for a few deep breaths. "Someone should have said *don't look down.*"

Finally, she dared to reach for the hole, stretching… *stretching…*

Too short.

Ruger made a noise of inquiry from the base of the rubble, concern in the *huff-huff-huff* that followed.

"Maybe I need to be bear after all," Mariska said, and her voice echoed dully into the open space below— although this time she knew better than to look. "I could try changing here—"

Ruger thought little of that notion, and a snort told her as much. Mariska couldn't help a wobbly smile, looking down on his massive form—all rippling pelt and muscle and strength. She doubted he realized he'd gone primal with her. No, he'd simply done the natural thing…bear to bear, no matter the form.

"Well," she told him, "I'm not going anywhere this way." She squinted upward, and fought a sudden squall of panic at the impossibility of it. *We have to get out of here! We have to stop—*

Ruger interrupted the spiral with a grumble as he headed for the rubble, one ambling step after another, his casual nature belying the care with which he placed those enormous paws.

"No!" Mariska said, sharply fearful. "What if it doesn't hold—" She hadn't expected to still be above him as he climbed, adding instability to the landslide. But he came on, inexorable and huge. Dirt shifted beneath him, sinking where it had held her, sharp objects jutting through.

"Oh, be careful," she breathed. And then, louder, "Just wait, I can figure this out. Give me a— *Oh!*"

Ruger froze, one paw reaching for security as Mariska's footing crumbled away. She flung herself up at the hole in the roof with an impossible jump, futilely grasping for handholds in the warped material—finally snagging a slippery root to hang over the edge, unable to gain so much as another inch. Barely able to keep what she had.

It's a long way down…

Ruger coughed a sharp inquiry from below.

"I'm okay!" she said, and spat dirt from her mouth. "I'm okay!"

Claws digging deep for traction, Ruger made steady progress below, leaving tumbling dirt and creaking wreckage in his wake. "Careful," she warned him, but even as she took a renewed grip on her pathetic little root, she felt a nudge on her calf, the brush of his nose along her thigh. Another nudge and she understood it was more than just a reassurance—it was suggestion.

"You're kidding," she said, not about to let go of the root.

::I'm not,:: he told her, from deep within the bear. ::Slide down. I've got you.::

She cursed, a heartfelt thing, and eased down—straightening her arms to the fullest and letting her knees rest on his shoulders. ::Hold on,:: he said, as her hands sank into the pelt of his neck.

She did just that, clutching fur, knees riding behind his shoulders. He tested his footing and heaved beneath her, rising along the slide until he'd regained the ground she'd lost, an absurdly large creature perching at an equally absurd height and using every muscle in his body to stay that way. He looked up at the ragged exit.

"Okay," she said, not nearly as certain as she sounded, but understanding well enough. From here, if she stood... she'd be just tall enough.

She thought.

She pulled the gear bag off over her head, steadied herself, and tossed it out through the hole, waiting for the satisfying thump of its landing. "You ready?"

He made a sound of assent, far too casual; she knew better than to believe it, and she knew that no matter how carefully she wanted to do this insane thing, the longer she took, the harder it would be on him.

She didn't let herself think too hard. She put her feet under her, found a hint of stability between his shoulder blades, and stood, swiftly reaching out to latch her gloved hands on the twisted structural beam at the edge of the hole. Ruger moved beneath her, surging in perfect synchrony with her push-off—sending her up with a power she hadn't expected. She cleared the hole with an elbow, bent metal tearing at her shirt—at her slacks as she once more slung one leg over the edge.

Below her, Ruger scrabbled to regain the stability he'd lost with that extra boost, and an instant of frustrated temper shoved out her fear—shoving out her awareness of the ground so far below her. She rode that fury right out through the hole, pulling herself onto the roof with determination more than grace, rolling instantly away from the edge.

::Mari?::

::I'm good!::

But there was no way he was getting through that hole. Not as bear, not as man. ::Mari?::

The question had a different feel this time—an urgency that reminded her he was still in the dark, while she had the perfect view of the area around the installation.

It took only an instant to absorb the first impact of the scene; she offered him visuals, pulling back slightly when he responded with a startled grunt, a sudden, audible lurch on his precarious perch.

Fallen and splintered trees from the ridge above, now resting in the hollow that held the installation; raw gouges dotting the earth around her... The ridge itself had crumpled overtop the installation's entrance—there'd be no approaching Ian and Sandy from that end. And here, she lay sprawled over a ruptured roof that probably wasn't anywhere near strong enough to hold her anymore.

She pulled back the visuals and scooted down the arch of the exposed roof on her bottom—and then, once she was well below the level of the hole and back on thick soil, she reached for her bear. It swelled up within her, strength and fiercely protective; she closed her eyes on the surging swirl of light and energy and expanded into herself. *Sharp scents of rent pine and disturbed soil, the breeze against her fur, the cool ground against her pads.*

The destruction looked no less impressive from her bear's eyes. She tread cautiously on the roof to reach the hole, hooking out splayed claws to catch metal and peel it away from the structural beam she'd found so useful, enlarging the hole in all directions. Within moments she peered down at Ruger—found him panting and perched at the apex of the landslide. The moment he spotted her, he collected himself, balancing, muscles bunching—*leaping.*

Mariska jerked back in surprise, unable to fathom how he could—how over a thousand pounds of *Kodiak* could—

The change bloomed around him, sparking color and light and motion; he thrust upward with the power of his bear and left the bear behind. The hands slapping into place on the beam belonged to Ruger the man. He jerked himself up, gaining an elbow over the beam; he hooked a leg over it. "Mari—" he said, a gasp behind it as the damaged beam creaked beneath his weight—and beneath her weight, all black bear as it was.

She understood with abrupt dread—rolling away to take back the human, and just as quickly scrambling back up again. She threw herself half over the edge, her hand closing around his belt at the hip—hauling upward with enough force to drive a grunt from her lungs—inching back as he gained a better hold, grabbing at his calf to tug him toward safety. Grabbing at anything she could reach, never mind how intimate the touch, until he finally slid back onto the roofing, his harsh breath matching hers.

The metal creaked as the beam buckled slightly;

Mariska abandoned dignity and scuttled away, down to where the building disappeared fully into the ground. Ruger did the same, launching away to land beside her.

Together they rose just enough to watch the roof section fall away in a rending clash of metals and a dull thud against the dirt below.

Mariska released a breath vigorous enough to stir her bangs, sat back on her heels, and glared over at Ruger. At the chances he'd taken to get them out of there, at his refusal to let her make the choices that would keep him as safe as they kept her. At his sliced back, on which he'd allowed her to clamber; at the toll taken on his body because he'd given so much to the effort of getting her out of that hole. "Dammit," she said, and hit him without pulling that punch in the least. "You make me so mad!"

Ruger's arm still stung. His back stung, a surface wound with the annoying sting of a giant paper cut. Mariska pulled his shirt from the bag and took his shoulder, turning him without so much as a by-your-leave.

Ruger growled low in his chest.

Mariska growled right back and dabbed the shirt against his back, slowly growing bold enough to take long swipes across his skin.

He had it in mind to turn on her and grab the shirt and stalk off; fussing at the wound wouldn't improve the situation one bit. But then he felt the tremble behind her touch, and then he let himself linger on how she'd thrown her bear on top of the unstable roof to enlarge the hole, and the impeccable timing of her change back to human so she could help haul him up.

He subsided—unsettled, wary, and standing braced with his head bowed while he listened to the woods around them. The scents of destruction raked his nose and sinuses with each breath, overlaid with the lingering skunk—but his ears…they could still assess the area.

Creaking, settling wood; shifting leaves. The birds shocked to silence; the small animals already fled. The rising breeze against his back, the sullen heat of a building monsoon storm against his skin.

Mariska's touch grew less brusque. She hesitated, fingers tightly tracing alongside the slash of the wound—telling him, for the first time, just how long it ran. "It's stopping," she said. "But it won't heal well if you keep moving."

He looked over his shoulder with wry amusement. "I've lost my healer's connection," he said. "I haven't forgotten everything I ever learned."

She made a face at him and tossed him the lightly stained shirt; he shook it out and shrugged into it, not bothering with the buttons.

Mariska looked at him with an unexpected wistfulness—but she shook it off quickly enough, lifting her head to look up the ridge. He didn't have to read her mind to know her thoughts. *Find Forakkes. Reach brevis. Get HELP.*

::Ian?:: he said, waiting only for the sense of the man's attention before raising his voice. ::Sandy?::

Mariska caught his eye and shook her head; there was no sense of either. Ruger kept his thoughts loud and clear anyway. ::We're out. We're going to find Forakkes. If we can break through the blackout zone, we'll get someone up here to pull you out.::

::Good hunting,:: Harrison said, the mind-voice of a man who held no illusions. ::If I manage to crawl my way out of here, I'll head for the ATVs—back to Maks' place. We can get a call out.::

Mariska caught Ruger's arm, her eye bright with question. *Maks.*

He shook his head. "I doubt the ATVs are still there."

"Still, if one of us went that direction, we might get out from under the blackout—"

"No," Ruger said sharply, and then made himself stop, scrubbing hands over his face with the impossibility of it all. He found her watching him with a stubborn reserve—her shoulders stiff, her arms crossed, her legs braced. He sighed. "I mean, I know. It could happen. But it's not worth the risk of splitting us up, not when we might walk out from under the blackout in this direction, too. Especially not when Forakkes knows exactly where Maks is."

Her arms dropped to her sides. "You think he'll have Maks blocked, too."

"I think we have to assume that if he launched an attack of this magnitude, he prepared for it. He's our enemy and he's every single thing we stand against—but he's not stupid."

"No," she murmured. "He's not stupid. I'm not sure I think he's sane, though." She shook her head. "Grenades in the national forest—! Surely not even the Core would welcome what he's done here, no matter the carrot he's got to dangle."

"I wouldn't care to predict what they're willing to accept if it means gaining any sort of control over us." Ruger lingered a final moment to hunt for signs of awareness from Ian and Sandy. Even now, if he could sense their needs, he could prepare brevis to deal with them—

"Stop it!" Mariska shouted at him—startling him with her closeness. "What is *wrong* with you?"

He stared at her, something close to dumbfounded, and she swiped her fingers over his bare upper lip, holding them up for his inspection. *Red and gleaming.*

He met her eyes, dark brown and glittering with anger, and had nothing to say. Mariska Bear, protecting him from himself, no matter how it frustrated him—flushed and mussed and beautiful. *Being who she was.*

He closed his hands over her shoulders—not gently, either—and pulled her in to cover her mouth with his, a punishing kiss that caught her up with a startled and then fervent response. He kissed her fierce and hard and not possibly long enough, and he broke away just as suddenly. "Mari Bear," he growled at her, and left her standing there in the shock of it as he headed for the ridge.

Her emotions simmered after him—*frustration, fury, desire.* He tore himself away from it, forcing focus—forcing himself to deal with their circumstances. *Survival.*

Not just for their team, but for the Sentinels as a whole.

When she caught up to him at the crest, the gear bag once again slung over her neck and shoulder, she'd composed herself; he felt only her lingering impulse to launch herself at him, and couldn't tell if it was from the fury or the desire.

Or both.

But outwardly, she'd regained composure. She joined him, standing beside the crater of a recently upturned ponderosa to look over the changed landscape. "Everywhere they go," she said, mourning in her voice, "they destroy. The earth, its people...*us.*"

"Forakkes is rogue," he reminded her, though the words felt token. "Not technically acting on behalf of the Core."

She snorted. "Do you really think they didn't know they were losing control of him? They could have stopped this—they just want it both ways. If he fails, they'll take him out as proof of their goodwill—and if he succeeds, they'll disavow him and use his work."

"Then we'll make sure he fails." Even as he said it, Ruger felt the absurdity of the words—standing half-naked and exposed at the top of the ridge, his team buried behind him, his backup out of reach. Standing beside a bodyguard with an amulet loose in her system, the smooth browns of her complexion still carrying that high flush, the corners of her eyes and tension in her brow still carrying signs of pain.

Mariska looked down on the destruction below and around them and scowled. "We'll make damned sure he fails."

"Let's not make that any harder than it has to be," Ruger suggested—and when she didn't quite get it, he nodded at the gear bag. "A little luck and your cell will have a signal."

Not likely, and she knew it, too. But she rummaged in the gear bag to pull out her phone, flipping it open long enough to confirm that even at this local high point, she had no bars, and then turning it off to preserve the battery. Ruger started walking the high ground—cutting over to follow in Mariska's earlier track, and moving quickly enough so he wasn't hunting precise sign so much as he was assessing the lay of things, seeing what Mariska had already absorbed not so long before.

She waited, letting him get that feel for things without comment. When he returned, she said, "I think we're going to have to circle wide to pick up any sign of them. Things here are too much of a mess." She made a face, wrinkling her nose in a wry sort of dismay. "Earlier today, I couldn't figure out what they were up to—all that effort to leave a mess of tracks and lay down scent. And the *skunk!* But now I get it."

"They knew we'd come looking," Ruger said, looking out over the woods as if he could see straight to wherever Forakkes was hiding. "If any of us survived. They knew we could find them."

"They planned ahead," Mariska said—agreeing with him, her expression still full of dismay.

But Ruger quite suddenly felt no dismay at all, following through to the implications of Forakkes' precautions.

He grinned out at the woods, now recovering from the shock of the explosions. *Room for a bear to roam. To hunt.* A flock of pine siskins tumbled past, flashing yellow against the lower branches of the ponderosas and scolding the world with wheezy, nonstop twittering. Overhead, the gathering clouds had turned glowering, and offered the first mutter of thunder. "It was more than just planning ahead," he said. "It was fear. It means that they're here to find—that they're *close* enough to find."

Room for a bear to chase down his prey.

Mariska took another look beneath Ruger's shirt, wincing at strong, smooth muscle marred by the slashing, shallow wound. It wasn't any kind of a threat; his body's accelerated healing would likely leave it alone to heal at a natural pace. And barring the miraculous appearance of Ruger's field kit or a tube of miracle salve from the sky, he was right enough—there was little to be done.

She wondered if the amulet effects still dogging her would fade away, or if they were a mere harbinger of what might be to come. And she barely heard Ruger as he surveyed the landscape surrounding the facility and then pointed randomly along one ridge.

Or not so randomly.

"They may have tromped the hell out of this area," he said, "but they're still human. Wherever this second hideout is, they needed decent access to construct it. And it's not so far from here that they weren't willing to trudge over on foot for their little attack."

"You're thinking of the logging road," Mariska said.

"And wherever they came from, they took the easiest path to reach this place. They might not even have thought about it. They just did it.

"Let's see if we can't pick up a track along that ridge." He tipped his head, invitation in his eye.

Mariska grinned at him. "They should have left us alone," she said, forgetting about the aches and cuts and bruises. "We'd have been too busy deconstructing that facility to come looking for them."

"They should have left us alone," Ruger agreed.

The look in his eye had nothing to do with healing at all.

Chapter 15

An hour later, Mariska found herself still smiling—at the growl in Ruger's voice, the look in his eye…the set of his jaw as he sent that glare of a warning out to the woods.

Now he led the way across the ridge—diagonal slashes up and over, hunting sign on both sides of the crest. Slow going. And if they found nothing…

Even as she thought it, Ruger stopped, looking behind them, his expression pensive. Darkening clouds grumbled above; a gust of rising wind briefly lifted the open shirt from his back.

No, not pensive. *Primal.* A bear on the hunt, the unusually softened high altitude light sliding along cheek and jaw, leaving his eyes dark, his brows drawn and expressive. Mariska caught her breath, yearning and wistful at the same time—knowing that the simple physicality of what they'd first shared had become complex and uncertain and infinitely more important to her.

She cleared her throat, as if none of that mattered at all. "Maybe one of us should take the bear…try scenting."

He nodded, still looking out over the woods. "It's all yours."

She handed him the gear bag without hesitation, remembering the invigoration of the last time she'd taken the change—how it had pushed aside the amulet's effects. She reach for her bear, welcoming the energy that surged through her aching fatigue, welcoming the feel of the earth against her pads and her sturdy bear legs, ready to amble.

She wasn't expecting the little sting of nerve pain that shot from her spine down her legs, from between her shoulders down her front legs and all the way to her toes. Her back end quivered and gave out on her; her bear ass smacked down on the ground.

Ruger jerked as if he'd felt some echo of the sensations, turning on her with an intent he just couldn't seem to help. She curled her expressive bear lips and sent him a coughing bark of warning, stopping him short; he stepped back, opening his hands in capitulation.

::I'm all right,:: she told him in the still moment that followed.

"You're not," he said, too sure to be guessing.

::Fine, I'm not. But it's passing.::

"It was the change," he said, still eyeing her—but respecting his limits, if not the ones she'd set.

::Don't know that.::

"We'll find out," he said, tipping his head at her—an oblique reference to the fact that she'd need to change back sooner rather than later. Then he turned away—not in the least shaken or alarmed at the ferocity or teeth she'd shown him. Not even bothering to call that bluff. She grunted dissatisfaction and got to her feet.

"Try downhill," Ruger said, looking down a slope slippery with pine needles and crusted with protruding rock. The wind flapped at his shirt and died again. "If there's scent to be found, it'll have drifted down. All we need right now is that confirmation; we don't need to track footsteps."

True enough. The first step was to know they'd come the right direction; after that, they had only to maintain a decent orientation to the scent.

"By the way," Ruger added, returning his attention to the ridge, "if you smell water…"

She huffed a quiet response, knowing their need as well as he—dehydration was just as much a threat as the Core in this high desert clime.

With her legs steady beneath her, she headed down the slope—a foothills slope in nature, the same as those cradling the installation behind them. Rugged and challenging, the descent nonetheless put her only a hundred feet below him. She softened her focus, no longer thinking about her footing—letting it take care of itself while her attention went to her sense of smell.

The air filled her sinuses with the dry scents of pine and disturbed dirt and Ruger and… She flared her nostrils, stopping her own progress to cast her head back and forth at the scent. ::Hold your ground a moment,:: she told him. ::Let me go ahead.::

Not that she couldn't readily distinguish Ruger's scent from any other she might encounter. But as long as it was there, it filled her mind so completely—*hard body beneath her touch, deep rumbling groan in her ear, big hands smoothing her hair, loving her curves, tightening on her hips as he lost himself to her*—she couldn't think of anything else.

Besides, he disturbed the ground. She needed to move away from that influence on the scent pool—then if she still scented fresh disturbance, that would mean something, too.

He responded with an inner vocalization that sounded more bear than human, and she had to stop and gather her thoughts in the wake of the wave of pleasure it gave her to have that common language—to know he'd used it without second thought.

Once she started to move again, she soon found what they needed. He'd been right from the start—the Core minions had come this way, heading toward a second location that had, decades earlier and just like the first, been constructed off the old logging access road. Mariska slanted upward, silent in her concentration—knowing Ruger would understand this, too, that she'd found enough to work toward a track.

In fact, he came down off the ridge, still hanging behind her in a slow and methodical search for sign. The moments passed in companionable silence—the faint shuffle of paw against ground, the trickle of dislodged rock…the forest creatures going about their own business, less disturbed by bear than they were by man.

It didn't seem like long before Mariska caught the hot, direct scent—one of those she'd run into that morning, a man with the clinging taste of Core corruption. The discovery came far too soon, in fact—while she was still happily immersed in being herself, Ruger a silent teammate. Reluctantly, she withdrew from that tight focus and reoriented to the rest of the world, discovering herself high on the slope with Ruger behind and just above as he crouched to examine the ground. Thunder rumbled overhead, and she discovered the clouds towering dramatically overhead, a roiling mass of blue-black shapes with startling white tumbles of contrast.

::Big one coming,:: she said to Ruger.

His satisfaction at finding the trail turned grim. "We need to do this thing before it hits—find Forakkes and get out from under this damn cone of silence. Ian and Sandy need help."

::I'm a bear,:: she said, giving him a toothy mental smile. ::I won't even feel the rain.::

But when the skies opened up, she was quick to change her mind. The rumbling thunder broke into a sharp, simultaneous flash of light and sound; she ducked her head and hunched her shoulders, and still wasn't prepared for the sting of heavy rain on her face. ::But I'm a *smart* bear!:: she cried, loud enough in her head to overcome the follow-up thunder.

So was Ruger—and he was already stripping off his wet shirt and jamming it into the bag. He tossed the bag out ahead of them and leaped into the bear, the energies splashing out around him in a flickering echo of the lightning.

Even as bear he looked disgruntled, with water dripping off his brow and beading on his muzzle. ::We can't track in *this*,:: he sent at her, dropping off a modest outcrop to slip carelessly over stone and needles. ::Head for cover!:: Mariska followed, heading for the hint of leeward overhang ahead—between that and the slant of the vicious rain, they would escape the worst of it.

But only if they poured on the speed. Typical big storm, black clouds spewing first rain and then hail as it opened up from full bore to something beyond. Ruger swore in mind-voice just as a pea gravel of hard and stinging force bounced off Mariska's nose, and hit full speed. Mariska broke into a lumbering run behind him, scrambling sideways on the steepening slope—and slamming into the marginal shelter close enough on Ruger's heels to call it a collision.

With no small amount of huffing and grunting, they arranged themselves into an efficient huddle, black bear and great brown. Mariska blew a final drop of water from the tip of her nose and said, ::Well, any rain is a *good* rain, right?::

Ruger coughed bear laughter, dark as it was. Yes, their friends were fighting to survive, half-buried; yes, Forakkes had developed a devastating weapon and had to be stopped; and yes, he'd blocked them from all contact with their people, leaving them hurt and sick and trying to track him down under impossible circumstances. But still, Ruger added the inevitable response: ::It's the desert. Any rain is good rain.::

They curled together with the hail rattling through the trees, a vicious squall that increased to a frenzy and then slowly eased back to a pounding rain. The wind shifted, blowing back spatter and spray into their shelter.

::I should take the human,:: Mariska said, only half-kidding. ::There'd be room enough if I hid behind you—:: But unexpected, startling fear clutched at her, rising from deep within her own mind.

Ruger was quick enough to pick up on the change; he nudged her with a wordless inquiry.

She couldn't respond—not right away. Not through the fear, a primal thing so deep that she wasn't even sure of its origin. Not until she went back to her own half-joking comment.

I should take the human.

::Ruger,:: she said, hardly daring to put words—even private words—to the thought. ::I don't know if I can take the change. It doesn't feel…*right*.::

::Do it,:: he said instantly. ::Do it *now*.::

::But the amulet—::

::Must still be working at you. *Do it!*::

She hesitated, thinking of their confined quarters and mixing energies—but Ruger swung his massive head to her shoulder and closed his jaws down with the slightest shake, just enough pressure to rattle her into action.

She reached for the human, a spurt of panicked response. The energies rose around and within her, pushing at her like an unfulfilled yawn—and just as quickly faltered. Panic sliced through her chest.

The amulet. He'd been right; her previous discomfort had come from the change going wrong and now she couldn't manage it at all. She was bear and she was stuck and she was going to lose herself—

::*Reach* for it,:: Ruger told her, pushing at her. ::Hang on to it!:: He flooded her with images and impressions— his first glimpse of her at the Celtic fair, his instant interest. Her expression as she hesitated in the town house doorway—her eyes gone dark, her lips slightly parted— her invitation clear. The heat of his response, the speed with which he roused—the moment he'd curled his fingers around her hips and the shock of pleasure as they came together.

::*Mari,*:: he said, sending her remembered hurt and fury, a hint of her expression gone stubborn, a perfect memory of the set of her shoulders…the perfect memory of her face, flushed with pleasure and asleep against his arm, bottom gloriously round against his thighs. ::Mari Bear, *reach* for it!::

Reach for it. It was the human who'd embraced Ruger, who gloried in his strength and the chance to be her uninhibited self. The human who'd thrown herself open to the glory of being just who she was, with just the man she wanted.

The human who'd fallen so very hard for that man and all his strengths that she'd scared herself into doing one challenging thing after another just to see how he'd react. *Reach for it,* the energies rising hard and fast, tangling with emotion and flaring brightly against the rock, whirling and changing and splashing against Ruger, her very human form falling against him just as hard.

"Mariska," he said, as changed as she. His arms closed around her shoulders, pulling her in close to his bare chest, stroking down her spine.

Naturally she burst into tears. Embarrassing tears, full of weakness and defeat.

He only held her closer. "There," he said, as if the rain didn't surround them, glancing off rock and scattering drops into a hard and swirling mist. *"Mariska."*

After a few moments of stupid crying, she pulled herself together for a deep if tremulous breath and held her hand out into the spray, gathering enough water to swipe over her burning face. "Now I guess you've seen it all."

He grunted, deep in his chest; she felt more than heard it, and felt the shrug in it. "You train hard, you run hard... you cry hard." He still held her close, pushing back hair that had become disarrayed to clear her cheeks for a nuzzle of a kiss. "You love hard, too."

She managed a wry expression. "You noticed."

"Noticed," he said, and kissed her again, the distinct gentleness of a big man, "would be an understatement."

"About that." She couldn't bring herself to pull away and look at him—not to meet his gaze and not to lose his touch. "I didn't mean to be so pushy about everything. I didn't mean to—"

"Yes, you did," he said, and this time the sound in his chest was a hint of laughter. "That's the whole point. You are fearsomely, awesomely *you.*"

She shivered, tucking herself in just a little smaller. "You say that like it's a *good* thing."

"It gets to my temper," he admitted. "But I'm beginning to think I like that."

She thought on it a minute, thunder filling the silence around them. "It makes you angry."

"It makes me *alive*," he corrected her. She shivered again; this time he joined her.

"Your back," she said, realizing it. "You don't even have a shirt. I think we lost the bag—"

"It's not far. Hold on." And to her astonishment, he left her there, bolting out into the weather. She squinted out into the driving rain, hugging herself tightly, the storm-cold air a slap against her wet skin. In moments Ruger was back, bag in hand—but he didn't dive back into the shelter. He worked with quick, deliberate movements, yanking things from the bag, doing something beside the outcrop—fumbling a little in the wet and cold until he quite suddenly joined her again, soaked and shivering, and still without the shirt.

"What?" she asked.

"Water," he told her. "There's a small pool in the rock—I tore up the shirt to wick water into the bottle."

"That shirt was for *you*," she told him with some asperity. "You should take the bear before you get any more chilled. Besides, I have every intention of sheltering with you if you do."

"I can't be the bear right now."

The ferocity of the storm eased up; rain pattered more gently around them, no longer spraying them with water. Mariska looked askance at him, perfectly aware that she wasn't going to like whatever he had to say.

A smile settled at the corner of his mouth in response—an acknowledgment. "I do my best healing work as the human."

She snorted. "You're not doing any healing work at

all, as I recall. Or have you forgotten what happens when you so much as try?"

He grumbled at her, a sound distinct from the rain that seemed to surround her in their enclosed space. In the wake of it, he rubbed thumb and forefinger over his eyes—and when he looked out at her again, his expression was more weary than she'd seen. "I'd be a fool to have forgotten. But I'm no less stubborn than you. And I need you in this—finding Forakkes, putting an end to his plans or at least to his cone of silence. I can't do it alone."

"There's no point—" But she sputtered to a stop when he put a finger over her lower lip.

"Mari," he said, "I don't have to be a healer to see that you're getting worse. All I have to do is care."

Instantly, tears prickled her eyes. "That's not fair," she said. "Don't you dare make me cry again!"

He lifted his shoulders in a hint of a shrug.

She withdrew from him, pressing herself back against the rock. "All right, then. Yes. Obviously. This amulet thing isn't going away. I don't know if I can take the bear again, and I'd be stupid to try unless I knew for sure I could get back to the human, too. After what just happened and all."

He made a generalized noise of agreement.

"But there's no point in risking you, too! You're already hurt—"

"And I can work on that, too, if you help me."

She gave him a suspicious glance. "What do you mean, *if I help you?*"

"I mean that you're right," he told her. "Every time I reach for a healing, I run into a roadblock that hits back."

"If that's what you call bleeding from your damned ears and taking a dive," she muttered.

"It hits back," he said distinctly, *"hard."*

She said nothing.

For the first time, he looked somewhat abashed. "The problem is, I don't see it coming."

She couldn't help her incredulous reaction. "Ton of bricks, meet Ruger? You don't see that coming?"

He could have growled back at her; he merely looked bemused. "Healing doesn't leave room for multitasking."

Mariska shivered. The sun slipped out through a big splash of blue sky and sparked over the wet ridge, and she longed to go lie in its warmth and bask the afternoon away, letting it bake out the chill in her bones that had nothing to do with the weather and everything to do with the amulet damage…with the circumstances. "What do you want to do?"

"I *want*," he said, "to hold you until this whole mess passes, because I'm a selfish bastard. But since that doesn't seem likely to help our friends or to stop Forakkes from wreaking havoc, I'd appreciate it if you would stand watch for me."

"Stand watch," she repeated, by way of question.

"Give me a nudge if things seem to be getting out of control." He lifted a single brow at her. "A *nudge,* I said."

"But…how does that accomplish anything? You start healing…I stop you. Neither of us is any better off—and maybe we're worse."

"Maybe," he agreed. "But maybe I can learn where the line is. Maybe if I do, I can keep from crossing it—and maybe I can do a little bit of good from there. Enough to keep us going."

"Huh." Mariska shoved herself past the emotion—past the conflicting impulses to protect Ruger from himself and the urge to let him take over. To let him take her pain away. She tried to think logically about it all instead.

Because he was right—she was a mess, and getting worse. He was right that their friends needed help.

And he was right that neither of them could do this alone.

Chapter 16

Ruger saw it happen—the understanding in Mariska's expression, and the change from resistant conflict to...

Resignation.

Maybe even a little bit of hope.

"Okay," she said. "We can do this."

He couldn't help but laugh out loud. She huddled shivering before him, skin pebbled and toasty complexion paled in a way that only highlighted the unnatural flush high along the strong bones of her face. He felt every inch of the slice along his back, every cut and scrape of their escape.

But together, they possessed such an accumulation of stubborn determination, it was hard to imagine anything but success.

"Just *nudge,*" he reminded her, and settled to sit cross-legged with his back to the rock and the slope spreading down before him. Overhead, the next round of rapidly shifting clouds rumbled a distinct warning; the rain wasn't done with them.

"Go slow," she warned him. "So I have the chance."

In answer, he held out his hand. She took it, her fingers wrapping without hesitation around his. "Is it easier this way?"

"A little," he told her. "Mostly I just want to hold your hand."

She might have smacked him then; he saw it in the press of her lips, the spark of her eye. But in the end she squeezed his fingers—and maybe there was even a hint of a smile.

Ruger closed his eyes, shutting out the world. He took a moment of indulgence to feel the nuances of her hand in his—the faint pressure of strong, short nails against his skin, the calluses on the knuckles and edge of her palm, the rough skin of a recent scrape. Her fingers twitched with passing restlessness, and that made him smile, too.

From there he slid not to healing, but to awareness. He started with the sharp pull on his back—feeling it as a healer would, and practicing the balance of perceiving without acting.

Harder than he'd thought, that balance.

Harder yet when he sought out Mariska—*deep aches, gripping chill, insistent wrongness*—and especially at the ice pick of a headache clamped down in her head.

Generalized healing. That's what he needed. Nothing fancy; nothing too targeted. Nothing that would eliminate the amulet working from her system, and just enough to spill over to his back.

Just enough to help.

He groped for the energies, struggling for balance—struggling to push his way through the thick wall of dead energy—but without shoving. Without falling into lifelong habits of *reaching*.

It used to come with such ease, this energy did. It used to flow like silk, not mud. It used to wash around the wounded like a cool balm. Now he grappled with sticky energy sludge, making little headway until in his impatience he *yanked*—

He startled wildly at the stinging slap against his face, his head hitting the rock behind him. "Son of a *bitch!*"

Mariska knelt before him, facing uphill with her knees nearly touching his, annoyance at war with grim concern. "You should have saved some of that shirt for your face."

"Nudge!" he told her, at a loss for words.

She rose up on her knees, pulling the hem of her shirt high and wiping it beneath his nose; when she sat back she displayed the stain to him. "I did *nudge,*" she told him. "I nudged the hell out of you, and it didn't help. What did you *do?*"

He swore, and couldn't keep the sheepish note from his voice.

"You got impatient," she said, and rolled her eyes. And then she rolled a knuckle against his chest. "That's a *nudge,*" she said—and then added, "Don't you growl at me."

Only then did he feel the residual vibration of that grumble in his chest. But by then she was stroking the spot she'd just knuckled, and his thoughts tangled on the sensation. He reached for her waist and tugged her closer, uncrossing his legs to make way for her.

"It was worth a try," she said. She didn't tug easily— not with her knees pressing into the ground—but she inched forward between his thighs and hardly seemed to notice it. "We'll just have to—"

"We're not done yet." *Not by a long shot.* Her waist curved beneath his hands, tidy and defined; he smoothed his hands up her torso until his thumbs rested just under her breasts. As if they belonged there—as if he had the right to touch her so casually.

Then again, the bear knew what he wanted. And so did he.

"What do you mean, not done yet?" She leaned closer, and the flush on her cheeks, the brightness of her eyes—they no longer came of fever.

He grinned. "How do you feel?"

"Just because you have your hands where you have your hands doesn't mean I'm going to forget—" But she stopped short, her mouth still open. She looked down on herself—at his hands, at her own; she put the inside of her wrist to her forehead. "Better!" she said in surprise. "Definitely better. But you didn't— *How*—?"

"Give me some credit," he said, sounding aggrieved even to his own ears. "Or did you think I was the most active field healer in brevis just because I can take care of myself?"

She pushed a hand off his shoulder in a quick shove, pulling back without managing to dislodge his grip in the least. "That's not what I meant and you know it." Her eyes narrowed. "You'd *better* know it." She subsided when he made a noncommittal noise. "It just wasn't long enough."

"It wasn't." He could still feel it in her—the wrongness, the lurking malaise. "I'm working with sludge. But now I know the sludge does something…and so do you."

"Sludge," she said. "You put *sludge* into me."

He rose to it, would have tightened his grip on her—but saw the tiny little smile at the corners of her mouth, the way her lips pressed together to suppress it.

"You," he growled.

She widened her eyes, clear enough. *Want to make something of it?*

"Maybe it wasn't such a good idea to sort you out."

"Oh, I think it was a very good idea. Imagine how annoyed Forakkes will be."

He couldn't help it; he laughed. "One more time, then."

"Don't get impatient," she warned him.

In answer, he closed his eyes. He skimmed quickly past the familiar feel of their needs, hesitated to ground himself in caution, and reached for the sludge.

It was all wrong, that energy—all wrong that he should labor so hard for such a basic thing. He wobbled to find the balance—enough effort to move the sludge, not so much that he paid the price.

He felt her nudge this time—knuckles pushing into his shoulder; he steadied himself. It was a crude thing, this healing—a barely directed flow of energy applied with a trowel instead of precision and finesse.

But he felt the faint burn of his back, and knew his body had claimed the sludge for its own purposes. He felt Mariska stiffen in his grip, holding her breath on a gasp, and knew that this time, she felt it, too.

Somehow, he kept that balance.

But then she poked him—harder this time—and he thought he'd likely used up his luck. It was a relief to let go of the sludge, watching it drain away from his grasp; it was a relief to step back from the stringent self-control that kept him from going after more. Mariska relaxed in his hands, inching closer. Her touch brushed over his shoulders, stroked down his arms—a soothing thing, as if she understood he needed time to make the transition back out.

Or else simply took advantage of the opportunity.

All right, then. It went both ways, this touching thing. He followed impulse—following the warmth of her in his healer's awareness, releasing his grasp of body and bone and wholeness to reach for something more personal. A place he'd never gone before, simply because his grasp of body and bone and wholeness had always come foremost.

The heat of what he found stirred through his limbs, turning liquid—turning her touch into something that sent a shiver right down his spine. He stroked her with it, in tune to the thunder overhead.

Her hands tightened on his shoulders; her words sounded strangled. "I didn't know you could do that."

He hadn't known, either. He would have told her so, but he ended up murmuring her name instead, turning it into an endearment—a satisfied hum, and yet full of awareness that he hadn't meant to go to this place and that he wasn't sure he could stop now that he'd started. She moved closer yet, her knees nudging inside his thighs. Her breasts brushed his chest through a shirt still wet, her breath brushed his neck and her lips brushed his ear. "We don't have time for this."

"We don't," he agreed, somehow managing those words in spite of his complete and total focus on simply being there with her. The tease of bear in her scent, her body both hard-toned and curvy beneath his hands; the very solidity of her, tangled with her lurking exuberance, the promise of unfettered enthusiasm. His breath came sharp on a surge of response, his balls tightening in anticipation. He grasped for words. "We don't…but we don't have much choice."

Her hands slipped over his chest, fingers scraping through crisp hair to wring a groan from him. But she shook her head. "Ian…Sandy…Katie's vision… We *have* to—" She shook her head again, pressing it against his in regret.

Just maybe she hadn't noticed that the sky had darkened again, the clouds tumbling to darkness overhead—but when thunder slammed together all around them, they both jumped. Newly roused energies spiraled through their little shelter, rising in a slash of desire and encircling them both.

"Not. Fair." She was still that close to his ear; she clamped her teeth on his earlobe.

His laugh was more of a gasp. "Not mine," he told her, pulling her closer with no mercy at all. She settled in on him, her knees hitting the stone behind them, her ankles hooked back over the top of his open thighs—flexible, at that, and spread so completely open to him. Another peal of thunder rolled through as he reflexively thrust against her, a groan behind his words. "Not that time."

"We should…" She lost track of those words, her hands stroking his sides, skimming up to his chest and down between them again to hover at his jeans. "Our friends. Forakkes. We should—"

"We *can't*." He lifted his hips to offer the wood buttons on the jeans, digging his heels into the thin soil of the slope below them. "Not until this storm passes. Or haven't you had enough fieldwork to dodge a high desert monsoon before?"

She paused with her hands on the top button and her teeth resting on his throat. "Are you messing with my temper? *Now?*"

"Maybe," he told her, as the rain started again, soaking into the legs of his jeans. He pushed her away, just enough to give her a satisfying and possessive once-over, not the least bit gentle inside. Wet strands of hair escaped her braid to wisp around her face; high color washed over her cheeks and brightened her eyes. The wet shirt clung to her skin, outlining every detail of the form beneath.

"Maybe," he said, and traced the line of her bra where it sloped close to the nipple, "I think I like your temper."

She swore and yanked at his jeans, then gave up and yanked at her shirt.

"Patience," he said, as if he wasn't aching to do the same, "I've been told it's a virtue. And we need what clothes we have left." But his head dropped back as the energies he'd loosed wove between them, tightening around them; he grabbed her hips to push against her, the groan deep in his throat.

She swore again; her voice rose in pitch. "You did that on purpose!"

Ruger spoke through his teeth. "Not while I'm still wearing these pants, I didn't."

Her fingers fumbled with the buttons to her shirt; he joined her, working from the bottom up so they met in the middle. She closed her hand over his, then, stilling him a moment; her dark eyes were full of conflict—passion and regret and the looming loss of control. "We really can't—? We're stuck here?"

"We really can't," he said, and pushed back an errant strand of hair to cup the side of her face, holding her firmly. "We're stuck here. Take the moment, Mariska."

She showed him her teeth, the wild flaring high in her eyes, her legs tightening around his thighs. "I'll *take,*" she said, as much warning as promise. She yanked the shirt off and tossed it aside.

He reached around for her bra fastener—only to stare at the sprinkling of pale lavender blooms over the swell of otherwise sporty material. "Flowers."

"What of it?" she said, stilling her hands to glare at him.

"Like 'em," he told her. He left the clasp alone to cup her breasts through the material, running his thumbs firmly over both nipples. *Perfect.* Her glare dissolved to grasping neediness, and he might have been smug about it had not the awakened energies surged up to include him.

Mariska emitted a sound of despair and jerked away,

hands at her pants even as she stood. The rain splatted against her back; she had to grab at the rock to maintain her balance on the slope, and by then Ruger had untied her shoes, pulling them off one by one as she lifted each leg to tug away the pants.

"See?" he said. "We *can* work at as a team."

"Shut up and do something about those pants!" She threw herself back on him just as she'd been, leaving just enough room between them to reach his jeans. But he was erect against them, painfully so; he fumbled the wooden buttons as if he'd never handled them before.

She shoved him back against the gritty angle of rock, leaving the whole of him sprawled out before her, and tackled the pants—more gently than he might have supposed, and with a whole lot more—

A whole lot more—

Touching. Stroking.

He growled, just to let her know he knew what she was doing, and she laughed. The growl turned to a groan as he tipped his head back against rock and pushed helplessly against her hands.

Wicked, wicked hands.

She played with him long after she tugged his jeans aside, touching him everywhere—adding a nip and kiss, small hands clever and bold. His toes curled; his fingers clutched at rock and dirt. More than once he tried to drag her up across his body—to get his hands on her. More than once she interrupted him. It took nothing more than warm breath and just the right touch—and it didn't help when she reminded him, "I owe you." Her voice hummed with heat and satisfaction, the energies he'd roused taking a life of their own to wrap around them both.

"You're just trying to make me—" *Cry,* he would have said. *Beg mercy. Just plain beg.*

But he didn't have the breath for it, his body going tight, tighter—

"Mari," he managed, teeth clenched and control a thing of the past. *"Mari—"*

"Good," she told him. "Because oh, I *want* you."

Before he knew it, she had him. She came down over him with a sharp cry of delight; he barely heard it over his own ragged gasp. Pleasure pulsed between them and he grasped for those energies, trying for control; they broke apart into wisps and re-formed, enfolding Mariska—enfolding Ruger. This time they soaked in—through skin, sinking into muscle and nerve and firing heated tension along the way.

Mariska breathed out a deep groan, leaning back to prop her hands on his thighs. It changed the angle between them—they felt it at the same time, a single, gasping cry from both throats. Ruger lost control of that energy—he lost control of everything. His heels dug into the slope; the rain pounded against his legs and he reared up to pound himself into Mariska. He grabbed her hips and slammed her down hard, feeling her strength, her easy ability to absorb him—to *take* him.

Oh, he lost control, all right. And so did she, and then the energies rose wild between them, and Mariska dug her fingers into his thighs and keened. Hot pleasure rose to take them both, and together they cried out helplessly into the thunder.

Chapter 17

Rain. On her face.

Rain on her face.

Rain.

Mariska opened her eyes only an instant before reflex tripped them shut again. Absurd to be so unwilling to move, when the big drops splatted heavily against her face and torso. Absurd to be resting against Ruger's thighs, folded back on her own legs, and downhill, at that.

Absurd to be so content with it, at the wondrous feeling of encompassing his hips—of being filled so completely, leftover pleasure pulsing between them with a delightful warmth.

He shifted beneath her, and that was delightful, too—just the play of muscle and sinew and strength, his whole body involved as he sucked in air. She could still feel the pressure of his hands—at her waist, and her hips, shifting as necessary but no holds barred.

No holds barred.

And she'd given it right back to him. Grasping at him, pounding over him...she'd shoved him, she'd grabbed him, she'd...

She'd been herself.

"I didn't know you could do that," she said, a non-sequitur piece of conversation that he could have taken wrong in so many ways, but didn't. As if she would be talking about anything else but that wild surge of pleasure that had tangled around and through them, wringing them both into completion.

Still, he responded only after he took in more air, his hands curling comfortably over her thighs and his legs strong beneath her—propping her just enough so she didn't slide right off. "Don't think I did," he told her. "I started it, maybe. Then…I think *we* did." And then, with hardly any hesitation at all, "Come in out of the rain, Mariska Bear."

A particularly dire rumble sounded above her; she sighed. "I wanted to wallow in this for a while longer." She levered herself up, settling firmly over him again and unable to hold back the smile at the stunned look on his face. "That was the most unique inclined sit-up *I've* ever done," she said. "I take it you approve?"

He made a strangled sound of agreement, pulsing inside her. She laughed out loud, and bent forward to kiss him lightly beside the mouth, brushing her cheek against his. His face was like the rest of him—strong-boned features with the perfect balance between size and refinement.

Perfect for me.

She sighed, settling herself against him, squirming a little to find just the right spot where skin, damp with sweat and rain, created friction. "I could almost forget that there's an amulet working running wild inside me, or that Forakkes is planning to do worse to the rest of us… or that we lost Jeckle, and Ian and Sandy and Heckle are waiting for help. I could almost not feel guilty."

He stroked a hand down her back, all the way down to cup and hold her bare bottom, his fingers so intimately placed that he touched both of them where they joined. "Nothing's changed. We can't do anything in this rain."

"We could try," she said, muffling her words against his shoulder and moving ever so slightly in response to the pressure of his fingers.

"We could," he agreed. "And we could stumble around messing up the track, being cold and exhausted and in no shape to do anything when we actually find Forakkes. Because we *will* find Forakkes, and we *will* stop him."

She sighed in a hum that vibrated down his neck. "Because we're just that stubborn."

"Because we're a team," he told her, shifting his hands and rocking ever so slightly beneath her. But then he admitted, "And because we're stubborn."

"We should try the phone once this passes." She scraped her teeth over his shoulder. "*If* it passes."

"Stupid of us to have taken the weather for granted just because we've been working underground. This system must have been building for days—it could easily cycle through the evening." So matter-of-fact, his words, while his breath stuttered slightly along the way.

Mariska made a noise of surprise at the new surge of warmth between them. "You?"

"Us," he told her, and let air out through his teeth. "God, Mari, I never want to let go of you. I never want to *not* hold you this way. You…you're…"

Perfect.

She wasn't sure if he said it out loud, or if she imagined it. She only knew that here, in the middle of the rain-pounded forest, with their enemy ahead and their friends behind them, she rocked gently over him and reveled in the slide of flesh on flesh and the sensation of his quiet touch where they came together, the slowly building wonder of it and the understanding that they did this to one another, they did it *for* one another…

And it was perfect.

"You still make me furious," Mariska told him, as if she wasn't snuggled up in the aftermath of the latest rumbling storm, looking out into the fading daylight.

Ruger pulled her closer, running a hand from her shoulder to the dip of her waist to her hip, where he let it rest on smooth, warm skin. "Want to fight?" he inquired mildly, knowing neither of them had the energy or the mood for it.

Rain or no rain, the itch to pick up Forakkes' trail worried at them both. The impulse to return to the collapsed installation pricked at him just the same. But they still couldn't track under these conditions, and it was much better to rest until morning and start anew than to battle fatigue and the weather—only to end up in enemy territory frayed to exhaustion.

He'd tried to reach Harrison; he'd tried to reach Ian and Sandy. He'd called for Annorah…and he hadn't even bothered with the *adveho,* the brevis-wide cry for help that would mobilize every Sentinel within hearing.

There wasn't any point. Not with the dull, dead working that covered this area, trapping his efforts within.

Mariska shivered and tucked her head against his shoulder. They'd withdrawn up into the scant shelter, no longer sprawling in spent passion, but curling up into the angles of rock and ground to avoid the worst of the rain. "No fighting just at the moment," she said. "But don't get complacent."

"No chance."

She spoke with a sudden vehemence that startled him. "I just wish—"

Hindsight wasn't a friend to either of them on this day. "Don't," he told her. "It's not our nature to make things easy. And we don't know that anything would have turned out differently." He tipped his head back against rock and breathed in the scent of her—a woman well-loved, the hint of bear beneath. "Besides, you and I had an understanding to reach. That can't be rushed—and it damned well makes *this* mean more."

"Hmmph," she said. "Maybe I was going to say, 'I wish my clothes were dry enough to put on.'"

He snorted. "No doubt."

He'd never quite removed his jeans; he wore them now, if only haphazardly buttoned. Mariska's clothes, wet and tossed aside, had picked up enough grit so she'd declined to put them on until she could shake them out first. But they'd drained the water bottle dry and set it out to refill, and they'd split an energy bar, and as the third cloudburst cycled through, Ruger had practiced another healing—finishing the work on his own minor cut, giving Mariska a breather from the amulet working.

He'd also cleaned up after another nosebleed, still struggling to find and keep his balance in the sludge—and still unable to do it without Mariska's help.

"At this rate," he said, starting right in the middle of that conversation, "instead of being the only brevis healer who can take care of himself in the field, I'll end up just another bear riding herd on the one who can do the healing."

Mariska growled and bit his shoulder, following his conversational leap with no problem at all. "There's no such thing as *just another bear,* and even if there was, you wouldn't be one." She breathed on the spot she'd bitten…and then bit it again, more lightly this time. "Besides, maybe it's about time you had someone watching your back. Maybe you can't always do both."

Ah, hell. That hit hard, even as he knew she hadn't meant it to. He sat up away from her, earning a startled glance as he grabbed up the damp gear bag and rummaged through it for her phone, movements brusque and purposeful.

"Hey," she said, in the voice that meant she wasn't going to back off just because he'd reacted to her words. "Maybe you *can't*."

"I *obviously* can't," he said, coming up with the phone. "I'm going to try the ridge while we've got a break in the storms."

"Ruger—"

But he'd left the overhang for the cool air of the mountains after a storm, his departure nothing more than flight—even if he didn't quite know why.

He took the phone to the ridge, tracing their steps back a quarter mile to hunt connectivity. "Can you hear me now?" he muttered, holding the phone up and finding, again, that it had given up completely. *Zero bars.* He turned it off again, thought ruefully of the buried sat phone, and headed back down the slope.

Mariska greeted him with pine needles all over her feet. She'd clearly been out and back, and now sat with her arms wrapped around her updrawn knees—goose bumps over the pale brown of her skin, her hair pulled from its French braid to spread thickly over her shoulders, her body chilling.

Ruger dropped the phone back into the bag as she said, "Ruger—"

He interrupted her with a wordless sound—a neutral thing of the bear. Before she could say otherwise, he sat beside her and drew her back into his arms—saying nothing, still unable to explain, and to some extent simply not wanting to try. He guided them down to spoon on the slope.

"But," she said, and then, *"Oh!"*—for he reached for the bear, surrounding them in a whirl of fierce blue-white intent. The energies engulfed him, swirling around and through her in a pleasant, intimate tickle.

When they faded, she lay snug within the embrace of the bear, and he warmed her with his fur and his body heat and his heart.

Jet curled up under the cabin porch, just as pleased to be tucked up under her wolf's tail as she would to be inside the cabin beneath a quilt. The latest storm cell raged around her, misting her with droplets; they glistened over her coat, bringing her the scent of fresh, damp earth.

The cabin remained dark above her. Empty.

And while Jet didn't mind being alone, she cared very much that her friends weren't where they were supposed to be. That they'd gone off into Core territory that morning and not come back.

And that no one had reached out to her, calling on the phone they'd left behind on the porch. Unlike the others, she couldn't hear Annorah; she couldn't send an *adveho* and she couldn't reach out to her friends.

Maybe they were simply later than usual. Maybe the storm had delayed them—or they were waiting it out, underground where they couldn't use any of the phones. Maybe they'd be back after the rain passed.

Maybe.

She'd give them a little more time, and then she'd go hunting, too.

* * *

Curiosity lured Ciobaka from his corner.

He hadn't forgotten and he hadn't forgiven. He watched Ehwoord with a hard, direct eye—the one that spoke so clearly and yet so few of the humans seemed to understand.

Not that they paid any attention. Too much activity, too many loud-pitched voices and sharp responses. A new scent permeated their cave-like human den, a thing of burnt and acrid stringency that had followed Ehwoord's people home.

He'd thought it a bad thing at first, but the people were not punished, and Ehwoord, for all he tried to maintain his cold demeanor, moved with excitement. He had even put aside his morning pastry and coffee to take a report— they still sat at the corner of his large worktable.

Ciobaka thought he might eat that pastry if Ehwoord had rejected it. He sat and flexed the stubby thumbs that had replaced his dewclaws, yearning to try them on a hunt. What rabbit would have a chance? Could he pounce and pin and bite and *hold?* "Fud," he said softly.

"You should have stayed to finish them off," Ehwoord said to the one called Yovan. Tarras had not been in charge of this activity, although he'd expected it; he still held his face and his shoulders with a stiffness that spoke of resentment.

The machine that powered the lights in this place stuttered; no one had told Ciobaka of the rain overhead, but he didn't need the machine or the dim light from the overhead tubes to know of it; he ached to be out in that sweet scent, scrubbing his shoulders into the dirt and laughing up into the sky.

Yovan said what he'd already said more times than Ciobaka had toes. "Nothing could have survived what

we did to that place. Even the entrance tunnel caved in."
And then he added, also again, "We wanted to be where
we could be of the most assistance to you."

The human equivalent of licking the lips of a superior
in the pack. Obsequious, just a little beseeching—except
the humans tried to pretend it wasn't. Not as honest with
their words as any dog would be with his body.

Ehwoord glanced overhead at the dim tube light,
smoothing a palm over his hair. It was less gray this
day, his lips were a bit less thin and his face a bit less
lined—yet his expressions and emotions were just a little
bit more jagged. "It's too late to go back out," he said.
"But we won't take them for granted. Tomorrow I want
to run the first field tests on the new working—if there
are survivors, we'll use them. And I don't want any annoying interruptions in the meantime."

Tarras, out of favor as he was, dared to speak up. "If
there are survivors, they can't get out. Not with the tunnel closed off. And they can't call out—not with anything they've got."

"I made sure of that," Ehwoord said, offering his disdain to the man—and then tipping his head to say with
far too much meaning, "I know how to handle the things
that annoy me."

Tarras took a step back—a step closer to Ciobaka's
cage. Ciobaka waited for Ehwoord to turn back to his
work—stroking the amulets with a touch more suited
to flesh and blood. He stuck his leg between the bars,
stretching…snagging Tarras' shirt with his hand-paw.
"Owwwt," he said softly. "We. Owwt."

Tarras turned on him, but Tarras' surprise—his *fear*—
didn't quite shape his face to a scowl before Ciobaka
saw it. "I'll feed you when it's time for it," he snapped,
as if Ciobaka had said something else altogether. More

of human dishonesty with words, saying one thing when he meant another. "Go chew a bone!"

But Ciobaka knew the reactive nature of a false dominant when he saw it. And he knew from Tarras' face that they both needed to find a way out of this place before Ehwoord became annoyed again.

Chapter 18

Mariska woke to a world still damp, the scents of the forest rising thickly around them as the sun warmed tree and rock. She discovered herself stiff and sore from the attack on the underground facility, wonderfully sated from the previous evening, and still warm from a bear's embrace.

She and Ruger went their separate ways into the woods, and Mariska returned to shake her clothes free of grit and ants, donning them in the distinct chill of the morning. "Do you suppose Maks is wondering about us?"

::Not likely.:: Ruger's response came tinted with the bear, claws scraping wood somewhere below her.

She understood immediately. "Oh, you're not!" Mock horror filled her voice. "Some poor black bear will find your Alaskan grizzly marks on his turf and never be the same."

::As it should be,:: Ruger said, full of satisfaction. A rustle, a flickering light showing pale in the light of the morning sun, and his very human voice replaced the one his bear had projected at her. "What about you, Mariska Bear? Going to be the same?"

"Don't get cocky," she muttered, tugging her shirt straight and turning to find him there—painted with sunlight, legs long and shoulders broad and stance easy on the uncertain footing. He grinned at her, and she scowled back. "About Maks—"

He shook his head. "Little chance of help from that quarter. There's no reason for him to be concerned just because we might have overnighted at the facility. We haven't checked in with them since the day we first came out here."

"He's not on active status," Mariska said, reluctant in her agreement. "I don't suppose he's likely to leave Katie just to see what we're up to."

"Not under the circumstances."

Pregnancy sometimes made the men crazier than it made the women, Mariska thought. But she couldn't disagree. "Jet might stir up some help. She knows we should have come back last night."

"She might. But we don't know. We *can't* know." Ruger scooped up the bag and tossed it to her with an easy ripple of muscle. "We were on our own yesterday. We're still on our own."

"Yeah, yeah," Mariska said, fitting the bag over her shoulder, hating the unspoken assumption that she wouldn't be taking the bear. Hating that it was right…and hating that she could still feel the amulet's effect on her, a deep wrongness she could only pretend to ignore. "We've got to find Forakkes and stuff his amulets up his—"

Ruger coughed amusement—one moment doing it as human, the next as a sharp sound from the back of a bear's throat. He headed straight up the slope, more nimble than any creature of a grizzly's size had the right to be.

She expected to be trailing him at some distance when

she finally crested the ridge herself—she expected him to be on the scent and ambling forward at a stiff pace. The rain had beat the scent into the ground, stirring soil and scant humus into a mix of rich odors. The trail might be obscured and it had definitely aged, but it nonetheless lingered.

But five hundred yards ahead, Ruger quartered over the ridge. When she reached him, he'd made no further progress at all.

Worse than that—when she reached him, rather than turning to her with his mind-voice, he instead took back the human. Whatever else he had to say, she knew what that meant—the trail was so utterly lost as to be unrecoverable.

"Dammit," she said. "If I could take the bear to help—"

"Don't," he said sharply.

She showed him her teeth.

"It wouldn't make any difference." He scrubbed his hand through his hair, leaving it in rakish disarray. "The trail was here...and now it's not."

That stopped her short. "Do you think he knows we're out here?"

He sent her a wry expression. "He's not subtle. I think we'd know if he suspected we were this close. He probably put this working up when Maks found the first facility." He put his back to a nearby tree, scratching his shoulder where the long slashing wound had been; his tone turned rueful. "There's a reason the Core generally keeps its amulet masters away from direct action."

"Too much power," Mariska murmured. "Even the Core knows better than to turn them loose with power *and* the authority to wield it."

"Too much power," Ruger agreed, but he didn't seem entirely dismayed.

Mariska narrowed her eyes, not hiding her suspicion. "What're you thinking?"

Ruger grinned. "I'm thinking that he's not a nice guy." Mariska sent him a *tell me something new* look, but it didn't have any impact. "I'm thinking that wherever he is, something is probably hurting."

He said it as though it had significance. She shook her head. "I don't follow."

"I *do.*" He took a few swift steps to close the distance between them, taking her arms to look down into her eyes. "I *can.* Follow, I mean. It's still foggy, but I can target that hurt. I can take us to it."

She couldn't hide her surprise. "From here?"

He slid his hands up to her shoulders, brushing one thumb over a collarbone and then up her neck to caress her cheek while he cupped the side of her head. She stood still, absolutely still—floored by the power of that touch and the flood of warm response in her belly, down her spine.

Dammit, she'd only meant to sleep with him that evening she'd hunted him in the park. She'd only meant to enjoy him, to experience his strength and to revel in her own without—for once—worrying about the reaction.

It hadn't ever occurred to her that he would revel in her in return—or that it would matter so much, so quickly.

He bent his head to her mouth, kissing her with a gentle thoroughness, and when he moved away, that thumb now caressing the side of her mouth, she mourned it. And she almost missed it when he said, "Yes, from here. But I need your help."

She wanted to hit him for having such power over her. She wanted to kiss him again and never stop. She wanted them safe and away from here, going in any other direction but this one. In the end she didn't move at all. She said, "What do you need?"

He hesitated; she thought he was finding the words hard to say. "I need you to watch for me."

That brought a frown. Not because she couldn't or wouldn't or even would think twice about it at all, but because it wasn't anything she hadn't already been doing. "Of course I will."

He shook his head; dappled sunlight slid over the rich texture of his hair, finger-combed into a scruffy shape that didn't begin to defeat the underlying curl. She kept herself from touching it. Barely. He said, "Not like before. This isn't healing; I won't go out on you. But it's…" He hesitated again, his mouth briefly flattening. "It's vulnerable."

Ah. The bear who could take care of himself, needing help. Truly *needing* it.

"Of course I will," she repeated, more quietly this time. With understanding. And then, in a rare moment of restraint, not saying again that this was why she had come, why she had asked to come—and why she had believed all along that he shouldn't bear the brunt of double duty in the field. Be the bear; take care of himself. Be the healer; take care of others.

But not both at once.

Ruger moved blindly through the trees, following the faintest awareness of distress. A small collection of distresses, in truth—hunger and aching and the sensation of being closed in coming so strongly that it bordered on pain.

He'd taken far too long to pick up on the emanations of need—far longer than they had time for, and far longer than he should have. But once he found them, he clung to them with tenacity, moving through the forest with unseeing eyes and Mariska's hand lightly touching his back as his guide.

I'm here, it said.

On occasion, she applied guiding pressure—avoiding a low branch or rough ground—and when they broke off to dip down between ridges, she pulled him close with an arm around his waist, wrapping him in a combination of strength and curves.

Through the thick veil of interference that had become his world as a healer, the faint sensations led him on.

Until Mariska stopped him, hooking her fingers through the waistband of his jeans to tug gently until he emerged from the meditative state he'd taken, dazed and blinking and with no idea where they were.

"Here," she said, rummaging in the bag and handing him the water bottle. "Drink."

He took the bottle without thinking, tipping it up for a few deep swallows and then letting her gently reclaim it—finding it as hard to come away from the tracking as it had been to dig that deep in the first place.

She squirted water in her mouth and swished it around, watching him as she swallowed. "You okay?"

Maybe it was because he was still half in that healer's awareness; maybe he would have noticed anyway—that in such a short time, the skin around her eyes had gone from rich to bruised, her face an underlying gray beneath the brown tones.

He shook away the remaining daze. "Are you?"

She shook her head with impatience, denying the question—but stopped herself, looking away. Beautiful lips of a wide mouth, even when pressed together for a moment before she spoke. "It's not good," she said.

"We'd better find them today if we're going to do something about it."

Alarm spiked through his thoughts—the instant understanding of how bad it had gotten in order for her to admit it affected her at all.

Unless she's accepting you. Trusting you. Allowing vulnerability.

"Let me help," he said, and made it a request.

Maybe because of it, she turned rueful instead of fierce. "Not yet. Let's know what we're up against, if we can. I may need to take the bear—"

"No," he said, refusing the sacrifice out of hand—knowing that even if she managed it, she'd never manage to change back. Or survive the attempt.

She gave him a steady look. "I may need to take the bear," she repeated. "And if I do, I'll want to be tanked up on healing before I do."

"No," he said, more implacably.

"You don't know what we'll be up against." She remained steady…implacable. "Has Forakkes got a whole posse there? Are they dedicated? Or is he working with a few minions who haven't managed to break free of him?"

"Or they're so tainted by him that they can't," Ruger added, sensible in spite of himself—in spite of his fears for her.

"The Septs Prince can't be happy with him," Mariska said. "Never mind the new regional *drozhar*—who's probably taking a lot of grief from the rest of them. The Core knows as well as we do that if our quiet little war gets loud, they'll suffer as much as we do. Either way, these guys are probably desperate to succeed. That makes them dangerous. And that means we might need not one bear, but two."

"Dammit," Ruger muttered. He ground his teeth together briefly and, without forethought, grabbed her arm to pull her close. "We don't need to stage a coup. We don't need to wipe Forakkes off the face of the earth. We just need to disrupt him—to buy some time."

"So he can get away again?" she said, looking at him with surprise. "Is that what you want?"

"They used rocket-propelled *grenades,*" he told her. "You can be certain they have guns—we know they have amulets. And we don't have anything but our personal wards and shields. They won't stop bullets and they might or might not stop an amulet working."

"It all depends on the working. I *know.*" Her face held a weariness that said she did indeed know just that. "Our best option is stealth. Find their air vents and block them. Lure them out one or two at a time. Lurk where we can pick off their sentries."

He relaxed, if only by degree. "You've been thinking about this."

"I've had time."

Right. Because he'd hardly been a conversationalist while she'd been guiding him through the forest. "Okay," he said, accepting it. She gave his hand a pointed look; he released her arm. "We'll do it your way. We'll pick our time for a final healing. *Unless* this thing goes too far."

She met his gaze, then, looking up with less defiance and more resignation. "I think we can pretty much guarantee it's going to go too far. I know Ian said the working would probably fade, but we've pretty consistently underestimated the awfulness of Eduard Forakkes. So if we can't stop it, it's *not your fault.*"

He'd been trying not to think of that possibility—and now he found himself unprepared for his reaction—the fierce denial, the heavy guilt…the wrench of what it would cost to lose her.

"Shut up," he told her, taking her recent words and trading the sharp tone she'd used for something no less intense but infinitely more gentle. "Just *shut up*."

"Make me," she suggested, a hint of her usual spark showing in her eyes.

He wrapped his arms around her, bringing them together for a crushing kiss, not waiting for permission. She didn't wait, either—she dropped her hand to cup him in a bold caress, one that made him instantly hard. He pushed into her hand, and felt her smile beneath his lips; he pulled away to pin her with an aggrieved expression.

She laughed—though the spark was back in her eye, and a bit of color on her cheek. "Remember that, the next time you think you should go macho on me."

"I didn't *think* I went macho," he said, stalking far enough away from her to regain control. "I *did* go macho on you. And it made you shut up, too."

"Whatever you say, dear."

He couldn't help a double take—still aggrieved, still aroused so profoundly that shifting himself didn't ease it…he wanted nothing more than to throw them both down to the ground and take her until both their eyes crossed.

Mariska laughed out loud. "Later," she said, and sent him mind-voice shorthand—quick glimpses of shifting bodies and frantic hands and heavy breathing, heavy moans.

He groaned.

Later, she'd said.

He'd damned well make sure they had a *later,* then.

Ruger came out of his tracking daze with a lurch and a stumble and no idea how much time had passed since Mariska had stopped him for their break. He straight-

ened to find he'd tripped over nothing physical at all—
and that the energies he'd been following had turned dark
and cold, a void of imperceptibility.

"What's wrong?" Mariska's arm tightened around his
hips, her touch both practical and as unselfconscious as
only a lover could be. "We haven't gone far—maybe a
quarter mile."

Ruger kept his voice low, pulling himself back into
focus as quickly as he could—scanning the rugged area
around them without much success, not quite there yet.
"They're gone."

She stiffened slightly. "Dead?"

"No, just…gone." He managed his bearings—finding
the sun, getting some sense of their orientation, seeing
that they stood in a dip between two sharp crests, and
seeing that the logging road cut up close behind them as
it wound along the base of that crest, nothing more than
two strips of dirt barely rutting the ground. Dread crept
along the base of his spine.

"Cone of silence?" Mariska guessed. She shifted uneasily, checking over her shoulder.

"Something like that." He nodded at the road; his feet
itched to take it. "We were right. There's the logging
road—the long way out."

"The easier way. Maybe we should—" She stopped
herself from finishing, rubbing the heel of her hand over
one eye. "I was going to say we should take it. But that
doesn't make any sense. Nothing's changed—this is still
what we need to do. Forakkes wouldn't have taken out
the other installation if he wasn't ready to move…we've
got to stop him. There's no time to hike out of here."

"It'd take us a day," Ruger said, shifting uneasily, still
halfway to heading for the road regardless, the impulse
so strong it made him frown.

"We don't have a *day*." Mariska looked up at him, rueful again. "*I* don't have a day. You'd end up carrying me." And still, she shuddered against him, her dread palpable. "I just don't know…I don't know we can do this—"

He turned to her, suddenly enough that she drew herself up with wary eyes. It didn't stop him from taking her shoulders, or even from pulling her aside, finding a massive ponderosa trunk as cover. "It's a working," he said, the certainty of it breaking through the dread. "Remember Maks' report? He ran into one when he first found signs of the Core in this area. No hiker would ever come through that gap and into this area to stumble over what's here. And it *is* here, somewhere. We're close, Mari, very close."

She frowned with resistance, caught up in the dread and unable to break free, to see that it wasn't her own. He gave her a little shake—a patronizing thing, diminutizing her.

She didn't bother with a slap or a kick to his shin or a good stomp on his foot. She drove her fist into his stomach, a swift, sharp blow for which he wished he'd been more ready. "Son of a—" He bent over himself, a hand pressing beneath his ribs.

Mariska blinked, more surprised, if possible, than he was. "Ruger! I didn't mean— Dammit! What did you do that for?"

"For that," he said, a little wheeze behind his voice as he straightened. "The dread working. To get you back to yourself."

"I'm *right here*. I—" She stopped, considering—looking around as if this little patch of forest now appeared entirely different to her. "Oh," she said, wincing. "I'm *sorry*."

He shook his head. "We've done enough *sorries,*" he said. "Are you good now?"

"I can still feel it," she told him, and annoyance crept into her voice—at Forakkes, at herself, at the situation. "But it doesn't have a grip on me anymore." Her expression hardened. "That bastard."

He grinned at her, not feeling much like a healer at all. "Time to let him know how we feel about it."

She tipped her head at him, wary in an entirely different way. Strands of her braid had come loose again, curving around her face in a perfection of disarray; in spite of the pallor behind her color and the faint wrinkle of her brow he'd come to recognize as a sign that her head ached, she looked herself—alert and ready to go. She asked, "What are you thinking?"

Mine.

The internal response came unbidden—the most honest, most personal answer to her question. *You are mine.* He swallowed it back. "I'm thinking we should just knock on the door."

She looked around the area in the most meaningful way—trees and bush and rugged ground, rocks sporadically scraping to the surface, and all under a bright blue sky with only a hint of building cloud. "Door," she said flatly.

"Cameras," he said, feeling almost cheerful about it. "You can bet they're here. Somewhere. Got wards up?"

Weariness briefly haunted her eyes; she shook it off. "Give me a minute. I never was much good at knitting."

Shields came easy to many—but they required a constant energy drain, and for some, constant attention. Wards came in knots and lines of energy, a woven pattern of protection that, once placed, held until dismissed.

But not everyone could set them, and fewer yet could set them well.

Ruger took her hand, and said, "Me, neither. But we need to be ready. We're right *here.* If we make him impatient enough, he'll send out his posse."

"You hope," she said darkly, but closed her eyes and bit her lip, her hand twitching in his in an unconscious echo of the ward she wove.

Ruger watched her—the sweep of black lashes against her cheek, the furrow of concentration in her brow, the faint flare of nostril in her straight, long nose. He watched her too long, in a moment not made for such indulgences, until he finally forced himself to look away and inward, pulling energy together for his own wards.

Ciobaka lifted his lips in a squint-eyed grin as Tarras approached Ehwoord's work area and hesitated beside his little jail. Small cages lined the back of the table; the middle cage held a small, flailing creature that had once been a giant tiger salamander and now wasn't anything much at all.

Ciobaka lifted one paw to show Tarras, flexing his thumb-claw to display the newly sharp, poisoned nail at the end. "Hurt 'oo."

Tarras spared him a scathing glance. "You stupid creature," he said, his voice low. "Don't you see what he's doing? Don't you know that you'll be next?"

Ciobaka's paw fell limp, dangling on the upraised leg so that now he only looked the supplicant. "Naht!"

"Yes," Tarras said. "You're no different than the rest of us. We're all expendable. And you're nothing but his biggest experiment, saved for last."

"Naht."

"Are you interrupting for a reason?" Ehwoord didn't

lift his head from his gruesome work, a clinking shuffle of amulets punctuating his words.

Tarras sent Ciobaka a warning glare. "Someone's made it in past the dispersal workings," he said. "I thought you'd want to see."

Ehwoord sat straight up, regarding Tarras with an unpleasant expression. "You fool. Of course I want to see. Immediately!"

You'll be next. Maybe after Tarras?

Ciobaka looked down at his new weapon. It had hurt when Ehwoord put it there. It had hurt a lot.

But Ehwoord had fed him. Ehwoord had made him special. The new claw made him even more special… more important.

Tarras moved briskly to the computer desk at the end of the worktable and tapped out a quick combination of keystrokes, swiveling the large monitor so Ehwoord could see it.

A lone man, standing among the trees. Shirtless, bigger than any of Ehwoord's pack, at ease with himself in the forest. Just standing.

Ehwoord cursed. "I warned you not to take them for granted! Where is Yovan?"

"Gearing up," Tarras said. "There's only one of him. Assuming he's Sentinel, he still won't be hard to take out."

"No!" Ehwoord snapped. "He is most certainly Sentinel, and I want him alive! He can take Ciobaka's cage. I must have him, do you hear me? Failure is not an option!"

His cage! Ciobaka whined under his breath. *"Nahhht."*

Tarras' mouth turned into a grim little line. He understood, all right. His hand dipped into one of the many pockets of the blotchy green pants he wore. "We may need to damage him."

"That is of no consequence, as long as he lives." Ehwoord swept the dead salamander from the table and into the trash and his notes on the creature along with it; he swept his amulets aside and yanked open a drawer, plucking out a series of amulet blanks and a few select, primed amulets; he seemed to have already forgotten Tarras' presence.

Tarras strode for the exit, turning beside Ciobaka's cage—well within reach of that new claw. "We'll turn all our resources on him," he said, glancing oddly at Ciobaka, his words distinctly formed. Ciobaka gave him lips and teeth in return. "I'm afraid it will result in some temporary confusion here below."

Ehwoord graced him with disdainful frown. "I may have overestimated you, Tarras. At times you seem quite simple. *Go get that man!*"

Tarras turned on his heel. On his way past Ciobaka's cage, his hand flicked out.

A metal key landed silently in the bedding.

Chapter 19

Mariska shifted on her perch of an arching pine bough, staying close to the trunk so the resulting tremble of the branch wouldn't give her away.

::This is a bad, bad idea,:: she sent to Ruger, letting her scowl color her thoughts and pretty certain that her worry leaked through, as well.

And there he stood, out in the open—out where they were so certain Forakkes would have surveillance in place. Just because after an hour of lurking less obviously—as if they didn't know they were so close—Mariska had run off into the woods to retch off the growing effects of the amulet working in her system.

"We can't wait," Ruger had said. "It could be days before they come back out. We don't have the time. *Ian* doesn't have the time, or Sandy."

"Maybe Jet—" Mariska had started, but it wasn't an argument she pursued. He was right. Maybe Jet would come to check on them; maybe she wouldn't. Maybe Maks would wonder; maybe he wouldn't. But by then it would be far too late for all of them.

It would clearly be too late for Mariska. And it would leave Ruger out here on his own.

And so he stood out there, exposed, tall and relaxed and shirtless. Easygoing and primal at the same time. *Bait.*

Mariska suddenly thought it was such a very, very bad idea.

They appeared without warning—two men toting guns, one with a rifle also slung over his shoulder. Gangsters at heart—just as they'd always been, all the way back to the start of it all, when the Roman-born son had persecuted his druidic brother. Mariska gave them a mental sneer.

::Steady,:: Ruger said. ::I see them.::

::I'm not sure where they came out.:: She let her frustration slip through that, too.

::They obscured it. It doesn't matter. I'll see it when I get close enough.::

::I don't *want* you to get close enough!::

::I know,:: he said, and that was all.

Dammit.

The Core minions stopped not far from Ruger—definitely out of reach, watching him with overalert wariness.

When Ruger spoke, he did it without moving—without threatening any further. "Take it easy—we're not at war here. At least, that's what your Septs Prince says."

From their expressions, they knew as well as Ruger and Mariska that their international prince was growing short in temper when it came to the trouble the Southwest regional *drozhars* had generated these past several years. But they were well-trained minions, decked out in matching black shirts and camo pants, similar features and black hair pulled back into tight ponytails—

and similar implacable expressions. The tallest of them said only, "Come with us."

Ruger didn't move; he didn't show any signs of concern. "Of course, you're all officially disavowed now, but I'm sure you'll be welcomed back if Forakkes gets his big working finished and tested out."

"We're not asking again," the man said, and shifted the rifle across his back.

"You never asked in the first place. You *told.*" Ruger's congeniality shifted, making way for a hint of the bear— an imperceptible shift in bearing as his voice hardened and his expression hardened, and Mariska felt her bear rise right along with his. "So now I'm telling *you.* This is your chance to get out of this mess. Go turn yourselves in to the new *drozhar,* and see if he lets you live. Because Forakkes is going down, and if you stay with him, you'll go down, too."

One of the men lifted his gun—or started to. He'd made his biggest mistake coming out here with the weapon still down at his side. Because for all his size, Ruger carried little bulk—and he was faster than either of them. Stronger than either of them. Buoyed by the bear, tempered by the human—the best of the best, working in concert.

When Ruger straightened, he pulled his strength in, calling on the bear. He said, so softly that Mariska wouldn't have heard it but for their connection, "Leave the gun out of this."

At the man's hesitation, Ruger added, "This isn't about whether I go back into the bunker with you. It's about whether you leave this place in one piece, or whether you never leave this place at all."

Neither man moved. Not for a long, long moment. Then the taller of them took a step back, not raising his hands so much as spreading them from his sides with open fingers, the gun barely held to his palm with his thumb.

Mariska sent Ruger her skepticism. ::Don't trust—::

::No,:: he agreed, and then jerked slightly, his expression grim with alarm. ::Mariska!::

It was the only warning she got, and she understood it well enough. The man's very acquiescence had been a signal to someone within, someone with an attack amulet to spare. Mariska threw energy to her shields, tightening her grip on the branch beside her, bracing herself—

Not enough. Even as Ruger faltered in the clearing, it hit her—a working of cruel, sweeping pain and sucking darkness. It slammed through her shields; it tangled in the wards. They shuddered, warping; Mariska gasped, suddenly bereft of air. The world swooped around her and she closed her eyes and *clung*—to the tree, to consciousness, to herself. *And it lasted forever...*

With a final reverberation of agonized, whiplashing energy, the wards snapped. Mariska moaned, her face pressed against rough bark, her hair catching in it.

But the working ebbed away, and she was still there. It faded into nothing more than a lingering stench. She scrabbled for her defenses, eyes squeezed shut against tears and unable to suppress a small sob of effort. *No more wards, no more shields...*

She had no defense against the next working. And Ruger was still out there—

Ruger! She forced her eyes open, hastily scrubbing them against her forearm—not daring to release her grip on the tree. He'd been stronger than she from the start, better protected than she. Surely he—

Yes. She found him there, still standing. He'd staggered but not gone down, and the overconfident Core minions hadn't yet realized he wasn't going to. They stood waiting—one smirking, one grim—and only belatedly responded when he lifted his head, baring his teeth in a ferocity they should never have roused.

They scrambled back, guns rising, and Ruger moved on them—slapping aside one weapon with preternatural quickness, whirling to ram his elbow into the man's chest. The minion dropped in his tracks, astonishment etched on his features.

The second man pulled off a shot before his weapon even came to aim; dirt puffed up from the ground and Ruger was on him, ripping the rifle sling off his shoulder and coming around to meet him with the butt of it. A blow to the arm cracked audible bone; a reversed follow-up to the side of the man's head and he went down hard.

Silence.

Ruger stood on braced legs, for that instant still in the fight. Then he straightened and stood quiescent, his gaze aimed at the place where the men had first become evident—the doorway still masked, but clearly not far.

Mariska couldn't see his face from this angle; she didn't have to. She saw the message clearly enough—the direct challenge in the set of his shoulders, the threat in the power of his stance.

Then he turned and walked away—heading not for Mariska, but lateral to her position, not giving her away. ::Two down,:: he told her, his background thoughts full of intent. ::We'll come back after dark and circle in the other way if the others don't come out for us. If not, we'll go looking for those air vents.::

She didn't respond at first, too full of dismay—too full of her own truth. By evening, she'd be no good to him. The hit she'd taken had undone his painstaking trickle of healing, and there was little he could do to stop the effect of the working now.

She dropped the gear bag; it landed on pine needles with a solid thump, and after a moment, so did she. She brushed herself off, hoisted the bag over her shoulder, and angled off to meet up with Ruger.

"Okay?" he asked, watching her with narrowed gaze. He still held something of the wild about him—a quality of movement, a look in brown eyes gone pale.

"You?" she asked, as if she'd answered.

He noticed, of course. He might even have asked again, had not someone from behind them snapped off a rifle shot that thunked hard into a tree to their right. Ruger grabbed her hand and tugged her onward—completely unnecessary, at that. She stumbled over nothing and caught up with him, even as another shot flaked bark to their left; together, they flinched away.

She might have called it coincidence, had it not happened again. *Right, left.* ::Don't like this,:: she told Ruger, not wasting her breath on spoken words.

Right, left.

Without warning, Ruger ducked behind a tree, yanking her around to do the same. She thumped up against him and they struggled to quiet their breathing, still gulping for air—listening behind, and belatedly understanding. ::They're herding us!::

::Yes,:: he agreed, a snarl still lingering in his thoughts. ::We're not supposed to figure that out. We're supposed to run straight out.::

::Let's not.::

"No," he muttered out loud, "let's not." He crouched low, one knee on the ground—drawing her down with him, albeit less abruptly than before. He nodded to their right—the direction that would allow them to circle out behind the Core—and pushed off, staying low.

White-hot slamming noise—

The forest exploded in front of them—sound and fury and shredding trees, flashing the world into chaos. Ruger pushed Mariska to the ground, landing on top of her—shielding her. ::Watch yourself!:: she cried, terrified for him—understanding now why they'd been herded. ::Watch—!::

Another explosion, closer—close enough to wash her mind with a concussion of sound, to slam the breath out of her lungs. Her ear stabbed with pain; Ruger jerked against her with a grunt she felt rather than heard.

::If we'd kept running...:: she said, dazed enough to let the thought trickle out.

::Then that would be us.:: His weight lifted from her, his hand lingering on her arm to give her a tug—not bodily lifting her, as he'd done before, but suggesting this time. ::Double back. They had this corridor set up. They'll be out to look for us.::

::Double back,:: she agreed, her gaze caught on the wreckage ahead of them. Only with effort could she resolve the jumble to perceive the shattered remains of a once-massive pine. ::Come up on them from behind.:: She pushed to her feet, staying low—staggering a step or two with the noises of her movement coming muffled through ears still ringing with shock. She cursed at herself—that, too, came strangely filtered.

Ruger's expression echoed her own—annoyed, a little off balance. He nodded at a nearby cluster of bushes. ::Can't hear a thing—watch behind, and I'll get us there.::

::Go!:: she said by way of agreement—checking over her shoulder as he slipped his hand in hers and drew her along. He stumbled, righted himself and threaded them between a tree and the bushes—solid wood at their backs, sheltering leaves before them. Ruger leaned against the tree. ::See anything?::

::A glimpse,:: she said, spotting black and camo movement along that same corridor—a single man, easing forward with unconvincing stealth. ::He's moving onward... didn't even look this way.::

::Hold on. They could be flanking us.:: He scowled as he straightened, and said as though for the first time, ::Can't hear a damned thing.::

Something in his mind-voice made her look twice. ::You okay?::

Puzzlement surfaced in his eyes—a part of him clearly still dazed. He shuttered it away. ::Still blasted into stupid.::

::How long until my ears stop ringing, that's what I want to know,:: Mariska grumbled. She returned her attention to the forest, raking it for movement—seeing only the retreating glimpses of the first man. ::Anything?::

::Either I missed him or they didn't send someone. Not many posse members want to defy their *drozhar,* never mind the Septs Prince. They were probably leftovers from Gausto's inner circle,:: Ruger said, his voice distant. ::Already in the same situation as Forakkes.::

::Disgraced and hunting redemption,:: Mariska agreed. ::The end justifies the means.:: Then she murmured, "It's all clear here."

"And here."

"I heard that," she said, with some relief, rubbing the ear that had stabbed with pain at the explosion. "At least, I think—"

He gave her a sharp look. "It's probably perforated. We generally heal fast from that injury, but don't count on hearing from that ear."

"Don't assume there's not something out there to hear, you mean." She made a face. "You'll have to be the ears, I guess."

"I can—" Why he stopped, she didn't know—just caught another glimpse of that earlier puzzlement. He shook his head slightly and completed the thought. "I can do that. Ready to move?"

"Before they come back." A distant sound caught her attention; she tipped her head at it, wondering if she'd really heard it.

Ruger sent her a darkly amused look. "They're frustrated because they haven't found us."

"Good," she said. "Let's frustrate them some more."

But when he turned from her to lead the way to the next cluster of trees and stiff, prickly bushes, her satisfaction dissolved to horror, her chest clenching strangely around her lungs so for a startling moment, she couldn't even draw breath. "Ruger!"

He paused with one hand on the tree for support to look back at her, and for the first time she saw the whiteness of his knuckles as he gripped the rough Ponderosa bark. For the first time she knew to look.

For the first time, she understood what she thought he still did not—that while his back was peppered with small chunks of wood shrapnel around the now healed cut from the facility attack, one of those missiles had struck deep.

It *still* struck deep, leaving room for a mere trickle of escaping blood, the skin closing around the small protruding shard that remained.

Mariska felt the blood drain from her cheeks in a tingling flush and breathed deeply, forcing herself to think. They were too close to their original path to stop here, and he was still on his feet. He needed to *stay* on his feet until they reached a safer spot. "Never mind," she said. "Let's get away from here."

"You're okay?" he asked sharply, though his voice bottomed out a little with strain.

She laughed; she couldn't help it. "As okay as I was before."

It wasn't saying much. Two wounded Sentinels, trying to save the world. Or at least to save their friends. *I'm sorry, Ian. And Sandy. And Heckle, too. We made the wrong choice. We should have hiked out for help.*

Chapter 20

Ruger didn't believe her.

Not even as she continued to watch their backs while he led them onward. She'd hidden things from him before, when she'd thought it was best—she'd hidden them with purpose.

The difference was, this time he knew she was doing it.

But he knew, too, that arguing about it wasn't the best course. And maybe it was only fair. He was hiding things, too.

Not that he could have articulated those things. Just that he was still reeling from the concussive effects of the grenades, when he didn't expect to be. That he ached strangely, that his legs grew more rubbery and not less, and he'd broken out into a clammy sweat in the afternoon heat.

"Ruger," she said, tugging back gently as they reached the best of shelters, the angled root disk of a pine torn from the earth and resting cocked against another tree. Her expression gentled. "You're hurt, Ruger. We need to take care of you. Right here."

Hurt? Hell, yes, he hurt. He looked down at himself, saw nothing but his own hairy chest and worse-for-wear jeans.

"Your back," she said. "We need to— No! Don't—"

He'd found it, running his hand over his back, his ribs—a shard of wood where it didn't begin to belong, dammit, and how the hell had that happened, anyway? His fingers scrabbled over it, got a grip—

"Don't!" Mariska cried.

The wood yanked free with a sucking sound and a flood of warmth and a bolt of shredding pain that knocked him to his knees. His lungs burned for air and his torso seized up—but when he finally drew breath it came with a bitter, coppery taste.

"Dammit, Ruger!" Mariska turned on him, grabbing at the bag she still carried and throwing it down beside him. She plucked the wooden shrapnel from his unresisting fingers and held it up in front of him, pine stained dark and so much longer than expected, the point of it as sharp as any spear. "Here," she said urgently. *"This* is what you just pulled out, and now you're bleeding like the proverbial pig."

Well, hell.

She grabbed his jaw with strong fingers and turned his head to look directly at her, crouching to eye level. *"Look* at me, dammit! What did this thing do to you? What are we up against?" She held it to her side, approximating position and angle. "Ruger! *Don't make me hit you."*

Shock. Of course he was in shock. And his brain wasn't working and his body was torn and his mouth was full of blood—

She hit him.

He bared his teeth at her, swaying on his knees. "Liver," he said hoarsely. "Bleeds like hell. Hepatic artery? Wouldn't survive that. Diaphragm. Lung—" He proved that one by doubling over with a sudden hack of a cough that sprayed blood everywhere.

"The shirt," she said, tossing the wood aside and grabbing at the gear bag. "I need to stop the bleeding—"

"Not where you can get to it," he told her faintly, and sweat flushed anew across his forehead, between his shoulder blades. "Mariska…I think…"

She swore resoundingly and dropped the bag. "That's our cave," she told him, jabbing a finger at the fallen tree and the hollow where the roots had torn from earth. "Me and you. Get your ass in there before you pass out, because you're too damned big to carry."

"Too late," he said, and knew only that she was there to catch him when he fell.

::Ruger.::

It was very far away, that voice.

::Ruger. Get back here.::

Too far away, really.

::Ruger Bear, get your ass back here!::

His eyes cracked open of their own volition. He showed her his teeth, putting a little growl beneath it. The display had no effect whatsoever, as he expected. *That's why you let yourself do it.*

Understanding came with unexpected clarity in his dully confused state. With no one else had he ever been able to release the underlying nature of the bear, simply because no one else would have taken it in stride.

Mariska only said, "Yeah, grrr. Now haul yourself awake and get to work."

He lay on his side in cool shadow, surrounded by earthy scents—dirt and dampness and the strong, sappy scent of pine. The root disk loomed above them, sharply angled and closing them in. "How—?" he asked, no less befuddled than before.

"I didn't drag you, if that's what you mean." Her comforting hand on his shoulder belied the matter-of-fact nature of her words. "Let's just say I encouraged you along."

He scowled, lacking energy as it was. "You poked me."

"You'll never know, will you? Now, you ready to work? We've got things to do." But still her hand was gentle, caressing him minutely before she reached to brush dirt off his face and lightly scrape her fingers through the hair over his ear.

"Sludge—" He caught his breath on a sudden shard of pain, fighting a cough—unable to hold it, as short on air as he was. The coughing took him over and he rolled into it, curling around himself and coincidentally around Mariska. He barely felt her hold him close, or her hands stroking along his back, firm and comforting and...

Possessive.

Possessive. He liked that. He liked the warmth of it, the comfort of it, the—

"Ruger!"

"Ah, hell," he muttered, floundering back to the surface again. "Sludge," he said again, on a gasp. And, "Wrong side. Help me turn."

"But—"

"Mari." It was all the argument he had left in him, gasping out on not nearly enough air.

She stopped arguing, delaying only long enough to grab a remnant of his shirt from the gear bag and hold it to his side as he turned, protecting it from the hard, sand-clay dirt. It left her kneeling at his back, her hands familiar on his body—one resting on his hip, one on his arm. "Better?"

He couldn't quite catch his breath against the tearing

pain of movement, the outraged reaction to the pressure against the wound. But he sent her an affirmative anyway. ::Better.:: It would be; he was already breathing easier, even as his blood soaked into the dirt.

Not even a Sentinel healed fast enough to offset an injury of this magnitude—the shock, the blood loss. He knew it, and he thought she might know it, too.

She might well have been reading his mind. "Sludge isn't going to be enough."

"Not enough," he agreed, and the words came in gulps of air. "Change of plan. Head to high ground. Get a signal. Get Annorah. Or Maks."

"Think again." But she had no argument in her voice, only regret. When he drew breath to respond, she closed her hand over his arm, staying him. "I hear you, Ruger Bear. But it's not an option. Before the Core blew you up, they got me. There's not much left of me."

::The amulet working,:: he realized, remembering how drained she'd looked when they'd met up in the woods.

"We still have to go after the bastards," she said. "*You* need to go after them. You drew them out—we know pretty much where that entrance is, no matter that they obscured it. So we need to be enough of a problem to buy time. It might not be soon enough for Ian and Sandy, but if Forakkes is ready to launch that new working of his on Sentinels, every moment we can buy brevis is critical."

He didn't have words for that; he had only sorrow and assent, and he knew she'd heard him by the way her hand tightened over his hip—and by the way she leaned over to plant a kiss on his cheek.

When she would have retreated, he snagged her hand—needing to see her face, her eyes. There was no snap in those eyes—they were merely huge and dark and sad. *Resigned.*

She used a scrap of his shirt to dab around the blood at his mouth and chin, and then she did just what he'd hoped, bending over his shoulder to take his face and kiss him with a firm possessiveness.

"Perfect," he told her, as she drew away again.

"*Perfect* is a good healing," she told him. "Not with any damned sludge, either. The real thing. The same work that's had healers talking in all the brevis regions—like what you did for Joe Ryan in Flagstaff before that ambush."

::I'm not that healer any longer,:: he said, mustering the energy to feel annoyance that she would even say it, even if he couldn't muster spoken words.

"You're not that *man* any longer." She settled down behind his shoulders and briefly rested her forehead on his arm, the only sign she'd given of her own struggle. "Don't you get it yet? You don't *need* to be. Quit trying to do it all at once, and let me help."

::You don't understand.:: A new wave of pain shuddered through his torso. ::Talk fast,:: he told her dimly, when he could. ::I can't…*can't*—::

She talked fast. "I know you can take care of yourself, Ruger, and I know that makes you invaluable in the field, but you *never* should have been asked to handle healing and protection at the same time. There should always be someone to watch your back—*always*." He snarled a panting denial, absurdly weak as it was; she ignored it. "That's why I wanted to come on this assignment and that's what I'm here for now. Think about it! You can't do both at once, not truly. And now that you were hurt so badly, how could you begin to let go of *protecting yourself* enough to let the healing happen?"

The words hit him like a blow, leaving him without words.

"I'm sorry," she said, and she sounded unutterably weary. "You can hate me for saying it if you like, as long as you *live*—"

He barely managed the words. "You're right."

"I… What?"

::You're *right*.::

He'd been hurt in Flagstaff—hurt badly. Deep down, he'd never let go of that fact. It had infused him with determination—*never let it happen again*. And the only way to do that was to throw all his energy—subconscious or not—into making sure it didn't.

How, then, was he supposed to put any of that energy into healing? Or even into getting past his own defenses? ::*You're right*…::

Her breath caught; it sounded like a sob of relief. "Then let me help."

He wasn't sure how. Or he thought it should make sense, and he just couldn't think it through.

"It's okay," she said, resting the side of her head against his shoulder, leaning against the breadth of his back—small and solid, full of curves and strength both. "I'm covering you. That's all you have to know right now. And all you have to *do* is let go of that responsibility and be the healer. I know it's not easy to heal yourself, but you can *save* yourself. I believe that. Do you?"

His breath caught; he struggled with a new stab of pain. *There goes the lung.* Collapsing.

"*Ruger.* Be the healer!" She poked him, hard, up high on his shoulder. He snarled reflexively and gasped in the wake of it—and she didn't let up. She poked him again. "Get off your metaphysical ass and do something about this!"

::Don't—::

"Then make me stop." Damned if she didn't poke him again, sending hot shards down his side.

He sent her a silent snarl this time, barely managing it through the tangle of fog and pain.

She didn't know what she was asking…she *couldn't.* She'd never tried to absorb her own pain, feeling it double as it wrenched through both healer and body. She'd never tried to think through that onslaught, or to direct delicate energies.

But she was still right.

He reached for his healer's calm, floundering through the chaos of pain to assess and target his own needs. *Too big…too much…* Teeth clenched, breath panting hard, just barely aware of her at all—just knowing that she was there, and that she stroked and petted him, her lips on his skin in a comforting flutter. His side burned, his blood flowed, his breath ached in his lungs…it slammed into him from the healing side and escalated until he writhed against it—and then her strong hands held him down.

But when he reached for the healing, he found only sludge. And when he pushed at the sludge, the pain grayed around the edges, the *world* grayed around the edges…

She did more than poke him. She hit him. She hit him *hard,* a punch to the shoulder that jarred him loose from the sludge and sent him whirling back into the pain. He cried out with it, as angry as he was hurting, even knowing she'd just kept him from slipping right away into the gray.

"Stop it!" she snapped, and hit him again. "Screw the sludge! I'm *here,* Ruger, and *I'm* doing the watching. Now *let go and be the healer!"*

The world tumbled away.

He had no idea if she touched him; he had no idea if he

cried out as he plunged back into that doubled agony. He had no sense of the ground beneath him, the roots above them, the distant presence of Core corruption... He knew only the pure clarity of pain and the sharply defined kaleidoscope of energies surrounding him.

He plucked at the energy, spinning it like wool and sending it spearing along the lethal flow of life from injured vessels. He found the wounded lung and infused it with a spongy pale essence; he found torn flesh and soothed it, soaking it with soft encouragement. He found the body as a whole—drained and exhausted—and nourished it with clear, cool sustenance.

And, quite suddenly, he found himself looking back out on the world. He looked up to the roots dangling above them, on his back with the fingers of one hand digging into dirt and the other hand clenched around Mariska's so tightly that it felt crushed in his own.

His side ached ferociously, but...he breathed. His heart pounded a galloping rhythm...but one that slowed, one that beat steadily and not erratically.

"Are you back?" Mariska whispered. "Did you do it?" She brought their hands up to rest her cheek against the back of his, leaving his skin damp. *Tears.*

"I'm back," he said, and tugged her back down, pulling her to him until she understood *come all the way* and stretched out right on top of him where he held her close and closer yet, until her tears no longer ran down his neck. He smoothed a hand over her hair as she lifted her head to meet his gaze from those close quarters, her face smudged, her cheeks full of high color, her eyes still gleaming. "I'm *back,*" he said again.

She kissed him, full of feeling, and then rested her head on his chest for long moments in which they did no more than breathe together, his chest rising steadily beneath her. Long moments in which he did nothing more than absorb the feel of her—her breasts pressing into his torso, the line of her ribs and the softness of her waist and the definition of her hips. He stroked her back, down her spine and over her tight round bottom. "Thank you."

And then he rolled over to his side, lowering her to the ground so their legs tangled and he propped on one shoulder over her. Hell, that hurt. But it was only pain.

In deep healing, he could mend a cut; he could resolve a moderate wound. But he couldn't take a body that had been deeply rent and do anything more than stop it from dying. He could stop it from bleeding and kick-start it to recovery, but not *fix* it. At least, not in one session. And over the centuries, they'd learned it was better that way— that support was better than brute physical change, even change for the better.

Mariska drew a deep breath beneath him. "We're not done yet, are we?"

"Not by far. We still have to find that entrance. We still have to stop Forakkes. And we still have to save Ian." He kissed her, as gently and thoroughly as she'd just done to him—not an arousing kiss, as much as his body responded to her. More of a statement—of intent and feeling.

They'd talk about how hard she'd hit him later.

"Can you stand watch for just a moment longer?" he asked. "Because my guess is that much as you've not said it, you're as done as I was."

He was surprised to see her lower lip tremble; she bit it as if that would stop her emotion, and then gave up. "God, Ruger—it hurts. Everywhere. Please make it *stop*."

"Watch for me," he said, and slipped into being the healer again.

* * *

Tarras was dead. Broken and dead and dumped in a corner along with Yovan.

Ciobaka hadn't liked Tarras. He hadn't considered him a dominant and he hadn't felt obliged to listen to him, only resentful of the artificial circumstances that made it necessary.

But he had *known* Tarras. And he had been aware that the man's presence was an intricate part of the balance in Ehwoord's pack.

Ciobaka hadn't *thought* that he liked Tarras. But already he missed him.

Ehwoord still raged, hours later. He'd gotten little work done with his amulets this day, and he blamed the dead men. Then he blamed the three men still alive for their shooting and their wasted grenades. He blamed the Sentinels for being so tenacious, for interfering with Core business.

He did not blame himself.

Ciobaka knew only that the Core itself was the biggest pack he could imagine, and he had the sense that Ehwoord's business wasn't in fact necessarily Core business. This he had learned because no one ever paid attention to his swiveling ears, and they spoke without reservation in his presence.

He curled up in his back corner to give his venison ribs a thoughtful chew, his hindquarters resting casually on top of the key Tarras had dropped. Maybe Ehwoord would send him out to hunt down the Sentinels.

He could do that.

"*Find* them," Ehwoord raged, flinging the thing that wasn't really a mouse anymore at the man named Doro. Doro's hand twitched as if he might catch the not-mouse, but he knew better. He stood stiffly still as it bounced off his hard chest.

He didn't know enough not to say, "They must be wounded, sir. We had them right in our sights only moments before impact. They can't threaten your work now."

Ehwoord's fury extinguished to hard, cold intensity—that which Ciobaka feared most of all. "Then you know nothing of Sentinels at all."

Doro's fear-sweat reached Ciobaka's nose. Ciobaka chewed on his ribs, crunching off a chunk of meat and bone in a display of great relish. Pretending he didn't notice things weren't right anymore, pretending he didn't care.

Pretending he hadn't learned so much these past few days.

Ehwoord brushed off the front of his immaculate black lab coat, all his anger gone. Just like that. Ciobaka had seen that, too—how as Ehwoord strangely grew less lined and less gray, his moods grew more volatile.

I am only a dog. I am only chewing.

"Never mind," Ehwoord said. "Of course you don't understand what I'm doing here. How could you? But understand this—those Sentinels are a threat to us until they're dead. And I don't want them *dead* until I have a chance to test my new working on them. It will save us weeks of remote field experiments, and it means we can abandon this compromised facility in short order."

That much, Doro certainly understood. None of the men wanted to be here anymore. Ciobaka quietly reached out to caress a thumbed paw-hand down the nearest bar.

"Now, if you would...*go find them.*" Ehwoord's voice rose to a dangerous pitch, then just as abruptly dropped back to normal. "On your way out, please find the box with Ciobaka's amulets. It's time to accelerate my protocol."

I am only a dog. I am only chewing.

Ciobaka's paw-hand closed around the key.

Chapter 21

Mariska flexed her hands; she ran them down her body. She searched herself for aches and pains and that debilitating sense of imbalance she'd carried for days now— and then, free of it all, she scrambled out of their little hollow and dared to reach for the bear along the way.

Mariska Banks, who takes the bear.

And she did, surging into her bear with accustomed ease. When Ruger emerged to unfold to his full height, she charged for him, as delighted to see him stand his ground as she was to leap at him. She reached for the human just in time to wrap herself around him, ankles hooking at his hips and arms around his neck.

"Feeling better?" he asked, just enough of a dry tone to make her laugh; his hands quite naturally cupped her bottom, supporting her. She kissed him by way of answer, and then, feeling the strain on his side, slipped away to her own two feet.

"No headache!" she said. "No lead feet! Now, let's see you." She turned him around to the sunlight, running her hand over his back. The peppered little wounds were nothing more than pink spots and scabs, some of them hard to see around the dried blood. She glanced overhead, hoping for more rain, but the afternoon thunderheads weren't voluminous or dark enough to be promising.

Her inspection grew more tender at the site where he'd been impaled. That wound was far from closed; it even still trickled a pale glisten of fluid—probably from her rough treatment of moments earlier. "Sorry about that," she said, running a hand down the ridged muscling of his side and abdomen.

His skin twitched beneath her fingers. "Worth it," he said, but he put his hand over hers, pulling her attention from his injury to his eyes. "Mari," he said. "You were right. You've been right all along. And you were the only one who had the strength to say it and *make* me hear it."

"Bear to bear," she told him, stunned at the pleasure his words gave her, at the warmth of them in her chest.

He shook his head. "Mariska to Ruger." And this time, when he framed her head with his hands and bent to kiss her, she knew what was coming—she knew it would be less celebratory than it was tender, and less fierce and needy than it was giving. Than it was *asking*.

She answered in kind, opening of herself to kiss him long and deep—and most of all, *aware*. He couldn't quite seem to let go of the moment—ending one kiss to begin another, this one full of regret at the inevitable moment when they would stop being two people in the woods— two lovers in the woods…*two people who loved one another* in the woods…

To start hunting again.

"Ready to go find some bad guys?" she asked. It surprised her anew when he held her tight, taking her up in his arms in a way that must have caused him no little pain. Then he took a deep breath, his chest expanding against her—the hitch in his breath so obvious with her head resting against him—and kissed the top of her head before he stepped back.

"Bad guys," he agreed. "Though it would be good to find water along the way. I lost a lot of blood—even forced healing won't replace it if I can't stay hydrated."

"Healer talk," she said. "So sexy." He snorted as she added, "With all the rain we had the night before, we'll find something pooled up somewhere. Maybe even a temporary creek."

"Take the bear," he suggested. "And we'll circle around the long way back to Forakkes, down into the low spots."

As the bear, she'd smell the water long before they ever found anything, even if it was only a surface pool on rock or tree. She agreed by stepping back to make room, still delighted to find her bear with little more than a twist of thought, the change energies swirling bright and strong around her.

"Show-off," Ruger said, and had the audacity to tug her furry ear. She curled a lip at him and loped on out ahead.

So it was that she smelled the water before he saw any sign of it, some forty-five minutes later, and led them down to the trough of land where the ground was still damp—more mud than water, but still oozing slightly.

"Dig us out a little hole, will you?" he asked, removing the gear bag from his shoulder with a care that told her she might feel like her old self, but he was still faking it. She pretended not to notice and did as asked.

By then he'd pulled out the well-used remainder of his shirt; he pushed it into the hole and up against the mud. The seepage started immediately, and Ruger sat on the slope nearby, digging his heels in downhill. "It's a good place to take a rest while this fills."

She gave him a critical look, and he met it steadily. "It is what it is," he said.

::If we have time, why don't you—::

He shook his head before she finished. "There's a fine line beyond which healing yourself becomes counterproductive. It doesn't come *free*." The quirk of his mouth turned wry. "Besides, we might need some of that later."

She offered him a little bearish hum of agreement and snuffled aimlessly at the base of the nearest tree. But Ruger's head had come up to alert, his eyes searching; he rose to his feet, tracking slightly uphill of the spot that had gotten his attention. Mariska inhaled, but the wind was against her and she got nothing.

Out of the following silence came a weakened voice, one that sounded far too much like a child. "'Ite 'oo."

Mariska did more than stop in her tracks; she recoiled, instantly aware of how vulnerable they'd been in those previous few moments.

::Ruger?::

"'Ite 'oo!" the child said, more urgently.

Bite you?

By then Ruger stood above the nearest cluster of young pines and scrub oak, his mouth flat in a grim line. ::Take back the human,:: he told her. ::Come on over.::

::But—:: She'd be seen. And one of their strictest tenets—shared with the Core—was that they not be seen in the act of the inexplicable.

But he didn't need to say anything more—not when the bushes spoke again. "Grrrr!" they said, vocalizing rather than growling—though the sound mixed with an actual snarl, one only an animal could make. "Grrr!"

There was no making sense of that—not from here. Mariska reached for the change.

"Beast!" the creature accused her, its pronunciation labored. "Grrr!"

"It's a dog," she said, looking down at it in surprise. A dingy, red-ochre dog with long legs, a brush tail and prick ears—no particular breeding behind this one, just pure survival in tough circumstances taking on a primal form. "Isn't it? Unless someone brought in a dingo…"

"Dog, I think," Ruger said. "And badly hurt."

"Grrr," said the dog, its ears flattened and its eyes rolling wild. It raised its lips in a dramatic snarl that was as much deliberate communication as fearful reaction.

Ruger looked down on it and said, more matter-of-factly than Mariska would have thought possible, "Would you like help?"

The dog watched them with eyes gleaming, gone still in thought—still enough so Mariska could see the twist of its front leg, the blood gleaming on its haunch and smeared along its face.

After a moment, its tail gave a faint wag, only the tip of it moving—a hopefulness that made her sadder than she could have imagined. ::As if we didn't already know Forakkes was a monster!::

"He'p?" the dog said, its voice very small.

"Yes." Ruger lowered himself to the ground with a flexibility surprising in a man of his size. "You're hurt. I can help with that." He glanced at Mariska, an unspoken request that struck warmth in her chest—that he'd so completely accepted, finally, the need for protection while he worked healing. That he'd so readily reach out to her for it.

She didn't have a chance to respond out loud, but maybe he'd read it in the way her head had lifted, or the way her eyes widened with pleasure, or even—yes, the smile still lingered at the corners of her mouth.

The dog said, "A-yes, 'oo he'p?" and its hope mixed with wary disbelief.

"I can take the pain away," Ruger said. "I can start your healing. You wouldn't yet be whole. But maybe you can help us in return."

The dog squinted his eyes in suspicion.

"Never mind," Ruger said, and sent a private aside to Mariska. ::Screw that. Who knows what this dog has been through already.::

::Just help him,:: she agreed.

"Do you have a name?" Ruger asked the dog.

The dog lifted his head with a defiant pride. "Tcheow," he said, forming the word with exquisite care. "Tcheow-baka. Ciobaka." He wagged his tail a little more boldly. "He'p?"

Mariska found herself standing watch while Ruger took the dog in his lap and slipped easily into the healing trance he'd so recently rediscovered, his big hands soothing the animal with a gentle stroke and ear rub while he was at it. The dog, at first tense and once going so far as to close his teeth around Ruger's hand, gave a final whine of surrender, shifted to quick, anxious licking, and then—finally—relaxed.

Ciobaka had not thought of it. Feral before he was a creature of Ehwoord's, then accustomed only to the cage and sharp adversarial exchanges and the constant change of his body and his status…

He had not known that hands could be gentle at the same time they were strong. Or that a man of power could touch him and leave him more like himself instead of less.

He had never cared for Ehwoord, but Ehwoord had been his dominant, and that meant certain things. It meant Ciobaka accorded him respect; it meant Ehwoord did, in some ways, look after him.

But a true dominant had benevolence. And in the end, Ehwoord had none of that. He had made Ciobaka less, and not more.

And in the very end, he had intended to hurt Ciobaka. To kill him.

Ciobaka remembered the moment he had closed his paw-hand around the key…the moment he had unlocked and slipped away from the cage. He remembered finding the amulet that controlled his pain and snatching it up by the knotted cord. And then there had been shouting and gunfire and slamming impact, his teeth sinking into flesh and blood on his tongue.

He didn't remember exactly how he'd escaped that place. More shouting, a scrambling, lame dash for the door, his thumb-claw scrabbling to grasp his way to freedom. He'd found himself in the forest, thirsty and broken and heading painfully for the scent of water.

He'd found this man, with his hands that made him more.

Ruger gave the dog the space to stand up and shake off and absorb what had happened to him.

Truth be told, Ruger needed time to absorb what had happened to *him*. To wallow in it, if he had to admit it.

He was a healer again.

Pure, clean, healing flow, nudged to the places where it would do the most good—following his vision for what *should* be instead of what was. Following knowledge borne both of study and instinct to restore flesh and bone.

Not that it had come instantly, or easily. He'd floundered at first. But—

Mariska. She stood nearby, as alert as any Sentinel

could be—scanning the area with her sight, her hearing, her energies...

And so he'd let go of the need to do the same, and felt the sweet rush of the thing he was born to do.

As the dog sat to scratch and then contemplate his foot, Ruger walked over to Mariska and wrapped his arms around her, filling himself with her as he held her tightly and lifted her right off her feet. Her laugh came muffled between them, and when he set her down he took her head between his hands and kissed her—not just deeply, but as if he had every right to leave her breathless.

"You're welcome," she said, laughing slightly in that breathlessness, her hands against his chest and fingers scraping through the crisp hair in the best possible way. She looked a little dazed while she was at it, and drew breath on words she didn't quite say—putting them aside to search his gaze. "Ruger," she said, watching his pale brown gaze grow darker, his expression just a tad fiercer. *"Ruger..."*

"Yeah," he told her. Understanding her...affirming her. *Yes. This is more than just the moment.*

This is just maybe forever.

The sloppy sound of a lapping tongue broke their connection; as one, they turned to the newly constructed water hole. Mariska's arm slipped around Ruger's hips for one more squeeze before she eased away, just as familiar with his bottom as he'd been with her mouth.

Ciobaka looked up, backing away with ears flicking uncertainly from upright to flat again. Ruger scrounged the water bottle from the gear bag, filling it as he could with a second, smaller piece of cloth over the top as a double filter—and then taking a moment to push a quick flash of energy through it, cleansing it. "We need to find Forakkes," he said to the dog, handing the bottle to

Mariska. Ciobaka didn't respond, and he added, "That's Eduard. Will you show us?"

"T'ras dehd," Ciobaka said, a whine behind the words. He looked off into the woods, his nose lifting into the breeze and his nostrils twitching, and Mariska handed the water back with a warning that it tasted like mud. Ruger drank, watching the dog, waiting...

They could backtrack the dog if necessary. But it would be so much swifter to follow him straight to Forakkes' little shop of horrors...and he might yet do it. Ruger suspected the animal simply needed time to assimilate all that had happened.

In fact, Ciobaka rose, shook off and trotted to the spot where they'd found him. He came back dragging an amulet with his thumb-like dewclaw, and dropped it in front of Ruger, nudging it farther with his nose when Ruger didn't pick it up. "'Akes hurr," he announced. "Kill it."

"Makes hurt," Mariska said, turning to Ruger. "Like what they did to Jet at first? Implanted her with one half of an amulet set and tortured her with the other?"

"Grrr," said the dog, which Ruger took as affirmation.

He bent to pick up the amulet and admitted, "I don't know how. But I'll keep it with our things until we reach the man who can deal with it." *Ian. Please still be alive.* He looked at Ciobaka. "His name is Ian, and he needs help that we can't give him until we stop Eduard. Will you show us?"

"Show 'oo," Ciobaka said, and trotted away, still limping profoundly but without hesitation.

Ruger gulped down the remainder of the water—*tastes like mud, but so sweet*—and tossed it back to Mariska, who refilled it as quickly as possible before she reclaimed the ever-useful remainder of the shirt. By then the dog stood waiting near the closest crest.

"'Oo hurr, too," he said, as Ruger took an awkward step on approach and recovered even more awkwardly. "Ehwoord?"

"Yes," Ruger said, gone grim at this reminder that he wasn't yet what he should be—that he *wouldn't* be. "But now we're going to stop him."

Chapter 22

The first time the dog hesitated, Mariska tucked the gear bag behind a tree. There was no point in getting that amulet any closer to Forakkes—and no point in bringing the bag along. Not until they figured out how to rig a weapon from the battered scraps of a shirt, a water bottle and the wrappers of the food they'd eaten.

The second time the dog hesitated, they crouched down to assess the land before them. The scent of shattered pine hung in the air; she would have known they were close even had the uneven dip of ground before them not looked familiar.

"See 'oo," the dog muttered, his brushy tail dropped low between his hocks.

"The cameras," Ruger said, glancing up in the trees as if he could spot them without the equipment they'd left buried in the old facility. "There's not much we can do about them."

"Then when we move, we'll have to do it fast," Mariska said decisively. "And maybe not so much through the door." When Ruger glanced back at her, she smiled toothily. "I bet this place uses those solar tubes, too. They're too narrow for us, but I'm pretty sure a grizzly can tear right through that roof once we find it."

"Helluva drop," Ruger said, but it was observation and not argument, and he turned to Ciobaka. "How about it? Sunlight coming through tubes in the ceiling?"

"Ayeah." But Ciobaka sat and gave his front foot a few quick licks.

"You don't have to come any further," Ruger told him. "But I hope you'll wait for us. We'll see that the amulet is destroyed…and we'll give you a place to finish healing—a place where it's safe to be yourself. If you go off on your own, you'll have to hide yourself."

"Hurr," the dog muttered to himself, the faint hint of snarl on his muzzle.

"Yes," Mariska told him. "People will probably hurt you if they discover the changes Eduard made to you. It's stupid, but they'll be frightened. It's the same for us. It's why Eduard and his people come after us."

Ciobaka gazed at them with wise almond-shaped eyes and trod silently to the nearest tree. He curled up in a small red-ochre ball and tucked his nose over his tail, watching them—watching as Ruger stepped over to touch his head between those big scoop ears. "If we don't come out of that place, there will be others like us who come looking," he said. "It might take a couple of days—but they'll help you, if you let them."

Ciobaka squeezed his eyes closed and stayed that way, and Ruger gave his neck a final rub, glancing at Mariska. ::When I find Forakkes…:: he growled silently, leaving the threat unfinished.

::When *we* find Forakkes,:: she corrected him, and gave him that toothy grin again. ::By the time I hit the ground in that bunker, I'll be bear. And this time, I'll be warded and shielded and not fighting his damned amulet.::

::And you won't be alone.::

No. She wouldn't be alone.

Once they moved, they did it swiftly—assuming that Forakkes had eyes on them, and that if he hadn't already noticed them, he'd do so imminently.

But finding the solar tubes was easier said than done. Stout, dull little plastic domes only fourteen inches in diameter, they blended with the forest floor, obscured by brush and shadow. Mariska and Ruger quartered the area in a quick pattern with no success, until Mariska sent him a shrug. ::Well, maybe we'll bring them out to us after all.::

::If they'd seen us, they'd already be out here—or Forakkes would have sent a working at us.::

::Maybe we've made a dent in their operations after all.::

Ruger snorted out loud. "There aren't as many as there were before we got here, that's for sure." But he couldn't hide his awkward steps or the faint glisten of drainage from his wound, and Mariska knew the truth—no matter Ruger's restored healing ability and what he'd done with it, there wasn't quite as much of them to go around, either.

Dull red-ochre streaked across the ground, a lithe four-footed shape at full speed. Ciobaka ran straight to an area of complex brush and shadow, dug furiously at the ground, and silently streaked away again, his terror displayed in every line of his body.

::He's seen too much,:: Mariska said, instantly heading for the spot the dog had marked.

::With Forakkes, there's too damned much to see.:: Ruger took the bear as he ran—a smooth, blinding transition to Kodiak. But once at the solar tube cover, he stiffened to raise a shaggy brown head, ears swiveling tightly. ::Shields,:: he said shortly, and Mariska strengthened hers in instant response.

She had no idea what kind of working Forakkes threw at them—only that it hit them both with an audible sense of sucking energy, distorting her shields and making Ruger grumble out loud. She fought the impulse to crouch and cover, making herself small and tight. It wouldn't help, and she'd only be more vulnerable—and of less use to Ruger. She forced herself to lean into the working, shaping her shields into a prow the working might more easily flow around, while Ruger shook his broad head and curled his pale muzzle in a snarl and reached out to the skylight with one massive foot, four-inch claws, and brute strength.

The plastic ripped away from the roof, flashing with a twist of tortured metal and bringing half the sky tube out with it. Mariska pushed forward in anticipation as a second effort peeled away a section of roof, exposing a structure beam. The Core working faded into little more than the stench of corruption around them, and she braced herself for another even as she assessed the facility below, shoring up her shields.

Instead, she heard a shouted command and looked up to see two men emerging from a camouflaged doorway— this time no longer obscured by the working that had hidden it on their first approach the day before.

Only a day.

"Guns," she told Ruger under her breath. Only the surge of energy beside her—and then his hand on her arm—told her that he'd taken back the human; she glanced to the hole he'd made and didn't hesitate, crouching to grab the exposed beam and swing down into the open space below.

She had the quick impression of the arching Quonset ceiling, a structure half the size of the one they'd left behind, crammed with equipment and bunk cubicles and a tiny kitchenette and with a single shelf of small animal cages at one end—and, directly beneath her, the large, barred cage that must have held Ciobaka.

Clever, clever little dog—giving them a way down.

She dropped lightly to the top of that cage, balancing on her toes with narrow bars beneath, and grabbed the side to lever herself over the edge even as Ruger swung down to join her, escaping the first sounds of gunfire from above.

Forakkes scrambled out of his chair; the other man in the room hadn't yet noticed them, his attention pinned to a monitor screen and his finger stabbing. "Ciobaka!" he said. "He's *helping* them!"

"Not for long, he isn't," Forakkes said, fumbling at a locked wooden box on his desk, taking it with him as he retreated—no fear on his face, only fury. But…his *face*… She recoiled from it. Hair a dry, straw-like mixture of black and gray, body bent with age but sinewy with stringy muscle, face smooth of wrinkles but skin leathery…

He looked like nothing so much as a living mummy.

Forakkes sneered at her. "Look good and hard," he said. "*You* did this to me. *Sentinels.* Your damned Maks Altán. Do you think I'll let you live?"

"I don't think you'll have any choice," Ruger said, as if he wasn't holding his side as he straightened.

From above came a few brief curses as the Core minions reached the torn roof and assessed the situation. Forakkes snapped, "Hold your fire! You'll hit the equipment."

More cursing; one man lodged himself in the hole

with his gun propped and ready but his finger over the trigger guard; the shadows of the others disappeared. *Headed back this way?*

"It's over," Ruger told Forakkes. "Not even your Core wants you out here now. Hand over that lab coat."

Forakkes' expression might have been a smile; it was hard to tell. "They'll change their minds when I prove my work," he said, and indicated the coat in question, festooned with pockets inside and out. "Which, as it happens, I'm just about to do." He jerked his attention to his assistant as the man made a strangled, fearful noise and dove for a desk drawer in desperation, fumbling to snatch out a pistol. "Stop, you idiot—!"

The man fired a wild shot as Mariska dove for him, covering the intervening space with a swiftness that visibly shocked him. She slammed his wrist against the long computer bench and twisted around him, still gripping the arm and neatly flipping him to the ground, jamming her foot on his neck—not with the killing force she could have used, but enough to make him gurgle with fear.

Forakkes clutched the box, his fingers working the latch but his glare on Ruger. "And you Sentinels wonder why we hate you so. How is it fair that any given people should have such speed, such strength? How is it *not* fair that we who know of it should work to balance the power?"

"Oh, boo-hoo," Mariska muttered, yanking the assistant up to his knees and half walking, half dragging him over to what had been Ciobaka's cage. She shoved him inside and would have snapped the lock closed—but it had no key. She glanced at Ruger. ::We might need it for the rest of them—::

"Leave it," he agreed, and she immediately moved to the nearby building entrance—just like the one at their

bunker, a tunnel that curved outside the bunker itself—
to press herself against the wall. *Waiting.* Ruger circled,
putting Forakkes between the entrance and himself, and
spared a glance at the caged assistant. "If he tries to come
out, kill him." He bared his teeth at the man—no longer
Ruger the healer, but Ruger the bear.

Angry bear.

But neither of them expected what Forakkes did
next—darting to that same cage with surprising alac-
rity, yanking the door open to slip inside…slamming it
closed behind him. He jammed the box under his arm to
free his hands and deftly slid the lock into place, clicking
it closed. From within the cage, he smiled his leathery
smile, his exposed teeth a sickly yellow and his gums
receded nearly to bone.

He held up the key.

Mariska bit back a curse, and Forakkes laughed.

It had an edge, that laughter…something not quite
right. She wondered suddenly if his brain had turned as
leathery as his skin—and to judge by Ruger's narrowed
eyes, he had his own suspicions.

But he didn't linger out in the open to consider them,
moving fast as he joined Mariska against the wall, flanking the doorway. ::He's not thinking this through. All we
need to do is find one of their guns, and that cage offers
him no safety at all.::

She nodded at the entry, and at the rustle of movement within. ::I believe some of those guns are coming
our way right now.::

"None of that!" Forakkes snapped. "Do you think I
can't tell what you're doing? If you want to talk, do it
out loud."

Mariska tipped her head at him, an invitation. *Or what?*
In the tunneled entry, the movement stopped, leaving

only a hint of erratic breathing. Ruger shifted, just a little more ready than he had been, and Mariska prepared for Forakkes to cry a warning to his people. His assistant might have done so, had he not been watching Forakkes, holding back—all too clearly unwilling to take an initiative with the man right there.

But Forakkes himself had other things on his mind. He worked the latch on the solid wooden box he'd grabbed, flipping the lid open as he jammed the container at his assistant. The man grabbed it out of self-defense, staggering back a step until he hit the bars—and the wall—behind him.

If Mariska hadn't been watching, she wouldn't have seen Forakkes flick his gaze at the entry—wouldn't have seen his sly satisfaction.

But she was, and she did.

::He thinks we don't know they're coming up on us,:: Ruger sent to her, just as aware.

Had come up on them was more like it. Those in the tunnel weren't so much biding their time as they were working up their nerve. *You shouldn't have hesitated,* Mariska thought at them. She sent Ruger not words, but ferocity. Readiness. She sensed more than saw his bared teeth of response.

But Forakkes shook his head at those in the tunnel, a barely perceptible command made sinister by the glitter in his dark eyes. He indicated the sprawling security monitor—cradling an amulet for display in his other hand. "A thing of beauty," he said. "I would say that your new four-legged friend shouldn't have helped you if he wanted to avoid this, but the truth is it was inevitable."

Mariska risked a glance at the monitor—at the giant grainy webcam image displayed there.

Ciobaka.

He crept at the edge of camera view, reluctance and fear in the form of a dog.

::He's coming to help!:: Mariska said, startled into a sharp intake of breath. Ruger's ferocity took on a grim tone, washing against her.

"Inevitable, but convenient that this step serves my purpose at this particular moment," Forakkes said. "Now, when this happens to you, you'll understand what it is, and why. Your fellow Sentinels won't have that privilege."

Ruger growled, so deep and low in his chest that Mariska barely perceived it at all.

Forakkes lifted the amulet and briefly closed his eyes. Mariska didn't want to look—she *really* didn't want to look—but she couldn't *not*.

And so she saw Ciobaka writhing on the ground, flinging dried pine needles in a cloud of dust…biting at his legs.

"He's far too clever with those thumbs," Forakkes said, tossing the dulled amulet aside. "And you've seen the results of my experiments, haven't you? Of course you have. No doubt you understand their brilliance. Maybe you've even figured out the whole point."

Ruger didn't respond, but Mariska's inner eye immediately flashed to what she'd seen of the caged animals.

"He'll do without dewclaws," Ruger told her, his voice low. Inside the tunnel, the nearest minion took a few deep breaths. *Getting ready…*

"And possibly without the ability to vocalize," Forakkes agreed, plucking another amulet free of its padded slot in the box. "But not likely without large sections of his brain that he'll lose after this."

"Just leave him," Mariska said, unable to stop herself.

Forakkes smiled. It didn't strike Mariska as quite sane. "I think we both know that I can't leave a *talking dog* out in the world." He lifted the amulet, and his gaze flickered—and the first tunnel minion struck, his altered breath the only warning.

Warning enough for Sentinel ears. He emerged with a gun on the rise and Mariska grabbed that wrist, wrenching the weapon away and using his resistance as an anchor—pivoting and driving upward with the heel of her hand not once but twice. His nose crunched, his mashed lip spurted blood—another shove and he flailed backward into the tunnel to crash into those who waited. Mariska got a scant glimpse of the other two men as she threw herself back at the wall and out of the line of fire.

Within the tunnel, the man sputtered and swore and groaned, and his companions made a great deal of noise as they dragged him away.

::Two more,:: she told Ruger. ::But I don't think they'll make it that easy again.::

He sent assent without words. He hadn't moved, trusting her to handle it while he divided his gaze between Forakkes and the monitor, his cold fury splashing against her.

Forakkes didn't seem dismayed by his minion's failure. He simply waited until they were watching him before he raised his hand and triggered the second amulet with a flourish—but Mariska refused to look at the monitor. She knew what she'd find; she knew she couldn't do anything about it. She wasn't about to give Forakkes the satisfaction.

Forakkes tossed the second amulet aside; it landed with a *clunk* and rolled out of the cage. "As I thought," he said, as inside the tunnel, someone thought himself stealthy, though Mariska could smell his fear. "If you could stop me, you would have done it by now."

"Or maybe we just think you're right," Ruger said.

"Maybe it's just no good to have a talking dog out in the world." He smiled tightly at Forakkes. "On occasion, the mutual interests of the Core and the Sentinels overlap."

"Would you have him dead, then?"

Hell, no! Red-ochre dog, caught up in something he couldn't understand and didn't deserve. *Back off, Forakkes!*

Ruger's anger reached her with the same undertone; in this, she had no doubt they felt the same. He shifted, a barely discernible gathering of intent. ::Mari—::

::I have your back,:: she told him.

Not that she had any idea of his intent. It didn't matter. Whatever it was, she'd have his back.

Forakkes plucked up a third amulet. "Dead dog," he said, "it is."

::You have my back,:: Ruger said, by way of warning—but not much, as his eyes rolled back and he slumped against the wall. The next tunnel minion took his cue from Forakkes—only this man came out with his pistol already aimed, firing the moment he cleared the tunnel.

She'd heard him coming; she dropped down, crouching well below the gun at chest level. He blew through six shots in quick succession without emerging the rest of the way, and Mariska hooked an arm into the tunnel, yanking one ankle out from under him. He fell hard, the wind whooping from his lungs.

Mariska cast only the quickest of glances back at the monitor—Ciobaka lay panting on his side, but not writhing, not dying—and then at Ruger. He pushed back against the curving metal wall, his hands flat to it and his jaw hard, his eyes flickering with movement beneath closed lids.

And Forakkes...

Forakkes was furious. Furious and baffled.

Unexpected pride surged through Mariska. She had no idea how Ruger thwarted the man—how he saved Ciobaka from that final amulet—but her job was still clear enough. *Got your back,* she thought, keeping it only to herself, and leaped up for the tunnel—going straight to the bear on the way and landing on the man she'd just taken down. She grasped his head in her clever bear paws and took him out, a mere ripple of strength—twisting just *so* in a very human way and then raising her gaze to the remaining two men, horrified and scrambling away from her. They stumbled over one another, only one gun left between them and no teamwork at all, and Mariska came on.

Got your back, Ruger Bear.

Chapter 23

Core corruption slapped against Ruger with a hard hand—another wave of it, another working, piling up on the one that had stolen Ciobaka's voice. The final working to kill the young dog, taking away all the changes to his mind...leaving him in pieces, just as Forakkes had killed all his previous experiments.

Just as he meant to kill Ruger and Mariska, ripping from them the very essence of the bear, and the way he ultimately meant to trigger his working on every Sentinel in the region.

The wild, yipping howl of a bereft wild dog, the wash of a vile stench... A hollow huffing sound, followed by a clacking, the surge of fear...a tremendous explosion. And then an entire chorus of grief, animal skins fluttering to the ground like sodden laundry. Wolf and bear, panther and boar, wildcat and stoat and deer. Crumpled up and discarded, and a nation of grief splashing in to wash it all away—

Ruger couldn't reach Forakkes—not physically. He couldn't *stop* Forakkes.

But the amulet working was, at its most basic, an *unhealing*.

What was Ruger, if not *healing*?

Got your back, Ruger Bear.

The whisper trickled through his awareness as he slipped into the cool, clear energies of healing—the ones that had always been there, and were now once again waiting for his touch, his direction.

The ones he now threw out ahead of the working to absorb the *unhealing* as it came on. Not just a wall of energy, but a whirling dance between the working and the healing—a race to keep the tumbling Core energies matched with equal energy from moment to moment. Ruger lost himself to it, spinning and diving and weaving of himself an antidote to the working. He shuddered in the reverberations of Ciobaka's terrified pain when a strand of power slipped through; he redoubled his efforts and watched the working fade, slowly losing its momentum and density...

Until it merely licked at Ruger's gathered energies, faint surges of destruction going nowhere.

He gave the working a final swipe of healing power and watched it dissipate completely.

When he opened his eyes, he had to blink away sweat. The facility smoldered with the stench of suppressed Core workings, closing down around him in resentful, sullen failure; Ruger straightened on legs that felt not nearly as strong as they should. *Not without price.*

From the tunnel, Mariska's bear coughed a roar of warning; a man screamed, and then screamed again—and then choked off into silence.

Forakkes glared at him from within the cage, his hand clenched so tightly around the burnt-out amulet that Ruger wondered those old joints could take the strain.

Older than they'd ever guessed, at that—old enough
so the age plucked at healer's senses sharp from recent
use. He followed that leaden demand—and he found that
which he'd only begun to suspect. *Layers of twisted scars
in body and mind, layers of corrupting energy, fused to
thought and will.*

"Enough," he told the man, his voice rasping with the
strain of what he'd done. "End this, Forakkes. You're
not well."

Forakkes stood straighter, his leathered face gone
even stiffer, even less natural. "You're a fool if you think
you've weakened me."

Ruger shook his head in a weary gesture. "I didn't say
weak. I said *not well*. All the years you've been working
on these projects, did we ever even come close to catching
up with you before now? All the loyalty your men have
given you…did you ever fail them before now? All you
had to do these past few days was sit tight, and instead
you threw away everything you accomplished before.
I'm a healer, Forakkes. Do you think you can hide from
me what's happened to you these past months? Workings to preserve yourself, failed. Workings to rejuve-
nate yourself—"

"Have performed perfectly!" Forakkes snapped.

Ruger said nothing, looking at the caricature of
humanity before him. Then he caught the eye of the
assistant—his hair cut more tightly than most, his silver
jewelry less ostentatious. "If you were making the choice
today, would you follow this man into defiance of your
drozhar and Septs Prince?"

The man looked not at Ruger, but at Forakkes, his
shoulders gone stiff. "I refuse to give credence to that
question with a response."

"You see?" Forakkes snatched a final amulet from

the box—one that sat apart from the others, strung on two cords connected at intervals by complex knots: an amulet of power and complexity. "Or maybe you don't. But you *will*."

::*Mari!*:: Ruger threw energy to his personal shields; he checked his wards.

And he knew, with gut-deep certainty, that they wouldn't be enough. Not to protect him from this amulet. He knew Mariska's wouldn't be enough.

Mariska appeared in the mouth of the tunnel, raising herself briefly to her hind legs in a threat—sending him a wordless sense of query and frustration at the sight of Forakkes, safe in the cage.

::Just be here,:: he told her, and maybe some of his desperation slipped through his awareness. *Outmatched.* They were healer and bodyguard, not shielding specialists or warding wizards. ::*Watch my back.*::

And then she was Mari again, short and strong and determined, and her hand slid into his. "You're not alone," she said, low enough so Forakkes would have to strain to hear it. "Never again."

Never again. Ruger tightened his hand around hers, drinking in the strength of her.

Forakkes lifted the amulet, and smiled until his lips stretched tightly over his teeth. "And so you lose."

Ruger didn't wait for the first flush of corrupted energies; he dove deeply into healing energies—a fresh, clear wash of golds and soothing blues and deep greens painting his mind's eye in a whirl of watercolor existence. He only distantly realized he shouldn't have left the rest of him standing against the wall—just as distantly felt Mariska catch him, propping him against her shoulder while she guided him down and then settled beside him, tucking herself close. Cradling him, as much as could be said when he sat so much larger than she.

The amulet working rushed up against them, slamming into their shields—thinning them and warping them and making Mariska gasp at the solidity of the blow.

Ruger floundered in it, the healing energies turned to chaos under attack by the same working that tugged against his bear-fingers, clawing around his soul to tear away at the essence of him. Gold turned muddy, blue turned dark…green bled away.

He couldn't heal *this* after it was done. There'd be nothing left of him by then. Nothing left of Mariska, and soon enough nothing left of the Sentinels at all—

::*Not alone,*:: Mariska told him, pushing into his turmoil. ::*Take me, too.*:: She cried out and twisted against him, her pain echoing threefold through Ruger. He felt it through his healer, he felt it through their connection, and he felt it in his own body—until they were no longer sitting together but crumpled together, and her moans reverberated against his skin.

He flung healing at the working, making of it a blunt barrier, nothing of finesse or direction. It gave him only enough surcease to realize that the working stabbed through such undirected force with ease, and inside him the bear roared.

::Take me, too,:: Mariska sent to him, a mere whisper. ::*Be not alone.*::

He didn't understand; he couldn't. She was no healer. She couldn't combine her efforts with his. She couldn't be what she wasn't—

Idiot.

She could be what she *was*.

And if it wasn't enough, then they would die together— completely and fully together.

He bought them an instant, shoving out another wave of what should have been healing. And in that instant, he reached out and wrapped his soul around her—accepting her, taking her in.

Beneath him, she gave a small sob—it might have been relief. And then the sense of her burst through him—fierce, sturdy Mariska Bear, a flood of warmth and strength. He spun it into himself, absorbing it—

Clean, fresh healing energies infused with the bear—infused with two *bears, given new tooth. Bold, primal energy surging forward to meet the enemy, ignoring the stench and the rake of pain to swipe at darting power, leaping forth in anticipation of clawing destruction—roaring into the throat of devastation.*

The working swirled, the currents of it disrupted into billowing chaos. Ruger herded it, surrounding it—driving it back and back and back again, until the energies turned darting and frantic and in search of outlet. In search of *undoing.*

Until they suddenly surged away from him, spinning tightly into a cyclonic whirl that swallowed itself from the bottom up, sucking away into nothing on the tail of a hoarse scream.

And then Ruger was alone again—

Except he wasn't. There inside himself, Mariska's essence overlapped with his, exhausted and quiescent, a gentle intertwining nudge. His skin tingled with it; his body gently purred with it.

But only until he finished passing out.

Mariska woke to chaos and snarls.

"Dead," said a voice that wasn't quite in the same room. "Torn to pieces. I think one of our bears has been here."

"Here," said another, pitched low and whisky-rough, mingling with the sounds of a steady tenor growl. "They are still here."

Jet—!

Mariska forced her eyes open, astonished at the effort of it.

"She wakes," Jet said, standing just inside the entrance with curiously passive body language and speaking into the tunnel.

"Dammit," Heckle said. *Harrison—free!* "I'm coming in there!"

"Do not," Jet told him without moving—nothing but her gaze, angled down and away from Mariska now.

Mariska saw him, then. *Ciobaka.* Crouching not far away with tail fully tucked—thumbless, voiceless, but his eyes full of intelligence behind gleaming white teeth and snarling lips. His message couldn't have been more clear: *I am terrified and I think I might die here but you had best not come any closer anyway or I will BITE!*

"Ciobaka," she said, and was surprised that it came out as no more than a whisper. She nudged Ruger, who lay mostly on top of her, reminding her that he was in fact a big, big man and too damned heavy when he wasn't wrangling his own weight. She couldn't even get a good look at him, not from this angle. "Ruger—"

Jet crouched without coming any closer, a fluid movement during which she deliberately angled her body away from Ciobaka. "His eyes moved," she told Mariska, which was her way of offering reassurance.

Mariska gave up on subtlety and *shoved.* Ruger startled into full awareness, shoving away with some vehemence in his effort to scramble awake and ready. *"Oof,"* she said, as he righted himself to kneel with his back against the wall. "Do you *want* to get bitten?" But she could see him now—see his confusion as he took in his surroundings, his relief as he saw Jet, his eyes widen as his gaze landed on Ciobaka. It was enough to put a glee-fully sharp edge in her voice as she added, "And I *don't* mean by Ciobaka."

He reached down to pull her upright, and hardly gently. Nor was it gentle when he hauled her in close and caught her up in a fierce embrace, burying his face in her hair and holding her so tightly she could scarcely breathe—and at that, she never wanted to let go of him. "Mari," he said, as if no one else in this facility had Sentinel ears. "Mari, *love*—"

She did the only thing she could, crushed up against him, the bear-and-man scent of him enveloping her as much as the embrace. She *did* bite him. Right on the meat along his shoulder, her small, strong teeth firmer than a polite scrape and gentler than the bear.

Ruger made a coughing sound; his body shook beneath her. She froze—and only belatedly realized he was laughing. *Laughing.* She jerked herself free of him to scowl from only inches away, as if his beautiful face wasn't drawn with strain and her hand wasn't damp from contact with his draining wound. A profound scowl, with eyes narrowed and mouth clamped—and one that lasted only until he pulled her back for the fiercest, most possessive kiss in the world, one that didn't last nearly long enough and that left her gasping when he broke away.

Jet's voice came as dry as a wolf could manage, which was plenty dry enough. "You are well, then?"

Mariska sucked in a deep breath and leaned against the wall beside Ruger, sliding down to go cross-legged. Ruger scrubbed his hands over his face and pushed off against his thighs—standing, but only by dint of the wall still at his back. "We're alive," he said, and looked down at Ciobaka, who still kept a wary eye on Jet.

"Ciobaka," he said. "Brave of you, son. This is Jet. She's a friend, and she's wolf. Not like us, a human who takes the wolf. But a wolf who has taken the human, because of what Forakkes once did to her."

"Ciobaka," Jet greeted him. "When I am wolf, you may sniff me."

Ciobaka looked at them all, his stiff tail drooping, his big scoop ears losing loft. He backed an uncertain step, then turned and slunk away.

"It's too much for him," Jet said, understanding better than them all. "He will be back."

Harrison emerged from the tunnel—dirty, ragged, and his expression simmering with lingering anger. Hardly the mild amulet assistant they'd left behind. His expression cleared somewhat as he saw Ruger and Mariska; she pushed to her feet, ignoring her own staggering clumsiness. "Heckle! What about Ian? Sandy? Did you hear from Maks? Has Katie got any news?"

"We all felt the changes," Jet said. "Too many things happening in this spot, and it stunk." She meant literally, from the wrinkle in her nose. "Maks stayed with Katie— she is not well with this. Annorah sent help and I brought them to the other bunker. Then I followed you out."

"The rain slowed us." Harrison's mouth went flat. "We don't know about Ian or Sandy yet." Then his eyes narrowed. "Did you call me *Heckle?*"

"Maybe," Mariska said cautiously—but her attention caught on movement in the cage, just as Ciobaka raised his muzzle to lift a lip in that direction. Ruger made a wary sound in his throat, started to move, and hitched over his side, a startled grunt of pain replacing his intent. She dropped beside him, bracing him—but kept her eyes on the cage.

Forakkes sprawled on his back, one arm outstretched and the amulet just beyond his reach, the cord still tangled in his fingers. His stringy musculature had gone not just lax, but soft; his hair clung to his skull in a wispy, gentle white. The angle made it hard to see his face, but Mariska had the impression of pale skin, wrinkles on wrinkles.

The assistant had flattened himself up against the back of the cage, the amulet box clutched against his torso with the lid still up—and one hand reaching within.

"Don't!" Mariska told him. "Ruger can counter the workings before they reach us—or didn't you notice your boss?"

"What—" The man swallowed hard, and made himself straighten. "What did you do to him?"

Ruger snorted gently. His voice held strain; he eased himself back down to sit against the wall again. "I healed him," he said, and looked at the hand he'd had pressed against his side. He would have surreptitiously wiped the fresh blood against his leg had Mariska not grabbed his wrist and taken a good hard look. "It's okay," he murmured.

"It's *not,*" she said with some asperity. Jet eyed him, too, her entire dark-clad, long, lean body coming to attention, her expression knowing.

Ruger only shook his head. "It will be."

The assistant didn't follow the byplay—didn't even notice it. His hand tightened around the amulet; the box shook slightly in his grasp. "What do you mean, you *healed* him? He's dead!"

"Did you *see* him before?" Mariska asked. "Did you really call that *living?*"

Ruger scrubbed a weary hand over his face, and

Mariska glared at the assistant—but Ruger rested that hand over hers when she would have spoken.

"You must have known he was not truly whole," Jet said, taking a step toward the man, her curiosity as honest as ever. "Find the key and come out of there. What Ruger did before, he can do again; your amulets are useless."

Mariska *hoped* he could do again. But then, she was the only one touching him, feeling the faint tremor beneath her hand as that big body slowly gave way before the insults of the past two days. She dared no more than a glance at him—seeing the strain in his jaw and around his eyes, the increasing list in his upright position. *No weakness, not in front of this particular Core minion.* The man had to believe what Jet said—had to believe that further attack would be pointless.

Ruger shook his head at the man—responding to both his fear and his defiance. "Forakkes was so tangled in workings it was hard to tell where he ended and they began." And even though Mariska felt the hitch in his breath and moved to position her knee so it blocked the man's view of that growing trickle of blood, Ruger's voice stayed even. "When I stopped that final amulet working—"

"The Amulet of Undoing," the man said, a reverence mixed with his bitter tone.

"—I did it with healing."

The man shook his head. Not Sentinel, not understanding.

But Mariska did. "Ruger healed us faster than the amulet could harm. He *healed* the working all the way back to where it started, and the splash-over must have reached Forakkes' amulets. It's what we do, you know. Heal. Protect. Preserve."

"You *kill,*" the man said, a wild look in his eye and

all his attention on Ruger. "You took away an old man's support workings—a master! You think I trust that I'm safe with you? You think I care if I die with you, if that's the way it has to be?"

Mariska snorted, loud enough to draw the man's startled intention away from Ruger suddenly drained of color, his breath coming faster, shallower. A man about to pass out, human enough after all. "Get over yourself," she said with no little scorn. "Forakkes wouldn't be dead if he hadn't triggered that amulet." She looked at the one the man held, knowing it took little more than a trained twist of will to handle a prepared amulet—and this man surely had more than that at his disposal.

Jet knew it better than any of them. "If you try to hurt us with amulets," she said, "Ruger will stop you. And instead of returning you to your people, we will shoot you through the bars with one of your own guns."

::Mari,:: Ruger said, and his inner voice sounded faint; his eyes flickered, as though only strength of will kept them from rolling up. ::Mari, I'm trying—::

Trying not to faint, she thought, and closed her hand on his shoulder, fingers digging in hard enough so he jerked with surprise, growling, and let her know she'd pay for this one. She caught the man's gaze and held it, hard. "Unlock the damned door, because we've got other things to do than watch you decide to go out in an illconceived blaze of stupid!"

The man looked at her—looked at the amulets in the box, his face contorted, his decision made. He upended the whole box, amulets clanking to the ground, twisting and tangling around their knotted cords, and fell on his knees beside them, digging his hands into the bunch of them.

Oh, hell, he's going to trigger them all—

There was no way Ruger could fend off such a glut of workings—and then they would be dead, and no one would know what had happened here; no one from brevis would have the chance to decipher the amulets, or to formulate defenses against them.

Oh, hell.

::Mari—:: The silent words held a gasp to them, a desperation. She dug her fingers in, glancing at Harrison and the gun he held, wondering if he was fast enough, ready enough, to pull the trigger before the man triggered the amulets.

Or if the man would be able to trigger the things even if he'd been shot.

Ciobaka yawned.

It was loud and ridiculous, with a long curl of rising sound at the end. The man startled, and for that instant his attention split.

::Mari—:: Ruger said, and this time she heard the request in it, and finally she understood.

::You aren't alone,:: she told him, responding to need—knowing that now, of all times, when he sat in the enemy's house with his wounds bleeding and unconsciousness pushing at him, he needed someone at his back. More than that—he needed everything she could give him. As the sharp stench of triggering amulets cut the air, as the assistant clutched at the pile of amulets, his eyes squeezed closed and his lips peeled back from his teeth in fear, a noise rising in his throat as though he charged to battle—

She opened herself wide, and suddenly there he was—wrapping around her and through her and leaning on her from the inside out—surging forward into one final effort.

The assistant's eyes rolled up in his head and he slid

bonelessly against the bars, the amulet dropping from his grasp.

In the silence that followed, Harrison lowered the gun and cast Ruger a sardonic look. "Tell me that was healing."

"He's tired," Ruger said shortly. His presence slowly receded from within Mariska, leaving her with only what he'd been trying to hide—the unutterable ache in his side, the gripping weariness—until that, too, withdrew back into Ruger alone. His voice faded. "He needed to… sleep. So he is."

And then, finally, his eyes rolled back.

Mariska dropped to catch him as he slumped to the side. "Sleep, Ruger Bear," she told him, holding him close. "You won't be alone."

Chapter 24

So much confusion.

Ruger heard it dimly, starting with Annorah's burst of excitement upon reaching through to them for the first time. She burbled about Ian and Sandy—*They're found! They're alive!*—and that the recovery team was already heading for Maks and Katie's cabin where the chopper waited. She told them the team would be coming for Ruger next.

No, he thought, and thought it hard. *Not yet. I need to—*

He hadn't sent that thought anywhere; he hadn't the focus. But Mariska was right *there,* and she knew—and once she took up the argument, he relaxed.

He knew she'd go after what she wanted. Or in this case, what *he* wanted.

Not to go back to brevis. Not just yet. Not when it would tear him away from Mariska and into the whirl of debriefings and brevis medical and the potential that she'd be rushed off to another assignment before he ever…

Before he got what he *really* wanted.

The argument circled around him; it grew to include Ciobaka's fate, and Jet's voice rose with the certainty of the dog's sentience and his ability to make his own choices. There came the noise of new arrivals, the small victory of acquiring the key to the cage, recovering the amulets and the assistant. The swirl of activity happened around him but not to him; it circled him without touching him.

He was tired, that was all. Way too tired to open his eyes, to join in the fluster, to argue his own case. For if nothing else, a healer's body knew when it was time to shut down and *heal*.

Ian and Sandy, safe. The bad guys stopped. The working that would have killed them all, stripping them of all they were…that was stopped, too. And Mariska stood watch over him, trusting his instincts over her own and standing her ground on it.

It was okay to sleep.

Mariska plucked one last berry from the sprinkled confectioner's sugar on her plate and popped it into her mouth, licking away the juice and powdered sweetness, slanting a quick glance at Ruger just to see if he was watching. Really, just to make sure she'd done the right thing, keeping them here in the cabin together as he'd wanted instead of sending him down to Tucson with the others.

He lay propped against pillows at the head of the king bed in their cottage, his stomach full of comfort food that was more about those berries than the French toast beneath. "I told you I'd make it to this bed sooner or later."

Yes. The right thing. He looked good. To Mariska's eyes, he looked just plain perfect—every ridge of muscle, every flex and sinuous movement. Not his normally indomitable self of size and strength, but getting there, with most of the color back in his cheeks—the drawn look gone, the gray undertones gone. *Healer again.*

Mariska stood and stretched, her own stomach full and happy. Her shirt—a tank top she wore only during her downtime, luxuriously without a bra at that—pulled up over her belly, and she tugged it down, giving him the eye. "Saw you looking."

"Do it again," he suggested.

She put a brisk tone in her voice. "You're hurt."

"I heal fast."

She snorted, and snagged her dishes from the foot of the bed, heading for the kitchen to leave them soaking. She heard him yawn in her wake, and smiled to herself. She'd woken him with that breakfast after fifteen hours of sleep. She imagined he'd done some healing during that time, at that.

He rolled out of bed and rummaged around while she headed back out to the front porch—homey noises of water running and a toothbrush clanking into the glass on the bathroom sink, the toilet flushing...

Ciobaka lay between the roots of a pine, the perfect shaded hollow for a nap. He lifted his head on her approach—and though he probably didn't mean to do it, the tip of his tail wagged, too.

"Do you need anything?" she asked him—though she'd dumped a fresh raw turkey into the yard the night before, and figured him to be fed for a couple of days. Jet had put a big metal mixing bowl in the shade of the porch for her own water supply, and now it served Ciobaka.

He didn't so much as flick an ear at her. He had no voice at all any longer—no whining, no barking, not even a snarl behind the expressive curl of his lip—but she'd had no trouble understanding him so far. Especially when it came to the very salient point that he would not voluntarily leave Ruger. She understood the feeling.

Too bad she was a Colorado bear.

The other cabin sat empty of Sentinels but full of equipment and still serving as a nominal sleeping base. Ian wouldn't be back even if he recovered as quickly and fully as expected; he had his hands full with the amulet stash. Sandy had asked for a teaching assignment once she went active again, and Harrison was still at the site with the new team, directing the action with vigor and a new confidence.

She and Ruger had been left in peace—and now Mariska had a conversation to face.

She returned to the cabin to find Ruger back on the bed, poking at his newly recovered bag of healing tricks. Packets of herbs sat beside him, along with several empty vials. She gave him a wary look. "You're not making more of that restorative, are you?"

"Yes," he said, and with some satisfaction. "That's exactly what I'm doing. Want some?"

"No," she said, without hesitation or regret. Not that she needed any such thing—he'd left her flush with health back when he'd healed them both at the fallen tree, and sleep had done the rest. But then, she didn't expect her mouth to keep moving. "What I want—" she started, before she got herself stopped.

Ruger looked up, his fingers closing over a pinch of herbs.

Well, hell. Go for it, then. "What I *want*," she said, "is to transfer to Southwest Brevis. Nick asked me."

He put the herbs aside.

"What I *want*," she said, "is to stay here with you. I want to know there's always someone at your back, and I want it to be me."

He stilled, holding her gaze with such intensity that it took all her courage to continue. "What I *want*," she said, "is to butt heads with you until we're both wrinkled old little Sentinels with blunted fangs and a million grandchildren, and to sleep beside you and fall into that dip your great big body makes in the bed, and to always have my hands on that great big body while I'm at it."

Ruger eyed her so long that her heart beat triple-time in her chest—doubting herself, doubting that *stubborn,* this time, was enough to do the trick. Doubting whether he'd done more than embrace the fleeting moments of their time together, just as he'd told her he intended from the start.

No matter what he'd said in that second bunker. No matter that he'd used the word *love.*

But Ruger spread his arms, and the doubt fled. She threw herself over him, scattering herb packets, and then—because he'd made her wait—she bit his shoulder.

He only laughed and pulled her in for a heated kiss, the tang of toothpaste on his mouth and his hands swiftly finding skin under her shirt. He tugged the hem of it upward and she slipped her arms free, breaking from him only at the last moment when he pulled it over her head, as well. By then her hands had found the fly of his jeans, and he joined her, working the buttons free until she could get her hands on him. More than that—until she could shed her soft sleep pants and settle right down over him, making them both gasp with the suddenness of it.

Then she pulled his hands away from her breasts and slammed them down on either side of his head, holding them there. "You called me bossy once," she said, and nuzzled not-quite-gently at the side of neck.

"I…might have," he said, through enough of a guttering breath the words were hard to understand. Sensations tingled at her, a faint skittering of familiar energies flowing just under her skin, pooling in every sensitive area and flowing outward.

"You called me pushy." She held him down with hips and hands, and gave him a little squeeze from within, nibbling the words along his jaw—reveling as he stiffened in response, recognizing the flood of sensuous delight as what she did to him, what she alone had ever done to him.

"Don't…know what…I was thinking," he managed, if barely.

"Too late for that." She caught his mouth and took it over, letting herself get lost in the sensation of his lips moving against hers, his body straining upward as she held him still, the friction of crisp hair against her breasts and the tight sensation of being filled with both his body and his energies.

When she broke away he would have followed, but she hadn't released his wrists—she held them yet as she bit her way down his neck and chest, firmly enough so he'd have to work to break free, not so firmly that either of them thought she could hold him if he truly wanted to. She licked a flat nipple and then bit that, too. A shudder ran through him, triggering delicious sparks of heat between them; he made a sound of protest, trying to reach for her—and subsiding when she didn't relent.

She closed her eyes to revel in what she'd brought out between them, allowing herself the faintest sob of pleasure. And she moved sooo slowly, so infinitesimally, remembering how he'd responded to the sensation on the ridge. His head fell back and he sucked in air, letting it out on a long groan. "Mari—"

"Shh," she told him. "I'm being pushy. I'm getting my way. And I'm liking it." She rocked over him, just enough to feel the movement—feel the rising tension in him as he swelled within her, his thighs trembling and his hips reaching for her. She closed her eyes, focusing on the thrill of his response—the building pleasure of the subtle friction, the dance of gathering sensation and the awareness that energies spiraled between them, just outside the edge of any control at all.

He made a despairing noise, touched with laughter. *"Mari—"*

"Shh," she told him again, loving his strength beneath her, the strain of his body and his willingness to play with her. She gave him inches of movement now, enough to up the ante without quite giving way to it. "I *like* being pushy."

His groan came in earnest, his wrists tensing beneath her hands with restraint, his breath delightfully ragged; the bed dented as his heels pushed into the mattress. She gave him more movement but not enough, feeling the sudden flood of warmth that meant she was close to release, the quiver in her low belly and thighs—in that instant she forgot about moving with any kind of finesse.

Ruger broke. He wrenched free of her hands, leaving her braced on either side of his head as he grabbed her hips and slammed them down, taking himself deep, *deep*—she cried out and so did he, a ragged shout that burst out again and again until they reached for one another, reached for sensation and energy and *being*—breaking through the *Ruger* and *Mari* of it so he suddenly flooded through her in every possible way, and the building heat centered not just at their physical connection but stormed through every bone, every muscle. Fiery sparks took over her mind's eye and then paled out altogether as the rest of her exploded, a wash of pleasure so intense she lost track of which of them felt it.

She would have collapsed against him then, but the

energies held them both in an echoing thrall, his groans against her lingering sobs for breath, a trembling series of aftershocks—until the energy suddenly bloomed hot and full and ecstatic again, entirely unexpected. She cried out in the surprise of it as he gasped, astonished, in her ear—holding her tightly, grinding upward with a groan that sounded as if it had been wrung from the depths of him.

Then she fell against him, damp with sweat and tears and limp with sweet, ebbing warmth.

He closed his arms around her, rolling them until he pressed her back into the mattress and freed himself to plant lingering kisses around her face.

"Mmm," she said eventually. "We should do that again sometime, you think?"

He stilled, even while his breathing still ran ragged, brushing against her ear; he nuzzled her, licking the rim of that ear in a most thoughtful way, offering one last thrust that was more about claiming her than it was about starting anything. He said, his words sounding like a careful choice, "I'm not sure that particular thing is something we can do again soon."

She felt the frisson of alarm he'd so obviously been trying to spare her. "Why? Are you okay?"

He stilled her with a kiss. "I'm fine. And so are you. In fact, you could say…you've been healed of something. In a manner of speaking." He shifted away until he could slide his hand between them—until it rested low on her belly. "Me, too. It wasn't intentional—"

She put her hand over his. *"Healed,"* she said, not knowing it had been necessary—thinking of that last surge of sensation, that sudden warmth—and suddenly understanding. "My protections?" *Their* protections. The very personal warding every capable Sentinel learned, and learned early; the reason their culture was so physically expressive, so physically giving—the reason young Sentinels were so carefully planned. "You healed me of— And you, too?" No conception protections…that amazing, final burst of pleasure, wrung from them both—and still faintly throbbing between them. "Then…that last… *moment*…when we…was that what I think it was? Did we—?"

"Ohh, yes we did." He stroked a hand between her hip bones, resting on the toned muscle under tender skin. "Mariska Bear," he said. "Meet Baby Bear."

The joy of it staggered her, grown hot and fierce and protective in an instant.

"*Our* baby bear," she said, and pulled him back to her, the happy tears of it all running from the corners of her eyes and into her hair. ::We aren't alone.::

Ruger bit her neck. ::We won't ever be alone again.::

* * * * *

Sentinels Mythos Glossary

Long ago and far away, in Roman/Gaulish days, one woman had a tumultuous life—she fell in love with a druid, by whom she had a son; the man was killed by Romans, and she was subsequently taken into the household of a Roman, who also fathered a son on her. The druid's son turned out to be a man of many talents, including the occasional ability to shape-shift, albeit at great cost. (His alter-shape was a wild boar.) The woman's younger son, who considered himself superior in all ways, had none of these earthly powers, and went hunting other ways to be impressive, acquire power. He justified his various activities by claiming he needed to protect the area from his brother, who had too much power to go unchecked...but in the end, it was his brother's family who grew into the Vigilia, now known as the Sentinels, while the younger son founded what turned into the vile Atrum Core.

Sentinels: An organization of power-linked individuals whose driving purpose is to protect and nurture the earth—as befitting their druid origins—while also keeping watch on the activities of the Atrum Core.

Vigilia: The original Latin name for the Sentinels, discarded in recent centuries under Western influence.

Brevis Regional: HQ for each of the Sentinel regions.

Consul: The leader of each brevis region.

Adjutant: The consul's executive officer.

Aeternus contego: The strongest possible ward, tied to the life force of the one who sets it and broken only at that person's death. In *Jaguar Night,* Meghan Lawrence places one of these on Fabron Gausto, reflecting any workings he performs back on himself.

Vigilia adveho: A Sentinel mental long-distance call for help.

Monitio: A warning call.

Nexus: The Sentinel who acts as a central point of power control—such as for communications, wards or power manipulation.

Atrum Core: An ethnic group founded by and sired by the Roman's son, their basic goal is to acquire power in as many forms as possible, none of which is natively their own; they claim to monitor and control the "nefarious" activities of the Sentinels.

Amulets: The process through which the Core inflicts its workings of power on others, having gathered and stored (and sometimes stolen) the power from other sources.

Drozhar: The Atrum Core regional prince.

Septs Prince: The Atrum Core prince of princes.

Septs Posse: A *drozhar*'s favored sycophants; can be relied on to do the dirty work.

Sceleratus vis: Ancient forbidden workings based on power drawn from blood, once used by the Atrum Core.

Workings: Workings of power, assembled and triggered via amulets.

HARLEQUIN® NOCTURNE™

NEW YORK TIMES BESTSELLING AUTHOR

HEATHER GRAHAM

THE KEEPERS L.A.: A NOVELLA

—

THE GATEKEEPER

THE GATEKEEPER

Heather Graham

Right when L.A. was on the verge of exploding with underworld activity, the Gryffald cousins were called upon to take their places as keepers of the peace between humans and otherworldly races. Hollywood, they were about to discover, could truly be murder....

Discover *The Keepers: L.A.*: a dark and epic new paranormal quartet, led by *New York Times* bestselling author Heather Graham, debuting in January 2013.

Turn the page now to sink your teeth into *The Gatekeeper,* the sensual and gripping prequel story.

Chapter 1

The City News and Herald
Las Vegas

Are Zombies Roaming the Streets of Las Vegas?

The scene on historic, neon-lit Fremont Street was an unprecedented bloodbath last night as a crowd of several thousand went into a panic, killing and trampling one another as they scrambled to survive a "zombie apocalypse." The frenzy began when the body of Marston Greenwood, thirty-eight, of Portland, Oregon, was discovered in the midst of an Old West display beneath a blazing green neon *Z*. The man appeared to have been partially consumed by some sort of animal, which sent the crowd into a frenzy just as, ironically, the cast of the new *Zombieville* revue appeared on the street for a promotional stunt—with tragically unfortunate timing. While eyewitness accounts vary, one survivor, Sam Nichols of Nunnelly, Tennessee, claims, "Some guy who walked like a mummy and had a serious skin rash stumbled toward a woman just as she discovered the body. She screamed, and the man next to her—I think he was a Texan, 'cuz he was fast on the draw—tried to protect her and shot the zombie or actor or whatever the hell he was. Then people were screaming, running like crazy. There was a giant hairy creature roaring down the road, and I couldn't tell the showgirls from the hookers or the actors. Music was blaring from somewhere, but you could still hear everyone screaming. Looked to me like zombies or werewolves or vampires or God only knows what were ripping through the streets, tearing into everyone."

Despite Nichols's claims and other similar reports, police, state and federal authorities have characterized the tragic incident as a case of mass hysteria in reaction to the combination of an unfortunate death and the ill-timed promotional performance by the *Zombieville* cast. The agencies have joined forces for the continuing investigation into the tragedy. Pending notification of family, the names of the dead are being withheld.

While the area is currently closed, Mayor Herman Langston is assuring the local population and tourists alike that the situation is now under complete control. "Vegas is open for business. Police are out in force, and while we're all shocked and saddened by the horrific events of last evening, we will not be shut down by this tragedy that has been visited upon our exceptional city. The local hotels and casinos are offering free rooms and entertainment, so if you already have plans to visit us, don't change a thing. And if you don't already have plans, then this is the time to make them."

Saxon Kirby stood in the morgue staring at the body of lynching victim Joe Moore. Art Krill, the medical examiner, was carefully removing the rope used to hang the man. He spoke in his dry monotone so the microphone clipped to his chest could record his findings.

"The deceased, identified as Joe Moore, thirty-one, resident of Las Vegas, Nevada, actor by trade, appears to have been in excellent health before his death. X-rays show that the deceased's neck was not broken, and that he died…"

Saxon didn't actually need to be there. There was nothing for him to do but stand around and watch. But he was a cop, a detective, and his presence was expected. He was pretty sure that no one needed a medical degree to figure out that the poor guy was dead, and that he had died slowly, ripping desperately at the rope around his neck as he kicked and fought before finally losing the fight. The smell in the room was rank, but then, hanging wasn't an easy way to die. The body gave in and the bowels emptied. There was no dignity in death. He'd met Joe Moore a few times. He'd been a decent guy and a half-decent actor who'd finally gotten his big break with a role in *Zombieville*.

Yeah, his big break.

Saxon looked out at the stainless steel gurneys filling the room. The statistics were horrifying: nineteen dead and forty-nine in local hospitals, some in critical condition.

He turned and exited the autopsy room, his strides lengthening as he left the morgue. Outside in the bright Las Vegas sunlight, he headed for his car.

"Detective!"

He stopped and turned.

Captain Clark Bower was there. It was unusual to see him at the morgue. Then again, this entire situation was unusual.

Bower was nearing retirement. He was a good captain, but at the moment he just wanted to finish out his last three months in office.

"Captain," Saxon said.

"You're leaving already? I thought—"

"Captain, what am I going to learn here that we don't already know? Joe Moore was hanged. Eleven died of gunshot wounds, and the others were stabbed or trampled. I was here earlier for the autopsy of the man who was…cannibalized—and that mattered."

Bower gritted his teeth, looking up at the sky as if asking the heavens how this could have happened now. "The mayor is down our throats, Saxon. The police chief—"

"The mayor wants to be reelected. This town runs on tourism, so naturally he wants an explanation for everything that happened, and he wants it fast and all wrapped up in ribbons. It's not like we can blame it all on some crazy with a gun permit. Every man out there—assuming we find every man—who shot his piece will claim self-defense. I don't need to hang around the morgue, Captain. I need to find whoever killed Greenwood and dumped his body on Fremont so something could chew his face off."

Captain Bower nodded. His jowls weighed his face down heavily. Bower had been in charge of units that had solved some of the most vicious murders in the city, but right now he looked as if he were a cast member in *Zombieville* himself. He was a big man, but it suddenly looked as if his skin was hanging off his bones.

"Yes—find who murdered the man. Or who found his

gnawed body and threw it into the street. Get to the core of this and—Lord help us all, Saxon—do it fast. I'd say you could start with—"

"I know where to start, Captain. I have connections on the street. I know what I'm doing," Saxon told him quietly.

Bower nodded. "Then do it."

Saxon turned and continued to his car.

But he wasn't really heading out to see a snitch.

At the Wolf and Crown, one of the newest and most elegant casinos to grace the Strip, he pulled up to the valet stand and tossed his keys to one of teh attendants, Billy Shield, a kid he knew pretty well.

Billy grinned as he caught them. "I'll have it ready the second you want it," he called. Billy knew that even though Saxon was a cop, he tipped.

Saxon headed past the flashing slot machines. He was barely aware of the din that filled the casino as he strode across the elegant marble floor toward the elevators, and he ignored one of the executive guard dogs who saw him, frowned worriedly and hurried in his wake.

The elevator door closed after him just as the suit rushed up.

Saxon knew the code to reach the level devoted to the private office of Monty Reilly, owner and CEO of the Wolf and Crown.

The elevator opened on Monty's floor.

And there was Monty.

He was still in his bathrobe. A silver coffee service sat on his desk. There was an urn of coffee on it with a large bottle of bourbon next to it. To his credit, Monty wasn't sitting there petting one of his scores of buxom fortune-hunting beauties. He was pacing. He'd dragged his fingers through his dark hair a dozen times and looked like hell.

"Saxon! I knew you'd be coming, but you got to believe me, this wasn't done by one of mine. I'm telling you—"

"Sit down, Monty."

Monty, who had the smooth look of James Bond—at least when his hair was combed—sat immediately and stared at Saxon. "It wasn't one of mine," he repeated.

Saxon walked over to the desk and leaned on it, staring back at Monty. "It all started with the discovery of a corpse, Monty. A corpse that had been eaten. Gnawed. Devoured."

He'd seen that body, and he knew a werewolf's marks when he saw them.

Monty swallowed hard. "Come on, Saxon. You know that a body doesn't last long in the desert without something eating it. A coyote, a—"

"A werewolf, Monty. And you're the Keeper of the Vegas werewolves. Your charges have been getting out of control for a long time. And I know you have a pretty good idea which one of them did this. I'll bet you cash money that a werewolf was responsible for the disappearance of that craps dealer two months ago, and for that pretty blonde singer who left work and never returned. And I know damn well that a wolf was responsible for those bones we found out in the desert last month. What the hell is going on, Monty?"

Monty looked away.

"Who is it, Monty?" Saxon sat on the corner of the desk, crossing his arms over his chest. "That new hotshot from Toronto who gave me grief when I kicked him out of the Wolf's Den? What's his name? Jimmy Taylor? Or how about the billionaire pulling your strings—

old Carl Bailey? He's been talking all over town about going back to the old ways. And God knows, he has both the power and the money to get rid of any witnesses. Then there's the new girl I've been hearing about, fresh in town, Candy Laughton. She's been working the elite clientele—'entertaining' them. Stripping, maybe more. God alone knows what really happens when she gives a guy a private lap dance."

Monty swallowed. "Come on, Saxon. You don't know that a werewolf is to blame. That guy from Toronto is just a jumped-up punk with a big mouth and too much money. Old Carl Bailey is all talk. And Candy…she's just another wannabe, even if she's an especially pretty one. Saxon, I'm telling you the truth—I don't know who did this. I mean, you don't even really know that it was a werewolf."

"We both know the truth, Monty. And when the first disappearance happened, you should have been right on it. Damn it, Monty, it's your job, your calling."

Monty rose. He was going to lose all his hair, Saxon thought, if he kept running his fingers through it so hard. The Keeper shook his head. "I thought everything was going well. I mean…what control do I really have? They're the biggest players in the city, some of them. You know that. They're powerful. They're— Hell, Saxon, stop looking at me like that! There really aren't any rules… no justice system for us to rely on. I can't haul anyone into court. I—"

"Monty, Keepers maintain control."

"That's not fair, Saxon. Sure, we're supposed to control the other races. But what power do we really have? It's not like everyone signed off on a bill of rights. Once it wasn't a big deal. The populations in the New World were small—hell, the worldwide population was still small—and it was possible to discreetly handle situations. But there's no recourse for me now, nowhere to go—and no real laws."

"You should find a way to handle it," Saxon said. "But since you can't, I will."

"This is everyone's fault—not mine!" Monty insisted.

Saxon felt tension riddling his body. He wanted to land a punch on Monty's clean-shaven jaw; he wanted to shake him out of his comfortable, suck-up position at the casino. Monty was a figurehead. He wasn't running the werewolves—they were running him.

But one thing Monty had said was true: there was no overall governing body for the Keepers to rely on when they were dealing with their charges; there were no real laws. Life and society had changed over the years. For well over a century now, the Keepers had been keeping control all over the world—preventing the mass extinction of human beings by keeping the werewolves, the vampires, the shifters and all the other paranormal races in check. But Monty was right. They were living in a world where populations had exploded. If a Keeper in one city was weak, hell, just move there and behave as irresponsibly—as violently—as you wanted.

Saxon cursed the fact that there was no judicial system for Keepers and their charges.

There should be.

Except he didn't even know who to talk to about forming one.

And for the moment he couldn't worry about it. He had to find the werewolf chewing his way through Las Vegas.

Hell.

Did he start with the kid, the billionaire or the stripper?

Chapter 2

The Rock Candy Club occupied the penthouse level of Candy Country, one of the few casinos that hadn't been built using Carl Bailey's money or ended up with Carl Bailey owning a huge percentage of the shares, whether by name or through one of his many business ventures.

Carl had wanted in; Saxon knew that. But one of the major investors was Reginald Holland, a vampire who held sway in New York City. None of Carl's goons were going to get to Reginald in his cement castle in the Big Apple, and Reginald could not be bought. Saxon had never met him, but he hadn't heard about any vampires causing problems in New York, so presumably Reginald was working hard at living the American dream—controlling his appetite for blood with domestic animals, the small forest creatures that inhabited Central Park or, most likely, blood banks.

Saxon smiled, pleased that Carl Bailey hadn't managed to take ownership of the entire city.

The Rock Candy Club was reached via private elevator.

The women who worked there weren't listed in

advertisements—nor, he suspected, on any IRS forms—as either prostitutes or strippers, though both professions were legal in the city.

The Rock Candy Club hired entertainers.

To be fair, the women were reputed to be quite entertaining.

There was a guard outside the elevator. It wasn't so much that you needed ID to reach the upper floors, but you did need an impeccable credit rating to reach the penthouse level.

Saxon produced the exclusive platinum card that he carried for precisely such an occasion. Sometimes in Vegas it was necessary to play the part.

The guard let him by, but there was another "host"—not as tall as Saxon, but massive and broad like a steel-hulled ship—ready to greet him in the elevator.

Werewolf, definitely.

Big, hairy, broad-faced werewolf.

"Welcome, sir," he addressed Saxon politely. He wore his suit well, though he did seem to chafe a bit in the tailored shirt, high collar and tie.

"Elven?" the guard asked politely.

Saxon merely nodded.

The man cleared his throat. "Begging your pardon, sir. I didn't mean to pry. We don't see too many of your kind here, on account of…"

His voice trailed off as Saxon pointedly ignored him.

Elven were invariably tall and generally blessed with exceptional looks. That was why so many of them had successful acting careers out in Hollywood; not only did they tend to be tall, blond and good-looking, they were usually also blessed with a considerable amount of charm.

Both sexes were also revered as lovers, endowed with

stamina and, in the males, sexual equipment to match their well-toned physiques.

"Actually," the guard said, "we don't see many of your kind in Vegas at all."

"I'm sure that's true," Saxon agreed.

"And certainly not…here. You know what I mean. Here. Looking to spend money on…entertainment."

Saxon wasn't feeling the patience for a pissing contest. On the other hand, he didn't want to start off on the wrong foot before he'd even made it into the club.

He grinned at the guard. "I've heard great things about this place."

The guard smiled back at that. "It's spectacular." He lowered his voice as an indication of confidentiality. "Ask for Candy."

"I hear she's new," Saxon said. "And exceptional."

"She may or may not agree to see you," the guard told him. "She's selective."

Luckily Saxon didn't have to continue the conversation any longer. The elevator had reached the penthouse.

The door opened.

At the end of a hallway stood a beautifully constructed glass enclosure, the customary pole at the center. The pole was wrapped in a shimmering sheath of fabric that matched the temptingly designed outfit worn by the dancer on display.

She was incredible. Lithe, her every movement was seductively smooth as she danced to a tune he knew well and barely heard.

She wasn't half-naked, like the typical Vegas entertainer, or even provocatively dressed. Clad from head to toe, her exceptional allure came from the figure within, which was tall and lean and wickedly curved. Limber didn't begin to describe the exotic way she could twist and turn. She moved around the pole with the animalistic grace of a cat.

Saxon was dimly aware as the guard behind him said, "Enjoy yourself, sir," and the elevator door closed. He continued down the short hall that led to the foyer—and the glass-enclosed dancer. The place was elegantly and tastefully furnished in antiques; paintings graced the walls. None of them were sexually explicit. One was of a medieval damsel clad in delicate draping white, bending down to draw water from a shimmering stream. Another was of a knight in shining armor, a fair lady gently carried in his arms. The rest were similar in subject matter and tastefulness.

Saxon barely noted them or the decor. His attention was fully caught by the dancer.

Her hair was dark—not black, but a sable color with streaks of auburn running through it. Her face was delicately, aesthetically, sculpted, yet her lips were almost supernaturally full.

Her eyes, when she deigned to notice him, were an intriguing mix of green and gold, as sharp and beautiful as diamonds, glittering like the fabric that covered her.

And when they met his, they filled with disdain.

Once she caught his eyes, she didn't look away. She stared at him and continued dancing as if he were no more than a fly buzzing nearby.

"Mr. Kirby?" someone murmured in a silken voice.

He turned. A blonde with the perkiest—and undoubtedly heavily silicone-enhanced—breasts he had ever seen was coming toward him. She was clad in something that resembled a stewardess uniform from the earliest days of commercial flight.

"Welcome," she said. "They told me you were on your way up. Please, if you'll join me in the antechamber, we'll discuss what brings you to us, what fantasy you would like fulfilled and what kind of entertainment will satisfy your heart's desire."

Antechamber? Interesting word for a business office.

He smiled. "Of course."

He was loath to leave the entry. He could almost feel the hot gold-and-emerald gaze of the woman behind the glass.

Not to mention her contempt.

He forced himself not to look back, though it was difficult.

But he followed the buxom blonde. She led him into an elegant office. Her desk—which still held the obligatory computer and phone—was carved ebony with handsome ivory insets. Her office chair was upholstered in a deep burnished crimson, like the massive chairs that sat across from it. Marble statuary graced the edges of the room, and a plate-glass window looked out over the sunbaked brilliance of the Vegas Strip.

"So..." she said, sitting down and folding her long-fingered, exquisitely manicured hands, and smiled. "What is your wildest dream, sir? How may we entertain you? Do you dream of angels or demons? Or perhaps something in between—a dance of innocents and vixens together? Is your dream girl slim or curved or...?" She lifted her hands, the fabric of her suit jacket stretching across her breasts. "We seek to entertain, sir. Our performances are among the most talented in the country. But we cannot entertain you unless we know what it is you seek."

He leaned forward and met her eyes, then gave her a charming smile. "Candy," he said.

She paled slightly. "We have Asian beauties who can twist and turn in ways that you've never imagined. We have Russian acrobats who sail across a room as grace-fully as the last great ships that rode the oceans' breezes. African women whose movements can rival the rhythm of any heart. Irish lasses who can dance their way into the bloodstream."

"Candy," he repeated.

His hostess sat back, perplexed. She pursed her per-fect cherry-red lips.

"Candy—despite the name of our establishment—has not been with us long. She is a rare and exotic talent, so rare that her contract here allows her to choose when to entertain privately."

He nodded. "Candy."

The woman sighed.

He tapped his platinum card on the table as if in thought. "Perhaps you would see if the young woman might be willing to give me just a few minutes of her time."

"I…" The blonde clearly intended to protest.

He leaned closer to her and deepened his smile, seek-ing her eyes and staring into them. "Candy," he said again.

She rose without breaking eye contact. "I'll speak with her."

He nodded, watching her go. Once she was out of the room, he was on his feet. He quickly made his way around the desk to the computer and looked up Candy's employee file. She was listed only as Candy—no last name. Her hours were listed as "general entertainment," and, as the blonde had said, there was a notation by her name that read "Will choose individual clients."

He frowned as he heard the blonde returning, her heels clicking on the marble floor.

By the time she entered the room, he was back in his chair. He quickly stood, looking at her expectantly.

"Candy will see you," she said, and turned. "This way, please."

He followed her down an elegantly paneled hallway until she stopped, opened a door and ushered him in.

Saxon stepped into the room, but he didn't see Candy. Nor did he notice when the door closed behind him.

A marble-floored entryway led to a large, richly carpeted room. Sunlight poured through French doors that led to a balcony and offered a view of the nearby fountains at the Bellagio and a stunning view of the entire Vegas Strip.

A huge Venetian-tiled whirlpool bath looked out toward the balcony. Heavy furniture in oak, mahogany and ebony filled the room, along with a massive bed whose hand-carved head- and footboard supported an elegant canopy.

He knew he was being observed.

He noticed an Oriental screen beside the whirlpool.

And as he watched, Candy emerged from behind the screen.

His breath caught in his throat when he recognized the dancer who had seduced and entranced and hypnotized him from behind the glass.

She wasn't dressed as she had been before, or as he would have expected of an "entertainer." She wore a plain white terry robe, her hair sleek and curling around her shoulders.

She was tall, perhaps five foot ten. Elegant in build, and supple, as he'd already seen when she'd danced.

She moved so fluidly that she seemed to float slowly across the room.

She wore no makeup. Her eyes, which seemed to

gleam with a hypnotic beauty, were unadorned by shadow or mascara. Her lashes were rich and thick all on their own, her face pure perfection.

When she spoke, her voice was a husky alto that teased his senses. "So, you have come just for me, I hear?"

"Yes."

She smiled and came closer. "And what is it that you desire? A dance? Ah, but you've already seen me dance. Perhaps you're looking for something more intimate, more...personal?"

She stopped directly in front of him and slid her hand up his shirt. Then she placed both hands on his chest, the subtle pressure of her body pushing him toward the bed. The backs of his knees met the mattress, and he held steady for a moment.

"What are you offering?" he asked her.

It was difficult to maintain his composure in the face of her pure sensuality. She seemed to offer the wildest and most intimate and intriguingly carnal pleasures the mind could imagine.

And he was Elven.

Also a cop—trying to stop a murderer.

He let himself fall back on the bed, wondering what her next move would be. In seconds she was straddled over him, and his wrists were imprisoned by her long fingers as she stared down at him.

"Elven," she said.

"Yes."

"And a cop," she added.

He smiled. Time to turn the tables. She wasn't prepared when he flipped her over and straddled her, pinning her wrists to the bed.

"Werewolf," he said, meeting her eyes. "Hunting your way up the Strip and through the desert."

Her eyes widened, and she stared back up at him. "What?"

"You heard me," he told her, but his gut told him that she had nothing to do with the rash of deaths.

He was fighting to keep his responses to her in check, but he could feel her beneath him with every fiber of his being.

"Elven cop, yes," he said. "And I intend to stop the death and insanity before more innocents die and their deaths bring our entire supernatural society crashing down."

She was still staring up at him, and her frown seemed real. "Get the hell off me," she told him. "Unless you... can't." Her suddenly seductive tone told him exactly what she was thinking.

"Don't flatter yourself. You invited me here, after all."

"Don't flatter yourself, Elven. I had to know what you were up to."

Those golden eyes studied him, reached into his soul. Then they suddenly cleared and turned innocent—even vulnerable.

"Just what do you think I'm doing?" she asked, making no attempt to hide her annoyance.

"I have no doubt that you entertain your audience. I just worry about how many pieces your audience is in when you've finished your performance."

"Don't be a fool," she told him. "I'm here to stop what's happening. I'm not causing it."

He stared down at her. How the hell do you trust a woman who could torment a man to insanity with her eyes alone? "Why should I believe you?" he asked.

"Because of Angie," she said softly.

He waited for her to go on.

"Angie Sanderson." He could have sworn that tears

glistened in her eyes. "She disappeared six weeks ago, right after Carl Bailey gave her a job singing at one of his casinos. She had the voice of a lark. If you're a cop, you must have seen the report."

He had.

And he had suspected that her disappearance was related to the case he was looking into—he'd said as much to Monty.

True, lots of beautiful, talented young women came to Las Vegas, and plenty of them ended up disappearing. Some simply gave up on their dreams and left. Some were consumed by the city, finding work but not the glittering careers they had come in search of. Some changed their names when they vanished into the city's seedy underbelly, because they didn't want their families in Kansas or South Carolina or whatever wholesome place they came from finding out what they were really doing.

But Angie...

He could remember the "Missing" posters that had gone up all over town.

She was blonde and blue-eyed, young and innocent. She had done her shift one night, singing her little heart out—and been reported missing when she hadn't returned to work the following day. The casino cameras had lost her once she'd mingled with the throng of humanity on the street.

"What do you have to do with Angie Sanderson?" he asked. "It's not your job to find people. And if you really are innocent, then you need to get out of here—since it's dead obvious one of your kind is up to something very bad."

Candy looked at him with her golden eyes gleaming with tears.

"I don't believe 'my kind' have anything to do with

this. As for what I have to do with Angie…she's my half sister. And I don't care if you're a cop, an Elven or an archangel come down to claim us all—I'm not leaving until I find her!"

Chapter 3

Saxon got up and moved away from Candy and that far-too-tempting bed.

He needed some distance. First the woman had been the embodiment of exotic beauty and erotic movement. Now she seemed like a little girl lost. It didn't matter which, really. When she looked at him, he felt as if he were being drawn deep into a netherworld where he could easily become lost forever—and he didn't dare take that chance. Especially not now, with a murderous werewolf on the loose.

"Your half sister?" he said, studying her. "Half... what?" He conjured the picture of the missing woman. Blonde, angelic.

Elven?

Candy shrugged, then sat up and ran her fingers through her hair. "Half sister. We share one parent."

"And?"

She took a breath, then said, "I'm a bit of an unusual... being."

"Go on," he said firmly.

"Our mother was the sweetest, gentlest and most

amazing woman you could ever meet. She met one of her own kind—an Elven—and they had Angela. Then Angie's father died."

Saxon felt his muscles tighten. Elven normally led very long lives. "Because your mother met your father?" he asked.

The look she gave him was so scathing that he felt as if he were melting in the pool of her contempt.

"Angie's dad died because he had it in his head that he should serve his country," she said quietly. "He was in the air force, and his plane went down in the water and he…died. I'm sure you understand."

Saxon nodded. Of all the underworld beings, the Elven had been the last to come to the New World. They didn't melt if they touched water, but they were creatures of the earth. Despite their strength and normally robust health, they couldn't survive long in or even over water. Because of that, they hadn't come to the New World en masse until flying became commonplace. A few adventurous and hardy souls had made it over via ocean liner, but the crossing had been difficult. Not everyone who attempted it had succeeded, and the weakened survivors had been easy prey on arrival.

"And your mother married a…werewolf?" he asked.

"You really are a condescending SOB, aren't you?" she said sweetly.

"Don't be ridiculous. I'm not a prejudiced man," he denied quickly.

She shrugged. "You are—but perhaps it's not entirely your fault. You're Elven."

She said the word as if no explanation was needed, and she was probably right, he thought.

"So, yes," she went on, "my mother married a werewolf, and I don't know a soul who doesn't like my father.

He was the best father in the world to my sister. He doesn't know yet that she's disappeared. Neither does my mother."

"And they don't know that you're working here, either, do they?" Saxon demanded.

She exhaled. She was obviously trying to come up with a good explanation, but then she simply said, "No."

He shook his head while looking at her. "So how are you going to explain to your father that you've been dancing in a strip club and pretending to be a prostitute?"

"That's the point, don't you see? My mother is an actress. Angie and I grew up in the theater. I've done nothing but act—act like something I'm not—since I got here."

"You've acted out wild romps with men?" he said incredulously.

"If you know so much—"

"I know you've agreed to see only a few private clients. But you're growing legendary—there's talk about you around town."

"Really? That's wonderful. I'm getting to where I need to be," she said, smiling.

He walked over to her and pulled her to her feet. "What's the matter with you? You're dealing with ruthless men—ruthless creatures who can rip you to shreds and scatter your bones across the desert. Have you actually slept with these monsters?"

"No!" she protested. "I told you—it's all an act. I'm trying to find out who killed Angela, and I think I know."

"What? Who?"

"I'm trying to get to know people who are close to Carl Bailey," she said. "Everyone's on guard, too intimidated by him, on his own turf. But people are less wary, more willing to talk, when they're away from work. Maybe

Bailey himself will even show up here one of these days. I'm certain he's behind her death, if he didn't kill her himself. He has his eye on this place, and I think he'd do anything to get it. If Angie heard something about what he was up to, something he didn't want her to know, he wouldn't have thought twice about siccing some killer werewolf on her. As for my…sexual activity, I accept very few private clients. Luckily for me, my performance has earned me the right to choose who I do and don't see."

"This is dangerous. You're dangerous!"

"Good," she told him flatly.

"And how do you get rid of those clients without… delivering?" Saxon demanded. He reminded himself that he wasn't her father. He had no right to sound so angry. But…

She was dangerous, all right.

She shook her head and offered a dry grin. "I make them believe they were involved in an experience that was pure magic."

"And how do you do that?"

"It's in the eyes," she said softly.

"You have werewolf eyes, animal eyes," he said. His voice was harsh.

"Yes. And I could have made you leave here without suspecting a thing, thinking you'd been to heaven and back," she told him.

"I doubt that," he assured her. "I'm Elven, remember?"

"And I'm half Elven—and half wolf," she reminded him sweetly. "Should we test it out? Or perhaps you should leave now. And make sure you arrange an exceptional gratuity for me, will you?"

He walked over to her, jaw locked, frustration boiling inside him. "What's the matter with you? Your sister disappeared. Do you want to disappear, too?"

"I'm forewarned—and I do have that wolf thing going for me, after all."

"You can stop that. Some of my best friends are were-wolves," he said.

She laughed. It was a nice sound. An honest sound. "Sorry, but that is so, so patronizing."

He flushed, then was annoyed with his own reaction. He was a cop, for God's sake. "It's not patronizing. It's just the truth," he said. "Listen—"

"I'm not going away. I'm free and over twenty-one. And here in Vegas, my activities—or whatever activities you suspect me of—are completely legal. You can continue on your quest—just leave me alone to follow mine."

She surprised him by smiling again. A real smile, not pretending to be a hardcore temptress or making fun of him.

"Let's start over, shall we?" She walked over to him, offering her hand. "My name is really Calleigh. Calleigh McGowan. From San Francisco. I'm a Libra—usually very fair in all things. I love long walks in the forest, and I think there's nothing quite so beautiful as a full moon rising on a clear night. And you're…?"

He couldn't help it; his lips twitched. He gave her his hand. "Saxon Kirby. Detective by trade—and inclination. I have a deep-seated need to help the underdog, and I loathe watching the powerful take advantage of the weak." He paused, shaking his head. "What the hell am I doing standing here still talking to you?"

"Admitting that I'm not going away, that I may actually be—" she paused to laugh "—of some help. Face it, Carl Bailey is always surrounded by security, and he may have half your department in his pocket."

"All right, back up."

"I said may," she stressed.

"And Carl Bailey may not even be behind these deaths. It could be any one of a whole list of suspects, including the new hotshot in town—that Canadian wolf who's been throwing around so much money."

She could manage a truly impressive stubborn set to her chin. "I'm telling you, it's Carl Bailey. He runs the werewolves of Las Vegas. The Keeper here is...weak."

Weak. That was an understatement.

"It's not like that in San Francisco," she said. "There are laws in San Francisco, and everyone knows you obey them or you pay the price."

Saxon frowned. San Francisco had laws—why couldn't the rest of the world manage it?

No time to dwell on that now.

"I should call your father," he threatened.

She looked away nervously, and he realized he'd hit on the key to keeping her safe.

"You don't know who he is," she said, but she still wouldn't meet his eyes.

"I'll find him. I know he's in San Francisco," Saxon told her.

She shook her head. "Don't you dare! He doesn't know that Angie is missing. He doesn't know that I'm here. He and my mother—"

"Listen to what you're saying! Do you want them to lose two daughters?"

"Care to let me finish?" she asked him coolly.

"All right." He stood back, arms crossed over his chest.

"Not too long ago, my father got a request from a Keeper in London, via Larry Miller, our Keeper in San Francisco. They were having some trouble in Chelmsford—a banshee rampage. Anyway, they were seeking my father's advice." She was quiet for a minute. "My dad has a background in law enforcement and the judicial system. He's gone to work with the English on a central plan so they won't find themselves in this situation again, and my mother's over there with him. It's very secret. I don't even have a way to reach him. He calls every few days to check on me. He thinks Angie is so busy with a show that she's impossible to reach, so..."

"So you've been lying to him," Saxon finished. "Your father is Theo McGowan, then? The former congressman?"

She didn't respond. She didn't need to.

He shook his head. "Great. Theo McGowan's daughter is in Vegas pretending to be a stripper, and he has no idea."

"You won't find him."

"Actually, I wasn't thinking about that. I was thinking how great it is that the San Francisco Keepers actually cooperate with their international counterparts. But that's not important right now. What's important is—"

"Finding Angie and stopping this killing spree," Calleigh said. "And that's just what I intend to do."

"Calleigh, listen, I'm a cop—"

"And I'm a big girl. You can't stop me. What you can do, if you want, is help me," she told him. "Meanwhile, your bill is getting higher and higher," she warned him. "You need to get out of here before you go bankrupt."

"Calleigh, I can't let you do this."

"It's not your call. Right now you need to go. We can talk later," she told him. "Trust me. If you don't give me away, I'm safe, at least for this afternoon, even if I can manage to lure Carl Bailey here. If—"

"Carl Bailey is old, Calleigh."

"And I'm young."

"My point is, he knows every trick in the book, and

he hasn't got a moral fiber in his body. He'd just as soon kill you as look at you if you were in his way."

"Then I'll have to make sure he doesn't realize I'm in his way. How about I meet you tonight and we can make a plan to work together?" she said. "Please. Frankly, I don't want to be responsible for a good cop going bad to pay his bill for my services."

He hesitated. "You're not lying to me to get me out of here?"

"No. I swear. I'll do anything to find Angie, so if you're really going to search for her and not think of her as a showgirl gone bad—"

"Calleigh, Missing Persons has been on it—"

"And done nothing."

"All right. We'll talk tonight. But if you don't show, I will find you here, and I will find a way to arrest you."

"I'll meet you."

"Where?"

She scratched out an address he knew vaguely. It was one of the local equestrian facilities where the members of the show circuit trained their hundred-thousand-dollar mounts.

"This is where you're living?" he asked her incredulously.

She nodded. "The house belongs to a man—a human being—named Dirk. He's in love with Angie, and he's going insane with her gone."

"And he knows what you're doing and hasn't tried to stop you?"

"Seriously? Even if he wanted to—which he doesn't—can you imagine any human who could stop me? I need to find my sister."

Saxon knew that he would find Angela Sanderson, no matter what. She was Elven.

He looked at Candy—at the hope in her eyes.

He could only pray that, with everything else that had been going on, there was the ghost of a chance that he would find her alive.

Chapter 4

Saxon had several hours to kill until he was scheduled to meet up with Calleigh.

He headed back to his station house, sat down at his computer and pulled up the information on the cases that he was now convinced were linked.

Two months back: bones found in the desert. They might have been the result of an accidental death—and the surefire way the desert had of cleaning up the dead. A forensic examination of the bones had been inconclusive. There were no chips or marks on them to indicate that a bullet or a knife had been the cause of death. There were tooth marks on the bones, but while the ME considered them likely to be postmortem, Saxon had his own theories on that. The dead man had been about six feet tall, between forty and fifty years old—and somehow he had managed to die ten miles out in the sand, where vultures, coyotes, beetles and whatever else had pretty much taken care of all his soft tissue. His dental records had led nowhere. He'd been wearing a denim shirt and jeans, size-nine boots, and a buckle that advertised a Tennessee country rock band.

He'd died minus a wallet or any other identification—
or someone had intentionally removed them.

Saxon had attended the autopsy, because the bones
had indicated a possibility that the victim had been one
of the Elven, who had strong, elongated bones.

But in the end the ME had determined that the skeleton had belonged to a man—just a man, and nothing
more. A dumb man—traveling in the desert on foot with
no wallet—but a man. Except that Saxon didn't think that
little of humanity. And no mortal man could have gotten
that far out in the desert on foot. It was too convenient to
think he'd simply lain down in the sand to die, then was
fortuitously consumed by the local wildlife. No, someone
had taken him out there and left him to die, or killed him
elsewhere and dumped him in the desert for the body to
be eaten and the evidence destroyed.

Murder number one, he thought. At least that he knew
of.

Then there had been the craps dealer. Rutger Heinz.
He had come to Las Vegas because he'd been entranced
by what he'd seen and read about the city while growing up in Bavaria. He'd arrived just five years earlier, attended the University of Nevada, then taken a job.

At Monty's casino. Which was mostly owned by Carl
Bailey.

Security cameras recorded Rutger's exit the night he
had gone missing. He could be seen getting into his car
and driving away. And then, somewhere in the congested
traffic of the Strip, he had disappeared. And he hadn't
been seen again.

Not long afterward, Angela Sanderson had disappeared. Exquisite, beautiful, Elven. Young, talented,
ready to take on the world. With everything to live for.

One thing he'd noticed on the casino security footage of both Rutger and Angela before they'd disappeared was that there had been a very high proportion of werewolves around. It was a tentative connection to the murders, but his gut told him it was real nonetheless, that werewolves were involved in the disappearances as well as the killings.

Then, yesterday, the half-chewed body of the Oregon tourist that had caused a disaster on Fremont Street.

Two officially dead—and his concern as a homicide detective.

Two missing and, he feared, most likely dead.

The dead man found right there on Fremont Street seemed to be a sign that the murderer wanted to be noticed. It was like a cry for recognition.

Why would a killer make such a point of calling attention to himself? One possibility: it could be a cry for help. Maybe he abhorred the killing, but couldn't stop himself and was hoping the police would catch him. Or maybe he was showing off for someone.

Another possibility: the killer was so mentally deranged that he was certain he wouldn't be caught; as a narcissistic personality, he considered his own desires of uppermost importance and couldn't imagine that he could be caught.

Yet no matter what else was true of the killer's psyche, the validity of this was not in question in Saxon's mind: the killer was a werewolf. A werewolf acting as pack leader, as alpha, and trying to convince the rest of the pack that it was time for the wolf pack to take their place as kings of the city.

Las Vegas was one of the pleasure capitals of the world, a neon-lit paradise where every vice known to man—and Others—could be indulged. Where money—

and women—changed hands from minute to minute. A city where Carl Bailey was already the de facto king.

What more could the man want? Saxon wondered. Why would he kill—or, more likely, have someone else kill for him? He had money, and hundreds of people working for him, worshipping his name. He had power, scores of mistresses, every conceivable comfort.

Maybe it wasn't Carl Bailey, Saxon reminded himself. He shook his head.

No, Carl had to be involved. The new wolf from Toronto hadn't been here long enough to make the kinds of connections you needed to kill someone and dispose of the body.

Still, it wouldn't do to count the guy out. A smart detective considered all possibilities.

He rose. He supposed he could pay a visit to Carl. But he wanted more evidence than what he had—which came down to pretty much nothing—when he actually accosted the man.

He wanted to arrest the bastard, just on general principles, but he had nothing to hold him on.

Besides, how much good would it do when he finally did have enough? How much sway did Carl Bailey have in the courts? Was there any hope the werewolf would actually wind up paying the ultimate penalty under the law?

There should have been another law. A universal law for the nonhuman races. The kind of law that the Keepers had surely used to rule over their creatures, once upon a very long time ago.

Saxon reminded himself that he was a cop. Even if he could prove beyond a shadow of a doubt that Carl Bailey was a murderer, the man was protected by his rights under the Constitution. Saxon couldn't just walk in with a silver bullet and shoot him down.

They desperately needed real laws for the Otherworld. With real consequences.

It was a waste of time to rue the fact that Monty Reilly was either as crooked as Carl Bailey or totally ineffectual. There were two lost people out there, alive or dead. One of them a woman who was, in a way, kin. He had to find them.

He put through a few calls and found out that the new wolf in town, Jimmy Taylor, was playing craps at one of Carl Bailey's casinos.

He decided he felt like gambling.

Jimmy Taylor was in his late twenties, tall, leanly muscled, and he had a thick lock of dark hair that fell over his forehead and the heavy-lidded bedroom eyes that women seemed to find attractive.

The guy could have made it in movies. He should have headed to Hollywood—the kingdom of stars—Saxon thought.

But he'd come here instead—to the kingdom of high stakes.

Carl Bailey's Galway Glen casino was, like all his properties, expensively and expertly decorated. There were salutes to Ireland throughout. The Tralee Tavern, located above the casino floor with a view of the action, was done in shades of green, and the bartenders were all female and all wearing short green skirts. Carl liked women—the prettier the better, the bustier better still. It was pretty much a given that if a beautiful woman wanted a job—and was willing to kowtow to Carl Bailey—she was guaranteed a job at the casino.

Saxon knew that Carl hated him. He knew from the minute he entered the casino that the security cameras were on him and his presence would be announced to Carl, wherever in the city the man might be.

He didn't head straight to the gaming tables but decided on a drink first. He settled into a green upholstered chair at the Tralee and took a minute to appreciate the ornately carved wood of the bar itself, designed to look as if it had been cobbled together from logs in a forest. Eyes peered out from between artificial branches, as if mischievous leprechauns were watching out for those who'd come to imbibe. A realistically carved female figure, one of Ireland's famous selkies, looked down from above the bottles of expensive liquor shelved behind the bar.

His waitress was in her early twenties. She shimmered a bit when she moved, and he instantly thought, shapeshifter.

"Good evening, Detective Kirby," she said. "Are you here to ask questions? Or are you…off duty?" she finished flirtatiously.

"I'm off duty. But I always like to ask questions," he told her. "I can start with how do you know my name?"

She flushed. "I guess you're not going to believe I've waited on you before and you introduced yourself?"

"No."

"Okay, so…the truth is, Mr. Bailey alerted the employees to keep an eye out for you to show up. He doesn't want to cause a stink by refusing you entrance. He does want you watched."

Saxon looked over at the selkie statue above the bar. He knew she had cameras in her shimmering eyes.

He waved.

"Why does he want me watched?" he asked innocently.

"He says you're on a vendetta—blaming the werewolves for everything that's been happening lately."

"Could be a shifter pretending to be a werewolf," he said with a shrug. "Or a person. It's not as if vicious serial killers can't be human."

"So what will you have?" she asked, apparently deciding not to pursue the topic of his intentions.

"I think I'll stick with the theme. A good Irish beer, please."

She left to get his beer, and his eyes idly tracked her journey back to the bar. He noticed that there was a platform in front of the selkie statue, and as he watched, one of the servers climbed up and took her place on it. Traditional Irish music started playing, and she began to dance, her feet moving with skill and speed to rival the best performer back on Irish soil.

The waitress returned with his beer.

"She's good," he said, nodding toward the dancer.

"Yes—we don't get hired if we can't perform."

"What's your specialty?"

"I'm a vocalist," she said.

"This is where that singer used to work," Saxon said, keeping his tone casual.

"What singer?"

"The one who disappeared."

His waitress shrugged. "Girls come and go in Vegas. You get a better offer, you move on."

She started to turn away, but he grabbed her wrist to stop her. "This girl didn't get a better offer. She disappeared."

She tried to wrench herself away from him. Without blinking, he made a vise of his hand.

"Damn Elven," she muttered.

"You don't need to fear the Elven. You do need to fear your boss."

"Let go of me. They'll notice, and I'll get in trou—"

"Then smile and act like you're flirting with me."

She smiled, and he kept his eyes locked with hers, so she didn't give the cameras a guilty look.

"Did you know her? Angela Sanderson?" he asked. She was obviously frightened, her eyes widening in shock, but she didn't say anything. "You did know her," he said.

She leaned close to him and laughed, as if he'd said something funny. "I replaced her," she said, swallowing. "They said she wasn't coming back. But that was before I knew…"

"Before you knew that she'd disappeared."

She looked even more terrified, if that was possible. "I have to go," she insisted, trying to pull away again.

This time he released her. When she was gone, he drank his beer, then headed for the craps tables.

He spotted Jimmy Taylor at one and took a spot at the other end. He bought in for several hundred, aware that Taylor was staring at him angrily. He ignored the other man and laid money down on the pass line.

A man at the middle of the table was rolling. "Lucky seven, lucky seven!"

The dice landed on four and three. The players applauded.

Jimmy Taylor continued to ignore Saxon as the run continued. The same man rolled an eight next, and more money landed on the table. He hit several more numbers, and then an eight again. The table cheered. There was money everywhere.

But Taylor didn't seem happy. And when the roller came up with another seven, Taylor actually looked relieved, though sighs went up elsewhere around the table, along with some applause for the shooter, who'd made a lot of money for most of them.

Taylor went to cash in. Saxon held his ground, putting down his money while the next shooter started. On a whim, he played a nice sum on craps. The shooter hit an eleven, and Saxon realized he was coming out ahead, a nice plus for his investigation.

He watched as Jimmy collected his money and headed toward the bar. He waited through the next roll, then cashed in himself and headed back to the Tralee.

There was Jimmy Taylor, his hands rough on a young waitress's shoulders. Saxon was tempted to step in, but he reminded himself that he was playing for higher stakes. And he knew Jimmy wasn't going to hurt the girl anyway—not in public, and not in one of Carl Bailey's establishments.

He followed when Jimmy left the bar. He thought at first that the guy was going to head upstairs, which could prove tricky. Carl's men would be on him like an infestation of lice if he tried to go up to the rooms.

But either Taylor didn't know he was being followed or he didn't care. Either way, he apparently had a destination in mind. Or maybe—Saxon warned himself—a plan.

Taylor headed out to the streets. Saxon followed him down the neon strip, until he took a sudden turn into a back alley. Okay, so a plan it was.

It occurred to Saxon long before he entered the obvious trap that he would need some help, which was easy enough to arrange. It was good to be a cop. But first he wanted about two minutes alone with Jimmy Taylor. After that, it would be great to have some help. He hit the speed dial on his phone and gave the code for "Officer in Need of Assistance."

Then he took a deep breath and ducked into the alley, keeping close to the wall of the building on his right, one of the smaller casinos and most likely another of Carl Bailey's properties.

There was a doorway marked Employee Entrance about thirty feet in, and Taylor was heading right for it.

Saxon hurried past boxes and an overflowing Dumpster, and before Jimmy could put his hand on the doorknob, Saxon grabbed his shoulder and spun him around, forcing his thumb on a pressure point in the younger man's throat as he slammed him against the door.

"Where is she?" Saxon demanded.

The other man couldn't breathe, which made him desperate. He tried to make the change, no doubt intending to rip Saxon to shreds with his teeth and claws, but Saxon just increased the pressure on that vulnerable point. And if the other man couldn't breathe, he couldn't make the change.

Jimmy sagged, giving up, and Saxon eased up just a hair, then repeated, "Where is she?"

"I don't know what you're talking about, so kill me if you want to. But you'd better be quick. You're going to die soon enough yourself."

"Not likely. You've got good hearing, right? I can already hear the sirens."

"Great. I'll have you charged with police brutality," Taylor told him.

"Where's your evidence? There's not a mark on you. Now, you have thirty seconds before I put a shade more pressure on your neck and zap your nerves. You'll be a paralyzed pup the rest of your life."

At last Taylor looked scared. "If I talk to you, I'm dead anyway!" he said.

"Dead is probably better than the way I'm going to leave you," Saxon said. "For the third time, where is she?"

Taylor blinked. "You're talking about that girl, right? That singer? I told him to leave her alone."

Saxon tensed, accidentally increasing the pressure on Taylor's throat. The werewolf let out a sharp squeal and started talking again the minute he eased up.

"I didn't hurt her. I didn't do anything to her. I just drove her out there."

"Out where?"

"His lair in the desert," Taylor said. "Five miles out Highway 15 there's a big stand of cactus. You can't miss it. His place…it's there, but it's underground. You—"

Saxon heard footsteps. He pressed Taylor's neck hard to silence him. It had to be Carl Bailey's men, and considering the speed with which Taylor had given in, he might be someone worth keeping around.

He spun around and saw four thugs heading his way. Two dumb human guards with no clue, along with a vampire and a werewolf. He smiled.

"We can go at it, boys, but I think you hear the sirens. Now, here's the thing. This young pup of Bailey's doesn't give the police any respect. He took a swing at me. He's going to spend a night in jail, and then the little bastard will be arraigned and dumped back out on the streets. I think we should leave it at that."

"You know we have to report this incident to Mr. Bailey, Kirby," the vampire said, assuming the lead.

"I'm counting on it," Saxon said.

"You okay, Jimmy?" the werewolf asked. "We look after our own, so if you want help, just say the word."

Jimmy managed a nod. "Damn straight I want help. You need to bail me out. Fast!"

"You bet, Taylor. And don't worry none—Mr. Bailey looks after his own kind."

The four thugs turned and left seconds before two patrol cars, sirens screaming, drove into the alley.

"Take him in. Assaulting an officer," Saxon said, shoving Taylor toward the officers emerging from the second car. Then he bent to speak to Keeghan McMurtree, the driver of the first.

McMurtree was a leprechaun. A tall one. Despite his race's reputed ability with money, he wasn't lucky at gambling. He was a damn good cop, though, driven by his disgust at all the killing he'd seen back in the old country—among humans and Otherworld races alike.

"Anything going on I should know about?" Saxon asked.

McMurtree nodded. "Just a warning. Captain is in a state, anxious as all hell. That business yesterday with the dead guy getting eaten, you know."

"I know," Saxon said. "I've got a few things to follow up that might put him in a better mood."

McMurtree nodded. "Take care, buddy."

"Will do. Thanks," Saxon said.

McMurtree drove away, and Saxon stood there for a long moment, considering the state of his investigation.

So…it wasn't the stripper and it wasn't the tough new wolf in town—who wasn't so tough, anyway. And he'd never thought it was a shifter in wolf's clothing, much less some human nutcase. Given everything he knew about the man and everything he'd learned today from Calleigh and Taylor, there was only one person—one werewolf—it could be.

Carl Bailey.

But that bastard was too clever by half. No way was he doing his own dirty work. Nope, Carl was definitely not working alone.

Saxon glanced at his watch. It was time to head out to ranch country.

He would keep his meeting with Calleigh brief, just long enough to tell her that he had what looked like a decent lead, and if she stayed home and played it safe, he had a chance of finding her sister.

But when he got to the address she had given him, Calleigh wasn't there.

He knocked, and the door was opened by an awkward young man with a baby face and the look of a dreamer in his eyes.

It had to be Dirk, human owner of the house.

"You the cop?" Dirk asked anxiously. When Saxon nodded, the other man rushed on. "Calleigh's been telling me about you. She said you sounded as if you really care. You have to help. I don't know what to do. Like now. I don't get it."

"What don't you get?" Saxon demanded. He grasped the younger man's shoulder, steadying him, looking into his eyes, demanding silently that he get a grip.

"I don't know what happened. She was here, right here. I was just out back, feeding the horses, and I heard her say someone was coming. I thought she was talking about you, but when I came back in she—"

"Dirk, where's Calleigh?" Saxon interrupted.

"That's what I'm trying to tell you! She's gone, and I don't know where!"

Chapter 5

Gone? Calleigh was gone? Saxon could barely wrap his mind around it. Was this revenge because he'd arrested Jimmy Taylor? Or had Calleigh's amateur investigation made her too noticeable—and too dangerous—in the eyes of Carl Bailey?

And did any of that matter in light of the possibility that she might have fought back against her kidnappers and gotten hurt, or been dragged away half dead?

"How long ago?"

"Ten minutes."

"Did you hear a car? Were the horses acting up?"

"Um, yeah." Dirk stared at him blankly. "Yeah, sure, the horses were going crazy."

Saxon turned and hurried back toward his car. Dirk ran after him. "Hey, what do you want me to do? Should I call more cops?"

Saxon swung around. "Don't do anything or call anyone. Get back in the house and stay there."

Saxon waited long enough to make sure Dirk did as instructed, then got in his car and drove away. He didn't go far, though: just down the road. Then he parked, got out and headed back toward Dirk's place, making sure to stay out of sight as he carefully approached the house.

He heard one whinny from out back, but that was it. Horses had a tendency to like Elven.

They were fearful around werewolves.

And Dirk had been dating an Elven, so he knew about the other races, which meant not only that he could have known what the horses' behavior meant, but that he had known it. So he'd neglected to offer the key piece of information: the horses had been acting up....

Saxon slipped close to the rear of the house, where French doors leading out to the back had been left slightly ajar.

He moved in closer, listening. He could hear Dirk talking to someone on the phone.

"Yes, I know for sure he headed out. He left five minutes ago, at least. If Jimmy told him what he was supposed to, he'll be heading straight out to the lair—alone. He even told me not to call any other cops."

Dirk never heard Saxon enter, never heard him move. All he felt was the cold steel of Saxon's semiautomatic as he pressed the muzzle next to his ear.

"Ask him about your reward," Saxon whispered.

He was afraid that Dirk was going to fall down, his terror was so great.

"Man up and ask, or you'll be eating bullets for your last supper," Saxon warned.

"Hey, um, when do I get what you promised?" Dirk managed. His voice wasn't entirely steady, but it would pass muster.

Saxon heard the angry words coming from the other end. "You'll get your payment soon enough. You gave us the one girl, we'll give you the other."

Saxon heard the click as the other man hung up. He

frowned just as Dirk finally collapsed, falling down as if he were a marionette whose strings had been cut.

Tears sprang into the younger man's eyes. "I'm sorry, I'm so sorry. It's just that…I had to give him Calleigh. He swore that Angela was still alive and that he'd give her back if…if I gave him Calleigh."

Saxon felt his fury draining away; this kid was a mess. He wasn't a criminal—he was simply cowardly. No, not even cowardly. He was just pathetically in love and utterly useless.

He dragged Dirk back to his feet. "Listen up. I'm going to go get both of them back. You're an idiot if you thought your girlfriend would be returned. Bailey considers them a threat, but he's a man with an eye for a pretty woman, and that means he's going to use them both up and spit them out when he's tired of them. They'll end up as more bones in the desert if I can't save them. I can't take you with me—you'll just be someone else I need to protect—but if you pick up a phone and call anyone, you'll be signing their death warrants and your own. Do you understand."

Dirk nodded, sobbing. "You have to understand…I love her!"

This mess of a human being was in love with an Elven, and apparently she loved him back. Sad. Truly sad.

"Who were you talking to?" Saxon asked.

Dirk was sniveling. Saxon had to nudge him to get an answer.

"Monty. Monty Reilly."

"Reilly is in on this?" Saxon demanded.

"He, um, he says that Bailey is going to rule Las Vegas and all of the desert. That there's no point trying to stop him. He said Angela and I could get out before…before the killing started if I just gave him Calleigh."

Dirk was full-on sobbing again when Saxon bent down beside him. "I need a horse. I don't want to take my car, because they'll be waiting for me."

"The mare…Mistress Mellora…she's like a speed demon, and she's used to the desert. She's a Thoroughbred-Arab cross," Dirk managed.

Saxon didn't wait to hear more. Time was of the essence.

He slipped out back and quickly found a bridle and a stall with a placard that read Mistress Mellora. In less than a minute he was on his way.

The desert could be unforgiving, but Saxon had come to know it well, because it was such an organic part of the place he had bizarrely chosen as home. And as he rode the fleet-footed mare across the rough terrain, he thought about how to use it to his advantage.

Carl Bailey had no doubt built his lair underground so he could carry out his crimes—and practice whatever depraved behaviors turned him on—undetected. It was also no doubt where he was preparing for the werewolf attack that would end with his takeover of Las Vegas.

But no wolf's lair would have just one entry, because then it would be too easily turned into a trap. The question was, where would the back door be? And how would it be camouflaged against the desert floor and sparse vegetation?

It would have to be hidden by either a field of scrub brush or a group of cacti.

Finally he found what he was seeking. It was actually hidden by both scrub brush and cacti, and shadowed by a small dune for good measure, but footprints—both human and wolf—in the sand gave away its location.

After dismounting, he stroked the horse and thanked

her in a whisper for the ride; then he gave her a slap on the rump that sent her running for home.

He crept low among the cacti until, just as he'd expected, he found a wooden hatch flush with the ground and hidden under the brush.

They might not be expecting him to come in the back way, but even so, he would be an idiot not to expect an armed guard immediately inside.

Silently, he worked the latch, grateful for the darkness that was swiftly falling over the desert. He glanced up before entering. Bad luck. The full moon was rising.

He quickly lifted the door and slid through, stopping at the top of a flight of stairs leading down into the lair. As he'd expected, there were guards on duty: two of Carl's chowhounds. Luckily they weren't taking their work seriously. They were standing together, rifles slung over their shoulders, extolling the virtues of the Cuban cigars Bailey had procured for them.

Saxon marveled at the fact that they were so involved in their conversation that they didn't see the sliver of moonlight that slipped in with him—or him. They didn't hear him, and they didn't smell him. Maybe Carl had convinced his crew that brute strength alone made them superior, but these brutes were capable merely of chewing up the unwary.

Whatever the reason for it, their lackadaisical attitude worked for Saxon.

He was able to step right up to the two of them as if intrigued by their conversation and equally enchanted by their Cuban cigars.

"Nice," he said.

When they looked up, he cracked their skulls together. They fell without a whimper.

He was hindered by the fact that he had no idea where

he was going or just how extensive this underground lair was, but he was also determined to succeed.

He moved quietly through the hallway, listening, barely breathing. He heard music—the kind of music that belonged in an epic fantasy film, accompanying a phalanx of armed horsemen as they galloped out to do righteous battle.

He turned a corner, following the music, then paused. He could see a group of about twenty wolves in human form inside a room, the same room where the music was playing.

And among the werewolves gathered there he saw his quarry: old Carl Bailey.

Old he might be, but Carl Bailey was anything but decrepit. He'd been around for centuries. Werewolves weren't immortal, but they aged very slowly.

Carl looked like a distinguished gentleman of sixty-plus. His hair was silver-gray. His posture was still straight. He had his share of wrinkles, but they sat well on his sharp-boned face, adding character rather than age.

He was gesturing animatedly, speaking over the music—stirring up the passions of a roomful of his fellow werewolves.

"It is time! It is time to rise up and become all that we can be! The rules—the laws we have forced ourselves to obey—they are not for such magnificent creatures as our kind. We are strong. We are predators. The laws of men are not for us. I am your rule. I am your law. And my law says that we are meant to live and conquer as the greatest force on earth!"

His words were met by a roar of approval.

"Show yourselves in your true nature!"

As Carl shouted, the men and women in the room let out a second roar—a roar that became a howl.

Saxon watched as Carl's followers began to change.

Most of the werewolves that he knew personally—friends, fellow cops—managed the change in as sleek and beautiful a manner as could be imagined.

This was not sleek or beautiful. This was something so low and brutal and ugly that he found himself staring transfixed, despite his repulsion. Clothes were ripped off. Teeth gnashed as they nipped at one another, trying to show dominance. Some changed fully, others were arrested in some blasphemous form, half human and half beast.

Only Carl Bailey had yet to change.

He pointed to four of the wolves in front. "You! The Elven cop is on the way. Go out into the night. Take him by surprise. Tear his limbs from his body and gnaw his bones. Rip off his face."

As they turned to obey, Saxon flattened himself against the wall. They were so eager to do their master's bidding that they raced right by him.

He followed swiftly. He hated this—hated killing. But he had no choice.

As soon as the wolves had rounded the corner, Saxon drew the knife he kept at his calf and made a leap for the one in the rear, who went down without a sound. The next wolf died just as easily.

The third made a sound low in his throat as he died, causing the fourth to turn. He bayed and came at Saxon, preparing to leap.

Saxon pulled out his repeater and brought him down with one silver bullet. In the close confines of the tunnel, the report sounded like thunder.

Saxon turned and braced himself against the onslaught he was certain would follow. When nothing happened, he moved silently back toward the meeting room and realized that the roar coming from within, combined with the music, was so loud now that they hadn't heard a thing. He pressed himself against the wall again and listened.

"My friends!" Carl announced. "Tonight I have the ultimate appetizer for the feast that will be our reestablishment of the old order. Tonight you will dine on the most delicate flesh."

Saxon tensed against the wall, readying himself for whatever was coming next.

From across the way, a door opened and a woman was shoved into view. She was dressed in white, as blonde as a ray of sun, and appeared to shimmer even in the dark fortress of the wolves. She stood tall, staring defiantly at the werewolves slavering at her.

That had to be Angela.

Saxon saw that her wrists were bound with stout ropes.

One of the half-turned creatures moved toward her.

Before Saxon could intervene, a second woman was pushed up next to her. She, too, was bound at the wrists.

Calleigh!

She stood as tall and proud as her sister, a Rose Red to Angela's shimmering Snow White.

And when the first monster half laughed and half howled as it moved closer, she had plenty to say.

"Look at you! You're pathetic. Are you foolish sheep when you should be wolves?" she demanded. "Follow this man and he will lead you straight to death! Do you think the vampires will stand idly by and let you destroy the precarious existence they've established in the world of men? That the Elven will let you rule viciously and unchallenged? Touch me," she vowed, "and so help me, you will pay a bitter price."

The monsters hesitated, but the bloodlust still gleamed in their eyes.

Then Carl Bailey roared out in fury, "Why are you listening to her? She's weak, a half blood, willing to say anything to save her worthless skin. Show her the true power of her own kind—a power she has eschewed! Show her what she should have known, what she should have been!"

He strode over to the two women and stood beside Calleigh. "She is tainted, of course, by the Elven blood she carries. She has sullied our line. But she has the wolf in her still. Watch her squirm and howl in helpless agony as you rip apart her sister—the Elven! And then let her, too, know what it means to suffer fury and death."

Saxon prepared to move, but the instant Carl reached toward Angela, Calleigh leaped between them and raised her hands, breaking her bonds.

And then she raked her hand across his face, her nails leaving gashes and long ribbons of blood that drizzled down his cheeks.

Chapter 6

Carl Bailey let out a cry of rage that seemed to shake the walls.

He changed then, for long seconds becoming some horrible parody of both wolf and man. There were split seconds of horror-movie recall in which it seemed he was nothing but bones, teeth and a macabrely grinning mask, sheets of sinew and muscle, and then…

Then he became the biggest, most vicious-looking silver wolf ever to walk the earth.

He cast back his head and let out a howl that seemed to shatter the earth.

Saxon dug in his pocket for his phone and hit speed dial, praying he would get a signal this deep underground. He knew that if the call went through, his fellow cops would have his location and hear the terrifying cacophony.

No more waiting.

Saxon leaped into the fray, aiming his gun and its specially made silver bullets at the crowd.

"Stop!" he demanded as the room went still. "Do you all want to die?"

"Take him, you fools!" Carl Bailey roared, back in half-human form. "He can't kill you!"

"This gun is loaded with silver bullets—I sure as hell can kill you!" Saxon responded.

One of the half-changed wolves stepped toward him. "Silver bullets? Sure!" He laughed.

Saxon shot him.

He dropped.

The crowd surged forward and Saxon shot indiscriminately into the wall of fur and flesh.

Carl Bailey took a standing leap that carried him over Saxon's head to take up a position behind his acolytes, where their flesh protected him from harm. His followers howled and screamed, shifting between forms in their fury and terror and pain.

"Control yourselves! He can't kill all of us!"

Saxon shouted to be heard above the din. "Let the women walk out of here with me and there will be no more death!"

For a moment there was silence except for the whimpers of those who had been wounded.

Several others lay dead on the floor.

"Stop this!" Saxon shouted. "Stop this cycle of death!" He walked into the center of the room, despite knowing that this action left his back exposed and that he didn't have enough silver bullets to take them all down.

But this was wrong.

It was wrong anytime any race or religion set out to destroy or enslave another, to take all the power and use it without mercy.

"You are powerful," he exhorted them. "And because you're powerful, your responsibility is to protect others, not use them and destroy them. What is the matter with you? There has never been a force so great in the history of the world that it has managed to subjugate all men, all races, forever. They will rise against you—and you will be exterminated. Follow Carl Bailey and they will find a way to hunt you down and kill you. All of you. Even the mortals—frail as they may seem—will show you abilities you never dreamed they possessed. What they lack in strength they make up for in cunning. They, too, are capable of cruelty—but they're also capable of laws and compromise and governance to protect the weak among them."

He heard growling.... But he also heard whimpering, a sound that could mean pain—or a fierce desire to heed his words held in check only by fear.

"Stop the death—including your own," he commanded them.

"Saxon!"

He heard Calleigh cry his name in warning and whirled to see one of Carl Bailey's die-hard lieutenants leaping at him.

He fired at point-blank range, and the wolf went down like a rock.

"Fools! He can't shoot all of you at once!" Carl shouted.

Saxon was grateful for his acute Elven hearing. Grateful that he knew one of the wolves was nearly on his back. He spun, thrusting an elbow into the creature's side with a force that sent his attacker flying back against the wall.

"The women! He can't shoot the women!" someone—apparently brighter than Carl—called out.

Damn! The creature was right. He had to reach them before the werewolves did.

He swung around, shooting the two creatures separating him from Calleigh and Angela. Then he leaped to join the women, who immediately flanked him. He quickly handed Angela his knife so that she could cut herself free.

"We're getting out," he told them quietly. "We need to back up along the hall and around the corner. Block the way, so they can't surround us. It'll force them to come at us a few at a time."

Their barely perceptible nods assured him that they'd heard him, and as a group they moved backward along the passageway.

He kept his gun on the crowd, and they moved as quickly as they dared.

"You'll never get out—this place is a labyrinth!" Carl warned. He was making his way through what remained of the hesitant crowd, but he kept two of his followers in the lead as lupine shields.

"You're killing your own people, Bailey," Saxon persisted. "Doesn't that matter to you?" Carl responded in growls, so Saxon addressed the throng. "Don't you see? You're expendable to him. He calls you magnificent creatures, tells you you're poised for greatness, but he treats you as puppets, as tools in his rise to power!"

"Stairs. Stairs behind us," Calleigh whispered to him.

His feet touched something.

He looked down, and his stomach rebelled.

He was very much afraid that he'd found the craps dealer.

He was a pile of bone and ripped clothing, broken and gnawed limbs, blood and death.

He heard Angela moan softly.

"Hold yourself together. You can do this," he told her. "You are Elven."

He sensed rather than saw her nod. She swallowed and kept moving with him. One by one, with Saxon going last, they backed their way up the narrow stairway.

"The door," he whispered to Angela, who was first to reach the top. "Just push it up."

He caught Calleigh's eyes. Beautiful eyes. They were wolf eyes, that extraordinary glittering gold shot through with green.

He'd known that werewolves could be remarkable, just as he'd known that all sentient beings came with a capacity for evil. But overall they were good, driven by the desire to live and let live. The fight for survival had made monsters of many in the past, humans included. But laws and rules created a world where everyone could live and prosper.

Until you threw a Carl Bailey into the mix.

Saxon kept his eyes trained on the wolves that were still stalking them, step by step.

He heard Angela open the hatch at the top of the stairs and climb through.

"Go!" he shouted to her. "Run!"

He felt Calleigh behind him.

"Go," he ordered her. "Take your sister and get out of here."

The minute she was through, he followed, slamming the hatch down and jamming the latch with a nearby rock. He felt Calleigh next to him and knew from the tension in her body that something was wrong.

He spun quickly…

…and found himself facing the captain.

Captain Clark Bower. The man who was so near to retirement—the man who had ordered Saxon to put an end to the chaos.

And he had a semiautomatic trained on the three of them.

Saxon stepped onto the wooden hatch to further delay the werewolves and weighed his odds.

Elven could heal almost magically, but they weren't immune to bullets, silver or otherwise. Elven had tremendous strength—but a bullet in the heart trumped the strongest muscle.

"Captain," he said, his shock evident in his voice. "You're in on this? You're human, for God's sake."

"Human, hardworking and tired as hell. I've watched monsters—human monsters—do terrible things, go to court, blame it on a video game and be acquitted. I've been shot, stabbed, beaten and nearly ripped to shreds by a junkie running on coke and adrenaline. And now—now I have a retirement package that wouldn't support a poodle for a month. Sorry, Saxon. You're a good cop, a good guy. But I'm ready to savor the fruits of a long career as provided by those with the true power. Carl Bailey will set me up in a penthouse for life with a monthly allowance that will keep me well into my twilight years."

Saxon could hear the wolves banging at the hatch beneath his feet.

"Step aside," the captain told him.

He held his ground. "Why is it that we can all be so incredibly stupid when we want to be seduced?" he asked. "Carl Bailey used Monty Reilly and dozens of others, and he's using you. He tricked a weak young man into doing his bidding tonight, and he's tricking you. He intends to kill everyone who helps him as soon as he's done using them."

The captain's gun remained on Saxon; his hands were steady.

"I'm an old man, Saxon. Old and tired. I know you. I know all about you. You can afford to let the years go by. You can grow very, very old and still be in your prime."

A board burst beneath Saxon's feet. The pack would be bursting free any second.

"Let the women go," he said to the captain. "Let them go—give them a chance to escape—and I'm yours."

"No!" Calleigh cried. "No, listen, Captain, please… please, look at me!"

Saxon frowned, about to protest, but Calleigh had already drawn the captain's attention.

Yet she just stared at him, hopefully, searchingly, as if speaking to him through the changing expressions in her eyes. What was happening? Suddenly Saxon remembered how he had watched her dancing in that glass enclosure, remembered how their eyes had met, the way she had watched him with complete disdain—and yet he had kept staring at her…hypnotized.

Just as the captain now seemed to be under her spell, his gun hand down by his side, his expression slack.

But before the captain relaxed so fully that he dropped his gun, there was a massive bang as the hatch shuddered beneath Saxon's feet, and the sound broke the spell.

The captain realized his imminent danger and pointed his gun directly at Saxon's chest….

The crack of a bullet split the night.

Time seemed to slow as Saxon braced himself for the pain. Yet nothing ripped into his flesh. Instead, as he watched, a red stain spread out over the captain's chest and he fell forward.

"Dirk!" Angela cried. An angelic smile illuminating her face, she rushed forward into the arms of the man who had come to her rescue.

Saxon stared in surprise. Dirk stared back. He was shaking, but his arm was around Angela, holding her close. His voice was barely a whisper. "I had to come. I love her."

"Great," Calleigh said. "Now get her out of here."

"Get them both out of here," Saxon snapped at Dirk.

The wood beneath his feet was splintering. "For the love of God, get them both out of here now!"

Everything seemed to happen at once. Calleigh shoved her sister and Dirk, pushing them away.

The hatch shuddered as it started to give, and Saxon moved to the side, ready to fight for his life.

Then the wailing of sirens resounded in the night, and flashes of headlights cut erratically through the darkness.

The cavalry was arriving at last.

Dirk finally grabbed Angela's hand and raced with her toward the road.

The hatch burst open.

Calleigh stood shoulder to shoulder with Saxon as the werewolves surged forth in full, vicious splendor. He started shooting and didn't stop, and they began to fall, the dead delaying the living and buying him time. But there were just too many of them, and one injured wolf hurtled into him, nearly dragging him down.

Calleigh whirled and shoved, using her strength to send the wolf flying.

They backed away from the hatchway, Saxon still shooting, but there were so many of them. Too many.

For every werewolf that fell, at least two more came.

But then he felt the ground tremble as the squad cars came roaring up, and dust rose around him as he was joined by Keeghan McMurtree and a horde of men in uniform, guns blazing.

"Werewolves… Your bullets…" Saxon began.

"Silver, of course," McMurtree said with a grin.

The wolves fell by the dozens then, dying as animals, twisting in their death throes, becoming human again. Someone rushed past Saxon, and he realized that it was Calleigh. She was carrying a tear-gas grenade that she'd taken from one of the cops, and she was streaking toward the open hole in the desert floor.

"Calleigh!"

He called her name just as Carl Bailey appeared in his mammoth silver glory. He raked out a massive hairy paw and brought her down, then dragged her against his massive chest and open, slavering jaws. The grenade fell into the hatch.

Choking fumes rolled out and filled the night air.

Saxon couldn't fire: he might hit Calleigh.

Saxon shoved his way through the stragglers still coming at him and pitched himself atop Carl Bailey's shimmering silver back. He clawed at the wolf with a strength he'd never even suspected he possessed. His gun went flying as he wrapped an arm around Carl's massive neck and tightened it in a choke hold.

Distracted by the attack, Carl loosened his grip on Calleigh, who slipped free as Saxon and the wolf rolled together through the dust and dirt. Cacti pierced Saxon's flesh, but he didn't feel a thing.

Finally Carl pinned the Elven cop beneath him, and Saxon looked up and saw Carl's predatory eyes on his. Saw his gaping maw. Saw his canines as he bent down, saliva dripping, to savage Saxon's throat.

Elven had strength, Saxon reminded himself.

And cunning…

He waited, then rolled at the last second.

The werewolf took in a mouthful of dust, and Saxon leaped to his feet.

Carl made a quick recovery, rising and standing for a moment, silhouetted against the moon, a giant silver-haired man-wolf in all his strength and glory.

And then a shot rang out and he fell.

Blood soaked the ground beneath his body as he melted back into human form.

Saxon turned and saw Calleigh holding his gun in a two-handed grip, arms still outstretched, ready to shoot again. And she was shaking.

He walked over and wrapped his arm around her. She was beautiful, tall, slender, vulnerable there in the darkness.

He didn't speak; he just held her. He could hear McMurtree and the others finishing their cleanup of the remaining combatants.

Calleigh pressed closer to him. "I've just killed my own kind," she said softly.

"You had to," he said. "You saved my life."

She flashed him a smile. "No, you saved all our lives. I'm not sure he would have been a match for you, but…"

"But?"

Her eyes met his. The same eyes that could seduce, that could kindle with pure wickedness, were, at this moment, completely giving, and as bright and beautiful as the sun.

"I don't like to take chances, you know?" she whispered.

McMurtree walked over to them and gestured at the bodies strewed across the desert. "How the hell are we going to explain this?" he asked.

Chapter 7

The City News and Herald
Las Vegas

Desert Raid Puts End to Militia Threat

A violent militia group with an underground strong-hold and vast cache of weapons was brought down last night in the desert outside Las Vegas.

Inside the secret underground complex police found evidence connecting the dissidents to the recent deaths and disappearances in the city. Police speculate that the militia leader orchestrated the violence to destabilize the city and facilitate an attempt to take control.

The death toll is still being determined, but police have revealed that two prisoners being held by the cult were freed in the raid. The names of the dead are presently being withheld, pending notification of next of kin.

Captain Clark Bower of the police is among the dead; his position is being temporarily filled by

Lieutenant Keeghan McMurtree, one of the officers who led the assault.

Further information will be made available as it is released to the press.

"Not bad," Calleigh said, putting down the paper.

She and Saxon had escaped the frenzy in Vegas and taken a suite in a luxury hotel in Reno. Calleigh was curled up next to Saxon on a deeply upholstered love seat. He was staring out at a view that, unlike what every window in downtown Vegas offered, was not of neon lights or man-made towers.

These plate-glass windows looked out over the majestic splendor of the mountains.

Calleigh touched his cheek. "Good story, don't you think?"

He nodded and opened his mouth to speak, but she kissed him, and that was the end of the conversation.

She was sleek and beautiful. She had skin like silk, radiated heat like the sun and demonstrated a range of passion to match the golden fires that burned in her eyes.

Her kiss had the power to turn his blood to lava. She could move as if making love were the most exotic dance known to man, and she had the ability to make him forget himself and the world, leaving him absorbed in a feeling of wonder that they were alive and together.

They lay in each other's arms on the floor in front of a leaping fire, sated and spent.

She turned and looked at him, stroking his face as he stared back at her in wonder.

She smiled slowly. "News flash. Elven cop seen with Vegas entertainer. Can a true Elven find happiness with a half-breed werewolf?"

He smiled. "I seem to be too worn-out to think of an answer."

She smacked his shoulder lightly. "Cut me some slack. I'm laying my heart at your feet."

He grinned and rolled on top of her. "You are half Elven," he reminded her. "Making love…it's a pretty amazing deal for the Elven, you know."

She touched him, intimately. Even now she could get him sizzling again, kindle another fire in his loins—and fingertips, muscles, tendons, blood, toes….

"I know," she told him wickedly.

"I know I won't ever let you out of my sight again," he told her.

They both jumped at a thunderous knocking at their door.

"Get dressed," he said to her, reaching for his jeans.

A moment later he checked to make sure she was decent, then made his way to the door, checked the peephole and opened it, his expression a mix of welcome and surprise.

Keeghan McMurtree smiled and walked in, accompanied by an entire group of Keepers. He immediately started making introductions. "This is Brad Thierson, Keeper of the New York City werewolves."

"And we're all appalled by what Monty Reilly let happen in Vegas," Thierson said.

"I'm Eamon MacDonald, leprechaun Keeper, Dublin," another man said.

The introductions went on, with Calleigh standing behind Saxon, both of them confused as to what the hell was going on.

"Think we can sit down?" McMurtree finally asked.

Saxon nodded, and Calleigh led the way, seating them and asking if she could get them something to drink.

"I'm not going to waste time here," McMurtree said to Saxon once everyone was settled. "You've been chosen to head a new council."

"What? Why me? And what kind of council?"

"A council of Keepers," McMurtree explained.

"But I'm not a Keeper," Saxon said.

"Doesn't matter—hell, maybe your independence makes you an even better choice," McMurtree told him. "You see the need for a centralized system of regulations, of checks and balances, the one to insist that the Keepers need to have the power to maintain control, so that they don't fall prey to the powers of the very beings they are born to control." McMurtree grinned. "All you have to do is set the date and the place, and Keepers from all over the world will be called to a summit. Bailey wanted a New World Order—well, we're going to create one, and it's going to be based on a code that's fair and rational and backed up by the power of a worldwide network of Keepers. It's complex. I realize that. But we need you—not just as a figurehead, but because of your ethics and your beliefs, your strength and your courage."

Saxon looked at Calleigh, awed, uncertain, even a little bit afraid of the responsibility that was being handed to him.

"Put your money where your mouth is, big boy," she suggested softly.

He stood. He was being given the opportunity to be part of something that could change the world—and not only his world—for the better.

"When do we begin?" he asked huskily.

"In the morning," McMurtree told him. "Invitations will go out across the world and a true governing council for the underworld races will become a reality."

With that announcement, McMurtree stood and pulled Saxon in for a hug.

Moments later the visitors were gone, and Saxon looked at Calleigh. "Is it possible?" he asked.

She slipped into his arms. "All things are possible," she whispered, her eyes meeting his. "All things. Because I'm here, with you."

He took her into his arms. When she was with him, he realized, he did indeed believe that all things were possible.

"News flash," he said. "Elven cop finds life, purpose and everlasting happiness in the arms of a half-breed werewolf."

And just in case she wasn't sure he meant what he'd said, he proceeded to demonstrate exactly how true his words had been.

* * * * *

When Vampire Keeper Rhiannon Gryffald moves to L.A., she finds herself in the middle of a vampire's killing spree. Joining forces with Brodie McKay, a gorgeous Elven cop, may be her only hope of survival as they discover a conspiracy that shakes the Los Angeles theater scene to its core....

Read on for a sneak peek of KEEPER OF THE NIGHT by New York Times *bestselling author Heather Graham.*

Hollywood, California

City of dreams to many, and city of lost dreams for too many others. A place where waiters and waitresses spent their tips on headshots, and the men and women behind the scenes—the producers—reigned as the real kings.

So many of the paranormal races—the vampires, the shifters, the elven and more—traveled there, and many stayed, because where better to blend in than a place where even the human beings hardly registered as normal half the time? With so much going on, no one set of Keepers could control the vast scope of the Greater Los Angeles underworld, and so it was that the three Gryffald cousins, daughters of the three renowned Gryffald brothers, were called to take their place as peacekeepers a bit earlier than had been expected.

And right when L.A. was on the verge of exploding with underworld activity.

Hollywood, they were about to discover, could truly be murder.

There was blood. So much blood.

From her position on the stage Rhiannon Gryffald could see the man standing just outside the club door. He was tall and well built, his almost formal attire a contrast to the usual California casual and strangely at odds with his youth, with a Hollywood tan that added to the classic strength of his features and set off his light eyes and golden hair.

And he was bleeding from the throat.

Bleeding profusely.

There was blood everywhere. It was running down the side of his throat and staining his tailored white shirt and gold-patterned vest.

"Help! I've been bitten!" he cried. He was staggering, hands clutching his throat.

No! she thought. Not yet!

She had barely arrived in Los Angeles! This was too soon, far too soon, to be called upon to take action. She was just beginning to find her way around the city, just learning how to maneuver through the insane traffic—not to mention that she was trying to maintain something that at least resembled steady employment.

"I've been bitten!" he screamed again. "By a vampire!"

There were two women standing near him, staring, and he seemed to be trying to warn them, but they didn't seem frightened, although they were focused on the blood pouring from his wound.

They started to move toward him, their eyes fixed on the scarlet ruin of his neck.

They weren't concerned, Rhiannon realized. They weren't going to help.

They were hungry.

* * * * *

Don't miss the dramatic conclusion to
KEEPER OF THE NIGHT
by Heather Graham.
Available January 2013,
only from Harlequin Nocturne.

COMING NEXT MONTH FROM

HARLEQUIN® NOCTURNE™

Available December 18, 2012

#151 KEEPER OF THE NIGHT • *The Keepers: L.A.*
by Heather Graham

When a series of gruesome murders rocks the Los Angeles theater scene, Elven cop Brodie McKay suspects a vampire serial killer is responsible. Going deep undercover as an actor, Brodie knows nothing—or no one—can distract him from the case. Until he meets Rhiannan Gryffald. Having recently given up her rock-star dreams to fulfill her destiny as a vampire Keeper, the gorgeous former musician may be his best ally—and his ultimate temptation.... Don't miss this first book in The Keepers: L.A.

#152 DARK WOLF RISING • *Bloodrunners*
by Rhyannon Byrd

"Dark wolf" Eric Drake has never trusted himself with a human, dating only pack females—and then the night comes when he finds a woman, Chelsea Smart, mistakenly trespassing on Silvercrest pack land. Chelsea has dedicated her life to the belief that a woman doesn't need a man by her side to make her complete. She's always done her best to avoid arrogant, overbearing, gorgeous alpha males...until the search for her missing nineteen-year-old sister brings her face-to-face with a mysterious man she finds impossible to ignore...or resist.

REQUEST YOUR FREE BOOKS!

2 FREE NOVELS FROM THE PARANORMAL ROMANCE COLLECTION PLUS 2 FREE GIFTS!

YES! Please send me 2 FREE novels from the Paranormal Romance Collection and my 2 FREE gifts (gifts are worth about $10). After receiving them, if I don't wish to receive any more books, I can return the shipping statement marked "cancel." If I don't cancel, I will receive 4 brand-new novels every month and be billed just $21.42 in the U.S. or $23.46 in Canada. That's a saving of at least 21% off the cover price of all 4 books. It's quite a bargain! Shipping and handling is just 50¢ per book in the U.S. and 75¢ per book in Canada.* I understand that accepting the 2 free books and gifts places me under no obligation to buy anything. I can always return a shipment and cancel at any time. Even if I never buy another book, the two free books and gifts are mine to keep forever.

237/337 HDN FEL2

Name	(PLEASE PRINT)
Address	Apt. #
City	State/Prov.	Zip/Postal Code

Signature (if under 18, a parent or guardian must sign)

Mail to the **Reader Service**:
IN U.S.A.: P.O. Box 1867, Buffalo, NY 14240-1867
IN CANADA: P.O. Box 609, Fort Erie, Ontario L2A 5X3

Not valid for current subscribers to the Paranormal Romance Collection or Harlequin® Nocturne™ books.

**Want to try two free books from another line?
Call 1-800-873-8635 or visit www.ReaderService.com.**

* Terms and prices subject to change without notice. Prices do not include applicable taxes. Sales tax applicable in N.Y. Canadian residents will be charged applicable taxes. Offer not valid in Quebec. This offer is limited to one order per household. All orders subject to credit approval. Credit or debit balances in a customer's account(s) may be offset by any other outstanding balance owed by or to the customer. Please allow 4 to 6 weeks for delivery. Offer available while quantities last.

Your Privacy—The Reader Service is committed to protecting your privacy. Our Privacy Policy is available online at www.ReaderService.com or upon request from the Reader Service.

We make a portion of our mailing list available to reputable third parties that offer products we believe may interest you. If you prefer that we not exchange your name with third parties, or if you wish to clarify or modify your communication preferences, please visit us at www.ReaderService.com/consumerschoice or write to us at Reader Service Preference Service, P.O. Box 9062, Buffalo, NY 14269. Include your complete name and address.